MASTER DEFENDERS

By: Matt Bhanks

MWBhanks.

To: Tate and Cohen

You two are true Masters!
Keep fighting for
success!

Jan. 2020

Editor: Jason Rankin

Special thanks to my family and friends for their support. Continue to have faith in everything that you do.

MASTER DEFENDERS (Recommended for ages 12 and up)
FICTION
MATTHEW BHANKS
MB BOOKS

ISBN: 978-0-920233-68-9

MATT BHANKS

MASTER DEFENDERS

FIVE YEARS AGO

"The things that you speak of right now...disturb me."

"Trust me, this will work. At last we will finally be able to liberate the nation from the predators."

"Look, even if it could work, the effects would only be limited to save our country, not the world."

"The crisis has caused total trauma to the public. Imagine a world where these beasts listen to us!"

"You can't unleash it. We were warned at Lasher Labs."

"Do you really insist on listening to one of them?"

"They know the danger that lurks ahead if you succeed in your process. I trust its judgment. You saw what these things can do to them. The Lashers are dead because of this. And don't forget their beloved son. He had a bright future ahead of him and now...he's gone. Don't go through with it."

"I'm spending three quarters of my budget on this project. I thought you would favour my decision, but I guess I was wrong."

"I understand that you're only trying to help, but is this truly a safe assistance for America? What about the President? Did he approve of this? Plus, first you would have to deal with the council."

"I run the agency that is from what I can see, really corrupt in nature."

"You don't run the agency and suppose you are the cause of it being corrupted?"

"Why must you ask so many questions?!"

"Because I stand up for what's right. Richard Rageous made a mistake by bringing the substances here. Messing with them isn't going to help us at all. Please, just scratch the entire operation for your own sake."

"The council will agree one way or another."

"And how do you figure?"

"They just need to be persuaded by the right people."

"They won't give in."

"Then I'll go with the plan anyways. I wanted you by my side. However, you seem to have this sense that the creatures are safe. That makes you no different from them. The time will come when you will see my idea as a success. When that time comes, you'll know who the real master is."

"I don't know how you got this way. I will stop you...whatever it takes."

"You come to me with a couple of firearms and I'll have an army. Names like Derwin Grant, Corometheus, Professor Shaw, Gustavo Salazar, Dark-Shallow, and Avinotch are enough to strike fear to the public. I've been watching over them for a while now. I can see the things they're capable of doing. My group will expand as time goes on. How do you expect to defend yourself?"

"I'll find a way."

<u>IMPORTANT NOTE</u>

All of the characters and events in this story were developed
throughout my childhood.

THEY ARE COMPLETELY FICTIONAL AND ORIGINAL!

In absolutely no way do I believe in magic, super-powered
humans, and malevolent spirits.

As for aliens…I haven't made up my mind yet.

-Matt Bhanks

MATT BHANKS

MASTER
DEFENDERS

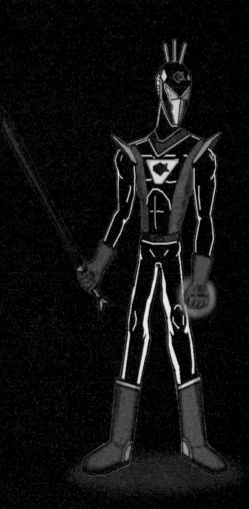

For my friends and family.

PART 1

THE GATHERING

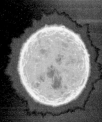

I

THE MASTER MISSION

THE BEST SEASON OF THE YEAR HAS TO be the brilliant season of summer. Who could resist its bright morning skies that fill the attitudes of children with spirits of joy? Regardless of the issue, the harmony is a pleasant one. Children playing on the swingsets, birds chirping lovely melodies, and the warm gentle breeze enhanced the soothing atmosphere. Should a tender environment such as this be put to question? Most times the answer would be a flat out "no". However, this was not one of those times.

Here is a list of the world's well-known generations: the Baby Boom Generation, Generation X, the Millennial Generation, the Homeland Generation, and now the Star-Pix Generation. They called it this because of the recent and paranormal event known as the Star-Pix Crisis.

The catastrophe was too great to be linked to any type of terrorist. It was an outburst of devastating creatures that somehow, some miraculous way, found themselves on our planet. The police as we use to know them are now the AIA, (Alien Investigative Agency). The agency is split into several sectors, each coming with their own form of cruelty. What pros and cons come from this grand event the world has seen? Anyone with half a mind can conclude that the side of the cons outweighs the side of the pros. What are the advantages? It has to be the sudden emergence of new heroes.

Captain Tina Truman is second in command of AIA East. The Caucasian lady was stunning as any woman. Her hair was chestnut brown and her jade eyes could stimulate any man. She had the curvature of the most attractive super models. It was a relaxing day for her. Her long and ravishing legs lounged on her large brown desk while she drank wine. It was her favourite kind. *"Dark Essence 1983"*.

Still, resting didn't come often. A man came to accompany her. He sat down across from where she was sitting.

Pretending to ignore the situation, Tina pulled a magazine in front of her eyes. This was of no use as the man knocked it down. They remained looking face-to-face. Strange enough, he held his hand in front of Tina. His five individual fingers clamped together to make a firm fist. She knew who the man was, in fact, she knew him for five years. He was her leader, (the first in command of AIA East). His name was Cyphrus Abel Reid, but he was better known as Cyfreid. As for his rank, he was recognized as the Commander.

Tina Truman understood the fist concept as an analogy. *As individuals we are nothing, but together we are powerful.*

The concept was rather confusing since it considered independency as nothing. Nevertheless, it was just Cyfreid's way of saying that a group brings better results than an individual. She nodded and smiled. Now was the time of union.

It has been eight years since the Star-Pix Crisis and so far only a number of humans accepted aliens to their dominant race. Many became overwhelmed by the whole situation and some desperately tried to avoid it. Tina was ordered to travel to Detroit, Michigan. When being there, she was to meet up with a group of miners; one of them was believed to be an extraterrestrial.

Only one word kept circling in Tina's mind in which her leader tried his hardest to stress. *Union* was what it was. Being an eye-catching agent of the agency, she realized that this was a classified mission. She spotted the miners in the distance and traveled by foot to greet them.

"Welcome everyone," she politely said but then was immediately corrected by a miner who said, "If anything, we should be the ones welcoming you."

If there was one thing that Tina hated, it was being interrupted, especially by a man. She stated, "I'll do the talking around here for now on...do I make myself clear?" The look on her face was greatly severe. All of the diggers agreed to label this woman as their instructor for the remainder of the evening.

Hours passed and evening became night. The miners sacrificed hundreds of sweat drops in order to find what Tina was looking for. One of the workers was more sensual than the rest. He was tall in stature and possessed a bushy mustache. He looked young, but that was not certain.

"Just what exactly are we looking for?" he asked. "Because if it's love my lady, I found my match." As Tina turned her head, she stared down the miner. Her response was plain and simple.

"Sorry wise guy, but you're definitely not my type."

"But my lady," he began. "You and I can make a nation of strong and attractive people. I have what is called *the key*, and you have what is called—"

Before he finished the inappropriate message, Tina swung at the sensual worker. Everyone watched as the miner was clouted in the face. The result was the vilest bruise that they've ever seen.

"My lady...that wasn't nice," he painfully said with his hand cupped on the swelling.

"Focus on the job you idiot! And that goes for the rest of you!"

They continued to obey the contentious female. The stars of the nighttime sky constantly sparkled. Each digger looked up at its fine beauty. Overall, the mood didn't fit with the task they were ordered to do.

A number of different minerals were extracted and ranged from copper to gallium and then iron. None of which was as extraordinary of a substance Tina scouted to find.

The substance that Cyfreid asked for was called Pixaliemain. This type of mineral was unknown to the public. Even Tina was slightly ignorant with some of its traits. Cyfreid believed that if this substance wasn't secured in the right hands, it could be the end of the human race. It was as if the pressure of the critical mission kept breathing down Tina's back. One thing was for sure and it was that the operation was going much slower than she expected.

"Please do me a dire favour and pick up the pace," the agent ordered.

"We are tired as it is, Tina. We need to rest immediately so why don't you do us a favour and stop treating us like dogs!" shouted a miner from the group.

Another worker stepped in the conversation and added, "We are being treated more like slaves than dogs!" The complaints grew. The workers set aside their obligations for another time, or perchance never.

This is pointless.

Cessation among them rose to a great extent. Some began to laugh aloud when finding the comment rather amusing. A little humour couldn't hurt them, even when being in the cold and quivering condition.

"Listen you slaves!" said the woman classifying them as undeserving and unfortunate workers. "My leader brought me here to command you fools. If there is one thing that slaves do, it's complaining to their masters. Therefore, the more y'all complain, the more I'm going to treat you like slaves. I'm willing to stay here all night if I have to. In fact, I'll do anything to ensure the human race continues!"

The miners' faces turned with confusion. One asked the question that was going through each person's head.

"What in the name of Jesus are you talking about? The fate of the human race is at risk?"

"Yes it is! That's why you must continue!" Tina screamed.

"What's *really* going on here? Who are you working for?"

"That doesn't matter. What matters is that you find Pixal—"

Tina stopped her sentence, remembering that there was an outlander nearby.

"Never mind," she concluded. They inferred the obvious; Tina Truman was up to something grand. They continued to search the deepest levels of the Earth's crust.

There's still nothing.

"My lady…you're as crazy as you're attractive. Just tell us what this substance is," suggested the sensual miner. Upon saying this, a loud voice was heard by a worker.

"Tina!" cried the echoing voice. "Tina, I think I found something!"

Tina and the others intensely sprinted towards his location. He was certain that what he just found was extraordinary. The remarkable substance was giving off an illuminating light. Tina smiled upon seeing it.

"Nice going, slaves!" she said only amusing herself. Everyone continued to stare at the glory of the rock. The light was bright blue; it was widespread and looked supernatural. The first half of the task was complete. The stunning agent was ready to shift to the second phase.

Her commanding officer happened to be correct after all. Pixaliemain was revealed to the public, but Tina had to act fast. She looked at each person only to see that the focal point of their attention was the precious light.

She realized that no matter what the circumstance, one of the diligent miners would not resist the substance. Certain tactics had to be improvised.

"Everyone move away from it immediately!"

The workers who were unaware of its traits ran away from the substance. All obeyed the female except for only one.

The agent walked towards the miner. He mumbled different phrases.

Tina was a very educated woman. She could speak all the different languages known to man, but she was unfamiliar with the miner's words.

"Are you deaf? I ordered you to move away!"

It was of no use. He continued to speak the phrases as if he was reading something mystical; a spell perhaps. The AIA agent was unsure of how to handle this. She contacted Cyfreid and explained the situation at hand.

After she explained everything, many screams were heard by Cyfreid.

"Stop him at once!" he shouted while being back at the confidential base. "Don't let him finish those words!"

With plenty of caution, Tina pulled out her pistol and aimed it at the mumbling man.

"Stand down!" she commanded. Still, this did no good as the miner continued to speak. It was an unnerving voice.

Tina had no choice but to shoot. When firing, the man turned to her completely unharmed.

"That does it! I'm calling the cops!" a miner said.

"I am a cop!"

"Lady I can't take you anymore! The boys and I are gone!"

At that very instant, the miners hastily departed in their vehicles. A farewell would've been respectful, but Tina had no time to say her goodbyes. The darkness of the night only added to the harsh drama she was experiencing. The swift breeze continued to wave her brown hair back and forth. According to the miners, the first option was departure; according to Tina, the first option was fighting.

The random phrases continued. Tina aimed her pistol one more time. The mumbling man stared at her; she stared back. As more outlandish phrases were said, his skin started to peel off. The outer layers landed and resembled wet mush. The human face dropped down like an old wrapping. The new look was horrid and grim. It was a creature with maroon eyes and gold-yellow fangs. Its skin was navy blue with multiple craters.

Tina fired ten times only to find out that the creature was barely wounded. The punctured bullet holes meant nothing. Some dropped, sprinkling down like spitting raindrops and causing high-pitched rings to her ears. The gruesome predator moved into attack position.

As it approached Tina, she pulled the trigger as many times as she could. Each shot pushed the creature back a step.

Tina's eyes were locked on the predator. She attempted to figure out the best target. There was a possible answer.

The enemy's mouth.

She thought that this way, all phrases would end. There was nothing to lose. Her breathing was heavy as she held the pistol at the charging alien. It jumped high, tongue swaying and dripping drool, teeth meshed and ready to finish its human prey.

Before it could, Tina blasted it in the mouth with one pull of the trigger and drop-kicked the predator. It gave a strident cry and then the scream eased.

At last, the agent was able to catch her breath. The incident wasn't traumatizing to her at all. She was trained for handling these tasks. She slowly walked towards the creature as it twitched on the ground with its mouth overflowing with plasma. She hoped that it was truly dead when considering that there was no more ammunition.

The head of the monster turned to Tina. It spoke. When seeing that the alien was speaking English, Tina hurried to find her communicator in her pocket. Something like this had to be shown at AIA East. The creature's words were as followed:

"You humans stand no chance.

Your race will be crumbled by the new authority.

Many will be killed and some will be forced to serve him.

Give up now and submit to Earth's new master.

Give praises unto the eternal reading.

All hail Xaliemer!"

Those were the alien's final words as it closed its eyes and died in front of Tina. She understood that this was common; she murdered many creatures in the past. Hunting aliens was her hobby; her enjoyment; her passion. The only thought that she had was its last words. The final sentence struck her the most. *"All hail Xaliemer."*

She wandered to find the substance. When she spotted it, she picked it up and was unafraid of what it could do. The rock didn't harm her at all. It was believed that Pixaliemain only had effects on aliens and not humans.

She scouted again, seeing if there were more traces of the substance. Not a single rock substance of Pixaliemain was found other than the one she possessed. Tina contacted Cyfreid once more.

"I almost died," she stated.

"I understand," said Cyfreid. "Did you retrieve a sample?"

"Yes, it's in good hands now."

"Excellent. There is much to be discussed."

"Who is Xaliemer?"

"I don't know…but whoever he is, his powers are linked to that reading. Trust me, I'm sure of it."

"You said the human race is at risk. Is it really that serious?"

"I'm afraid so. Tina, I need to tell you something. There are more traces of Pixaliemain in North America. If it comes in contact with any alien, then it's the end. I'm ordering you to travel to Washington, D.C. and when there, you'll await further orders. The time of union is here. We must build a special alliance to counter the Governor. I feel that we are already too late. Tina…we need Canavin."

The words coming from her master almost filled Tina with anxiety. Many aliens—or Pixalians as they preferred to be called—settled on Earth and even acted as humans in disguise. Tina lowered her head with disbelief. Any mistakes and the world will be at war, and probably for its final time.

A bright light shone behind her. As she turned to look, she sighted the rising sun. Night had now shifted into morning. The entire extraction process, the battle with the predator, and the search for remains of Pixaliemain happened to take the entire night. She checked the time on her watch.

"6:45 a.m." she read.

The morning resembled the relief she now had after killing the creature. The problem was that morning will always shift to night.

With that being said, there were greater circumstances waiting. If it was the end, it would take a group of special individuals to defend the planet. Such talented and well-trained individuals cannot be ordinary, but instead must be extraordinary.

II

HELP IN DISGUISE

THE ELEGANT MORNING WASN'T SPENT with an average breakfast and speedy rush to arrive at work early; at least this wasn't Tina's morning. Reaching the capital was crucial.

As for Cyfreid, his vision hauled his yearning heart for change in the world. The Star-Pix Crisis left a pure sign of torment. Nobody was truly safe from the menacing Pixalians. Some of them were believed to be harmless. Others were labeled as beloved heroes.

AIA East was no ordinary base. It was located directly above the capital and was surrounded by multiple clouds that gave it a heavenly atmosphere.

The main asset—the probable field leader for the Pixaliemain issue—was Pixalian himself. His evident name reached every nation, fueling society with hope.

"Canavin".

The saviour used to reside in Cyclohoma City—a metropolis placed just beyond Los Angeles, California. Now, the favoured Pixalian lived in outer space inside his very own base called the Canavin Station.

When Canavin was a youngling, he had a firm bond with his father. Close and encouraging.

Yet, everything shattered. A group of humans led by a man named Richard Rageous invaded his home world. Thousands of Pixalians followed humans back to Earth and this was indeed the Star-Pix Crisis.

Canavin was about six foot four and wore armour with blue, black, and gold shading. His most unique traits were the three antennae on his head and the black mask he wore to shield his golden face. At first, he wore the mask to hide his alien identity, but now the identity was revealed and he was well-respected by humans.

Cyfreid sensed the urgency. He couldn't visualize grappling a greater circumstance.

"Stan," he ordered a young agent at the base. "What's the status for the Canavin Station?"

"Nothing yet sir," replied Stan.

"Did you clarify that the matter at hand involves Pixaliemain?"

"N-no sir…I forgot to add that."

"Do you want your job?"

"Yes sir."

"Do you wish to be fired?"

"Yes sir. W-wait no sir. No sir I do not wish to be fired."

"Then do me a favour and persuade him and his 'sidekicks' to arrive here no later than today."

"Yes sir, I mean Captain, I mean Commander Cyfreid sir! Right away."

Tina was tired, worn out and empty. Her interest gradually degraded. Then she remembered the task at hand. The thoughts of the predator in Detroit flashed before her jade eyes. The mission was undoubtedly a success. Still, there was more, much more.

Who am I supposed to find? How many people are qualified in total?

She insisted to figure it all out by phoning Cyfreid.

"I'm here," she said. He replied saying, "Perfect, now you need to act fast. You are to find Silvert. His name basically speaks his appearance."

"Wait, what about Canavin?"

"I'll deal with him. In fact, I'll deal with another one on the list. Remember your old boyfriend?"

"Cyfreid, you know he quit for a reason. The things you made him do…"

"Mistakes Miss Truman. Those were mistakes."

"I don't know if that's a good idea. Anyways, where would I find Silvert?"

"Just look around the city. I know you'll find him."

"It's a big-ass city, Cyfreid."

"Relax yourself. Trackers indicate that he's not too far from you."

"Okay, I'll report to you when I'm finished." The conversation ended. Tina gave a lengthy sigh. The man had to be found.

Silvert wore an affected silver necklace which empowered him significantly, giving full strength, agility, and jet-like flight travel. It was an ancient crystalline amulet, providing his entire body with the ability to morph into silver metal. While in his sparkling silver form, the necklace is merged with his skin. The recruit was also positively attracted to various silver objects. He as well as Canavin earned respectable names.

Tina searched everywhere and there was no success.

Maybe this is a test? Cyfreid's given her many, but she couldn't grasp the idea of why he would now. The task of trying to achieve a team of heroes would be a checkpoint far from reached. She walked along the streets in a disguise that would best fit the atmosphere of local citizens.

Her outfit was simple: dark shades with a purple dress-shirt and a black purse to carry. She continued to stroll around until her curiosity lured her to a newspaper. She picked one up and buried her face on the front page. Her eyes remained motivated on the recent news.

The page talked about the fascinating story of Sherman Bawnder (another asset to Cyfreid's dream team). Upon seeing this, she immediately signaled Cyfreid.

"Did you talk to that Sherman Bawnder guy?" asked Tina.

"Already did that. Apparently he's still trying to process the situation. This is even though I clearly stated what was at risk. Tina, I have no idea what's wrong with these people. It's as if the very thought of working in a group doesn't suit them and being solo is in their best interest. I might have to force some of them."

"Well I still don't have this silver freak. Maybe I should just—"

A salient sight cut her off. She blinked twice to see the reality. It was a combatant, someone with credible artistry. She recited the name when it filled her memory.

"Titanium Titan."

His real identity was Hiro Matsuo—a Japanese male whose suit had a strong crimson exterior.

"What about Titanium Titan?"

"Titanium Titan?" Cyfreid's eyes squinted.

"Yea, Hiro Matsuo."

"He didn't qualify."

"We're going to need all the help we can possibly get. You said that yourself if I'm not mistaken."

"Go for it. It's your call."

The disguised Tina Truman came within Titanium Titan's reach.

"Excuse me mister," she began. Titanium Titan observed her beauty; Tina became faintly nervous.

"What is it?" he asked.

"Can I have your autograph? You're my favourite hero of all time!" said Tina fibbing while holding up her pen. His arm stretched forth to take the pen and accept the woman's offer.

A collection of shrieks penetrated their ears. Countless amounts of people were departing from a local bank across from where they stood.

"Hold that thought," he said. He agilely ran towards the bank. Each footstep pounded hard with crimson metallic boots.

As Titanium Titan arrived in the immense area with scattering civilians, he spotted the cause.

It appeared to be a knight; the armour was aged and corroded. Titanium Titan didn't understand any of it. He advanced to the cavalier from behind and sternly asked, "Are you lost?"

The head spun around to face him with its body still frontwards. The act caused Hiro's heart to tremor. He stepped back, unaware of who the knight was or his capabilities.

Tina hid with her back pressed against the outer wall. She popped her head as her inquisitiveness rose.

"Where is the Pixaliemain?" asked the knight.

"The what?"

"Where is it?! I sense that it's near!" The body twisted and fronted Titanium Titan. The cavalier reached for his grey scabbard and drew out his gleaming rapier.

"Look," started the hero. "I don't want any trouble."

The rusted knight gave his first strike. Hiro felt a gust of air as the blade narrowly missed his neck. Death was around the corner and the titan had no intentions for its arrival.

He held up his fists. Even though he originated from Japan, Titanium Titan was a kung-fu specialist. He learned the skill from his sensei many years ago.

Time was escaping him. The hasty attempts from the knight scarcely tore Hiro's attire. He avoided every swift slash with sufficient caution; each one was a step closer to meeting his flesh.

Tina remained witnessing the battle as it grew with plenty of intensity. Titanium Titan kicked the glossy blade out of the knight's hands. He threw seven quick blows to his gut and gave a massive uppercut. It sent the devoted warrior out the window into a pool of several sparkling fragments. Tina was impressed. Titanium Titan leisurely loomed near. His conscience flooded his mind, whispering the path to his notable benefit.

The nunchucks it solemnly said. Hiro reached for them. They were made from titanium. He quivered inside as his soul ached. Nervousness entered and he didn't know why. He desired to use the weapons another time.

"You give up?" he asked, hoping that the answer would be 'yes'.

"Where is the Pixaliemain?!" cried the gallant cavalier. He stood up with his feet planted on the ground and found his sword. He briskly hurled the rapier to come rocketing for Hiro. The titan ducked his head, almost meeting the road. The blade propelled and returned to the cavalier like an impressive boomerang.

"I have no idea what this Pixaliemain is!"

"I feel its presence!"

Tina fled the sight when finally realizing the answer. It was her. The rock was safe in her jet that wasn't too far. Somehow, the cryptic knight could sense it. Her jet settled on the top of an edifice. Her repetitive footsteps advanced closer and closer to the building. Then she stopped.

I need to help him. She looked back at the clashing warriors.

Or perhaps not. This was Hiro's opportunity; being victorious would prove him a true consideration for the squad.

Hiro's gaze journeyed over the contentious knight and marked a floating silver figure; a man of boldness.

Oh no...not you. He sharply hissed his teeth.

"I will find the Pixaliemain," swore the knight. "You cannot defeat me alone."

"Maybe he doesn't have to," said a voice. The vague silver man soared down and landed. The dazzling sunlight shone from his shimmering silver body.

"You mind if I help you out?"

"Stay out of this Silvert!" Hiro ordered. "This is my fight!" From far off, Tina saw him. Her quest came to a halt.

"I need the Pixaliemain!" the cavalier bawled.

"What's this medieval misfit talking about?"

The cavalier dipped his blade for Silvert's metallic chest. The metals sparked with his glossy exterior scratched.

"Now I know what a car feels when it gets dented," said Silvert staring at the mark.

"Can you just leave?!" asked Titanium Titan.

"I'm not leaving when this moron scratched my chest." He marched towards the knight, insisting to remove his pothelm. Silvert placed his hand on top.

"Hey buddy, how's about you take your—"

Upon removing the tarnished helmet, silence filled them both. It was a skull, grey and bloodcurdling, sending instant alterations of thought to the heroes. Silvert and Hiro couldn't resist viewing the eye sockets as green haze ran out like evading wraiths.

"Okay, so we established one thing. This sure 'ain't' a human."

"Silvert please, just go. I got this covered."

"No, I don't think so. I'm going to end this." He readied his hand to eject his silver rays. The energy emerged, forming a bright signature.

"Wait!" shouted Titanium Titan.

"For crying out loud, what is it?!" He touched him on the shoulder, being utterly demanding.

"Let me take care of it. Please, I need this."

"Okay, let me think…"

Silvert fired the blast to send oxidized armour and timeworn bones flying.

"Not a chance, buddy. Maybe next time." He patted Hiro on the back.

"You said that last time," thought the combatant. The threat of the hostile cavalier was no more. Silvert wandered the area, eyeing the dispersed pieces. He sighted the dark skull and picked it up.

"It's crazy that this is what caused panic, don't you think?" He began to laugh.

"Where is the Pixaliemain?!"

"What the…" He gasped and immediately dropped the skull out of anxiety. It glared at them both as the mist continued to leak out of the holes.

Hiro viewed Silvert's expression. *Oblivious and alarmed.*

The knight's skull spoke with a vulgar and brutal tone. The jaw constantly bounced and clamped its hoary teeth when they met.

"I must have the Pixaliemain! The directors sent me here to retrieve all of them. Identymous will have his revenge."

"Identymous?" asked Silvert.

"Hold on," Hiro said. "Who are the directors?" The knight's head continued.

"They're called the directors of the—"

There was quietness. The skull couldn't finish, but desperately wanted to. With the head detached from the body, it somehow choked on its words and gave a deafening cry. Hiro and Silvert sheltered their ears. The vapour soared out and vanished, never to be visible. The skull crumbled like soil and sank into shadowy ashes.

Tina saw everything, including the speechless heroes. The agent left, working up all the levels of the building and reaching the rooftop. She opened a compartment and there it was: the lustrous Pixaliemain. She programmed the jet to return to base without her. Another plan was in mind—one that involved a new disguise. It was essentially symbolic, though she hoped nobody would think so: *A homeless woman*.

Silvert kicked parts of the tarnished suit and witnessed the bones dissolve into ashes, just like the skull.

"Well that's something you don't see everyday," he said smiling at Titanium Titan. The kung-fu specialist folded his arms.

"Why do you always do that?" he asked.

"Why do I always do…what?"

Titanium Titan couldn't believe how clueless Silvert actually was. He explained saying, "For just one time—that's all I ask—one time I would prefer to be recognized by handling a task on my own."

"Your name was recognized many times."

"Yes, but that was back in the day. You know, before I met you. And I wish I had the opportunity to relive those precious days of being solo. If you were smart, you would realize that the result is always Silvert and Titanium Titan, but never Titanium Titan and Silvert."

"Okay," said Silvert calmly. "But it sounds better when it's Silvert and Titanium Titan."

Reporters and journalists swarmed them with endless questions. One of the reporters asked, "Silvert, how did you and your sidekick defeat the invading cavalier?" Hiro hung his head with disbelief.

"Well it was actually easy. He never really helped me to begin with." The flashing lights bounced off his body. He treasured the fame and the people.

"You know what," said Titanium Titan. "Forget all of this. I'll see you later…hero." He left the celebrity.

Why does he always get all the credit?! Nothing mattered except for another shot at a new start. Trying to be a solo warrior came with its disadvantage: *Silvert*.

Silvert watched Titanium Titan leave, but locked his attention on a woman, someone more favourable in his mind. Her beauty attacked his heart like a pounding pugilist. Still, there was something odd. Her clothes; the pants was filthy and the torso was shabby as if it was lacerated by rodents. Nothing matched the vehicle she stood beside. The dark-coloured car was fairly new.

She held up a sign that would be expected to say *"Spare change"* or *"Will work for food"*. Not even close. The sign actually stated, *"No time to explain. World is at stake. Get in the car now!"*

Silvert scurried his way out of the crowd and entered the vehicle. He was curious. He sat down in the passenger seat. The door slammed shut on its own. He leaned his head, seeing the true determination in the woman's eyes.

"Is everything alright Miss?" he asked.

"Look forward!" she commanded. The car shifted to autopilot and zoomed down the road.

Silvert obeyed, though he could witness her movements in his peripheral vision. She was changing clothes. He wished to take a glance.

"You heard what I said, right?" said the woman. He insisted to wait until she was done. As he continued to look forward, the woman said, "I'm Captain Tina Truman. I'm an AIA agent for the invasion protection center." Silvert nodded, but still understood that staring wouldn't be respectful.

Tina told him everything; the Pixaliemain issue; the thought of a legion of heroes; the notions about a lurking beast. He only responded saying, "Do I have to keep looking forward?" She replied, "No I'm done now, Jamal Vertison." Silvert turned to his left and felt dread crawl through his skin. One question stayed in his head. *How?* He saw Tina wearing the uniform for her sector.

"H-How did you know my name?" he asked.

"Really now, I mean come on," she began. "You followed a woman who was thought to be homeless inside of an AIA vehicle. You didn't infer that I would know your name? I know everything about you Silvert. But don't be alarmed. You're not the only one that has his or her secret identity in AIA records. You can trust us."

"I hope I can," Silvert said. "And besides, if this Xaliemer guy still has not shown up, then I don't understand the concern."

"The concern is that any Pixalian can summon him! There are four more samples out there and one of them belongs to Cain X. And I know for a fact you're familiar with him."

Silvert stayed silent. Cain X, or more commonly known as Governor X, was Silvert's chief adversary. He led AIA Central: a sector secretly responsible for the deaths of many citizens.

Silvert lowered his head. He was very compelled to act fast or else whatever Governor X was planning, it'll bring the world to its limit.

"I'm in," he stated with caution. Tina grinned at the remarkable response. She only hoped that every recruit would have similar intentions.

A fortunate man arrived in his adorable kitchen. It was ornately gorgeous, being only one of the finest rooms in his exceptional mansion. He sat down to watch the awaited news on his favourite broadcasting show entitled: Marvelous Munroe, starring Alyssa Munroe. To add to his life in the colossal mansion, he had an attractive maid by the name of Laura. She had striking brown eyes and alluring blonde hair. As the man sat down, Laura came and served him a simple meal of tea and bagels.

"Thank you Laura," he gently said as he watched. Alyssa Munroe began to speak.

"Laura, please turn up the volume. I want to hear this." She did exactly that. Alyssa Munroe's voice was exceedingly audible. She was talking about the latest news that happened in Cleveland about two weeks ago.

Alyssa said, "In other news, cleanup continues after the *Bon-Fire* attack of Cleveland. The officers with Spec-Ops agent Luke Crimson that have banded together are now saying their goodbyes. They are hoping for another opportunity to work together in the future. However, the real story is about their leader, Sherman Bawnder. This man was believed to have died years ago, but think again folks because he is alive! He stands right here beside me. Sherman, can you please explain to the world how you survived that incident two years ago?"

The incident which seemingly killed Sherman was a match between him and an abominable predator. The man kept gulping his tea as he listened to what Sherman had to say.

"Well," Sherman started. "I don't know if you're going to believe it...but I was some type of corpse who rose from the grave. Then after some special meetings with a classified agent, I am now indestructible. I can't die. I'll repeat myself once again...I can't die. Truth of the matter is that I don't know if that is a good thing. Regardless, I'm going to have to live with it."

As the news show ended, Alyssa Munroe concluded saying, "Well that's it for today's news. I'm Alyssa Munroe, signing off." The man turned off the television. He sighed and said, "Even Sherman is making the news." The maid approached him, ready to give a vital message.

"Laura, remember Sherman Bawnder? Well apparently he claims that he can't die. He considers that he's immortal or something. Man I tell you, these people. They think they're heroes."

"Someone is waiting for you at the door." The wealthy man looked at her with confusion. He usually never had guests at this time.

"Who is it?" he asked. Laura's eyes rolled up as she tried to recite the name. "I believe he calls himself...Cyfreid. Should I let him in?"

The man pushed himself from the table with his chair wobbling. He stared Laura down and roared, "Don't let him in! Do you hear me? Do not let him in!"

"I'm afraid you're too late," said a voice behind them. They looked back and spotted Cyfreid in the kitchen, eating the crispy bagels.

"Your maid makes a fine lunch. I should hire her someday."

Laura walked down the hallway to leave them alone. She knew Cyfreid was a particular visit from his past—one that was better left in the shadows.

He and Cyfreid sat around the dinner table for several silent minutes. He observed the officer as he sank his teeth in the meal—his meal. *He hasn't changed one bit.*

"Why are you here, Cyfreid?" He requested an immediate response. "And did it ever occur to you not to creep into people's homes?" Cyfreid took his last bite, chewed, swallowed, gazed up, and said, "That was delicious."

"Cyfreid!"

The Commander stared at the rich man and recollected an array of memories. The times they shared together, he missed them dearly.

"What happened to you, man?"

"What do you mean what happened? I moved on."

"You used to be the one guy who I could count on. You were a person who could hunt down any prey. You were definitely not afraid to get blood on your hands. Please tell me how come the one and only Curtis Kareem refuses to return my phone calls? Or should I call you by the name you used to prefer. Don't you remember…Sharp?"

Curtis Kareem, otherwise known as Sharp, exploded with a rampaging voice.

"My name is Curtis Kareem you idiot, not Sharp! Picking codenames wasn't one of your specialties. Do you know why I left you?! It was because I realized the real Cyfreid! You're a person who doesn't know when to stop! You have absolutely zero boundaries! It's always about hunting down creatures, some of which were good and respectful! Some Pixalians settled here only to start new lives. They didn't want any trouble, and yet you made me create more graves! And don't forget the worst thing you made me do. Your mistakes made me slaughter humans because you felt that some of them were aliens in disguise. I am sick of you and your agency!"

"Okay, okay relax yourself. However, I'm still going to call you Sharp. It's your codename, so accept it."

"I mean what did that stupid nickname even mean?! Strategic Hero Animalized—"

"Curtis…it's your name. I gave it to you for a reason. Please believe me because I truly understand that I messed up a couple of times. It didn't mean you had to leave me and use the money I gave you to build a mansion, hire a very gorgeous maid, and modify your basement into an entertaining movie theatre. Don't ask me how I know that. Sharp, regardless of the life you live and the people and experiences you come across, you'll always be remembered as one of mine."

"What do you mean one of yours?" he asked. Cyfreid sat up and gave an encouraging smile to Curtis.

"That's why I came here," said the Commander. "I'm building a team and I want you to join. So what do you say?" His arm stretched to the main entrance.

"Get out!" he ordered. Cyfreid remained in the kitchen.

"Come on, Curtis. The agency misses you. I miss you. Even your girlfriend misses you."

"Tina Truman is my ex you fool. And don't give me that crap saying she misses me."

"Yea, I guess you're right. I mean, she is a lot to maintain." Curtis scowled, wishing for his inner prowling animal to emerge.

"What about Gary?" he asked aggressively. "I'm sure he's enough help for you."

"Gary is…different."

"Forget it Cyfreid. I'm not coming. The door is right there. Be dismissed."

"Sharp," said Cyfreid as he rose from the table. "When you used to work for me, there was a moment when you told me about your dream. Do you remember what it was? It was your dream that someday the world would call for a group of courageous people. You wanted to be a part of this faction. Well guess what, now's your chance. There is a threat of a great force that vows to enslave our race. I need you, Sharp. I refuse to leave until you agree to the offer."

As critical of a persuasion, it made no progress.

"It looks like you're going to be staying here for now on because I'm not joining your stupid team," said Sharp with a little humour. Cyfreid couldn't believe the answer and was ready to erase Sharp from the enrollment list. He thought of a new strategy.

"Alright then," he said. "My aircraft is waiting outside, but I'm sure I could stay. And besides, it's not like I'm going to annoy you, wear your clothes, and eat your food. That last part already happened. How long would it be before I wear your clothes? Oh well, I guess we are going to be spending a lot of time together for the remainder of our lives. That is what you want, right?"

This was all sarcasm, but true in the same sense. Curtis despised every word that came out of his mouth. Those words formulated a vision inside of his mind—a vision of a life with Cyfreid disrupting his privacy. The very thought had to be avoided at all costs. He looked at Cyfreid and hollered, "Fine! You win! I'll join your team! But after this is all over, you have to promise never to visit me again."

"You see, now that's the Sharp I remember."

Curtis told Cyfreid to wait as he rushed to a secret room. He opened one of his closets and found his old uniform. The torso was dusty grey with elastic army-green gloves. After putting on the hated attire, he returned to Cyfreid's company.

"The suit still fits you," Cyfreid said. Sharp replied with the statement, "Let's just get this over with." Laura saw Curtis in the leather garment.

"I'll be back, Laura. Keep the house nice and tidy."

Former relationships were placed aside from the undertaking. Commander Cyfreid and Captain Tina were proceeding in the gathering process.

III

PIXALIAN CALLING

SEVERAL CONSTANT MESSAGES WERE transmitted to the Canavin Station that hovered above the planet as if it was some type of massive satellite. The station was heavily equipped with pernicious defenses that even the agency was unaware of; they would only be used if the alien-hero agreed.

Canavin stood with his golden Pixalian face reflecting from the enormous windows lined around the station's equator. He was accompanied by his three companions or as Cyfreid called them, *his sidekicks*.

His tech-specialist, Frankie, was one of them. There was Celestica, attention-grabbing and valiant. Zan Genrax was the last, strong-minded and Pixalian just like Canavin.

The only thought that roamed in Canavin's mind was Celestica. Her identity was Vanessa Allen. They fought alongside each other since the third year after the Star-Pix Crisis. After five unforgettable years, the two of them grew very fond of one another until the feelings reached their pinnacle of attraction.

Zan and Frankie discussed the future of the base and Vanessa noticed that Canavin was hushed. She walked up to him and only saw how he continued to gaze upon the millions of stars with Earth at the center. He pretended to ignore Vanessa's approach, but failed. *She was too entrancing*. She serenely asked him, "What are you thinking about?"

The alien with the three long antennae on his head turned to Vanessa. Then he moved his sights back on Earth.

"What if I haven't decided to protect the humans? Would I be living a better life?" Vanessa didn't know the proper response and also was muddled by the question. Before she could make her decided answer, Canavin asked another question. "What if…"

He paused, trusting that it wouldn't cause any harm.

"What if I decided to protect the citizens of Star-Pix instead of the citizens of Earth?"

"Are these rhetorical questions?" she thought to herself. Did they really require a response? If so, what would be the most acceptable answer? She tried to exchange one.

"Then you wouldn't have the reputation you have now," she answered. Canavin's eyes pinpointed her beauty. Her dark-brown glimmering eyes corresponded with her dark skin and her black, long, and dazzling hair. Her face was innocent looking, but he didn't let that fool him. He knew the anger that she was able to carry out.

"Reputation?" he asked. "It's because of the good reputation I have on Earth that gives me the poor reputation I have on Star-Pix. I was their Prince and soon-to-be King. I let them down."

Vanessa, as quick as she could, took Canavin by the hand and said, "No, you didn't. You did what you felt was right. You saw the corruption on Earth that no other Pixalian dared to correct. If you chose not to aid us, then you wouldn't possess this outstanding station." Canavin grinned and added to Vanessa's appreciated answer.

"I wouldn't have met you," he replied softly. His entire face shifted to his human form: a man of colour. Vanessa and the others were already familiar with this look along with many people on the planet, including Cyfreid.

"Stop that," Vanessa spoke. She was amused by how handsome Canavin looked as a human.

"Stop what?" Canavin wondered.

"Stop looking at me like that."

"Looking at you like what? I can't look at you this way?"

"It's disturbing."

The hero switched his appearance, returning back to his Pixalian body. Then he swapped back to human, then back again and again. He was playing with Vanessa, and it was working. She tried her best not to laugh at the continual shifting. She couldn't help it. Vanessa wailed out excitement. Canavin did the same as he converted to the alien form and remained that way. His merriment ended; the gold-faced Pixalian stared back at the limitless space.

"What's wrong now?" asked Vanessa.

"Laughter has always reminded me of the experiences I had with my father...before he was murdered."

"Then let laughter have a positive effect on your life. You said that it reminds you of your father. You loved your father, so learn to love laughter."

Canavin followed her advice. He laughed some more with her. The others watched them.

"Look how happy they are," said Zan. "It pleases me to see two individuals strongly connected by love. Except its odd because one of them is a human."

Frankie gave Zan a disorient look. It was as if his painted expression said, *"What are you talking about? It is clearly odd that he is an alien."*

His eyes angled to his screen with several similar messages.

Nineteen messages were listed and then immediately there was one more.

"Well that's twenty," said Frankie.

"Twenty what?" asked Zan.

"Twenty messages all coming from this Stan character."

"You never told me that today we've been receiving messages."

"Well I am right now."

Zan took a glimpse. All of them were listed as *Agent Stan*. He asked, "What are these messages about?"

Frankie reacted with a difficult pronunciation of the main subject.

"Pixal, Pixal...Pixaliemain," he stated finally getting it correct.

Fear sailed from the depths of Zan's gut. He was temporarily muted from the word. His outsized alien eyes widened to become greater than ever.

"What did you just say they were about?" He prayed that he heard Frankie wrong. The tech-specialist repeated the word, this time pronouncing it correctly on his first attempt.

"I said that the main subject of each message refers to Pixaliemain. Do you have any idea what it is?"

It was easy for Frankie to notice apprehension on Zan's face. He was speechless, wishing that he didn't have to convey the dreaded words to his leader. Still, it was necessary. He promptly turned to Canavin who adored his talk with Vanessa. He walked with each of his steps advancing to deliver the news. The delight of Canavin and Vanessa finished when Zan had no aims to smile.

"What is it?" asked Canavin.

"Does this word ring a bell to you…Pixaliemain?" His smile died. Vanessa didn't know what the word meant, but figured that it wasn't a pleasant one.

"Did you just say Pixaliemain?" he asked back.

"Yes, Canavin."

Canavin dashed for Frankie's monitor followed by Zan. Each message was in video format having Agent Stan explain the emergency. Both Zan and Canavin watched the recent one. Vanessa, being curious about the turmoil, joined the three of them. Stan's message was as followed:

"Attention Canavin Clan, this is a critical message. I repeat, this is a critical message. After recent actions with a substance known as Pixaliemain, it appears that the rock samples emit unidentified wavelengths. These happen to enable certain creatures to read an ancient hex of unleashing an extreme abomination to Earth's population. We fear that at any moment, this great threat will arise. This is an urgent calling for your team to unite with Team Valor and the world's most courageous fighters in order to defend the planet, just as you've been doing time and time again. We request an immediate response. The world is calling. If you choose to accept or better yet when you choose to accept, you will be

required to report to AIA East which is directly above the latitude of 38°, 53' North and a longitude of 77° and 02' West. We'll see you there."

What only Canavin and Zan knew was that each precarious stone originally belonged to Canavin's father. Before his death, his father hid the samples so that the traces will never be able to reach Earth.

"Can you explain more about Pixaliemain?" Vanessa asked Canavin, eager for an immediate answer.

"Not now," uttered the Pixalian.

Nobody was supposed to be exposed to Pixaliemain, not even humans. The roots of the ill-fated reality linked to Commander Cyfreid.

AIA East would provide a home of answers. He remembered Cyfreid and his decadent deeds. Yet, the true source wasn't the eastern base, but the planet where it all started. Star-Pix.

Canavin's senses tangled with one another, trying to determine the best route. *AIA East or Star-Pix.*

He and Zan were the only ones that knew where the Pixaliemain rocks were supposed to be hidden. A quick observation was crucially necessary.

"Star-Pix it is," he thought.

Canavin told Zan the plan. When he agreed, the two of them sprang into their ships that were located on the base's landing pads. Their ships had astonishing features: a light speed system and traits similar to the defenses of the battle station. Vanessa and Frankie watched as the two aliens said their temporary goodbyes.

"We're going to Star-Pix and we'll be back shortly," Canavin said while being consumed by Vanessa's enthralling beauty.

"Stay here at the base to make sure it's fully functional," said Zan as he flew off. Canavin gave a final wave to Vanessa. She offered a wave back to him and he flew away. The view of the cruiser shrunk to a twinkling star in the distance. It disappeared.

She put her head down, distressed by whatever the rocks could do. She tried to portend the future; she had slight moods of agitation. What wired her spirit more was the fact that she never heard about the Pixaliemain rocks for five years being a part of the clan.

Even after the Star-Pix Crisis that caused aliens to populate on Earth, Star-Pix still remained an alien-diverse planet. Creatures from all over the galaxy settled there and all followed orders from their new master, King Flern.

Canavin was supposed to be next in line, though he had vital responsibilities on Earth.

The journey to Star-Pix was nerve-racking. The world of various creatures wasn't too far off, yet the thoughts of Pixaliemain made the excursion displeasing.

When Canavin and Zan landed and jumped out of their cruisers, they sighted the number of ethnic Pixalians. Some wore regal robes. Others were mere peasants who willingly roved the streets in search for wealth. Then, there were the scoundrels, flagitious and loathsome, who gave Canavin and Zan malicious looks. That didn't bother them, specifically not at the moment.

Instant chants from crowds of creatures rallied their way, all saying the same welcoming words.

"The Prince has returned yet again!"

No delight was decorated on Canavin's face from the cheering Pixalians. The two warriors hassled themselves in the royal palace to speak with the King who possessed his imperial guards at his sides.

"Ah…Canavin. The wielder of the Pixcalibur blade has returned yet again. I see you also brought Zan with you. How are you two these days?"

"We are here to discuss Pixaliemain," said Canavin.

King Flern waved his arm to tell the guards to leave the throne room at once. With their presence gone, he dropped his tone. Every Pixalian did this when they were to bring up the issue of Pixaliemain.

"What about it?" whispered the King as he looked around for prying eavesdroppers. Canavin's response was plain and simple as if he was giving an order to the King.

"Does it matter?" he stated. "Those rocks belonged to my father. I deserve the full right to see them." Flern's face exposed slender dismay. He feared the son of the original King as if he was a god. The notion posed by Canavin was accepted; Flern allowed them to search.

Just watching the two Pixalians wander around his throne room built concern. Their pacings troubled him greatly. He had nothing to hide, but it seemed that way. He was like any other King who had a round belly with an admirable cape and exquisite crown. He had two enormous black eyes just like Canavin and Zan and possessed five antennae on his golden head.

The Pixalians scouted the room for every corner. They found nothing. Canavin assembled the memory. He saw his father carrying the rocks and hiding the substances the last time someone tried to snatch them. Saved by the restoring knowledge, he remembered the exact place where they were kept.

"Zan," he began telling his companion. "Take down that portrait of my father." He looked to his left and sighted the portrait of the former King. Zan took it down and behind was a passage vault attached to the wall.

"It needs some type of password," Zan said to Canavin.

"Relax, I already know the code."

He had a fascinating aptitude for recalling certain phrases and words, especially during dire times.

Zan and the King observed as Canavin punched in a variety of letters. The code was the name of Canavin's mother. He never knew her, but heard stories about her when he was a toddler.

After punching in the letters, there was a sudden rigorous ringing that lasted five seconds. The small vault creaked as it opened slowly. The desperate moment, the chance for revelations of pleasure or panic, it encountered them. Canavin's heart pounded when the tension of the awaited answer was torrid. He speedily swallowed gulps as perspiration escaped him. He hoped that the Pixaliemain stones would still be there. The vault opened fully and his faith shattered like glass.

Nothing. Absolutely nothing was within the vault except excessive dust. *How did the Pixaliemain get stolen?*

"Nothing," Canavin sadly murmured. Zan turned and paced bitty steps. His head elevated and he inhaled a deep breath, probably the deepest breath ever. He took in everything: the broken hopes of finding the rock samples, the threat of Xaliemer, and the very idea of joining a group of people he regarded as misfits. He exhaled and faced Canavin.

"Then you know what we must do," he said with much concern. The two departed from the King and were speechless. When the Pixalians cheered once more, Zan and Canavin ignored. Their ships were ready for takeoff. Canavin looked up and envisioned his father's face sheltered behind the foggy clouds; it was a sad face. Everything was crucial to fix.

The King hassled himself off his comfy throne and jogged out of the noble palace to see the ships ascend in the Pixalian sky. His dashing cape fluttered from the gusting wind. Canavin and Zan soared away. As the clouds concealed the cruisers, Flern returned to his seat. He generally never left his throne; he was quite languid and denied to do many things. The King sat and recalled the exposed fact.

Pixaliemain was gone.

He became rather alleviated, not understanding the concept of why the rock samples were missing in the first place, or better yet how they were missing. A question hit him.

"Why should I care?"

He referred to the situation as a blessing for his people. The curse of Xaliemer has been upon them for as long as he could remember. Flern couldn't grasp the idea why Canavin cared for the humans. He felt that staying on Star-Pix and never leaving in the first place would've been the smarter option. The humans were the ones who invaded his planet; the threat of Xaliemer would be the perfect revenge.

The intensity of the missing Pixaliemain wrenched at Canavin's heart. His feelings for Earth were just as strong as any human. Earth was the second planet he ever stepped foot on. Being there for eight long years has allowed him to call the world his home, just as he did when he was to discuss Star-Pix.

As the voyage to the station was complete, Canavin and Zan spotted Vanessa and Frankie awaiting their arrival. She smiled when they came out of their cruisers. When seeing Canavin's face, she smiled more, hoping that he would exchange one back. He didn't bother. Canavin ordered them to grab their belongings.

"Zan and I decided that joining AIA East is important. It turns out that unfortunately, all the samples of Pixaliemain are missing. Only Cyfreid knows of their location."

Frankie's face lit up with confusion.

"Cyfreid?" he asked Canavin.

"I'll explain on the way. Just hurry because the quicker we leave, the quicker we can get to the bottom of all of this." Vanessa rushed herself to some of her weapons. When she grabbed what belonged to her, she asked, "What about the station?" This formed a soundless juncture. The three of them turned to Canavin for the answer. Canavin told them not to worry one bit.

"Since our last incident, I installed a lockdown method so just in case anyone or anything gets by our defenses, the base's operating systems wouldn't be affected."

"Very smart," stated Frankie. He looked towards the others with admiration. They were thankful to have a leader like Canavin and wouldn't trade him for anyone else. They each went into their own individual cruisers. Within Canavin's ship, the alien put on his mask. He contacted Cyfreid on his monitor.

"Hello?" said Cyfreid. "Ah yes…Canavin. I'm so glad of you to finally respond to the offer. Have you met the man sitting beside me? His name is Curtis Kareem, but his codename is—"

"Shut up Cyfreid! Why is Pixaliemain on Earth?"

"Okay…obviously you have some questions and they'll be answered…just not at this moment. I'm trying to recruit people for the team that you're now joining. You are joining, right?"

"I guess so, now seeing that you doomed the human race!"

"I didn't do anything. Like I said, I'll explain later, but I need you to do me a favour."

"What is it? And this better be good!"

"You viewed Stan's message right? Well, he spoke about your clan uniting with Team Valor. Do you remember them?"

Canavin recited the group. The team was comprised of five members that Canavin worked with a couple of times in the past.

"Yes, I remember them."

"I need you and your team to make them agree to the grand offer. They haven't responded yet." In that instant, before Canavin could decline the mandate, Cyfreid ended the transmission.

"Sometimes I hate him," said Canavin.

IV

INFILTRATION

COMMANDER CYFREID TOOK CANAVIN'S tone to great consideration. The purpose of the alliance was to counter Governor Cain X. The intimidating Governor was sure that his plan will be achieved.

Soaring across the skies in his jet, Cyfreid was relieved that he finally persuaded Curtis to join. He felt that it was critical to aquire someone like him. There was a predator deep within him and Cyfreid valued that side. The man turned to Cyfreid after he turned off his communicator.

"Canavin," he started. "It's so urgent that you had to contact Canavin?" All Cyfreid could do was grin.

"Yes, why not? His knowledge of the substance is beyond what our minds can handle."

"Whatever you say. So who are you going to annoy next?"

The Commander wasn't too amused. He handed Curtis a piece of paper showing a brief biography of his next target.

"Actually, the person we're going to get *is* annoying. His name is Lynx, otherwise known as—"

"I don't want to know identities," explained Curtis. "You know for a fact that knowing those kinds of secrets is not my intention."

"Very well," said Cyfreid. "Anyways, if you honestly believe that I'm annoying, then you don't know the meaning of the word. Lynx has a mouth, one that for some strange reason, doesn't know when to shut up. The bottom line is that we are lucky to have him on the team."

"Don't you mean *if* he joins the team?"

"Absolutely not," said Cyfreid. "He'll join…trust me."

"*Sure* he will."

Cyfreid trusted the documents. The words explained the full character of Lynx: his likes and dislikes, the academic institutions he attended and dropped out of, and his current location in New Orleans, Louisiana.

His abilities were enabling internal lightning bolts. Curtis read all of this on the biography paper.

"It seems like this Lynx guy is pretty powerful. Anyone else I should know of that might *piss* me off?" Cyfreid was soundless.

"Anyone?" asked Curtis again.

"I'm sorry but did you say something?"

Curtis was annoyed once more. He couldn't even imagine how anyone could be as disturbing as Commander Cyfreid.

Canavin and his team watched as the view of the base got larger. The Pixalian warrior recited what Cyfreid told him.

Recruit the cunning Team Valor.

The Canavin Clan assisted Team Valor years ago. It was a hectic time that involved the smuggling of drugs by a crafty syndicate. The organization was led by Derwin Grant, a prominent drug lord. People called him the Optimistic one, or Professor Optimistic. After their success, the two factions never stayed in touch.

Team Valor was one of the strongest, yet oddest groups of gifted humans.

There was Fusion Fighter: an amalgamation of a man named Mark Foland and a Pixalian-mutated pterodactyl gone wrong. He had enhanced strength and flight.

The other was Meditation: a numinous woman named Sasha Grey. She was able to cast multiple hexes on her adversaries. The mystical energy was similar to black magic, but truly derived from extraterrestrials.

The third member of the team, DeMarcus Howard, was a spirit himself called Breath-Stealer. Thankfully, he was able to change his form.

The fourth member—and undoubtedly the most outrageous—was Alicia Eve Tavern. They called her Evesdrop. The name was determined by her advanced hearing. She had remarkable reflexes in battle, but that wasn't all. On her mantis green skin, there was a nauseating, yet useful trait. Her eyes, all one hundred of them that scattered all over her body, bulged out of their blinking sockets to see incoming threats.

The leader of the team was Valor, who was also recognized as the Valor Project. Nobody, including himself, knows his real name.

The story of Valor was a tragic one. When he was a young boy, he was with his mother and father. Being the only child, he traveled with them everywhere. They were in a plane; there were many passengers at his sides. Everything was perfect when the boy received the warmth of his mother and the leadership from his father. A random man, short in stature with trendy clothes, happened to be an alien in disguise. The time was before the Star-Pix Crisis, which only set the notion that Pixalians were among humans before they knew of their existence. The creature revealed itself; its scaly skin continued to shed as it approached the parents. Its presence led to a sky-high carnage.

The trauma rushed through the child. The creature gripped his feeble body. It slowly breathed on him and gave a baleful smile. The boy cried out for help, but nobody risked their own safety. The Pixalian clutched his neck firm and tossed him out of the plane.

After he fell all the way down, the young boy finally plopped into rippling waters. A group of sailors saw the event and hurried to save him. They found his body and he was pronounced dead.

Rather than bringing him to a hospital so that professional paramedics could give the final word, one of the sailors brought the youngling to a man named Chief Renegades. He had a systematic plan for saving the boy and predetermining his future. It was called the Valor Project which announced a new chemical: Valoric Energy.

The substance was injected into the boy and worked its magic of creating brand new cells and muscle tissue. The operation was a remarkable success and succeeded in saving the child, but he suffered from amnesia. This gave Chief Renegades an idea to make the boy a weapon. Valoric Energy had negative effects on aliens that eventually led to death.

At the age of 20, he was given two firearms called Valoric pistols and the qualities of them were the cords connected to his wrists. Each wrist had two cords: one cord sucked the energy from him and the other pumped more. His codename became Valor or in other words, courage.

Valor was led by Chief Renegades until his sudden death. He went solo and then was captured by a classified company. Soon, he was saved by four individuals that later formed the group of five currently known as Team Valor.

Canavin sent a transmission to his team while they flew for the base.

"Guys, I spoke with Cyfreid."

"Once again, who is that and what did he say?" Frankie asked.

"He's the Commander of AIA East and claims that this whole Pixaliemain issue wasn't by his own actions. Anyways, he wants us to find Team Valor."

"Not those chumps again," said Zan wishing for a better task.

"Yes, and there's nothing wrong with them. They make good allies. Y'all know that for a fact."

"Where are they?" Celestica asked Canavin.

"According to my readings, they're currently in Chicago."

"And how do you know this?"

"Just a gift I have." The four cruisers each made wide turns away from the AIA East base. Illinois was their new destination.

After enabling their light speed systems, Canavin, Zan, Frankie, and Celestica reached Chicago.

The cruisers landed as the four of them stepped out. They watched the luminous nature of the sun decay to broiling blistering rays. Dusk reached the eminent Canavin Clan.

"Alright, we're here. So where are they?" wondered Frankie.

"I'm not sure exactly," said Canavin. "Everyone split up and report your status in twenty minutes. Go!"

They went their separate ways in order to find Team Valor; Frankie went left, Zan went right, Celestica traveled north, and Canavin dealt with the area around him.

A similar greeting of praise was shown by the people just like on Star-Pix. The citizens of Chicago applauded and gave their respect to the world-famous Canavin.

He scouted far and was unsuccessful. Frankie and Zan got the same results. As for Celestica, the woman was lost in a state of awe. She phoned the others saying, "You guys might want to check this out." Each of them was unable to trace her coordinates.

"Where exactly are you located?" asked Zan. Canavin joined the conversion from his location.

"Did you find Team Valor?" Celestica said nothing. Her stillness deeply concerned them. The Pixalian repeated himself as everyone listened in.

"Celestica, did you hear me? I'm asking if you found Team Valor." Not a single word.

"Frankie, Zan, find out what happened to her. From what I can guess, she should be located around that tall..."

Canavin paused while the sight stirred his thoughts. A tall skyscraper was his target. It was called the 'X' Center. From the title shown, the letter 'X' stood out to be the largest.

"Canavin?" the worried Zan asked. "The tall what?" It took several seconds before Canavin realized the voices of both Zan and Frankie. He continued to hear Zan ask again and again what he was referring to.

"Look for the tallest building." Just viewing the edifice splattered plenty of wariness. From their locations, they concluded the obvious. The building was none other than the office of Governor Cain X, whose illegal acts were well known by Canavin's team.

Canavin worried about Celestica. The mere fact that she refused to speak meant that she was either experiencing the same type of wonder, or something else—something that would require major assistance.

Canavin understood both of these insights and had to act fast.

"We'll meet up there," his voice said. "And keep your guards up. Something doesn't feel right."

It took long minutes before all three of them met up at the front of the building. Frankie asked the other two, "So what do we do now?"

"Walk inside of course. Celestica should be in there. She was around this area at the start."

"I have a bad feeling about this," Zan added.

"Good," said Canavin sarcastically. "At least you're feeling something right?"

They entered and spotted three surveillance cameras above them. They looked at each other, smiled, and somehow shared the same idea.

"You ready?" Canavin asked as he held up his hand and slowly generated a pulse beam. Zan did the same and Frankie prepared his handgun for a clear shot. At the same time, Frankie and Zan said, "Ready."

They simultaneously fired. Broken pieces from the cameras dropped as smoky curls gradually evaporated. Then the thought came to Frankie.

It doesn't make sense for us to walk into a government building and start violating personal properties.

This happened to give Canavin an idea of transforming into a disguise. Having the ability to do this, Canavin and Zan shifted to their human forms.

"Okay," said Frankie. "But you still can't afford to be shown in that armour." Canavin and Zan had their average clothes underneath. They split up again and changed. When they returned, Canavin—whose human identity was Connor— had the appearance of an ordinary business man. Zan was a blue-eyed Caucasian male wearing a caramel-coloured jacket. All who was left was Frankie, who looked exactly the same but was in a rich and 'sharp' suit and tie.

Canavin decided that now would be appropriate to call Celestica and figure out what happened to her. The silence he heard increased the concern for her well-being. Each person remained together and rummaged every floor of the institution. The search neared its end and as Canavin looked through one of the office windows; all he sighted was the night sky.

They had to pick up the pace. Glancing into each room led them to the final area. The door that presented itself in front of them required one thing: a DNA scan.

"Great, all that searching for nothing," Frankie stated.

"What do you mean all that for nothing?" said the human-looking Zan.

"A DNA scan, genius. We're never going to pass now."

"Never say never," said Canavin.

Frankie hoped that the two aliens in disguise had a plan that would have to be put into action rapidly. He couldn't quite understand the concept of having such a passageway in the first place.

"It has to be X's DNA," Canavin confirmed. "I'm also guessing it'll accept a retina scan. Zan, are you thinking what I'm thinking?"

"That depends," said Zan. "Does it involve going back to the station and forgetting this ever occurred?"

"No, it doesn't."

"Then I have no clue what you're thinking."

"You know for a darn fact that I only have one human form," Canavin said. "However, you have several. See if you can transform yourself into the Governor."

Frankie added to Canavin's words saying, "Better yet, just change your retina to match his. We've dealt with him before so try and see if you can copy it." Canavin stared at Frankie, not understanding why he even said that. When he asked him what was the difference, Frankie said, "I don't like the way Governor X looks, that's all." All Canavin did was shake his human head.

The entire makeup of Zan's eyes shifted from sapphire blue to cardinal red. It resembled the very eyes of the Governor.

The red-eyed Zan stepped face front at the door. He opened his right eye and stood there, hoping that the plan would be a success. A green beam of light shot from the retina scanner. It focused itself on the eye and tried to match every detail necessary.

"This isn't going to work," said Frankie. The scanning process came to an end and a voice stated, "*Access granted.*"

"You were saying?" Canavin said to Frankie as the door finally opened on its own. As Zan's eye changed back to blue, he complained, "My eyes are hurting."

This only amused Canavin who felt relief that now they were able to pass. Beyond them was a long hallway. They walked further and when reaching the end, they sighted another room. It was larger than the rest and possessed multiple portraits of the Governor.

"My goodness, he's hideous!" shouted Frankie.

"You need to grow up," said Zan.

"Both of you shut it," whispered Canavin. It was unclear to Zan and Frankie why Canavin was whispering, and then they figured it out. There were sounds, multiple sounds that later became clearer to their ears. They were ongoing voices. Canavin looked to his left and noticed an automatic door. Upon seeing this, he pointed in the direction. The other two nodded and they carefully paced towards the door, keeping their distance to avoid setting off the sensors. The curious fighters tried their best to interpret the conversation between two people. They heard this:

"What do you mean it won't work?"

"I'm terribly sorry sir, but stabilizing the level of heat from the satellites you asked for is...impossible."

"Impossible you say? Why don't you do me a favour and make the impossible um, what's the word I'm looking for...possible!"

"It's not as easy as you think, sir. We're working harder than ever, but what you request generates a tremendous amount of heat. All of the devices in orbit will be destroyed."

"Find a way!"

"I told you that we can't. We just don't have that kind of tech. Again, I'm sorry but it is imposs—"

"Find a way! I've been planning this for years! Now you're telling me that I came all this way just to fail in the end? You must be crazy! Don't you know that I always get what I ask for? All of you get back to work! I'm the Governor for crying out loud!"

Those were the last words heard by Canavin, Frankie, and Zan.

"Well that pretty much explains everything," said Zan. He and Frankie turned to Canavin. The Pixalian was disturbed. His senses grew to a level that caused him to recite events from his past—his childhood. His head was still, eyes almost sighting a returning vision as if it wavered before him. He believed that it was some sort of omen. Someone, another Pixalian, stood out the most.

"Canavin, are you okay?" asked Frankie. Under his mechanical mask, the warrior blinked twice with his mind already foretelling the next approach.

"Avinotch is near," he told them. Frankie never heard the name before.

"Avinotch? And who might that be?" Zan brushed passed Frankie, not going to close to the door.

"Avinotch is his cousin," he said.

"Okay, so what's wrong with that? Let's meet him."

"He's not the nicest person to be around," explained Zan. "Canavin and Avinotch go way back. However, after the crisis, he chose to turn against Canavin. He hated your kind in every way possible, though tended to favour Cain. The Governor has many apprentices. Avinotch is the only one who is Pixalian."

He looked at Canavin who was prepared for what waited on the other side.

"What is he up to?" Canavin wondered.

"I don't know but I'm ready to find out," said Zan who was about to change his appearance back to Pixalian form. Before he was able to do this, Canavin placed his hand on his shoulder and said, "Wait, not yet. Let's walk in just as we look so it's not obvious." Zan agreed and so did Frankie. They took one step and the door slid open for them to proceed.

The three of them saw a number of revelations. It was a larger room than the one they were previously in. The massiveness of the area was confusing. It was as if there was a facility within a facility. It shocked them intensely and there was more.

They saw Governor Cain X with his blood red eyes who wore his signature suit which had an 'X' on the left side. He was tall in stature and had a fat cigar in his right hand. He took a nice puff and smiled at his assisants as they brought a lady to his company.

It wasn't Canavin's first time seeing Cain, but his appearance always made others feel uneasy.

"Let go of me!" cried the voice. It was Celestica who was in steel handcuffs which were used by the Governor from time to time. Canavin looked at Frankie and Zan. He knew that he had to formulate something to free her. One of Cain's assistants walked her passed the three of them. Celestica recognized them immediately. She smirked a little but didn't draw too much attention.

"That's why she never responded," Zan whispered. "It was because this idiot captured her."

"Vanessa getting captured?" Frankie thought. "I never thought something such as that would happen."

"Those steel cuffs are difficult to get out of," Canavin said.

"Can we fight these morons now?" asked Zan who was desperate to teach them a lesson.

"Wait," said Canavin. He directed his eyes to Celestica who still complained. The assistant tightened his grip on her shoulder.

"Get in your cell and join the others!" he commanded.

"What others?" Celestica asked being unimpressed. Canavin, Frankie, and Zan wondered the same.

Unexpectedly, the floor opened from where she was and a cell rose from the ground. It had narrow lasers to resemble the bars. The prison carried five individuals: Evesdrop, Breath-Stealer, Fusion Fighter, Meditation, and Valor. Team Valor was found at last.

V

CENTRAL DANGER

WHILE THE DISGUISED CANAVIN AND HIS companions were in Governor X's fortress, Captain Tina continued her travels with Silvert. The only thought that was locked in Silvert's mind was ending the Governor's plot. He was so depressed that he decided to drive. Tina watched his anger as he stomped on the gas pedal.

"You know you can put it on auto, right?" she said to Silvert. He paid no attention and continued cruising. Their destination was the 'X' Center in Chicago.

"Silvert?" Tina said, being a tad worried.

"What?!" the silver man yelled while watching everything that came his way on the road.

"You need to calm down a little."

"Calm down?! Don't tell me to calm down when the matter involves the Governor!"

"Okay, don't worry. We'll stop him."

"Yea, we better!" He clenched hard on the steering wheel. "This guy Cain, he's a psycho menace! Did you know that he created a cyborg version of me? He's too obsessed with power. I thought my days in Chicago were enough to change him, but now I'm seeing that I was wrong. This time his ass is going to prison and staying there, you here me?! Heck, I don't even know why we're in this scrap metal when I can just fly us both there."

Tina turned to him and asked, "You really want to risk that with your speed? What if it falls?"

"What are you referring to? Wait, are you saying that you have…"

The agent smiled with her flawless teeth and had her jade eyes direct Silvert to a compartment in the vehicle.

"I have one with me," she stated.

"Well let's see it!" he said very excited.

"No, not yet. Wait until we reach Cain's office. But outside of this whole concern, I noticed you two having a commotion hours ago."

"What do mean 'you two'? Who are you talking about?"

"You know…Titanium Titan."

"There was nothing going on between us."

"Are you sure? It looked like he was pretty upset with you."

"Titan? Upset with me? That's not true." He pretended his cockiness had nothing to do with Hiro leaving him. It had no progress of persuading Tina. He forgot that she witnessed the whole situation. She told herself before that she had a plan to enlist Titanium Titan, and it was already put into action.

"Why do you even bring that scrub up? He doesn't even care for my assistance. In fact, he never has cared."

"Well," said Tina being hesitant to speak. "It just so happens that on the way here, I sort of called him and explained the Pixaliemain issue." The rolling tires screeched to a stop on the side of the highway.

"You did what?!" shrieked Silvert once more to Tina.

"It wasn't hard. You were so fixated on taking down Cain that I called Hiro without you noticing. It was about an hour ago. All I had to do was call 'Hiro Services Inc'. He was a little defensive at first. The truth is that he'll probably get there before us."

"Why is that?"

"I say this because I had an agent of mine escort him in a private jet."

"How come we don't get a private jet?"

"Just drive and stop complaining." Silvert pressed the gas pedal harder than ever. The dark vehicle blended with the pitch-black sky and accelerated. They were certain that Chicago was near when they got a good glimpse at the destination boards. It stated that their location was twelve miles away. Relief was shown on each of their faces.

"Speaking of Titanium Titan, he and I fought that numskull of a knight—and I mean that literally. The cavalier spoke about the directors. Do you know what he was talking about?" She thought about it and explained, "Not a clue to be honest. Directors of what?"

"That's what I'm trying to figure out. He also mentioned someone by the name of Identymous." Tina's relaxed mood snapped in half as she promptly turned to him. She spoke with a vigilant tone.

"Jamal," she started. "Identymous shows up on my Commander's most-wanted records. He's Pixalian. Any Pixalian that is on his list is considered lethal." Even with the concern exposed on her face, her beauty still caught Silvert's eye. He thought about how he met her hours ago.

"Why was it that you were dressed as a homeless woman?" Tina sighed not wanting to explain, but she did anyways. She said, "I'm a master of disguise. It's a part of the reason I ended up in the agency. I guess you can say it reminds me of my past."

"You used to be homeless?"

"I was a high school dropout, got kicked out of my house, experimented with…I was a *street pharmacist* as they call it. I don't feel like going into details right now."

"Dang, I'm sorry. I never knew. You can tell me more when you're ready to do so. But I mean, do you ever wish that your life was normal?" The agent took his words in greatly. It wasn't the first time someone asked what she regarded as the *fundamental question.* She shared a relation to Silvert and the other heroes on Cyfreid's biography papers when understanding that the Star-Pix Crisis was the cause of their current lives. She responded with the same answer she gave everyone.

"No," she simply said. "Not really. My life, hunting creatures, arresting Pixalians, I truly enjoy it. I consider it to be thrilling for some reason. I don't know, I guess it's just my way of being…*somebody.* I don't expect you to understand."

"Actually, I do. It's sort of the same thing for me except I don't think of myself as a Pixalian assassin. I just love saving lives. It feels *right*, you know."

"I only kill the malevolent ones—which is a lot. Cyfreid gives me a list, and I hunt them down. Simple as that."

It has been a tiresome day for Tina Truman. She received absolutely no rest the night before, added Silvert to the team, and now had to travel to Chicago with hopes to confront Cain X and receive another piece of the alien substance. She was fatigued from the necessary voyage.

"I have to sleep," she said yawning aloud.

"Sleep?" Silvert said confused. "Why on Earth would you do that at a time like this? Would your leader, Commander Cyfreid, allow you to do that?"

"No," she stated calmly. "But I'm allowing myself to do it." While in the passenger seat, her head dropped to her side. She slowly closed her eyes and began to sleep, though it wouldn't serve her any form of true rest. They were less than twelve miles away and the threat had to be prevented. Silvert didn't complain about her choice. He just joined the so-called "heroic team" and had no idea what Tina had gone through just to make it a reality. He thought about Titanium Titan; the way he annoyed him; the way how the credit deserved to be split between the two of them. He fully understood the mistakes he made and wanted to make it up to him. Now would be the perfect time to do just that.

While speeding passed all of the other cars, he noticed the city in the distance. Its beauty was captivating when seeing such a futuristic metropolis, especially with Governor X's office standing out. After a few minutes, Silvert made it to the city; Tina woke up yawning once more.

"How long did I sleep?" she asked scratching her head, still somewhat tired.

"You only slept for seventeen minutes," said Silvert.

"That's it. Only seventeen?"

"Yes and if you haven't noticed, we're here in Chicago."

She looked to see the buildings and the bright lights projecting from several cars on the streets. She drew her sight to the 'X' Center in the distance. She readied herself to being up to speed with the operation.

"Be prepared," she said to Silvert. "Anything can happen."

"C'mon, remember it's me you're talking about. I'm always ready for a challenge."

Within the vehicle, there was a miniature screen on the dashboard. It turned on with difficulty of receiving the signal. Finally, Commander Cyfreid appeared. He called out Tina's name while looking at Silvert. He realized that she wasn't driving.

"Where's Captain Tina" he asked.

"To your left," said Silvert.

The Commander turned his head and saw Tina staring back at him.

"Tina, what's the status?"

She said, "As of right now we are in Chicago. Where are you exactly?"

"I'm currently in New Orleans," said Cyfreid.

"New Orleans? Wait is there a substance over there?"

"Not exactly, I'm just—"

Sharp butted in and said, "He's trying to get some fool named Lynx. Who's the silver freak?"

"I'm Silvert," the hero said.

"Can we all just stop with the introducing garbage," said Cyfreid. "We'll have plenty of time to say our hellos when we meet up in person and take down X."

The transmission ended. Tina revealed her weapons to Jamal and loaded each pistol. The corners of her lips rose to a tender smile, slightly sinister, but still pacifying. She took out a bunch of papers from a different section in the car. When Silvert asked what they were, she said that they were documents of each and every hero the agency planned to gather. Silvert asked, "Does that include Titanium Titan?" She shook her head.

"However," she told him. "I saw what he's able to do. He'll make a perfect addition and a nice ally." Her words were absorbed. The more she talked about Titanium Titan, the more he felt guilt that had to come to its end. He drove further down the streets making X's office more evident.

Jamal and Tina saw something else. A great number of AIA agents who worked for the eastern sector swamped the venue with a specialized jet on the property.

He and Tina exchanged smiles.

"Reinforcements," Silvert said to Tina. "I like that… I *really* like that. You knew all along didn't you?"

She said, "I guess it slipped my mind." Several agents blocked vehicles from coming near the building. As Silvert reached, an operative walked up to the car. Silvert lowered the windows and the man said, "I'm sorry, this area is restricted. Please head somewhere else." The words meant nothing when Silvert told the agent that he was accompanied by Captain Tina. He took out his flashlight and pointed it inside of the vehicle, only to see Tina becoming impatient.

"Let us pass," she commanded the officer.

"Captain Tina, my apologies, I didn't think—"

"Shut your mouth."

"Yes ma'am."

"Now let us through."

"Of course." The nervous agent gave them the right to proceed. Silvert parked the car and took a nice and relaxing stretch.

"That feels better," he said. He watched Tina as she gathered a collection of items. She spotted her reflection from his metallic glow. She asked, "What is it?"

"Aren't you forgetting something?"

"Forgetting what?" The answer already came to her mind. She carefully looked around to make sure they weren't being watched.

"We're here now so let's see it," he replied. She sighed again and nodded. Her arm stretched for a compartment. She gradually opened it to expose a blazing sapphire light with an intense energy signature. It was so bright that even Silvert had to shield his eyes. The force was certainly penetrating and possibly blinding. She shut the compartment to hide its splendor.

"You get used to the light after a while."

"So that's what this sector is fighting over. That's what the cavalier wanted."

"Yes. It seems everyone wants Pixaliemain."

"Well, Cyfreid was wrong about one thing."

"And this is what exactly?"

"He said we were all going to meet up here, but the fight is going to be over before that."

"Don't be too sure." Tina opened the car door on her side, came out, and took a stretch just as Silvert did. Silvert also walked out and marked a familiar face that spoke with the other officers.

Titanium Titan. Silvert only hoped Hiro forgave him.

"Hold on," he said to Tina. "I'm going to apologize to the scrub over there."

He approached Titanium Titan and with each step, he tried to formulate a proper apology. Tina didn't know how Hiro Matsuo would react. When talking about what the significant form of attack would be, Titanium Titan saw Silvert coming towards him.

"You!"

Silvert stopped, then continued his approach. The agents also left when they understood that this was to be a private negotiation.

Silvert faced Titanium Titan and said, "Look, I know I can be sort of…um, what's the word I'm looking for?"

"Annoying, idiotic, disturbing, conceited, cocky, spoiled, you choose."

"Yes, all of those words…except for spoiled. I don't agree with that one. Anyways, let's forget all that and start all over. We made the best duo back at the capital. And I promise, in no way do I consider you my sidekick. So basically, can you forgive me?" Hiro pondered his words briefly and came up with his answer.

"Nope," he said.

"I'm sorry, what was that?" Silvert thought he heard the response wrong.

"I said no. Just because we're on the same team, correction, just because we're working together again doesn't mean that I forgive you. It's just something you're going to have to settle with. You're selfish Silvert. Just accept it."

He stepped away and walked towards the agents. Silvert stood like a statue, unable to move any limbs of his body. Tina arrived behind him.

"Did it work?" she asked Silvert. He felt that the troubling response from Titanium Titan was completely erroneous.

"No, it didn't work."

"Okay, just move on. Who cares?"

"*Of course.*" The meaning of the last sentence from Hiro was taken too broadly.

More vehicles arrived at the scene. Countless agents slammed their car doors. A tall bearded man in burgundy clothes stepped out of one of them. He recognized Captain Tina and asked, "What's your sector doing on our property?"

The man, waiting for a sudden reply, was from AIA Central. Captain Tina turned, arms crossed with her face front, ready to disobey any order the man might give. The eastern agents observed as Tina didn't say anything.

"Lady, I said why are you on our property?"

She expressed no fear.

"You know for a fact what my name is. It's Tina Truman so get it right. Also, we're not leaving the premises."

"You're telling me that Cyfreid sent you here?"

"So what if he did?"

"Listen Tina, my crew and I work for AIA Central. Are you familiar with us? We work for Governor X."

"Well I'm sorry to burst your bubble honey, but I really don't give a damn."

"Very well," said the man walking away. The eastern alliance continued to commune with one another as they accepted that Tina brought them relief. Silvert and Titanium Titan felt the same way.

The bearded man gave a nodding signal to the rest of his crew. They took out their guns and aimed it at Tina's agents.

"Fire!" the man commanded. Bullets zoomed their way and hit some agents. Officers dropped, pressing on their wet wounds only to find more shots strike them. Tina watched as some of her friends perished before her eyes.

"Watch out!" she screamed pulling out her pistol. She knelt down and shot at the AIA Central agents. The others who were in good condition did the same.

It was an AIA civil battle that occurred right in front of Cain's office building. Some eastern agents hid themselves behind the jet.

Titanium Titan and Silvert were the only ones who had exceptional gifts that would tremendously aid the AIA East agents. Before Titanium Titan could help, Tina ordered, "Titan, go inside and find the Governor! Do you hear me? And make him give you the Pixaliemain! Whatever it takes, go!" Hiro rushed inside and had to act fast.

The shots from both sides kept firing. The popping bullets collapsed against one another, terrorizing local citizens who were awake at such a late time.

Jamal hurried himself beside Tina and shot silver blasts at the opponents; the energy beams were quite effective. Although he was trying to help her, Tina gave Silvert a command.

"You go inside too! You're the only one who knows where he is located!"

"Hold on, why should I go when that—"

"Would the two of you grow the hell up?! As you can see, I'm a little busy right now!" She got up and dodged the incoming ammos. Clamorous moans coasted her way as Tina viewed more agents being shot down in cold blood. Silvert flew to the entrance. He paced inside and shouted, "Titanium Titan! Where are you?!"

"I'm up here. Try not to shout. There could be danger."

"I'm *sure* there is," Silvert said. "That's the whole point. It's so you can attack the fools. Speaking of fools, you mind taking back what you said about me?"

"I'm going to go with this answer…no."

"You *would* be immature about it. Grow up already."

"I'm here to find Cain X and confront him."

"You're not going to do that alone."

"Why not? You've done it many times."

"Look, how's about I show you where he is. I know this building inside and out. Actually I've been here too much."

"I'm sure you have. So where to?"

Silvert grabbed Titanium Titan and soared passed all of the stair levels. He traveled faster than he normally would only to bother Hiro. Slight anxiety gripped the combatant's face as Silvert landed in front of a hallway.

"Something's not right," said Silvert.

"What do you mean?" asked Hiro, recovering from the flight. Jamal could recite every door, crack, and window. Something was truly out of the ordinary. He looked at Titanium Titan and said, "The door leading to this hallway, it was left open." Hiro glared at the door which possessed a retina scan.

"Judging by the retina scan, it was most likely Governor X who walked through here."

"But that's what is different. Don't you get it? It couldn't be the Governor because he would never leave this passage open to others. Trust me, it had to be someone else."

"Who else could it have been? It requires a retina scan only Cain could provide." Silvert noticed that the statement by Hiro was correct, but not entirely. He broadly smiled at his old companion.

"I believe we have aliens in our midsts," he confirmed.

VI

REALMS OF TRUST

IT WAS ESSENTIAL TO MAKE SURE THAT

Governor X's reign would come to a close. A way to end the cause would be to enhance the team. Lynx was Cyfreid's next and last target. Proven by the documents in his folder, acquiring him would add to AIA East's success.

With the great population that New Orleans had, Sharp couldn't understand how Cyfreid would be able to find him.

"Where to now?" he asked. The Commander stroked his grizzled beard a couple of times and replied, "I'm actually not sure."

"You brought me all the way here just to tell me that?!"

"Calm down Curtis, I know where he is. Gosh my man, you haven't changed one bit. You might want to save that anger until we reach Illinois."

"I get angry when I want to."

"Whatever you say."

"And remember Cyfreid, when this stupidity is over, you're bringing me back home to Washington. A deal's a deal."

"Your wish will be my command, *partner*." The jet began to land on the roof of a building. Cyfreid hopped out with Curtis. The talk of going back home made Sharp more anxious to complete the mission. He valued his life after working for Cyfreid.

He realized that Cyfreid was telling him the truth when he said he was aware of the exact location of Lynx. It was something that Cyfreid was the master at doing. He could receive little clues here and there and then before anyone knew it, he would track down any person.

"Can you explain to me why we're on the roof of—"

"This building happens to be the office of a car company."

"So what's your point?"

"The top floor however, happens to be the penthouse. You ready for a little fun, Curt?"

"No and why would I be ready for that?"

"*That's too bad.*" The Commander found the staircase that led to the party. He went down, not even saying another word to Sharp. Sharp stood there on the roof understanding that he was supposed to follow. The response spoke to him.

"*Come downstairs anyways.*"

He took a breath, just hoping that this would all be over soon. Sharp walked down the stairs.

He caught up with Cyfreid and was greeted by the atmosphere of the penthouse: the rich and elegant people, the up-tempo music, the gamblers, and the erotic dancing.

Curtis wasn't used to these types of places. Instead, he preferred his nice and peaceful home with a helpful maid to do all his chores. His mansion was his sanctuary and he desperately wanted to go back. He said, "You brought me to a club? Some leader you are."

"Thanks Curt, I appreciate it," said Cyfreid not even noticing the sarcasm implied by Sharp's voice. They ambled around the top floor through hordes of billionaires and players. Sharp didn't care about the number of them with their strange gapes. He had to accept the remarks people gave.

"*Halloween's coming early this year, boys!*"

"*Who brought the creep in the dress?*"

Cyfreid did nothing to defend him. It's been a long while since Curtis wore his uniform and he understood that the magnate wasn't as famous as other heroes such as Canavin, Silvert, or even Team Valor.

Cyfreid led Sharp to the bar. There were two seats left and they took it upon themselves to sit down. A man beside Curtis with a classy tuxedo had both of his arms spread out, holding two gorgeous ladies. Curtis ignored the laughter that came from them. Cyfreid called the bartender. He was quite bulky, having multiple tattoos and piercings.

"Get me the best thing you got, and pronto." The bartender nodded and sighted Sharp.

"What? Are you going to laugh at me too?"

The fat bartender smiled and said, "No, what would you like to drink?"

"Get me some tea would'ya." The bartender and the ladies' man cackled.

"We don't serve tea, you knucklehead. At least not here anyway. Now hurry up, what do you want to drink?"

"He'll take the same thing I'm having," said Cyfreid.

"Best on the house, coming right up!" He grabbed an old bottle and provided pilsner glasses for the two of them.

"Please, shots only," said Cyfreid. The overweight man nodded and obeyed the request. Cyfreid took a sip with the taste being nothing short of bitter. He was used to it. His sight targeted the wealthy man beside him. Sharp thought Cyfreid's eyes were pinpointing the beautiful women, insisting that he desired a share of the craved pleasure. He poured more and held up the small glass.

"This stuff is 'good' isn't it?" he said loudly, trying to get the man's notice. He guzzled the gold sparkling liquid and placed the glass down firm.

"Do you know what else is good?" The man had no idea and said, "I'm not sure old man. Now leave me in peace with these wonderful angels."

With his lustful beam, he winked at the girl on his right, then the girl on his left. Sharp watched and was slowly putting the pieces together.

"My apologies," said Cyfreid. "I made a mistake in my sentence. What I meant to say is, do you know *who* else is good?" Hearing more from the stranger with his costume friend, the man pushed his sight away to be stunned by an angel. He smoothly ran his fingers down her soft arm. Cyfreid repeated, "Well do you?"

"Can you shut up old man?! I told you, I'm busy with my women!" Cyfreid despised being called *old*, especially twice. He wasn't even that old at all. The prideful ladies' man didn't stop there.

"Why don't you do me a favour and leave my presence! And bring your pet clown too! He's hideous and looks like a confused fan boy. The geek convention was last week buddy. I think you missed it!" The girls taunted and cussed them out. Instead of angels, they revealed their true nature of being more like demons.

Sharp was baffled by the man and had his hands to his sides. His fingers were shifting to become narrower. His pupils enlarged with his mouth ready to foam from the excessive anger. Cyfreid saw what he was doing and didn't want any trouble.

"Curt, not now please. I got this."

Sharp hoped that he was right, for the man's sake. Cyfreid continued even though the playboy showed no sense of caring what he had to say.

"Look," he told him. "I was simply asking you a question. Do you know who is good? Well I'll tell you. It's that Lynx character. Do you know him?" He was soundless; his dates couldn't understand why.

"Never heard of him," he finally claimed.

"You never heard of the great Lightning Lynx? Are you from New Orleans?" Sharp clued more into the situation.

"Can you stop with the questions?!"

"No, you're going to stop yelling." Cyfreid opened his green jacket and dug his hand, fiddling through a pocket to search for an item. He took it out with significance.

It was a detonator.

The ladies escaped the loving hold and bolted faster than track runners. The lonely playboy freaked with his heart stinging and his conscience wailing for safety.

"Put that away man! Are you trying to kill us?!"

"I don't like your tone young man. If you were smart, you would notice that I come from AIA East. Now I'm telling you to shut up before I blow this floor to kingdom come!"

"You're crazy! You'll die too!"

"I'll take my chances!" Sharp heard the statement and didn't want to die. All he wanted was to be granted the opportunity to return home. He observed the rage straight from Cyfreid's soul and forgot all about it. The last time he expressed that much crassness was when he nearly attacked Sharp the day he quit his job of hunting. His vulgarity and forceful attitude was an ongoing problem. Most times, Cyfreid didn't mean it.

The man agreed to shut his mouth and listen to what Cyfreid had to say. The officer deactivated the detonator and hoped to never pull it out at a place without predators again. His temper dwindled, but not completely.

"My name is Commander Cyfreid and this is...special agent, Sharp. Do you know where we can find Lynx?"

"No I don't."

"Don't lie to me boy!"

"Okay, okay. I'm sorry, just don't shoot me or blow up something or whatever it is you agents do. He's a close friend of mine."

A different man, a lot bigger than the playboy, came and sat beside him. He wore a tight shirt, possessed ripped arms, and had a mullet that women adored. Apparently, he and the quaking ladies' man were good friends. The bigger man asked, "This guy giving you trouble?" Cyfreid, with more of his anger beginning to unfold, ignored the new visitor and continued to stare down the prosperous man.

"Focus on me kid," said the agent. "You're coming with us."

"Why?! I don't understand!"

"It's because you keep lying to me. I know who you are, Lynx."

Sharp was puzzled, though not to a full extent. He noticed the words that came from the man prior to Cyfreid's threat. It was all much clearer.

"Lynx has a mouth, one that for some strange reason, doesn't know when to shut up."

"Shade, help me out please!" shouted Lynx. The other man came to his assistance.

"And who are you supposed to be?" asked Cyfreid.

"Fool, the name's Axel Ramone. But everybody calls me Shade-Master. I have the ability to open up wormholes. So if you ever threaten my friend again, I'll send you to an infinite realm never to return! You got that?"

"Wormholes," the Commander thought. "You know what, I heard about people like you. You're a realm-bender. There's only a small portion of your kind on the planet."

"A realm-bender?" wondered Curtis.

"Yes Sharp. Most people think they're myths, but they became more evident after the crisis." Curtis turned to Shade-Master.

"So you can cross realms?"

"Easy as pie," replied Shade-Master.

"How do we know you're from this dimension?"

"Well that's the thing fanboy...you don't."

All the Commander did was glare at Shade-Master and say, "You're hired."

"W-what? I'm hired for prison?"

"No, the reason I came for Lynx was because I needed his help. Now that I met you, I'm allowing you to join."

"Help? For what?" asked Lynx.

"Let's just say that we're dealing with Governor Cain X. If we don't stop him soon, our lives will be limited."

"Everybody's lives are limited," Shade-Master claimed. "How long are we talking about?"

"From my calculations, I'll say probably two days, or one if we don't defend ourselves well."

The two of them became motionless and remained that way for a while. Lynx drank more, almost coughing from the rapid gulp as the thought of *one day of survival* circulated around his head. He never imagined a person such as Cyfreid asking him for help.

"Alright, count me in," he told Cyfreid.

"Excellent, the rest of the team is in Chicago."

"Team? Hold on a minute, you never said anything about that."

"Must have slipped my mind...*boy.*"

"Okay, let's get this straight. So, you're coming to me because I'm some sort of quick-paced electrical being and my boy Shade is able to perform tricks like a well paid magician. So tell me, what made this creep a draftee?" He pointed right at Curtis.

Curtis spread his fingers out. The edge of each finger molded to barbed claws. As the the claws became slender, they expanded three times their length like extending branches. Lynx and Axel stepped back. Curtis's claws didn't tear through his elastic gloves. They shrank back to human hands.

"Well after seeing that, I guess I'm in too," said Shade-Master.

"Everyone follow me to the jet. We have much to discuss."

"Wait a minute," said Lynx. "You want us to go with you and travel in a jet?"

"It's on the roof. Don't tell me my new 'draftee' is scared."

"No, not that. You said this team is in Chicago dealing with the dreaded Governor X himself. Not to be rude, but I doubt this plane of yours will get us there before things get messy."

"Then what do you intend we do?"

Shade-Master told Cyfreid and Sharp to follow him. Axel led them to a separate room on the top floor.

"I'm going to open a portal that'll send us straight to the 'X' Center in Chicago."

"So why are we in here?" Sharp asked.

"It's because this way nobody will see us disappear. Would you really want to blow our cover like that?" Sharp didn't say a word.

Axel held up his arms. A tiny dot, strangely hovering like a floating dust particle, appeared in front of them. It expended itself broad to form the portal. Its center was foggy and pitch-dark, leading the others to contradict whether it was directed to Cain's office building or not. Even Lynx was hesitant to go in.

"Hurry on in there," Shade-Master said to them.

"Alright," said Lynx. "I trust you." Lynx took his first step into it and was straightaway sucked inside like a vacuum would suck up dirt. This made Cyfreid and Sharp more appreciative of using the jet.

"Both of you go!" The first to go in was Cyfreid. Sharp felt edgy about walking in. There was no telling where it truly led. He took a profound breath and went inside. Shade-Master followed. The portal shriveled back to a dot and disappeared into thin air.

The gateway opened right at the side of the building in Chicago. All four of them rolled out only to hear blaring gunshots. Lynx was wearing his famous blue and yellow attire.

"When did you put that on?" asked Sharp.

"Trust me I'm a fast changer…and the realm was dark enough." Sharp shook his head. Cyfreid spotted Captain Tina and several AIA East agents firing at AIA Central.

"The three of you, head inside and find X!"

"Wait a minute? What are we even trying to do?" questioned Lynx. Before Lynx could receive an answer, Cyfreid ran off to assist Tina.

"I'll explain soon!" yelled Sharp dashing for the entrance. The three crashed through the main doors just as Commander Cyfreid reached his partner.

The officers haven't seen each other since Cyfreid ordered her to travel to Detroit. He shot at the corrupted agents.

"Did you miss me, Captain?"

"How did you get here so fast?" she asked continuing to shoot.

"An addition to the team, that's how."

"I just wish we had more help down here."

"Relax, we can hold X's agents off. The real battle is inside."

VII

ALLIANCES AT WAR

EACH HERO WAS INSIDE OF THE LARGE office building of the Governor while Cyfreid and Tina fought at ground level. It was Sharp's responsibility to inform Lynx and Shade-Master about the Pixaliemain circumstance. He took it upon himself to lead the others even when being unaware of Cain's location. Lynx stopped.

"Is this really an important task?"

"Cyfreid already told you that this was important," said Sharp. "If I recall, there are these items—not quite sure what they are called—but basically if any Pixalian bum gets a hold of these things, it triggers their minds to say an ancient scripture. This scripture will then lead them into summoning a being called Xaliemer."

"How big is this Xaliemer?"

"I don't know, maybe as big as your intelligence."

"Thanks for the compliment." Lynx tried to create strategies for getting up to the top. While he was diligently thinking, Shade-Master and Sharp walked towards the main elevator. They watched as Lynx awkwardly spoke to himself. Time couldn't be wasted.

"Lynx, you coming or what?"

He turned and felt stupid, realizing that the way to get up was the obvious.

They waited to reach the pinnacle of the edifice, the eightieth floor. The lengthy delay tested Sharp's patience, something he wasn't quite good with. He asked Shade-Master, "Why didn't you just teleport us up there?"

"Sometimes I like to take a break from using my powers," he explained to them.

Lynx nodded in agreement but he was still somewhat confused about that concept. They watched the numbers change as they reached each floor. It remained on the sixtieth level and the doors opened.

Awaiting the elevator was a colossal, cumbersome man. Hefty spikes stuck from his back resembling mischievous horns. He wore leather pants, giant boots, and frothed from his foul mouth like a ravaging pit bull. His bellicose breathing disturbed them. It troubled Lynx the most, making him press the button to deny the man's request. Before the doors were able to shut, the man stopped it from closing and pushed the doors open. Craving a fight, constant globules of saliva slobbered down. The doors were unable to close; they couldn't understand how he was that strong.

"Uh, Shade," started Lynx. "Now might be a good time to use your powers." The enraged man grabbed Sharp and pulled him out of the elevator. He ferociously heaved him across the hallway. Sharp slowly got up to his feet. His temper rose as his fingers grew to claws. They were able to cut through anything.

Sharp swung his arm towards the man with hopes of gouging his body or possibly his face. After scraping him, he jumped and brought the brute down upon landing.

"I hate idiots who think they can fight!" Sharp cried. The brute rose up with the crimson wound, being barely harmed.

"You ready for more?" Sharp asked with his finger-claws spread out.

"Sharp, let's go! I'm going to transport us to the top!" yelled Shade-Master.

"That's something you should've done a long time ago," Lynx added while watching Sharp and the brute take part in the vicious match. Sharp continued to attack, avoiding all of the brute's moves and creating tactics of his own. After Shade-Master opened the portal, he asked him one more time if he was coming.

"Just go already!" he shrieked at the top of his lungs. "I'm not finished with this scum!" Lynx followed the orders and hurried himself inside of the portal. When trying to keep it open a little longer, Shade-Master watched Sharp scream at the large man. The ferocity only prepared him for what was to come.

"Good luck," he said jumping in the portal. At the corner of Sharp's eye, he saw it shrink to a floating particle and vanish.

His hasty movements slit more of the man's flesh. The inner prowling creature was unleashed at last. The scars didn't seem to strike the brute as an issue. He grinned. He sighted Sharp's chest and charged for his fierce attempt.

The momentum made Sharp fly straight at a wall, smashing a desk in half. Sharp inched up with bleeding lips. He sucked it in and then spat it out.

"What kind of brute are you?" If his claws weren't enough, he didn't know what was. The man clenched his fists.

"You just said it. They call me Brute-Spine!"

"Clever name…you don't mind if I *break* your spine do you?" He sprinted towards him with one arm up ready to claw his face again. The vile beast swiftly clutched his arm and chucked Sharp to the other side of the hallway.

"Things haven't been the same after you left, Curtis." Sharp couldn't stop sweating. He cleared his throat and asked, "How do you know my name?"

"How do I know you?! If you stayed working for Cyfreid you would've figured out that your best friend was turned into this, this…this thing!" He was referring to himself: the spikes that came out of him and the overweight appearance.

Sharp pondered Brute-Spine's identity. He thought hard, though was still determined to continue the fight.

My best friend. Can it be…no. It couldn't. Impossible.

"All those years ago, my best friend was Gary Herman."

"You're looking right at him!" His body trembled, senses speaking to him insisting that the brute was lying.

"No. That's not true."

"But it is true, Curtis! It was Cyfreid! He turned me into this! It's his fault!"

"No! I don't believe you!" Then he thought again. It was as if everything around him froze, even Brute-Spine. In his moment of remembrance, he recited the words Cyfreid gave at his mansion. They were said very carefully.

Gary is…different.

The resemblance was finally apparent. He compared the traits with the differences. He still couldn't believe it.

"What did Cyfreid do?!"

"Why don't you ask him, Curt!" Brute-Spine threw continuous punches. Curtis couldn't handle any more of the hammerings from his so-called friend.

"Why don't you take it out on Cyfreid instead of wasting your energy on me?!" His mouth was flooded with redness.

"Because I remember how you felt about the Commander. You treated him like a mentor! You wanted to be just like him!"

"I think you got me confused with someone else."

"Shut up! I know what I said. This is your end, Curt. I'm going to miss the times we had together. Maybe they'll flash before your eyes as your life finishes! Oh, and your other friends—those two simpletons—they're in for a little showdown on the top floor."

"Showdown?"

"Yes you weak trash! If they're even smart enough to find the Governor, they'll end up against a legion of the nation's most well-known criminals. I'm *afraid* they're going to suffer the same fate as you…death!"

Sharp scurried in the opposite direction, leaving a dripping trail. He hewed a door that led to an office. The room was free of workers. He cut up the light switch and the lights turned off, providing a necessary advantage until he could think of something else. Sharp crouched behind a bookshelf.

Brute-Spine rushed inside of the room only to see darkness. He sniffed. Curtis's tender scent filled his nostrils. For the first time in a long while, Sharp agreed that he wasn't the hunter. He was the prey, the hunted, the one who wished to be thrown in a better circumstance. Being on the top floor would be the accepted choice.

Sharp lowered his breathing. His sweat merged with his wet wounds.

"You can't hide from me, Sharp! I know your scent so I'll find you, even if I have to break every single thing in here!"

It was a nightmare. Curtis never got nightmares when he slept. He actually rarely had dreams.

While being in the secured position for the time, the portal expanded on the top floor. Lynx and Shade-Master walked out. The gateway closed and the two of them saw a hallway. At the end of it was an open door.

"Secret passageway, that's pretty sweet," said Lynx. Shade-Master refused to agree with his fellow friend. He only hoped that Sharp had everything under control downstairs. Lynx observed the door and realized that it previously needed a retina scan.

"After you," Lynx said gesturing his hands towards the alleyway. Shade-Master advanced, Lynx followed. The two found themselves in a silent room and spotted an automatic door.

On the other side of Lynx and Shade-Master was Silvert and Titanium Titan. They stooped behind storage boxes that said *X Center Industries*. The spiteful Cain X continued to smoke his cigar.

With fifty storage boxes in total, they were both at the end of last box. They sighted a group of six heroes trapped inside of an electric cell.

"All right," Silvert whispered to Titanium Titan. "Let's review. There's Governor X and he's holding Team Valor and a fine lady captive. We heard him talk about a number of doomsday devices located in space. The question is, what do these things do?"

"Well this is all about that rock substance right? Most likely these devices summon that monster."

"Okay," said Silvert. "Not a bad theory there, Hiro. How do we find and destroy these things? What if they're indestructible or something?"

"We'll find a way. What's your line of approach?"

"We attack Cain and threaten his assistants on my signal. Are you ready for this?"

"I'm ready for anything. But I still don't forgive you so stay out of my way when I save Team Valor. You got that?"

"Sure thing. You rescue Team Valor and I'll save the damsel in distress and possibly get a lovely kiss. I'm the real hero so I deserve it."

"You never changed. I'll make sure to tell the press that when they honour my abilities."

"Fine, whatever makes you sleep at night."

"Alright, fine!"

"Fine!" After Silvert got the last word, both of them realized that they were yelling.

In the same room was Canavin, Frankie, and Zan; the Pixalians remained in their disguises. Frankie waited for Canavin's signal to strike. He whispered, "Can we just fight this guy already? I'm tired of picking up on his little schemes. We have a strong chance."

"Wait for it," said Canavin. He was watching to see what Governor X was going to do next. Cain tossed his cigar. He held the Valoric pistols and approached Valor. He dangled them, insulting his talents and plans to somehow escape.

"You see these, Valor?" he taunted. All Valor did was stare at the red-eyed man. Many crucial thoughts wandered through his head if he were to wield his weapons. Regardless, he wanted to kill Cain; cruel thoughts like this were completely normal.

"Well do you see them or not?!" the Governor hollered. Valor remained silent and still imagined the things he would do to the vile man. He wore a helmet which hid his expressions, but it made no difference. He only had one feeling at the time: hatred.

"I swear if you don't answer me then I'll—"

"I see them," Valor inaudibly replied.

"Finally you answered. Well they're mine now. It's such a shame that the great Valor would never be able to use his toys again."

"You're a man of your word right? Well so I'm I! I'm going to get out of this cell and when I do…"

"If you get out you'll do what? You stopped."

"My point exactly. It's too intense to say out loud."

"You and your threats, sitting in prison. How relaxing." Cain turned and moved towards a vault. He opened it and there was a glistening stone.

"This is the key to a better life! Do you know what it is?" The soldier became clueless. Cain reached inside the vault and took out the rock. From outside of the electric bars, he held it to face Valor. He listened closely for any unfamiliar phrases. Upon hearing not a single word, he said, "So you're not one of them. That's good to know. You see Valor, this entire private operation is all because of this rock sample. The creatures call it—"

"Pixaliemain," said Celestica interrupting him from inside.

"Well done my lady. How did you know?" She answered, "Just a guess."

"A guess that was right on the money," he said back to her. "Are you sure that you're not Pixalian?"

"Positive." He walked back to Valor and noticed the soldier's weary squad.

"All of you should get some rest. I mean you might as well because there's no escape. So get comfy. That's what the cell is for." Valor refrained from listening to the madman.

"Get me out of here so I can shoot you down!"

"And why on Earth would I do that?"

"Because you're asking for a fight and I'm not afraid to give you one! In fact, it'll be the most fun I'll ever get!" Being amused, Cain looked at the time.

"I'm sorry but it's getting late."

"Passed your bedtime?"

"You are funny, do you know that? I should've made you a jester just to humour me. Anyways, I'm leaving to meet up with a very special creature by the name of Identymous."

While hearing this, Canavin looked at Frankie and Zan.

"That's our cue," he stated.

Silvert and Titanium Titan hustled faster, revealing themselves to the affluent Governor from behind the storage boxes.

"Your time is up, X!" yelled Silvert to his adversary. He calmly smiled as if he was pleased to see the familiar lustrous face.

"My goodness, if it isn't Silvert. I thought you resided in the capital. Why did you come here to your old city? Do you miss me?"

"Not a chance! I'm shutting you down!"

"Okay? I have Team Valor behind bars and you think that you and your little pal can stop me? You and what army?"

Unexpectedly, Canavin shouted, "He has me by his side."

Everyone targeted the members of the famous clan. Frankie tore his suit and possessed his well identified uniform underneath. Zan changed from human to Pixalian. Canavin altered his form to return to his blue and black armour. He put on his mechanical mask with his gold antlers facing out. The presence of the Canavin Clan shocked Silvert and Titanium Titan. Still, they were thankfully amazed.

"So, the great Canavin is here too. Do these surprises end? Do you think you can stop me? Canavin, I'm sorry to say it, but even you're finished." The wretched face led them to see another passage way. A group of people showed themselves to the heroes.

"Feast your eyes, Canavin Clan, on my most impressive league!"

Each person of his expert faction was malicious in their own special way, having numerous special abilities. Some of them were familiar. This was especially Derwin Grant, the drug lord who dealt with Team Valor and the Canavin Clan. He carried an array of tazers and firearms.

"Optimistic," whispered Valor behind the electrical bars. Others included Gustavo: a resilient man who originated from Brooklyn, New York. He had the ability of telekinesis.

The next was Corometheus who had the power to control light in all of its forms.

Another was the Titanic who had super strength.

There was Bloodblast, an alternate version of Valor from a different dimension. Instead of two Valoric pistols, he carried a high-quality bazooka.

Another was Dark-Shallow: a mystical being with powers similar to Meditation.

Next was Professor Shaw who was originally from Cyclohoma City, (the metropolis where Canavin spent most of his eight years on Earth).

Gold-Mine was another one. This man was Silvert's first rival.

Canavin's insights were accurate when he sighted the only Pixalian on the opposing squad: Avinotch, his cousin.

"There's no hope," said Cain X. He took many steps away from the rogues. Before he could order them to attack, streaking bolts of electricity shocked Dark-Shallow. He loped to a corner to recover from the sparks.

It was Lynx who was accompanied by Shade-Master. They ran inside and firmly stood by the other heroes. Canavin knew that he and Lynx were simply an addition from Cyfreid. Shade-Master screamed, "This ends now!"

Canavin shot cobalt Pixalian rays at Professor Shaw while Silvert took on Gold-Mine. Titanium Titan only had one adversary in mind: the Governor himself. He dashed for his target and kicked Cain in the face with enough fury.

Cain grasped his left cheek. Titanium Titan continued with hopes of obtaining more fame by succeeding in the match.

"You're going to pay for that!" howled Cain while holding the painful cheek.

Titanium Titan was tapped on the shoulder. He rotated to see an average man, roughly the same height as him with no weapons. He tilted his head at Hiro.

"Do you mind? I'm trying to fight the one and only Cain X." The strange man frowned, and then became infuriated. Darkness engulfed his eyes as if he was possessed by a vindictive spirit. Hiro observed his anger. Wide wings grew out from his back. The winged man grabbed Hiro and soared high. He flapped around in circles, forcefully trying the make Hiro woozy.

After a full swirling minute, the winged man released him. Titanium Titan landed and heard some cracks in his body. He rose up in hopes to find X. Yet, the Governor already gathered his items and was ready to depart.

Shade-Master noticed that Team Valor and Celestica were still caged. He transported himself inside of the cell. The alarmed Vanessa jumped out of fear, and then realized that Shade-Master was there to help. He opened a portal to escort them.

"All of you, get in now!" he commanded.

"And who are you supposed to be?" asked Fusion Fighter.

"Shade-Master, now get in! It's the only way out!"

"Works for me," said Breath-Stealer. He slithered his ghostly self inside along with Fusion Fighter, Meditation, Evesdrop, and Celestica. All who remained was Valor.

His sights were on Bloodblast. He detested his alternate version with the immense bazooka he carried.

"You need to get in now," stated Shade-Master. He had no choice but to fight, even if it meant doing so without his pistols.

He entered the shady swirling portal and then Shade-Master followed. The gateway opened outside of the cell, immediately spitting out each member to clash with an opponent. As Valor came out, he was struck with the bazooka's Valoric blast.

The explosion blew him across the large area; he was able to withstand it with his inner Valoric energy.

His helmet became slightly tarnished. Bloodblast came closer.

There wasn't much that Valor could do to defend himself. Canavin, who decided to contend his cousin Avinotch, noticed the Valoric pistols on the floor next to him. Governor X mistakenly dropped the weapons while trying to escape.

Cain covertly snuck out of the lair which was now a battlefield. When Canavin located the pistols, he retrieved them and called for Valor.

"Valor! Catch!"

The Pixalian warrior threw them directly in the soldier's hands. The two cords on each blaster connected to his wrists. He felt reenergized as if the pistols were the batteries to his power. He looked at Bloodblast, cleverly smiling under the helmet. Valor pulled the triggers.

The blasts were astonishing green static beams that sent Bloodblast soaring across the room. After returning the "favour", Valor said with a sly voice, "Now the party begins."

The crafty Valor gave a signal of thanks to Canavin who was too occupied with Avinotch.

There was a story behind Canavin and Avinotch, a story that Canavin felt was better left untold.

"Avinotch!" he bawled out. "We can end this! Quit working for Cain and leave!"

"You honestly believe that you can tell me what and what not to do?" His powers were similar; his inner Pixalian energy was strong. Avinotch back flipped and directed his impulsive beam at Canavin. Canavin fired back. The energy blasts collided with one another, forming an illuminating force at the center. It moved its way closer to Canavin. Avinotch's force ultimately lowered the hero's stance. Canavin refused to quit as he gave it his all, hoping that the capacity would move away and closer to Avinotch. The more he attempted to stand tall, the more the energy brought him lower. He could feel his end approaching. Canavin retracted his blasts and swiftly hopped over to his side to avoid the explosive blow.

"Same old Canavin," his cousin started. "Always a coward!" Avinotch felt his old scabbard and took out the blade he used back on Star-Pix. Canavin's heart pounded at a wild pace.   If negotiating didn't work, then there was a more efficient possibility.

Whenever the valiant Pixalian was trapped in a challenging circumstance, he would wield his notable rapier called *Pixcalibur*. As a youngling, Canavin received the sword from his father before he was killed. It was truly important and very effective.

"I'm not a coward," he boldly said to Avinotch. "And here's my chance to prove it."

The fearless Canavin took out Pixcalibur, revealing its mighty reflection. It was a crystal-like blade that was more durable than it appeared.

"You want to fight?" Canavin asked. "Let's fight!" Canavin rushed at Avinotch and swung Pixcalibur multiple times, lacerating his gold skin to create rounded gashes. His strikes caused complete harm and distress to his cousin.

The battle of the cousins stood out the most with various separate duels behind them. The heroes understood that it was all a diversion.

The real concern was retrieving the Pixaliemain, but being too engaged in battle with Cain's alliance only meant that the Governor had the essential chance to reach Identymous.

The Canavin Clan was fully aware of the creature. If Cain X was to meet him without being ceased, Identymous would be the Pixalian to unleash the world's next great threat.

VIII

TOGETHER WE ARE POWERFUL

EVERYONE HAD THEIR OWN HOSTILE matches within the lair. Valor against Bloodblast, Canavin versus Avinotch, Lynx against the colossal Titanic, Shade-Master against Corometheus, and Titanium Titan handling a combat battle against Gustavo Salazar. The rest of the rogues were against the four members of Team Valor and the three from the Canavin Clan.

Sharp had to focus on escaping from a nightmare. This was Brute-Spine, his lost and tormented friend. He still couldn't understand why and how Gary became such a thing.

The dark, gloomy room had a strong relation to the miserable and sinister character of Brute-Spine. The smooth breathing of Curtis was expected to come to its final end. If there was one thing about Curtis, it was that he was too smart to know that he wasn't alone.

"Resistance is futile, Curt!" shrieked the monster. There was not a sound that came out of Curtis's mouth; continuing not to speak only added to its uselessness. He had his long claws fully extended as he felt Brute-Spine come closer and closer. He actually saw the body of the beast within the shadows of the office. He was also sure that Brute-Spine was about four feet in front and had his bristly back facing him.

"I found you!"

"No," whispered Sharp. "I found you."

As cunning as he was, Sharp screamed for victory, leapt up, and then jabbed his finger-claws right in Brute-Spine's back; the spikes were avoided at all costs. The large beast toppled down on his fat belly while Sharp dug his claws deeper. His aggression increased. He yelled louder than ever. Memories were returning to him. Every mission, every task Cyfreid gave him, was nothing different from his actions with Brute-Spine. His pupils grew. He felt the rush; the thrill; the pleasure from a good hunt. Then it hit him at last.

Gary Herman. This is still Gary Herman.

The terrifying screams from the incensed Curtis Kareem came to a close. Brute-Spine just stayed there.

"Gary?" he asked Brute-Spine.

No movements, no fury, no sadness, and no happiness. Overall, there were no emotions.

"Gary?! Speak to me!"

What Sharp believed he did was heartbreaking in every way imaginable. His claws condensed to fingers and he slowly moved off Brute-Spine's back.

A drop landed on his hand. He stared at it for a while and then saw another drop. These drops were tears of regret. Curtis Kareem rarely cried in his life; probably only five times in total to be exact. This would now be the sixth as he moaned for the evil he has done. Yet, things weren't as they seemed.

Brute-Spine got up from being jabbed in the back. He noticed the miserable Sharp and then grabbed him by the neck with his humungous hand. He held Curtis up to see his cruel face. He pushed on the Adam's apple, almost reaching the vocal cords. The choking Sharp cried out in agony saying, "Gary! Gary, please!" Brute-Spine gave a menacing laugh and squeezed harder.

"I promise that you will not live another day! Oh and for the record, those ten stabs in my back only tickled."

"Gary," Sharp slowly said as he continued to lose oxygen.

"What is it, Sharp?! What are your final words of life?"

"I missed you."

The affection caught Brute-Spine off guard. Sharp grew his claws and tunneled them into the monster's wrist to release the grasp. When free, he bolted for the way out of the darkness and back to the elevators. He pushed the button that signaled up, but all patience disappeared upon seeing Brute-Spine charge for him.

"Come here!" the vicious man yelled. His steps sounded like exploding bombs.

All Sharp wanted was his friend back. This was added to his *list of wants* which included returning back to his mansion and living the exquisite life.

There were two elevators: one that worked like any other carrying machine and the other which was unable to go up or down since Brute-Spine gave damage. The monster came closer and the working elevator doors refused to open. The other one was his only option.

While being in there, Sharp came up with a plan. He used one finger and drew a wide circle on the carrier's roof that was big enough to go through. The plate fell and he hurried, only to get above to his waist.

There was a pull; he felt that he was being sucked down. Brute-Spine was yanking him by the legs. The anxiety and pressure filled Curtis once more. In order to keep himself from being pulled completely back, he clamped his sharp fingers on the surface of the carrier. After seeing the tips of the fingers from inside, Brute-Spine shouted, "You think that's going to hold you Curt? I'm stronger!"

I've got to think of something else.

Curtis used his other arm for the same survival method. The pulling from Brute-Spine made him scrape the top surface.

"Closer!" said Brute-Spine.

"Let go of my legs you fool!"

"Your life belongs to me!"

Curtis began to panic until he found a solution. He took one hand from the carrier's roof and reached for the cords. While stretching all the muscles in his body, he was just about five inches short from snapping them. He tried to stretch more, or somehow make his claws extend further. The distance increased as he was monotonously yanked. He was about ten inches away, then twelve, and then fifteen. It was either death or survival.

Sharp vividly imagined the ways how Brute-Spine would end his days on Earth. The thoughts included throwing him off high heights, piercing his body, and choking him to death. Each thought was able to become a reality. When Sharp noticed the other carrier finally come down to his level, he decided that pain was his only escape.

He screamed using all the force in his body to finally reach the cords. Then it was finished. His index finger hewed the dark ropes. The carrier fell down and in an instant. Sharp was free and hopped over to the next elevator carrier. The massive Brute-Spine was unable to fit through the carrier's hole. He fell with the elevator to the very bottom of the 'X' Center. Curtis heard a faint crash below him.

The hero was relieved. He noticed the way to reach the top floor. He had to rapidly climb to the preferred height.

AIA East symbolized the side of the heroes as they battled against the antagonized AIA Central agents. Tina and Cyfreid were cautious of their surroundings. Looking over to the rest of the agents, they saw how they were injured. Some even retreated regardless of Tina's orders to stay put and attack. Their quest for survival seemed impossible, but if a simple jade-eyed woman could destroy an alien, then there had to be a solution to defeating the Governor's henchmen. Tina fired more bullets beside Cyfreid.

"We need to head inside! You said it yourself! The battle is not here, it's in there!" Tina and Cyfreid were both crouched down behind the jet.

"That won't be fair to our team! The Governor's agents would simply follow us to the lair. Once there, it will be a greater battle which will cause Sharp, Silvert, and the others to be misguided." Tina didn't want to admit it, but Cyfreid was right. If they were to bring a bunch of vile AIA agents to the heroes, it would create a more disastrous circumstance.

"They're heroes! It wouldn't make a difference if these pawns follow us!"

"You see, you just said it my tired second-in-command. If these are truly pawns, then we should definitely win."

"I hope you're right for my sake. I need to sleep right now!"

"When you work for the AIA, you never sleep." Cyfreid got up and gave the agents all he could. The will of wanting to succeed would lead them to success. Captain Tina did the same. The two of them combined their attack to fire an exceptional amount of bullets. While doing this, they were surprised that they still weren't out of ammo.

The bearded man got a phone call from the Governor, who was just about to depart from the building's peak.

"What is it master?" he asked Cain X.

"I got the word from Identymous. It's time to leave."

"Yes sir." As Cain hung up, the agent held up his fist to give the halting signal. He called for Tina and said, "I'm sorry miss Truman, but we are going to have to finish this another time."

"How's about we finish it now!"

"I wish we could. Just be glad that your death isn't at this moment, but it could be within hours." He turned away and ordered his men to retreat. Cyfreid and Tina didn't hold back their fire. They were able to wound a few of the central agents, though the others ended up being too far in the distance.

The cars drove down the street at swift speeds. When seeing that the injured central agents limped for freedom, Tina gave strict orders to her men to get every word out of them. The eastern operatives who were in good condition arrested the remaining central agents.

"Now's our time to head in," said Cyfreid.

"You always speak the obvious," she replied. The Commander and Captain made their way through the entrance and were surprised to see that one elevator was open with Brute-Spine. Gary was out cold from the traumatic fall. When seeing this type of creature, Cyfreid became familiar with him. He told Tina to use the other elevator. She pressed the button and waited for the carrier to come down.

Sharp, who was still climbing his way up, saw this happen. The elevator was far beneath him. He contacted Cyfreid.

"Hello?" Cyfreid asked from down below.

"Where are you?"

"I'm with Tina and we just entered the elevator."

"Elevator?" It was coming back up; Sharp had to hurry. It would be a while before they were to reach, but as more time went by, it was clear that the carrier was closer than ever. The thoughts were circling around. He would have no room from the top of the carrier and the end roof above him. The reality would be a crushed Curtis Kareem.

He clambered quicker with some fingers unable to pierce through the walls. By straining his neck, he saw the upcoming carrier as if the floor was rising to catch him. He exaggerated his movements from hesitation. Claw after claw, he climbed for freedom. After seeing that it was directly below him, he jumped on its surface and looked up to see how many floors he had left before his demise.

Three more left.

Sharp drew another circle on the surface in order for him to jump in. He punched his way through; a circular plate fell right in front of Cyfreid. Tina stood in the corner and readied her weapon. Sharp took another glance above his head and when noticing the end come closer than ever, he hopped in the carrier, sweating in fear.

"Sharp?" said Cyfreid surprised to see the man appear from above him. "You were supposed to lead Lynx and Shade-Master to Cain. What happened?" He refused to give a full answer. The agents noticed his bloodstained gloves. Sharp looked at Tina. It was the first time seeing her in person for a long time. He looked back at the Commander and said, "Memories."

Tina didn't know what or who he was referring to. Sharp kept it to himself. Cyfreid somewhat had a clue about what was on his mind. The doors opened and they walked out. Tina's mood grew to a new level. Her eyebrows curled down, her hands squeezing the grips of her guns.

"Where's Governor X?!"

"Patience," said Cyfreid. "He should be here somewhere."

"Wait a minute," said Sharp. He listened for what seemed to be loud noises of explosions, energy blasts, and several shrill screams.

"You hear that?" Cyfreid and Tina also listened and heard the sounds.

"Over there!" shouted Cyfreid as he pointed the same way where the other heroes went. They ran in and saw the automatic doors.

After entering, they found themselves in the middle of a brawl between heroes and rogues. Cyfreid was ready to fight and at the same time, he was enlightened to see all of the heroes working together for a common cause. He was pleased to see the Canavin Clan, Team Valor, Lynx, Silvert, Titanium Titan, Shade-Master, and now Sharp as he aided them in battle.

Their presence made the Commander really honoured and proud to call himself, *the one who made all of this possible*. Personal satisfaction had to wait. He saw Canavin finishing his match with Avinotch.

After securing the filthy Pixalian to the ground, Canavin held Pixcalibur up to Avinotch's neck.

"Do it," said the cousin. "Are you finally going to kill me? You've had so many chances and now is the perfect time."

"You already know the answer." He removed the tip of the blade from his cousin's neck.

"You're always trying to do the *right* thing. Just see how far that takes you."

"It's gotten me this far. I could've killed you a number of times, but I didn't. You know why? It's because you're family. The *One* wouldn't appreciate me being a murderer."

"You and your beliefs. When are you going to move on in life?"

"When the time comes." Canavin ambled away to help the others. Avinotch tried to get up, and then stopped to mend himself. He was too weak from the power of Pixcalibur. He remained there to see his heroic cousin; the way he fought for truth and justice; the way his faith could never be broken. He thought about how life would be if he was like Canavin, but didn't want to fully envy his qualities. It was too difficult to let go of his hatred.

Canavin spotted Commander Cyfreid shooting at a number of mutated humans. Using Pixcalibur to reflect the blasts, he told Cyfreid, "I hate you! I just wanted to get that out!" He didn't mean it completely. The situation they were in only increased the tension.

"You're not the first to say that," said Cyfreid.

"And I won't be the last!" Cyfreid smiled at Canavin and continued to shoot.

"Where's Governor X?" he asked Canavin.

"You see that's the problem! I don't know! He left before I could retrieve the Pixaliemain!"

"You didn't get the sample? Do you know what that means?"

"Of course I know what it means! It comes from my planet!" They noticed Silvert who fought Gold-Mine.

"Silvert!" Canavin yelled. "We need to find the Governor!"

"I know but I'm in the middle of something right now!"

"Come to your senses! What's more important? Facing whoever this guy is, or retrieving the rock!"

"You know, when you say it like that, it doesn't seem like it's that important. But I know what you mean. I'll track him after I'm done with Gold-Mine."

"You won't stop me!" his opponent said.

"What's wrong with all of you stupid crooks?" asked Silvert. "Y'all way too negative."

There was a certain trait about Silvert—one that many knew, including other heroes that shared the same amount of fame as him. It was one of his most destructive powers: Silver Explosion. When used, it creates an energy outburst of Silvert's silver form and abolishes everything in sight except for him. He never used this ability against pawns such as Gold-

Mine. It always came in handy when matters were more challenging.

While the seemingly endless battle went on, Fusion Fighter, Breath Stealer, Meditation, and Evesdrop fought alongside each other. Dark-Shallow and Derwin Grant opposed them.

The magician known as Dark-Shallow was especially focused on his heroic counterpart: Meditation. They used spellbinding: magical powers which were obtained by an ancient Pixalian source. Meditation had special relations with different sorcerers.

Breath-Stealer, the ethereal spirit, slithered his way into Dark-Shallow's body. As if the magician lost his soul, the spirit controlled Dark-Shallow to make the spellbinder attack himself.

It was Breath-Stealer's way of overcoming many obstacles. All Fusion Fighter and Meditation saw was the menacing man, beating himself as if he had a mental disability. After Breath-Stealer left the body, the spellbinder found himself in a world of confusion.

With a tactical hex in mind to cast, Meditation caused Dark-Shallow to temporarily lose his eyesight. She called for Fusion Fighter's assistance.

The pterodactyl man cracked his knuckles and went for a punch. Dark-Shallow grasped his arm and threw him to the floor.

He forced his eyesight to return and stated, "You forget, I got tricks as well. And for my next act, I'm going to make Fusion Fighter disappear."

"How's about you talk less and fight more!"

"Ah, but there will be no fighting madame." The mystic rogue held up his hand. A swirling pool of black matter formed in his palm. He recited enigmatic phrases to cast his intended spell. Before anyone knew it, Fusion Fighter vanished.

Meditation took out her spellbook and flipped through countless pages, scanning over the sections in order to find the right counter-hex. She slammed it shut upon discovering the proper one.

"You know for a fact that I can bring him back."

"In time you will, but within that time you'll be defeated." Dark-Shallow targeted Evesdrop.

The blinking eyes along her arms and legs were aware of the number of miniature battles. Her eyesight was divided one hundred times.

Every eyeball that protruded from her lime sockets shifted to a pale colour. She labeled Meditation as her adversary. As she slowly approached, Meditation asked, "Evesdrop, what are you doing?"

The several eyed Evesdrop had her fists ready for combat. She swung for Meditation and upon dodging the move, she hollered to obtain her alleged victory. Frantically trying to snap her friend out of it, Meditation said, "Evesdrop, it's me! Do you remember?"

"You're finished Dark-Shallow!" Thinking about what she just said, Meditation finally understood.

"I'm not Dark-Shallow! He is!" But all Evesdrop saw was Dark-Shallow pointing at Meditation.

"No! You are lying! That's Meditation!" Dark-Shallow snickered behind her, gesturing his arms to control Evesdrop's movements.

"Evesdrop, you have to trust me!" The more that Meditation tried to convince her, the more it made Evesdrop believe the opposite.

The numinous woman insisted to rely on Breath-Stealer. It was too dangerous for her to cast another spell; two spells at once could lead to mental instability.

When the spirit attempted to aid in the situation and merge with the body, he unexpectedly changed forms.

"What in the world just happened?" wondered Breath-Stealer who was DeMarcus Howard at the moment. He attempted to change back but couldn't succeed.

"I already told you people that I have a few tricks of my own. Evesdrop is going to finish you off, and without your muscular pterosaur, I'm afraid it's finally the end of Team Valor."

Hearing those words from afar, Valor shot his electrical blasts at Dark-Shallow. He slowly advanced close to the spellbinder and stated, "It's never the end of Team Valor."

"Valor!" cried Meditation. "Evesdrop is possessed! Do something!" He sighted Evesdrop with her clouded eyes. Four eyes on her forehead blinked at the same time. She was pleased to see the soldier, though it wasn't the right form of a congenial greeting. Valor was presented as a new target in her pale sight. She attacked him; Valor knew he couldn't pull his triggers, even when having a clear shot.

Evesdrop—Alicia Eve Tavern—was a close friend. After having her strikes blocked, Evesdrop yelled, "I will not fall for your lies, Bloodblast!"

"What are you talking about? Does it look like I have a bazooka on me at the moment?"

"Yes! Now hold still so I can make Valor proud!"

"I am Valor!" he screamed. Evesdrop was blinded by the works of Dark-Shallow.

The magician tried everything he could to resist the sting of Valoric Energy. When seeing him limp his way, Valor grabbed him by the collar.

"Release her from your stupid spell!"

"Sorry but I'm a little hurt from the electricity that—"

"Release her!" Valor brought his pistol to Dark-Shallow's forehead, pressing the muzzle hard, leaving a mark that was nothing short of being unbearable. His antiheroic intentions dramatically grew. Swallowing sundry gulps, Dark-Shallow lifted the curse. The vague matter flushed itself away. The pupils returned on all of the eyes.

"Evesdrop, are you okay?" Valor asked.

"W-what happened?" she asked. Meditation was glad to answer the question. She said, "First you attacked me thinking that I was Dark-Shallow. Then Valor came, but you thought he was Bloodblast. You were under Dark-Shallow's spell." Evesdrop watched as Valor continued to threaten Dark-Shallow.

"He's going to pay for that!" she screamed.

"I got first dibs!" replied Valor as he held both pistols at him. The spellbinder twiddled with his fingers. He had no explanations or excuses.

"Now listen up! First, you're going to lift the spell off of my boy DeMarcus! Then, you're going to bring Fusion Fighter back!"

He was tormented by Valor, Meditation, DeMarcus Howard, and Evesdrop.

Derwin Grant loomed near. He had a good shot at Valor—probably the best he's ever had in years. Before he was able to shoot, Valor's instincts kicked in.

"Don't even think about it," the soldier said with one gun pointed at him and the other at Dark-Shallow. The drug lord dropped his weapon and knelt down with his arms up in defeat.

"Well?" Valor began. "I'm waiting, magician."

"Alright! Just point that pistol somewhere else!"

"Then hurry up!"

With a snap of his fingers, Dark-Shallow made Fusion Fighter appear out of thin air.

He was confused—just like Evesdrop was earlier—but quickly put the puzzle pieces together and was ready to join his team. DeMarcus was able to shift back into his spectral form.

"You're lucky you're alive," said Valor, confirming his team's victory over them.

He led his team to Commander Cyfreid and Canavin. When getting there, he asked the warrior, "What's the status?"

"Let's see," said Canavin, still reflecting countless blasts with his saber. "Cain X can't be found at all and he has the key to end the world! That's the status!"

More of the heroes saw the concern smeared on their faces. They continued to fight in their own individual battles.

Governor Cain X returned to the top floor that was an overwhelming battlefield.

"Everyone halt at once!" The convicts, added with the supernatural beings, stopped attacking the heroes. The faction of heroes did the same; they wanted to hear every word the menace had to say.

"Cyfreid?" he said while looking at the Commander. Cain took another glance. There were slight differences, yet it was the same old Commander of AIA East.

"Oh my goodness, you're behind this? Commander Cyfreid has built a team of heroes to counter my alliance?"

"The threat is over!" Cyfreid hollered. "Now hand us the rock and nobody gets hurt!"

"I wish it was that easy," said Cain sarcastically. "Unfortunately, I need this substance. You see, I'm not the *bad guy*. Soon you will understand my logic."

"You don't know what you're getting into!" Canavin shouted as he stood beside Cyfreid. "My world had to suffer the consequences of the beast you're trying to unleash. Do you know how many died?!"

"Do I care? You're just a Pixalian, Canavin. You don't have the same values as a human. None of your kind does. I would've preferred your whole planet to be destroyed!"

Frustration filled the two Pixalians of Cyfreid's squad.

"For God's sake, just give us the damn rock!" screamed Valor ready to unleash his energy. Cyfreid held him back.

"Not yet," he calmly stated to the gunman.

Sharp was ready to charge full speed at him, but Tina copied Cyfreid by holding him back as well.

"You have a *feisty* team of individuals," said Cain. "But as members of the AIA, it is our duty to come to a consensus. So here it is. Join me and I'll reveal the answers to save mankind. I assure you that I am not the enemy here. By stopping me, you'll end a perfect opportunity of freedom. I wish I could explain it all, but I'll only do so if you accept my offer. Are you in or out?"

The Canavin Clan, Team Valor, Shade-Master, Sharp, Silvert, Titanium Titan, Lynx, Tina, and Cyfreid thought it over. The only person who really knew what Cain X was plotting was Cyfreid and Canavin. As the leader, Cyfreid gave himself the liberty of giving the final word.

"Hell no! My team and I will stop at nothing to ensure you are arrested. You're in violation of *regulation 16* which states that all sectors have a responsibility to fully follow the guidelines of ensuring health and safety for mankind!"

"Then I guess this is the end, Cyfreid. It's a shame it has to be this way. I'm terribly sorry." He gave the signal and his alliance was prepared to continue the fight. Cyfreid's team of heroes was ready to defend.

The illuminating Pixaliemain rested in Cain's palm. He sealed it tight and paced his way out. He brushed shoulders with a man he never encountered.

The man wore a faded laboratory robe, just like a number of Cain's assistants. To whatever degree, Cain couldn't recognize him. Cain stepped closer, squinting his fiery eyes at the the specious supporter.

"What is your name?" The man didn't answer. He only continued to organize files; his eyes rested on the glorious stone.

Still not replying, the Governor elevated his voice in frustration.

"I said, what is your name?!" The tone attracted everyone. The heroes and Cain's rogues fixed their sights on the visitor, awaiting his response.

The strange man swiftly knocked the Pixaliemain out of Cain's hands, making the precious stone roll over to a dusty corner.

"You idiot!" the Governor screeched. His hatred, cruelty, and embarrassment united. The Governor drew out his pistol and sent a flying bullet through the man's chest.

"That does it! I'm going to shoot this fool!" screamed Valor. Even when seeing the squalor of Governor X, Cyfreid still stopped him.

"Hold on there Valor. Take a look."

The soldier and everyone else observed the man as he reached into his chest in search for the bullet. Upon finding it, he tossed the object away. He simply smirked and slipped his way out of the pastel coat. Being fully unaware of who or what the man was, the staggered Governor took plenty of steps back when he witnessed the chest fully heal.

The man walked towards Cyfreid. The other heroes did the same, standing side by side, forming a barrier of truth.

He glared at the Commander with him staring back. At last, Cyfreid smiled and said, "Sherman Bawnder."

The presence of the indestructible Sherman Bawnder meant that he was persuaded to join. He returned a smile at Cyfreid and was ready to aid the team.

"Kill all of them!" roared the dramatic Governor.

Cyfreid's extensive team was essential. All of the enlisted members were finally together for a common purpose: defeat Governor Cain X and save the world from the threat of an alien abomination. One more battle would settle the conflict. Tina and Cyfreid turned to one another. The reality was a true accomplishment. Seeing every hero together made their thoughts speak bold words of encouragement.

Together we are powerful.

Canavin, Celestica, Frankie, Zan, Valor, Breath-Stealer, Evesdrop, Fusion Fighter, Meditation, Titanium Titan, Silvert, Shade-Master, Lynx, Sharp, and now Sherman Bawnder made an alliance of fifteen extraordinary defenders.

PART 2

INTERNAL CIRCUMSTANCES

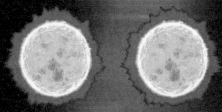

IX

TRUST IN ACTION

THE INTERNAL CONFLICTS FILLED WITH hatred and vengeance only expressed a mild feeling for the Governor. All of the gifted humans and aliens clashed to what appeared to be a miniature version of the last world war. Cyfreid's team didn't get too caught up in the action—an action that was actually considered "fun" to sly-like beings such as Valor and Sharp.

Even though Sharp still had the dreaded thoughts of Brute-Spine, taking care of a bunch of less complex opponents would be enough to ease the mental pain. One thing for sure was that he was going to have some serious words with Cyfreid after the raid was over.

He stared at his old master and saw the way how he shot at the opponents and took command of the heroes. Cyfreid looked back at him and saw that his old pupil was vicious as ever. He said to Sharp, "Are you okay?"

All Sharp did was turn around and leap towards his next target. Alongside Cyfreid was Tina. She also witnessed the troubled Curtis Kareem.

"What's gotten into him?" she asked.

"I'm not sure," he replied, fairly giving a lie. To take his mind off of it, Cyfreid called for Canavin.

The Pixalian warrior marched close, still with Pixcalibur out to reflect anything that came his way. Cyfreid stated, "We are going to surround the Governor! Call for the others at once!" He nodded and signaled everyone to his side.

Governor X wasn't as elusive as before. He found the shimmering stone in the corner. He picked it up, dusted the ancient object, and placed it inside of his dark jacket.

Canavin and the team surrounded Cain, ready to fight or just retrieve what they came for.

"The rock!" shouted Cyfreid to Cain X.

"You really don't understand. I must have this! And it looks like your chances of stopping me are over."

Cyfreid, Tina, and the fifteen heroes saw the villains slowly approach them. Their presence created feelings of resentment, but for some it was excitement. They clashed as Silvert, Valor, Canavin, and Cyfreid watched the Governor flee the area.

"Canavin, follow him!" commanded Cyfreid.

"No Canavin," said Silvert. "Stay here and help the others. I'll take care of the Governor."

"Excuse me but I'll make the orders around here!"

Canavin calmed him down and said, "He's right Cyfreid. I'll remain here and Silvert will head for Governor X. He knows his ticks better than the rest of us. Plus, he has a power unlike any other." Cyfreid looked at Canavin and then back at Silvert.

"Would it be too much?" he asked.

"It might be," said Silvert. "But what other option do I have?" There was no answer and it only proved his point.

They were all referring to his Silver Explosion ability. The only disadvantage was that it will temporarily shift him to his human form. Valor didn't quite understand the significance of the ability. According to him, the greatest power was Valoric Energy. The soldier watched curly wisps of smoke vacate his firearms.

"If the three of you don't mind, I'm going to kick some ass." He raced for the "fun" as he called it earlier.

"Alright then," said Cyfreid. He turned his attention to the silver hero.

"Please be careful!" he stated. "Your explosion could possibly destroy the substance and relea—"

"It'll take more than Silver Explosion to destroy Pixaliemain," said Canavin. "Besides, the result of the rock's destruction is close to a very small nova. The beast won't be free...I guarantee it."

"A nova?! Did you just say a nova?!"

"I said a very small one. Don't worry, Silvert isn't strong enough to destroy it. Nobody *really* is."

"We have a lot of talking to do. Still, I guess you know it best."

Silvert saluted them and took an extra communicator from Cyfreid. He quickly departed. He went through the doors and spotted a stairs to the roof.

When he reached the top, he sighted Cain quickly climbing a rope ladder that led into a jet. Wind blew in his direction as he saw the aircraft ascend and streak away like a bullet.

Silvert crouched down and lowered his head in defeat. There was no way he wished to report the news to Cyfreid. And he didn't have to. He stood right back up and took a deep breath. The jet was a twinkling dot in the night sky.

His sorrow reformed to anger. When refusing to quit the mission, Silvert rose in the air and zipped away, leaving a silver trail to match the same speed as Cain's jet. It would take time, but he was willing to do anything to save the human race.

"Stop at nothing! Be sure to demolish all of them!" These were the very words of Gustavo Salazar as he telekinetically threw hefty storage supplies at the heroes while he levitated.

"Watch out!" cried Valor. The energy blasts from his pistols were enough to protect him. He wasn't quite sure about the others. They managed to avoid the materials, but Gustavo kept going at it.

"Where do these misfits come from?" thought Valor. While he stood back to back with Canavin, the soldier agreed that Gustavo was a major irritant.

"Just how exactly can we stop this guy?" asked Valor. "I can't get a clear shot at him because of this scrap metal! Got any ideas alien?"

Canavin scanned around to view each member of the alliance as they were too engaged in swift combat. His eyes landed on Sherman Bawnder. He called him over.

"You! You can't die right?" asked Valor anxiously, tasting trickles of sweat under the rusted helmet.

"Well, I don't like to brag but—"

"Fusion Fighter!" The pterosaur strolled near for assistance. Valor could feel his straining veins from the intense firing. He shot down a mutated man from behind. Then he continued.

"You like using your strength? Well then come over here and toss this freak to the other freak!"

"Wait, so I'm a freak now?" asked Sherman.

The bulky Fusion Fighter picked Sherman Bawnder up by the waist and used all of his strength to fling him to Gustavo. The agent screamed aloud and glided passed the materials.

He flew right into him and they banged themselves on the floor. Valor, Canavin, and Fusion Fighter ran to them. Sherman got up and readied his shotgun.

Gustavo attempted to use his telekinetic force. He felt powerless upon being in the center of a heroic circle.

Canavin had the tip of his saber at his forehead, Valor had his pistols, and Fusion Fighter stood showing nothing more than his pterosaur appearance.

"Crap," whispered Gustavo under his breath.

"It sucks doesn't it!" shouted Valor. He was famished for the electrifying attempt. His index fingers bounced on the triggers, not pressing them all the way to eject the shocking beams from his blood flow.

"Now where's Governor X going?" asked Canavin. "Where is Identymous?"

Gustavo inhaled nippy gasps as he was heedless of what they were going to do to him. He quietly chuckled and then explained, "I'm not sure. Something about a different sector of the agency…but I don't know all of the sectors."

"You're lying!" said Valor as he exploded with contradiction. He brought his pistols closer. "You obviously know what the sector is!" Canavin thought about it.

"I think he's telling the truth," said the Pixalian.

"What makes you so sure?"

"Well…I know Identymous. And based on that fact, I think I know what sector he might be at." Canavin turned his head for a brief moment, but then was disturbed by a lurid energy blast. He looked to see Gustavo being electrocuted by a massive green voltage. The sparks jumped high to consume his full body. He looked at the soldier.

"Valor…c'mon now. Why'd you have to do that?"

"Yes, um…my fingers slipped." The four of them watched the villain twitch and roll on the floor, weeping for help. His cries got choppy. His shuddering hands became still. The static flashes formed to hazy fumes that waved from a charbroiled body.

Trying to avoid Gustavo's *shocking* condition, they turned around and walked away. Valor smirked under his helmet when his conscience knew that the event was intentional.

They saw Shade-Master open a portal that was ready to suck up a mutated fighter spewing flames from his mouth. There was a sudden sound of fluttering wings.

"Behind you!" Canavin yelled to Axel.

Shade-Master looked back. He was picked up by the winged man. Some feathers sprinkled down from the intense height. The man's talons clamped firm on Axel's shoulders, pinching him a tad. Shade-Master attempted to generate more realms. The human-bird avoided each one that tried to pull him inside. He journeyed in circles.

The crimson armoured Titanium Titan gazed at the flapping mutant with Axel in his clutch. He was certainly glad that he didn't have to deal with the winged man again.

Titanium Titan was known to be full of selfishness. He wished to be the key to end the entire operation. A part of his desire for inner pride was from Silvert's comparable egotism. He looked around in search for him. He was nowhere to be found. When Canavin and the rest caught up, Titanium Titan asked, "Where is Silvert?"

"He's taking care of X," said Canavin.

"What, why him?!"

"Because it makes sense for him to do it."

"I'm the hero! Me!"

Pounding footsteps rallied near. Canavin and the combatant turned to see the oversized Titanic. His ashy fists slammed together, knuckles cracking as they met. He crashed his fist into Hiro's gut and added a cogent uppercut.

Canavin was sure that helping Hiro would be the most appreciative unasked request. He brought Pixcalibur to the Titanic's throat. The massive man halted as he felt the blade's tip slit thin pieces. Hiro stood up with his metallic boots and screamed, "I'll handle this!" Canavin lowered the crystalline sword.

"Are you sure?"

"I have it covered, Canavin! I don't need help from you or Silvert!"

"Silvert? What does he have to do with this? He's not here right now."

Fury overflowed Hiro. The combatant listened for a whispering voice, wise and sonorous. His beloved sensei, somehow speaking to him.

Hiro, use the nunchucks. He cleared his mind from the punch and only envisioned his triumph. His hand hovered over them, feeling its texture, its metallic coating. His smile rose, his sight locked on the Titanic as if he was an ideal prize. The colossal man, as hulking as he was, could feel the dread clamber up his ripped arms. At last, Hiro revealed the nunchucks.

Canavin sensed the ominous look on Hiro's face. It was just as wicked as any scoundrel on Cain's alliance. Hiro took another glance at Canavin, insisting for the Pixalian to leave immediately. He spun his nunchucks to send air tendrils in the Titanic's direction.

"Just letting you know, this is going to hurt...a lot."

Canavin gradually stepped away and focused his attention on Frankie, Zan, and Celestica. When walking, he could hear the piercing screams from the Titanic with the metal clanging off his thick bones.

Canavin settled with the fact that that the violence was better left unseen. Being taught by his father to fight the honourable way, Canavin never had intentions to brutally torture anybody. Valor, Sharp, and now Titanium Titan fought with a more appalling style. The warrior thought about it.

Something else had to be bothering him. He arrived next to his crew members as they fought more rogues with various uncanny abilities.

The electrifying Lynx also arrived with Bloodblast and Corometheus on his tail. Corometheus—the controller of light—wore a grey and black attire with crackling cobalt flames as hair.

"They just *love* you don't they?" said Canavin.

"I can't see why?! A little help here would be nice!"

"From what I can see, you can generate electricity internally. C'mon now, you don't need any of *my* help."

"Canavin! This isn't funny!"

"Alright fine." Canavin emitted azure light rays. They only managed to strike Bloodblast. As for Corometheus, he absorbed the light as if it was a meal. He rose above Canavin and Lynx.

"Well that can't be good!" Lynx cried. "Any other suggestions?! Let's get Valor over here or something because it looks like *Bloodblast* isn't too happy." They watched his bazooka suck the static flow.

"I think we're dead man...dead!"

"Would you calm down?! This is nothing that we can't handle!" Canavin ascended to face Corometheus.

"Oh yea sure," said Lynx. "You take Corometheus when I have to deal with an insane rage man with a bazooka! I mean it's not fair! Who carries a bazooka?!"

"I'm going to enjoy this," said Bloodblast.

"And I'll remember that when I'm in heaven." Flickering static shielded his hands. The sparks danced around his fingers. He shocked Bloodblast with everything that he had. Several bolts filled Bloodblast's helmet, though did no good as he said, "That tickled."

"Okay…would the blast from your bazooka tickle me? Please say yes. I really beg you." He felt that he could humour Bloodblast long enough until Canavin was finished with Corometheus.

The floating warrior used the Pixcalibur blade to his advantage. His internal Pixalian energy would serve him no justice against the controller of light.

Lynx wished for him to hurry. He was able to see the Valoric Energy charged up inside of the weapon. He thought about using his agility. Then he figured it was pointless. Bloodblast wouldn't resist hunting him.

Within the area, Sharp stabbed a mutant, and then sighted Lynx with nowhere to run.

Bloodblast fired the flare. Before it was able to hit Lynx, Sharp leapt from the side and tackled him to the ground.

"Are you okay?" Sharp asked.

"No," said Lynx. He began to whine like a child.

"Why, what's wrong?"

"Your claws are jabbed in my thighs."

Sharp looked down to see his pointed fingers deep inside of Lynx's flesh. After taking his claws out and seeing blood, he smiled and said, "You'll be alright."

The injured Lynx remained on the floor, careless of the battles that occurred around him.

Sharp dashed straight towards Bloodblast and cut through the bazooka with one claw. Both of them watched the rocket-propelled weapon break apart.

"Impossible," said Bloodblast. He was hopeless, dumbfounded by Curtis and his barbed fingers. The slender claws extended more to cut Bloodblast's helmet.

Canavin finished his duel against Corometheus with a slash of his own that caused the man to have a pitiful fall. He descended down and noticed Sharp.

"Why is Lynx down?" he asked Curtis.

"Never mind that. How do you think Silvert is doing?"

"He has it covered, trust me."

"He better have it covered," said Cyfreid approaching with Captain Tina.

"Wait a minute," said Sharp. "Where's Shade-Master?" Canavin pointed up and they all saw Shade-Master who was still flown around the outsized room.

"This has to end!" he shouted. Axel stretched out his arm, still feeling the locked talons in his right shoulder. He generated the entrance to a realm filled with sizzling fire. The flames poured out from the gateway, almost landing on the watchful heroes down below. The winged man gulped fear and unlocked his baneful clutch to make Shade-Master fall all the way down on his back. The wormhole carried the flying mutant into the pit of flames. It sealed itself tight. Shade-Master dusted himself upon standing.

"Man," he started. "With powers like that, you have to have a nice codename."

"How's about Hell-Hawk?" said Lynx as he tried to recover from his lacerated thighs. "I mean, did you see his eyes? It was like he was controlled by *something*."

"Well, the flaming realm I sent him should make a pretty nice home."

"Can't you just do that with all the crazies here?"

"Yes, but I can only open one at a time. Also, Valor told me that it won't be as *enjoyable*."

"I'm with him on that one," stated Sharp.

"You guys are messed up," said Tina.

"Agreed," added Canavin.

"I'm going to contact Silvert and see how he's doing," said Cyfreid. He sent a transmission and waited for an answer. Upon hearing nothing, he hung up, nodded, and then gave a mild growl.

"I knew *you* would've been the right person."

"Don't give up on him," Canavin calmly said. "If you call yourself the Commander, then wouldn't it make sense for you to have faith in your team?"

Cyfreid thought about it and realized that the Pixalian was right. He selected each hero for a reason. They were all well-trained, very unique, and gifted with remarkable abilities he could only dream of obtaining.

"I'm sorry," he told Canavin. "I guess I forgot everyone here is equal…including someone as irritating as Lynx."

"Hey, I heard that!" yelled Lynx standing with one hand pressed on his drenched thighs.

"Well then, now what?" asked Sharp.

"We finish this!" shouted Valor who walked near with his squad.

Celestica, Frankie, and Zan came towards them after they defeated the supernatural mutants. The immortal Sherman Bawnder arrived as well as the furious Titanium Titan.

"Alright team," said Canavin. "Silvert hasn't returned yet, but the least we can do is show some credibility. He offered to retrieve the Pixaliemain so in the meantime, let's finish these scrubs once and for all!" The Pixalian placed his hand in the center as they surrounded in a huddle.

"We're the masters now," he said.

Everyone placed their hands in and they all shouted, "Together!"

Their combined chant produced a glorifying moment of unity. They stayed together in a cluster, waiting for the villains to come to them, focusing more on defense instead of offense. When the remaining members of Cain's alliance attacked, they stood no match against the team effort of Cyfreid's heroes.

Even with their nifty attempts, the heroes sensed the lurking mutants. They were notified by Valor, Canavin, Cyfreid, Tina, and even Evesdrop with her scattered blinking eyes. It was the same analogy given by Cyfreid:

As individuals we are nothing, but together we are powerful.

A dream come true to say the least.

There was an ongoing silver streak across the dusky sky that was moderately becoming blue. Morning was on the horizon. According to Silvert, it only meant that he had to hurry. He could see the AIA jet in the distance, bringing hope and making him travel even faster. The closer he got, the more he became determined and relieved by the clear fact that he didn't fail the team. The sky voyage went on for another five minutes. After bolting farther, there was a cunning smile on his polished silver face. The silver saviour reached the Governor's jet at last.

"More coffee sir?" asked a lady from inside the plane.

"Don't mind if I do," said Cain. His coffee arrived and he slowly picked up the mug that had an 'X' on it to take a gratifying sip. He looked outside to see the rising orange sun. Its presence relaxed Cain as he announced his victory over Cyfreid's team of heroes. He took a big taste of the rich coffee, just hoping that it would quench his thirst. With the liquid still in his mouth, he glanced at the sky's beauty again. He immediately spat it all out.

"What?! You're kidding me!" He sighted Silvert from the outside in his shot to foil his plan once more. The ferocious Governor marched to the pilot and screamed in his face saying, "Explain to me how Silvert was able to catch up!" Some of the Governor's disgusting spit made its way on the pilot's cheeks and lips. Before the pilot was able to wipe it off, Governor X yelled again.

"Lose him! Do you hear me?!"

"Yes, r-right a-away sir," said the pilot almost stuttering in his response. He turned the jet over to the left, but Cain was still able to see Silvert from behind.

"Can't this thing go faster?!"

"I-I'm trying but—"

The Governor dropped his tone.

"Silvert...we're talking about Silvert. Do you know what he's capable of doing? Do you know the power that's actually within him?"

"Well, um...not exactly sir."

"He has Silver Explosion you imbecile!"

"What is that exactly?"

"Well if you don't make this jet go faster, we might just find out!" The hesitating pilot didn't want to figure out what the inner power of Silvert could do to them. He made it his

personal mission to make sure the jet was completely out of
Silvert's sight. Before he was able to boost the acceleration,
glass shattered behind them.

"X! This is the final time! Hand me the Pixaliemain
now!" Cain looked around to try and formulate a plan to
escape. Nothing came to his mind. His bloodshot eyes
emphasized the anxiety. Silvert clamped his fists together, only
to make Cain think, *"Pathetic."*

"Or what?" he asked with folded arms.

"Or I'll just have to take it from you!"

"Really? You're going to use mere fighting skills to
take it? How original."

"I'm going to count to five," replied Silvert.

"Go for it. See if that's going to do anything."

"One," the hero began.

"You're pathetic."

"Two," he continued.

"You're a failure and the rock is mine!"

"Three four five."

"What?"

Cain noticed Silvert's crafty smile. He turned to the
pilot and said, "I guess we are going to experience it."

Throwing a glimpse at the sparkling stone, Cain leapt
for the substance and gave his trembling pilot a farewell. The
reality of death was one to refuse.

"Not this time," he thought. As soon as Silvert used his
Silver Explosion, Cain forced his weight to crash out the
window, sacrificing himself, though both options were
sacrificing.

The light from the hero's energy signature shot out like
an exploding star. Silver blazes consumed the jet, burning its
interior with the struggling pilot still inside. The massive jet
ruptured into tumbling pieces. As for the pilot, he was no
more.

Cain continued to descend from the obliterated plane
with no parachute or any aiding devices from his corrupted
sector. The wind shot dust in his heated eyes, raising his shady
hair with pale highlights. He noticed the sight of the city

expand and he accepted his defeat. The cerulean Pixaliemain was still in his grasp.

Silvert flew down and snatched it out of his hands. He was utterly careful from a startling shift of form.

The Governor screamed aloud when realizing the rock was gone and in Silvert's possession. Being an honourable hero such as Canavin, Silvert saved Governor Cain X and brought him on top of a skyscraper. Cain laughed from all of the trauma and the fact that the person he hated, Silvert, still allowed him to live.

"You just couldn't let me die, could you?" the Governor said. He closed his eyes and rested, not caring about what Silvert would do to him.

When the Governor slept, Silvert got a call. It was Cyfreid who had great news.

"Cain's alliance is defeated," he said. Then he asked the most critical question.

"Did you get it?" Silvert took in a breath of relief and excitement. He looked at the glimmering rock in his palm.

"Yea," he finally said. "I have it."

From where Cyfreid was located, the team shouted with cheers of success.

"Excellent!" said Cyfreid. "Meet us back at the 'X' Center." After hearing the Commander, Silvert unexpectedly switched forms back to Jamal Vertison. He panicked a little, and then noticed the sleeping Cain.

Jamal put the rock in his pocket and said to Cyfreid, "It's going to take me a while."

"Alright, but make it here as soon as possible. Over and out."

The conversation ended and Jamal was able to descend down some stairs that led inside of the edifice. He was anxious for rest until he was able to return to his silver appearance. The faith in the dream of a united group of heroes was now a reality.

X

CLOUDED REVELATIONS

THE BRIGHT SUN ROSE UP AND IT TRULY resembled the astounding achievement of the heroes. As soon as Jamal Vertison reformed to silver metal, he returned back to the 'X' Center which was now taken over by AIA East. Several villains were taken into custody by orders from Captain Tina. Commander Cyfreid watched his beloved pupil command the other eastern agents. He was amazed by how much she matured over the years.

After Tina made it clear that the central sector must vote for a new leader, Silvert was spotted in the blue sky. He landed and walked towards the Commander.

"Take this and find a safe place for it," he said to Cyfreid. The Commander grabbed the rock from him, but his expressions were concerning.

"What's the matter?" Silvert asked.

"Come, there is much to discuss." He followed Cyfreid and was honoured when each hero patted him on the back for his exceptional bravery. All of them did this except for one: Titanium Titan. Hiro simply gave a forged smile.

"So what now?" asked Breath-Stealer.

"Glad you asked that. We're all going to the east sector. It's great that we shut down the operation, but I fear that there are more troubling circumstances waiting."

"Hold on," Valor started. "My team was led into that filthy Governor's trap after searching for Derwin Grant and Bloodblast. Never did we fully agree to this…fraternity."

"Fraternity? This isn't college Mr. Valor, this is war."

"Doesn't seem like it." Lynx stepped in and added, "To tell you guys the truth, Valor is right. I mean, all of this for a bunch of rocks? That definitely doesn't seem like a war."

"Then I think you need to turn your attention to Canavin." Everyone looked right at the alien, hoping that he would end the confusion. Instead, he told them to listen to Cyfreid's orders of going to AIA East. While there, he would explain the entire story.

"Now that we have that taken care of, let's head to the base. Shade, you know what to do."

"Cyfreid, from my understanding this base is very...secretive. It's not as public as the 'X' Center. I don't know where it is." Then Meditation offered some assistance. She placed her hand on Cyfreid's head and closed her eyes.

"What's she doing?" he asked.

"Relax," said Evesdrop. "She's reading your mind." It was a strange experience for Cyfreid as he tried his hardest to avoid any unnecessary thoughts. He focused his mind to the very location of the base which was hidden among the clouds above the nation's capital. The majestic woman lifted her hand and gently told Shade-Master the location. He nodded and created the portal. As heroes walked inside one by one, Celestica remembered the recent circumstance.

"What about our cruisers?" she asked Cyfreid.

"Don't worry about those things," said Tina as she finished talking with the other officers. "I've told some of my men to pilot them to the station. It will take a while, but in the meantime we can set our next course of action."

"She's right, now get in before this closes!" yelled Shade-Master struggling to enlarge the gate.

Celestica, Frankie, and Zan entered followed by Cyfreid and Tina. All who was left was Canavin and Titanium Titan. Before Hiro walked in, the armoured Pixalian grabbed him by the shoulder and asked, "Hey, are you okay?" His altered personality was becoming quite evident. He moved the alien's hand off from his shoulder.

"I'm fine," he said. After they stepped inside, Shade-Master sprinted through the transporting realm.

AIA East was a humongous and metallic floating facility. Deep beneath the base was the city of Washington, DC. The heroes were speechless by the greatness it possessed as they stood on a hovering base plate. There were countless amounts of AIA East operatives who gave tasks to one another and trained like elite soldiers. It impressed Valor although he still preferred his team's facility.

"Everyone," said Cyfreid. "Welcome to AIA East, the invasion protection center. Over here we have state-of-the art technology capable of tracing any alien threat. In fact, the base was originally approved by Area 51 before the Star-Pix Crisis even occurred."

"How did you become the Commander?" asked Frankie.

"That my friend is a story for another day."

"There won't be another day," said Valor. "Because I already told you that my team is fully able to handle this mission. We don't need to be a part of this."

"I think it's best for your team to decide rather than you." Cyfreid looked at the four heroes and waited for an answer.

"We appreciate all you've done," said Fusion Fighter. "But Team Valor is our main priority."

"Just give us a chance," said Tina to the four of them.

The several agents observed and gave Captain Tina and Commander Cyfreid a salute as they led a bunch of heroes through the main doors.

The first person who Cyfreid brought to their attention was Agent Stan. Stan's sight lit up in amazement when he actually saw the fifteen recruits in person. Becoming a little jittery, he gave them a bow of honour.

"Boy, stop that foolishness!" complained Cyfreid. Being embarrassed, Stan turned his brown eyes to Tina.

"Is it safe?" he wondered.

"Yes it's safe with the agency."

"Safe with the agency?" Zan asked being muddled by Tina's response. "Hold on Miss Truman, but I think—"

Canavin stopped his fellow Pixalian from continuing his words and gave a demanding expression.

"You think what?" she asked.

"Nothing," said Zan. "Nothing at all."

AIA East wasn't a mere training facility that operated Pixalian surveillance cameras and had invasion armed weaponry. It was also a home for Cyfreid, Tina, and the other high ranked agents. The group of fifteen was led into an enormous room.

"This is the Collaboration Hall," said the Commander. "In here is where we negotiate certain creature files and decide on what the best form of punishment should be for them. We actually allow aliens into this room who act as solicitors for their clients or even their own species. The parties then collaborate specific legal terms that ultimately lead to a successful plan of action that satisfies everyone."

"You lost me at Collaboration Hall," said Lynx.

"You mean, this is also like a court office?" Sherman asked.

"Exactly, my immortal friend." Cyfreid took a couple of steps forward and then added, "However, it's also a room where you are all free to…relax yourselves."

"Oh finally!" shouted Lynx hobbling to one of the seats. "Do you guys have a couch anywhere?"

"Well actually the couch is—"

"Go get me a couch." Refraining from doing it himself, Cyfreid gave Stan a glare that basically said: *Go get him a couch now.*

The agent threw his arms high to complain. Cyfreid always took advantage of him. He was young, assertive, and zealous for more chances to hunt creatures just like Tina and Curtis. There was nothing he could do when it came to Cyfreid. He grumbled when proceeding out of the room in search for a comfy couch.

"And while you're doing that," Lynx said. "Can you *please* get me some damn ice?! My thighs hurt way too much!"

"Lynx, be a man," said Tina. "You're not the first person Sharp has done that to." Her words put Lynx in an awkward position. He looked at Sharp who didn't deny it by saying, "You see, she and I used to—"

"Yea, I get it," Lynx stated. He directed his attention to Tina. "And I am a man. I was just testing you."

The Captain nodded her head and was smart enough not to believe those words. She was awfully tired and now was the perfect opportunity to rest.

"I think I'm going to hit the bed," she calmly said to Cyfreid after she dramatically yawned.

"Alright then," he said. "You did a superb job today. I'm proud of you." She went through an entrance to a hallway of considerable rooms. As for the other heroes, they followed Lynx's advice of relaxing themselves with Agent Stan being their personal gofer.

Lynx took advantage of the young Stan by constantly giving him new orders. Some included bringing up more couches, junk food, magazines, and even videogames. The most needed request was a television screen that was seven feet in height.

Everyone was having a thrilling time. They revealed secret identities and past experiences in their hometowns. They bonded together despite their differences.

When Silvert was sitting down talking to Shade-Master, Lynx, and Team Valor about his success retrieving the Pixaliemain, it made Titanium Titan leave the room. He passed Canavin who continued to observe his changing character. Hiro Matsuo shook his head in disappointment; Jamal was too busy laughing with his new friends.

Sharp sat alone with his claws retracted. Then, after he enabled the humanlike hooks, he talked to himself.

I'm not a man, but a 'thing' instead.

Cyfreid was aware of his distressing look and decided that it would be best to speak with him in private.

"Silvert get over here!" he commanded almost with a congratulating voice. The hero was just about to tell one his funniest jokes; it had to wait. He went to the Commander who gave him some files.

"Take these," he said. "They're documents about the locations of the other rock substances. Bring them directly to the Captain."

"Yes sir. Although, Valor was right. I don't understand why I have to listen to you. I'm one of the greatest heroes in the nation if you must know."

"Then why don't you take that cockiness out of my station because we don't need that garbage."

Silvert became nervous. He nodded his metallic head and accepted the request about the documents.

"And make sure you knock first," the Commander said. Silvert took the papers and left the room for the hallway. He stopped at one of the doors that said, *Truman*.

He knocked three times and waited. The door opened slowly. Her presence ignited his mood, sparking plenty of interest when seeing her dressed casually. She wore small shorts and a slim green tank top to match her jade eyes.

"What is it?" she asked him. Silvert asked if he was allowed to enter for a moment. She saw no problem and gave him permission. The silver light was highlighted in the darkness of the room.

"You know you can change your form, Jamal." The hesitating hero refused.

"It's alright, I already know what you look like," she added. The silver exterior began to flush itself inside of the crystal he wore as a necklace. Revealing his identity, he changed forms once again to Jamal Vertison. He was relieved that he was able to do this in front of an agent who he could call his friend.

Tina sat on her bed and noticed Jamal continuing to stare at her. She lazed and closed her eyes as she pretended to sleep. Then Jamal brought something to her attention. He said, "You never fully explained your past." She opened her eyes and rose up to see Jamal's desire for a response.

"Why do you want to know so badly?" she questioned.

"Is it bad to know?" he replied.

"Well it's my business, not yours."

"You can trust me. I bet you never shared the story with much people. I won't tell anyone if you're *that* ashamed."

She patted on her bed for Jamal to sit. He paced near and sat beside her. Their eyes were glued to each other. To avoid it, she quickly pulled her sight away. She remembered her past, the one she tended to keep confidential. The agent felt that maybe Jamal actually cared for her. She somehow sensed a connection, a warm feeling that bloomed with her ex. Tina brought her eyes back to Jamal. She began to explain her story.

"Well if you really must know," she started. "It goes like this. Eight years ago, I was a senior student at my high school. But I wasn't any ordinary student. I had the top academic average in the entire school. You would think that I would've been a doctor or a teacher."

"Yea, I guess that would've made some sense."

"Anyways, even though I was the smartest student, my real passion was acting. I starred in several high school plays over my career and so, I wanted to go professional. One play was turning out to be a complete disaster. So, since I was so talented, they asked me to act as seven different characters. I had an unusual ability of quickly switching costumes."

"Master of disguise."

"Exactly. But the time came when I got used to the desirable nature of drugs. Anything that you can name in your head, I most likely tried it. It's still shocking to me how I survived with so much. I'm not proud for the things I've done since it led me to drug dealing. I probably had the strictest parents on the planet. They were so hard on me. I couldn't imagine how they would react if they had a son. They ended up finding out about my addiction and immediately told me to stop. Everyday, I refused to listen to them, so the result was my ass never allowed back into my house."

While listening to this, Jamal noticed a tear curve down her face. There was another tear and before she knew it, she was crying with full remorse.

"I yelled at them Jamal," she said with the tears. "I yelled at them, I swore at them…I told them I wished they weren't my parents. And then I walked out of the house. At that time, I had no love for them. I was very disobedient, but I didn't seem to care. Never Jamal, I mean *never* did I know that it was the last time I would ever see them."

"What happened?" asked Jamal becoming concerned.

"I slept that night being homeless. No food, no proper clothing, no warmth, and no water. Just me sleeping on the concrete ground in an alleyway. I begged that night when I heard the footsteps of strangers stroll pass me. They couldn't spare any change whatsoever. I tried to make myself comfortable. I had my phone, but it was that device that made everything worse. In the morning, I-I got a phone call from my friend Sabrina and she told me…"

The tears were flowing more than ever. Jamal got up and gave her paper to wipe them off. After doing this, she finished her sentence.

"She told me my parents had been murdered by aliens—hooded Pixalians of some sort. I didn't believe her. I had to know the truth but…I returned home and there they were. Two slaughtered bodies. My parents, they killed *my* parents." Jamal felt the inner pain. He waited until Tina was ready to continue the story.

"So there I was. My parents were dead, I said words that I can never take back, and I was in a terrible position. I went from that enthusiastic arts girl to someone I hated. The rage from the death of my folks made me indulge in drugs so much, that I looked in the mirror one day and actually forgot who I was for a moment. After enough dealing, I finally made enough money to rent a decent apartment. Still, nothing really ended. I dropped out of school and I made new 'friends' who robbed many stores, banks, and even homes. Each day was a new task that led to the grand job. They insisted to rob the newly formed police called the Alien Investigation Agency. I didn't know why I agreed, but I was pressured even more when one girl gave me a gun."

"Damn," Jamal said.

"I know," she said with dried tears. "But I went with it anyways. In the end, we were arrested by several officers and charged with intrusion and violation of AIA property.

Refusing to go to prison, I pointed the gun at a man named Captain Cyfreid before he was able to lock me in the handcuffs."

"Captain Cyfreid?"

"At that time he was the Captain. When I was ready to kill him on the spot, he simply said, *'Shoot me'.* I struggled to do it and my 'friends' made it worse."

Shoot him! Shoot him and run away! Do it Tina, save yourself!

"He repeated himself once more by telling me to shoot him. He even dropped his weapon and ordered the other agents not to help. When I was about to pull the trigger and retreat, I noticed something different about him. It was as if he knew everything I had gone through. This was the one moment where I had the choice to be a coward or become an adult and face my punishment. I dropped the gun and held my hands out to be locked in the cuffs. But he didn't arrest me. Instead, he brought me to the Commander whose name was Euro. Cyfreid said the words I will never forget."

This crook is special.

"That's truly amazing," said Jamal smiling.

"Cyfreid offered me a job at the agency. I worked my way up in months. I went through all the training simulations and succeeded more than anyone. My scores were shockingly high for a girl at my age. Two years later, Euro retired and Cyfreid became the new Commander of the east sector. The base was then moved to a hidden station among the clouds. The Captain of the newly formed AIA East headquarters was supposed to be a man named Jabyus, but Cyfreid insisted that I take the role. I was honoured to be at his side. We fought many battles together and met unique people including Curtis Kareem. I also got the liberty of meeting Canavin who taught me that not all aliens are cruel and deceitful. I guess you can say that my story *did* have a happy ending after all. The conclusion is that Cyfreid saved me, Jamal. He ended my addiction and he taught me everything about killing creatures. He transformed me and raised the assassin I am today."

After she finished, Jamal was delighted that Tina became someone of high standards after losing everything. The two of them were silent for a while in the room and then Jamal said the words, "Do you love him?"

Tina looked him once more in the eyes and said, "Well of course I love him. Who wouldn't? I mean he's smart, he has a strange sense of humour, he's loyal to his teammates, and he has the vision that only intelligent workers possess."

"I didn't mean it like that," said Jamal who this time refused to keep his eyes off of her.

"Do you *love* him?"

She finally understood the question and only answered saying, "Look, Jamal…you and I—"

"Cyfreid wanted me to give this to you," said Jamal cutting off her sentence. He handed her the files and agreed that he didn't want to figure out what her response was. She took the files and politely smiled.

"Thank you," she said. The documents showed a few locations of their next targets.

"Jamal, something isn't right."

"What is it?"

"There are five Pixaliemain rocks. We have two of them, but these papers explain the locations of two as well. One is missing."

Jamal grabbed the files and read them over. She was right. It didn't explain the destination of the last rock. He couldn't explain why. Tina called Cyfreid who was in the Collaboration Hall.

"Cyfreid, the documents were brought to me by Silvert. But where's the location of the last Pixaliemain?"

"That's the problem Tina, I don't know. In fact, nobody in this sector knows and it's making me very anxious. I'm holding a meeting in the Collaboration Hall very soon. And tell Silvert to come with the others this instant. He's been there too long. I don't know what you guys are up to."

Tina marginally blushed and hung up. When ready to leave, Jamal was glad to actually see her emotion.

"I got to go now," he said. "I don't want your boss to explode." She laughed and this amused Jamal. He was joyful for everything that has happened so far which included him joining the significant team, confronting the Governor, retrieving the Pixaliemain, and now him beginning a friendly relationship with the Captain. The hero switched forms back to metallic silver.

"I'll see you at the meeting," he said opening the door.

"Indeed you will."

He shut the door and walked back down the hallway and into the Collaboration Hall.

The heroes continued to celebrate their success. Food and drinks were everywhere, including a countless number of videogames and a lot of dirty plates. Most of them were considered young adults, but the appearance of the room suggested that they were teenagers once again.

Silvert saw Cyfreid who continued to stare at Sharp. He approached the Commander and asked, "If we're having a meeting in here, shouldn't this place be cleaned up?"

"You're absolutely right," Cyfreid said. "Stan! I want this pigsty gone in five minutes!"

"That's not fair at all Cyfreid!"

"Stan, we've talked about this. Do you want to get fired?"

"No sir."

"Then do as you're told."

"Yes, Commander Cyfreid." He began to pick up plates and empty glasses. In time, the celebration will end. Three more Pixaliemain rocks had to be found and one of them was unknown to the sector. Cyfreid called for all the heroes and stated, "There will be a meeting right here in the Collaboration Hall in ten minutes."

Sharp left the area upon hearing his words. Seeing his departure from the others caused Commander Cyfreid to become deeply worried for the guileful Curtis Kareem.

MASTER DEFENDERS

CANAYIN

Pronounced (Canayvin), is an alien warrior and former Prince of Star-Pix. His abilities include enhanced strength, combat fighting, and Pixalian energy. He is also able to fly.
Human name: Connor
Weapon: Pixcalibur Blade

SHARP

Sharp is an incredible being with the sharpest claws known to mankind. His codename stands for Strategic Hero Animalized for Rupturing Predators. He received his powers from an accidental alien reaction.
Identity: Curtis Kareem
Weapon: Claws

SILVERT

Silvert is a silver saviour to the public. His abilities derive from his silver necklace that has a material similar to certain Star-Pix minerals.
Identity: Jamal Vertison
Critical Power: Silver Explosion

CHARACTERS BY: MATT BHANKS

MASTER DEFENDERS

VALOR

Filled with Valoric Energy, Valor has similar traits to an antihero. He is known for his aggression and physical behaviour. He leads the impressive group of heroes called, Team Valor.
Identity: Unknown
Weapons: Valoric Pistols

TITANIUM TITAN

Titanium Titan is also known for his aggression. He is a kung-fu specialist and his abilities date back to his days with his sensei. He has the will to become the best hero in the nation.
Identity: Hiro Matsuo
Weapons: Titanium Nun chucks

FRANKIE

Frankie is a member of the Canavin Clan and specializes in alien hunting. After he was asked to hunt down Canavin, he accepted but lost the battle. Later, he became the alien's companion.
Weapons: Various AIA tech

CHARACTERS BY: MATT BHANKS   TITANIUM TITAN BY: MALCOLM BHANKS

MASTER DEFENDERS

CELESTICA

Celestica is another member of the Canavin Clan. She is a former member of AIA West. Her fighting style is compared to some of the most fierce agents in the league.
Name: Vanessa Allen
Weapons: Various AIA tech

LYNX

Lynx is a supercharged being who is known to be a constant nuisance. He is able to unleash electric bolts with amazing timing. In addition, he has enhanced speed and agility.
Identity: Unknown
Attack moves: Electric Strikes

SHADE-MASTER

Shade-Master is a master of Psychology and the realms of the universe. He also has outstanding strength and is Lynx's best friend.
Identity: Axel Ramone
Attack move: Realm Trap

CHARACTERS BY: MATT BHANKS   LYNX BY: MALCOLM BHANKS

MASTER DEFENDERS

Fusion Fighter is an amalgamation of a man and an extraterrestrial with similar features of a pterosaur. His abilities include flight and strength. Generally, he is the co-captain of Team Valor.
Identity: Mark Foland
Attack moves: (Various)

Zan is a Pixalian hero and has an alien appearance that is very comparable to Canavin. He is a member of the Canavin Clan and also the brains behind the construction of the Canavin Station.
Full Name: Zan Genrax
Power: Pixalian energy

Meditation possesses magical powers that derive from the Pixalians. Her tricks range from the simplest spells to the most dangerous attacks.
Identity: Sasha Grey
Main ability: Spellbinding

CHARACTERS BY: MATT BHANKS

MASTER DEFENDERS

Breath-Stealer

Breath-Stealer is a swift-moving spirit who is able to switch forms on command. He can also control his visibilty and is able to touch solid objects in his spirit form.
Identity: DeMarcus Howard
Attack move: Insertion

Evesdrop

Evesdrop has multiple eyes that are not only on her forehead, but also all over her body. She is able to control each one effectively. Surprisingly, the mutated being is not an alien.
Identity: Alicia Eve Tavern
Abilities: Enhanced sight and impressive combat skills

Sherman Bawnder is an agent of the Triple O Organization. Whether he prefers it or not, he is unable to experience death. The cause of this was because of a vicious match with an alien predator.
Years with Triple O: 9
Advantage: Indestructibility

CHARACTERS BY: MATT BHANKS

MASTER DEFENDERS

Agent Stan Bradley III is a first time member of AIA East. He is relatively young but is known as an impressive pilot. Often times, he is ordered by Cyfreid to complete undeserving tasks.
Role: MINOR OPERATIVE
Weapons: Shotgun, agency blaster

Captain Tina Truman is the second-in-command of AIA East. She is well-trained and is a master of disguise. She likes to keep her past confidential.
Role: CO-CAPTAIN
Weapons: Various AIA tech, holographic shield generators

Pronounced, (Syfreed), is the Commander of AIA East after former Commander Euro. He is often questioned about the choices he makes. However, he is always thinking about the safety of the human race.
Role: COMMANDER
Weapons: Various AIA tech, Thermal detonator

CHARACTERS BY: MATT BHANKS

XI

BETRAYAL

THE ENTERTAINING TIME OF RELAXATION

was up and now was the period of strict revelations. Commander Cyfreid deliberately called out the meeting for clarification purposes. They sat around a large table, almost like a banquet table, and the television screen was set up to show a visual of the Earth.

"Alright you misfits," he said sarcastically. "If any of you were smart, you would've already understood that this is a map of the world. About forty eight hours ago, I ordered Captain Tina to head right here." He pointed at the screen and the map enlarged to get a clearer view. It was pinpointed at Detroit, Michigan.

"Eight years ago when the five Pixaliemain rocks were unknowingly stolen from Star-Pix by Richard Rageous, it had to be kept a secret. We tested one of the rocks on an alien species at Lasher Laboratories, directed by the famous Lasher family. Luckily, a different creature informed us of the dangers we were getting into. Thank God for that alien, otherwise none of us would be here today."

"Either way I would still be here and you know it," said Valor.

"As I was saying," continued Cyfreid. "By that time the entire Alien Investigation Agency had been formed. We had a conference just like we're having right now. My Commander told me to meet up with a Governor by the name of Cain X. After Cain joined the agency, he told me the secrets of what the rock could actually do. It was called Pixaliemain and as you all know, it has a force of attraction among certain creatures. He said that the rocks could mean the end of the world. So, it was up to him and me to hide the items and never speak of them again. But three years from that time, I received a call from Cain. He was overjoyed and told me that the solution to the Pixaliemain issue was simple. He said that allowing just one extraterrestrial to speak the dreaded ritual would be alright. Of course, I told him he was insane but he continued. He said he had satellites in construction that would take about five years to complete. The generating rays from these devices would have a certain type of energy signature, the same from the Pixaliemain rocks. He believed that with some slight modifications, the beast—or Xaliemer to be exact—could be controlled. So, if he could control Xaliemer—"

"He would control most of the Pixalians on the planet," said Canavin who knew that none of this was *new* information.

"That's right Canavin. What the Governor realized was that being the leader of AIA Central wouldn't be enough for the council to legalize the plan. So, over five years, he put together a team of criminals and called them the 'X Viles'. I couldn't allow that threat to prosper. Therefore, AIA East has been watching all the newly emerged heroes over the last five years. The thirteen of you have been listed as the best of the best."

"Thirteen?" asked Celestica.

"Yes ma'am. You see, at first Shade-Master and Titanium Titan were not...scouted as you may say."

"Whatever, I'm okay with that," Shade-Master said.

"But I don't think Titanium Titan is," added Canavin. To such a coincidence, Titanium Titan entered the room and sat down. Inside of his pocket, there was an AIA shield device that he stole during his wandering trip around the base.

"Hey titan, guess what!" began Lynx. "At first, you weren't—"

"Shut up," Silvert whispered. Cyfreid stared at Tina and gave her the permission to speak.

"While I was in Detroit, I had a battle with a predator that almost unleashed the beast. This video was uploaded from my communicator. It's a recording of the creature's final words before it perished." The video clip played on the screen showing the defeated alien say the words:

"You humans stand no chance.
Your race will be crumbled by the new authority.
Many will be killed and some will be forced to serve
him.
Give up now and submit to Earth's new master.
Give praises unto the eternal reading.
All hail Xaliemer!"

The speechless heroes became uncomfortable about the cause.

"And if you think that's freaky," said Cyfreid once more. "Then you have to watch this next clip." They each sat up and turned their attention to the large screen.

"This was a video delivered by the surveillance cameras from Lasher Labs eight years ago. The man you see analyzing the Pixaliemain is William Lasher. Beside him is his wife Tanya and the young man is their son named Hank."

In the video, it showed William pick up the substance and place it right beside an alien. Then there was complete darkness.

"What's going on?" said William.

Strident cries lasted for one minute. The heroes could hear the raucous gashes from the film. Smashing test tubes sprinkled its sounds to combine with dynamic roars. The screams ended and the lights turned on as if it was on their own. The alien, along with all three Lashers, suffered death from an unknown force. The clip ended.

"My guess is that the alien panicked," stated the Commander.

"Hey I got a question," Lynx said. "If there are five rocks, does that mean that there are five Xaliemers?"

"Not exactly," said Zan. "Any *single* rock can unleash the beast. There's only one Xaliemer, but its spirit lurks through each rock. Once he's released from one of the rocks, the remaining ones will combine."

"So how come you and Canavin are immune to them?" The others agreed that this was the best question asked by Lynx.

Canavin explained, "If you really must know the entire story, then I'll tell you. When I was very young and my father was still alive, a plague was sentenced to destroy our race. This was the threat of Xaliemer. He was a massive being who communicated through the mind. Being the King, my father joined forces with other ethnic Pixalians to create an alliance called, 'The Star-Pix Defenders'. They fought gallantly against the beast. In the end, he was defeated. Almost the entire population praised them for their victory. However, the beast was not fully dead."

They looked at each other with confusion.

"Since my father was a spellbinder, sort of like you Meditation, he sentenced the beast to be trapped inside a colossal rock that could only be released by a ritual my father knew. But the more times that Pixalians came near the rock, he noticed changes in their speech. It was concluded that Xaliemer was aware of the reading and to try and free himself, he would control the Pixalians that came near the substance. Over time, the rock split into five pieces. My father knew that using his powers to make the population immune to Xaliemer's control would be necessary, but he only had enough energy to save me, my cousin, and a couple other families—Zan was part of one of them. When given the name Pixaliemain meaning *rock of Xaliemer* on our planet, the five rocks had to be kept safe. Over these eight years, I thought it was still on Star-Pix. I was wrong."

"Basically, this is your daddy's fault," said Lynx. Canavin wasn't amused by his response.

"No, it was Richard's fault for stealing it all those years ago."

From hearing Canavin's story of the origin of Pixaliemain, Cyfreid revealed the known locations of the two rocks.

"Believe it or not, the destination of one of them is in the *Grand Museum* located in New York."

"Museums…perfect," stated Frankie.

"The other is located in the hands of one of Cain's most fierce apprentices. His name is Version X."

Version X was a cyborg copy of Silvert. Jamal dealt with the android during his days back in Chicago.

"Silvert, I want you to take *care* of him."

"It's nothing new to me," he confidently replied.

"Unfortunately, I don't know where the last Pixaliemain is, and the computer isn't picking up its wavelengths."

"Maybe that Identymous alien knows," suggested Tina.

"We don't need to worry about him anymore," said Cyfreid. "It was obvious that Cain wanted him to unleash Xaliemer. But thanks to Silvert, the Governor is no more. He is no more...right Silvert?"

Jamal scratched his glossy head and tried to avoid the question. When most of his team fixed their eyes on him, he said, "Well actually, he survived the 'Silver Explosion'."

"He what?! I thought you told me that you had it under control!"

"Hey, we're talking about a person's life here! Killing the man wasn't part of the plan! I was after the Pixaliemain and that's all that mattered!"

"Do you know what this means? He'll be back! Who knows, the entire 'X Viles' might be back! He has his ways of escaping. It can be anything like hidden firearms or agents secretly working for the central department. He might even meet up with Version X and then Identymous!"

"Well, why does he want this Identymous 'thing' to unleash him?!"

"That's what I'm wondering," said Canavin coming into the conversation. "I mean, he was willing to travel that far just to meet up with one Pixalian. Something has to be up. And I think I'm starting to figure some things out."

"Wait...you said 'that far'," Cyfreid spoke. "So you know what sector Cain was going?"

"Yes, I've fought against Identymous before. It's the West Sector, located in—"

"Cyclohoma City," said Cyfreid finally understanding.

"That's right."

"So Gustavo really wasn't lying when he said he didn't know about the sector," said Sherman Bawnder. "Because I don't think he's ever been to Cyclohoma City."

"You better hope that the Governor magically died!" screamed Cyfreid towards Silvert. Upon witnessing the furious behaviour of her boss, Tina refused to contradict his words.

"We have to act fast! I'm giving Canavin the role of the field leader. In battle, you will receive orders from him. If he's not around, then you will receive orders from either me or Captain Tina. Do I make myself clear?"

"Hey! You dragged us into this mess!" yelled Valor. "So I don't need you to tell me who is in charge!"

"You know what Valor, I'm going to pretend that you're not in the room right now."

"Well I'm going to pretend I don't kill you this very moment! Like I said…it's just pretending."

"Easy man," said Fusion Fighter. "Just bear with this, okay. Everything's going to be fine. Lower your weapons."

"Big boy Cyfreid better not tempt me next time!" When Valor was calmed down by Fusion Fighter, the Commander added, "Canavin, you and your squad along with Sherman and Captain Tina are to head to New York. Valor, you and your team are to join up with Silvert and Titanium Titan to locate Version X."

"Wait, I'm with Silvert?" asked Titanium Titan desperately.

"Yes you are. That's not a problem, is it?"

"N-n-no…not at all. I was just making sure."

"As for the rest of us, we are to stay put until I can figure out where the last rock is. This meeting is adjourned. For those who have a task, move your asses out of here! If this scum arrives, it'll be the greatest invasion known to mankind."

"To be honest with you Cyfreid, it won't," said Canavin. "There's more to come whether you like it or not."

"I'm going to ignore that."

Team Valor, the Canavin Clan, Captain Tina, Sherman Bawnder, Silvert, and Titanium Titan departed from the Collaboration Hall. And as soon as the Commander left, Lynx got up and asked Shade-Master, "Okay…you up for more snacks?"

Commander Cyfreid told Captain Tina to wait. He spotted Sharp in the distance who missed the entire meeting. Curtis Kareem stared out of the large-scaled windows. The view of the clouds was enchanting, though it didn't seem to benefit his current mood. Cyfreid reached Sharp's presence and said, "You missed a very critical meeting." Curtis kept his eyes at the charismatic clouds as he tried to avoid the Commander.

"Sharp?" said Cyfreid. "Is everything alright?" The displeased look that Curtis gave him only meant that quarreling was soon to come. Tina also arrived being concerned not only for Sharp, but for Cyfreid as well.

"What did you do to Gary?" asked the troubled Curtis. Hearing this, Tina said, "Okay, I think it's time for me to leave."

"No, hold on," insisted Cyfreid. He gradually paced near, facing the alien hunter.

"Gary? What are you talking about?"

"Don't play games with me Cyfreid! What did you do to Gary?!" His voice was raised to a level that threw discomfort inside the Commander. Cyfreid tried not to reveal it by laughing a little.

"Look," he said. "In the alien infested world we live in, some things have to be done in order to secure maximum freedom."

"So it is true! You bastard—"

"I did what I had to do! You left the agency and I needed some extra help taking down monsters!"

"And that meant turning an innocent man into an abomination?!"

"Brute-Spine, I mean Gary, was a success! But over time he lost himself and became demented! The creature took over him!"

"I can't believe this! I can't believe you dragged me into this mess! You wanted me on this team because you knew

I was the only person who would stand a chance against him! He was my best friend!"

"As if I really knew you would find out! I had no clue he was working for X!"

"It just goes back to what I said before…you have no boundaries."

"Why are we even talking about this?! He's not the problem right now! The problem is that the Governor is still alive! Curtis, you're the Strategic Hero Animalized for Rupturing Predators! I told you that you were one of the best! It's an honour for me choosing you!"

"Maybe I'm going to suffer the same fate as Gary! Who knows because right now, I feel like I'm losing myself!"

His fingers protracted. Avoiding the still small voice inside of him, he labeled Cyfreid as his prey. A spiteful snarl trundled out of him. He bared the teeth of a predator when he had the chance to slice Cyfreid. Tina loaded her pistol and aimed it at Curtis.

"You do that and you would leave me no choice," she said.

"Fine!" he yelled withdrawing his sharp fingers. "I quit."

He turned away and left both of their sights. Cyfreid followed and was stopped.

"Maybe it's best if I talk to him," Tina claimed. The Commander agreed and returned his thoughts back to the things that really mattered.

Tina caught up with Sharp and defended her actions saying, "You know I wasn't going to shoot you right?"

"It wouldn't have worked anyways. Actually to tell you the truth, right now I feel like dying."

"Don't say that."

"Why shouldn't I?"

"Because we need you on this team. There's too much at stake."

"How could he turn a man like Gary into a monster? Gary is not a hunter like you and me."

"Cyfreid showed the same faith that he had in you with Gary Herman. He only wanted what was best for the agency."

"Do you hear yourself right now?! When will you realize the true nature of the man? I'm done working for that, that, that—"

"Fool, jerk…asshole? You think I haven't heard people call Cyfreid those names before?" She invited Sharp to sit down and calm his mind. When he sat, the hero asked, "Why do *you* still work for him?"

"Curtis, of the many years you worked for Cyfreid—and when you and I used to date—I don't even think you know who he is."

"I know *exactly* who that man is!"

"No," she immediately replied. "I don't think you do. Cyfreid isn't perfect, and neither are you. Do I have to remind you what you did to me? You made me kill—"

"Don't talk about that."

"Fine. Anyways, Cyfreid says things and he does things that even I disagree with time to time. But no matter what, he's always thinking about the safety of the human race."

"What are you trying to say?" Tina took a breath in and then exhaled. She said, "Although sometimes Cyfreid may seem like the *villain,* that doesn't mean he's a bad person. You just haven't figured that out yet." The Captain got up and before she left, she added, "Look, if you want to go, then go. But just know what you're walking out of."

This got the animalized hero thinking: leave the league and return back to the mansion assisted by a loyal maid or stay a part of the group and ultimately save the human race.

To his realization, both choices were equivalent with each other. It was shocking as he expected the choice of returning to the mansion to be the better option. It seemed as if the past day and a half reminded him that no matter what, he was and will forever be a hero.

Curtis looked at his hand and watched as his fingers rose back to claws. He accepted the creature he really was; he was still very much indecisive. Whatever choice it would be, he vowed to stay focused on that decision.

Canavin waited for the others to prepare themselves. He looked out and saw his unit's cruisers land. The agents riding them stepped out and gave him the signal that the ships were ready for him and his three companions. Valor approached the alien and said, "So…you're the field leader."

"I guess so. But I don't think you're going to take many orders from me…are you?"

"No, not at all. Maybe some…actually a few to be exact." The alien laughed being very familiar with Valor's way of saying: *I'm the best and you're one level below me.* It didn't matter to him. Yet, he still had thoughts about Identymous. To his surprise, Valor asked him a question about the creature.

"Do you think that the last rock is with that Identymous alien?"

"Well like I said, I don't think so. If that was the case, Xaliemer would've already been unleashed."

"Good point there."

"I'm still trying to figure out why he's more valuable than the other Pixalians on the planet. I have an idea but…it's too insane."

"What type of Pixalian is he, as in, what powers does he possess?"

"He's a shape-shifter." Valor was stunned by the words as if his heart skipped a beat.

"A shape-shifter? Do you think—"

"I hope to God not," stated Canavin. Silvert arrived and asked, "You boys ready for some action?!"

He noticed the concern on Canavin's face and how Valor didn't answer.

"You guys okay?" he wondered.

"Oh yea we're *fine*," said Canavin. "The question is, are you and Titanium Titan okay?"

"What do you mean?"

"You know what I'm talking about. It's like you guys had a bet as to who is the better hero."

"We sort of did. Is that a bad thing?"

"Well, all I'm saying is that it's not the esteem-needs that matter. All that's important is that the right thing was done."

"I understand."

"And the fact that you allowed Cain to live *was* the right thing. You have my respect. Don't worry about what Cyfreid says. Always be the honourable person, right Valor?"

"Whatever. If it was me, it would've been a whole other story."

"Then I guess it's a good thing it wasn't you." Valor simply nodded to show that the alien was too moral.

"You know what," Canavin added. "The three of us are pretty powerful. If we could combine our rays, it'll aid the others greatly in battle."

"I don't think that'll ever happen," said Silvert.

Tina Truman came and said, "Looks like one person could be gone." They were unaware of what she meant until thinking back to the meeting, realizing that only fourteen of them were in the Collaboration Hall.

They came to the understanding that it was Sharp's decision on whether to remain a part of the gifted alliance or plan his departure. Tina gave Valor some documents about Version X.

"We've tracked him down to be located in Toronto, Ontario. Find him and get the rock. Do whatever it takes. I really don't care."

"I like the sound of that." He called his teammates over and they entered inside of one of the AIA jets called the *Regime 5*, piloted by a man named Draymond.

Titanium Titan arrived and also entered to place his nunchucks safe on the seat. Before Silvert entered, he looked at Tina and hoped that it wouldn't be his last time admiring her beauty. The doors of the jet closed and then the silver man took his seat.

"You ready Canavin?" Tina asked the famous Pixalian.

"Are you ready?" he asked back. The Captain nodded and Canavin, Frankie, Zan, and Celestica walked out of the main entrance of the facility and located their parked cruisers.

They each went into their own and noticed the changes in their ships. Some slight modifications were made by the AIA agents including a more advanced communication system. While in the cruisers, Tina appeared on the screen with Sherman beside her. She was inside of a ship called, *The Ark Eagle*.

"Alright, follow my lead."

"We don't need to follow your lead," said Frankie ready to start up his ship.

"Why is that?" asked the Captain.

"Because, everybody knows where New York is. And that's even if it means being hidden in the clouds."

They noticed the other jet ascend and fly off downwards. Tina scowled and clamped her fists.

"Hey! I didn't tell Draymond to leave! What gives?"

"Valor's in the jet right?" asked Frankie.

"Yes he's inside."

"Well there's your reason."

XII

SWIFT FEAR

THE CANAVIN CLAN'S CRUISERS ALONG with *The Ark Eagle* left AIA East headquarters in their attempt to make it to New York.

During Cyfreid's crucial meeting with the alliance, the X-Viles escaped from a detention center back in Illinois. It was all thanks to the crafty Cain X. Hours ago, after waking up on the edifice, he grinned with his thoughts still locked on the initial plan.

The Commander's concerns were slowly coming true. Cain selected three members of his faction for a very critical task in "The Big Apple". The outlaws' target was the same Pixaliemain rock in the Grand Museum.

Within several lengthy minutes, the Canavin Clan members looked down to view the famous statue of liberty.

"Here it is, New York City," said Zan.

"We'll be landing shortly," said Tina to the others. The jet with the four cruisers flew across the city skies with the many New Yorkers and tourists getting the opportunity to take pictures. Soon, they landed on the museum's roof. When the group of six prepared themselves, the situation caused Frankie to ask, "Why does Cyfreid need five of us to do this? Well, I mean six if you want to count yourself Tina."

"You don't know what to expect," she explained.

"She's right," said Sherman. "The opposition here is unknown. We must be cautious."

"I'm not scared of a bunch of New Yorkers."

"I don't think they're scared of you either." She gave Frankie the idea that he didn't resemble someone who could express such stern and startling emotions.

"Exactly what floor is the mineral on?" asked Sherman.

"Cyfreid was the one who hid it," Tina explained. "According to his words, it should be on the third level."

"Okay," said Frankie this time. "So we go in, steal the rock, and get out. That sounds easy to me."

"It's not really considered *stealing* since it belongs back on my planet," said Canavin giving a peculiar stare towards the Captain.

The look informed her that all five of the Pixaliemain rocks deserved to be in Canavin's possession. She believed the choice was up to Cyfreid. Canavin inferred that Tina Truman was too loyal to the man.

Tina, Sherman, Frankie, and Celestica went down the rooftop stairs while the Pixalians flew out and around the museum to spot the third floor. As soon as Canavin was about to smash the windows, Zan stopped him and asked, "Canavin, what if this isn't right?"

"C'mon Zan, they're just windows."

"No, not that. What if this team 'thing' isn't right? I mean, it seems like our *dear* Captain is planning to not give us the rocks in the end."

"Zan, I promise you that every broken piece of the rock of Xaliemer will be with us. As of right now, it seems like she would await Cyfreid's orders. But either way, I'm not letting humans have control of Pixaliemain. Anyways, this is my fault. I should've watched over the substance."

"Don't blame yourself, you didn't know."

"You're right, I didn't."

"All of this is because of these humans."

"What Richard did was wrong, I get that. But I must remind you that we have two human allies on our squad. Remember, not all humans are immoral."

"The same goes for us."

"Then be sure to practice what you preach."

Zan was very proud to be a strong Pixalian alongside Canavin. They braced themselves as they crashed through the windows to create rowdy cries from a tour guide and multiple sightseers.

It was until a tourist called out, "Hey wait a minute, that's Canavin and Zan!"

The two names were enough to convert their fear into exceptional gratitude. The chants continued even when Tina and the others reached the level.

A female tourist cried, "Everyone look, it's the indestructible Sherman Bawnder along with Canavin Clan members, Frankie and Celestica. I don't understand why an AIA officer is with them."

"My name is Captain Tina," she said introducing herself.

"Sorry, but you're not famous like the rest of us," Frankie stated.

"Sherman, have you joined forces with Canavin's team?" the woman asked.

"Well not exactly. You see, this is..."

"This is none of your business," Tina clarified. "I have strict orders from Commander Cyfreid to acquire that rock substance."

The tour guide and everyone else followed her line of sight.

"That's just an average meteor fragment," the tour guide explained. "It even says so on the label."

"Ma'am, I'm not going to go into detail, but we came here for that rock. Just let us have it." The so-called average meteor fragment was sealed in a glass container. The tour guide allowed Tina to proceed until she asked the question, "What's so special about it?"

"That information is highly classified." After hearing those words, the tour guide along with the museum tourists closed their mouths. Tina marched to the container and was ready to fulfill Cyfreid's dire request. She felt myriads of breaths collect on her neck and run down her back. She tried, but couldn't retrieve it. The excessive drafts made her temper escalate. She bawled out, "As of right now, this level of the museum is closed! Please find your exits!"

The moans drifted her way. There was nothing that they could do. She was authority, a mark of attraction and severity fused together. Each of them left except for three men in sable trench coats wearing black shades.

"What are those guys doing?" Celestica wondered. Hearing the question, the Captain was lacking patience. She cried out once more, "Did you fools hear me? This floor is closed! In fact, I'm about to close this entire museum if you three don't leave!"

They ignored her words; the fact that five unique people were around didn't worry the men at all.

The mission was never in the heroes' intentions to retrieve the Pixaliemain in front of witnesses. The process was supposed to be quick and effortless.

One of the three walked beside the glass-sealed rock.

"Such a fascinating stone this appears to be," said the man.

"That's *great*," said the Captain. "Now you and your friends leave the premises."

"I'm afraid that's not going to happen," the man said.

"What the hell did you just say?! Do you know who you're talking to?!"

Her fuming reaction was only enough to curve an intimidating smile on his face.

Canavin noticed the traits of them from under his mechanical mask. The more that he stared, the more he knew that each of them were familiar in some sort of way. One of them stood out the most, being awfully huge and had his face covered with livid swellings and blotches.

The man continued to be near the vast glory of the stone. He chuckled while eyeing Tina's riling expression.

"Tell your Commander that his days are numbered," he said to her.

Tina stretched her arms to brandish her pistol at the man's chest. Her threats did nothing. She gripped her hands tight even with the understanding that he was only a fascinated citizen.

Or was he?

He swiftly kicked the gun out of her hands and called the larger man to shatter the glass.

He charged directly for the Pixaliemain. Frankie tried to prevent him from his goal. Though, he realized that the overweight man wasn't going to stop sprinting. To save himself, Frankie ran out of the way and witnessed the glittering shards ascend and scatter on the ceramic floor. They each removed their trench coats to reveal themselves; Professor Shaw, Derwin Grant, and the Titanic.

"Stop him now!" Tina screamed. As quick as she could, Celestica fought against Derwin Grant with Frankie and Zan to support. Canavin and Tina faced Professor Shaw. Sherman was left with the unwanted task of going against the the oversized Titanic.

His face was shaped with blatant lumps and wide lesions from Hiro's nunchucks back at the lair.

Sherman had the most important challenge considering the Pixalian rock was in the Titanic's hands. The Titanic clutched the stone to shield its brilliance. He turned and ran with the substance. Sherman followed and the chase continued out of the floor.

Celestica, Frankie, and Zan were confident in their match against Derwin Grant. With a three on one advantage, they each took turns of getting a fair amount of strikes.

The drug lord was equipped with plenty of tasers. He took one and used it on the clan members. It had no effect on Zan. As for Celestica and Frankie, they dropped like vacant puppets and excessively twitched. The menace ran off with Zan to pursue him.

The great Canavin and Captain Tina squared up against Professor Shaw. Shaw was the former head of AIA West located in Cyclohoma City.

"How did you escape from the detention center?!" asked the infuriated Captain.

"Now really, Miss Truman. You think I'm actually going to explain *that* to you?"

Canavin and Tina remembered the frustration from Cyfreid during the meeting, the mere fact that he was so outraged by Cain's survival of the eruption. Cyfreid's theoretical fears were slowly arising.

Canavin took his eyes off the Professor to notice his tased friends. Shaw seized the opportunity by firing an energy blast at his stomach.

The alien looked down; nothing seemed too serious. He reached for his scabbard to draw Pixcalibur and then was blasted again.

The warrior flew ten feet back from the blow and landed to see corroded streaks on his armour. He knew that if it wasn't for the dark cobalt exterior, death would be the reality.

Tina shot at Professor Shaw who shockingly avoided every hit. Canavin gradually got up to his feet. He had the easy ability of defeating Shaw with Pixcalibur. As he placed his hand on its grey hilt, he decided that it wasn't needed.

The Pixalian energy within him, his true fuel for achievement, was charged at an intense level. The alien watched the blue ring of light expose itself around his fists. Without any hesitation, he unleashed the energy blasts at Professor Shaw, sending him twice as far back. Shaw constantly coughed. The wrathful Canavin picked him up by the collar.

"W-what are you going to do to me?!" Shaw cried out.

"Where's the Titanic going?!" Professor Shaw gulped. The air was tough when going down his throat. He said, "The Titanic is going to be transported in order to reach Identymous! Honest, I swear!"

"Where's that?!" *It was obvious.*

"Cyclohoma! Cyclohoma City! Remember the good times we had back then?! Only during that time you were a bratty teenager!"

Canavin dropped the pathetic man. Tina approached him and aimed for Shaw's leg. She wasn't going to pull the trigger, not yet.

Canavin couldn't believe he was hearing that name again. Identymous had a special role in the Governor's plot. The alien-hero feared the worst if Sherman wasn't successful in snatching the rock from the Titanic.

The Titanic carried the Pixaliemain that drastically illuminated in his hand. The terrified citizens around the museum ran down the New York streets. To make room, the bulky man raced through the enormous crowd, causing poor civilians to fly up and break bones when landing.

"Move out of my way!" the Titanic hollered while forming his own path.

The cautious Sherman Bawnder sprinted down the pathway that the Titanic created. He wished to have time to service the injured New Yorkers, but the chase was too critical. Seeing the man rush his way down the road, Sherman remembered the one extraordinary aspect about himself: death was impossible.

"Hey you!" he called at the Titanic. "Why don't you stop running and face me like a man?!"

The criticizing words made the Titanic stop. There was a distance between Sherman and the Titanic. The large man saw his opportunity.

"This is going to be *fun*!" he screamed sarcastically.

"I bet it is," replied Sherman. With the Pixaliemain in his hand, the Titanic sprinted to build enough speed. His wild footsteps were repetitive, sounding like an aggressive heart beat. Sherman stood firm. He was partially scared yet confident at the same time.

Wind moved around the Titanic as he charged for Sherman. When he finally came close, he prepared himself for a brutal smash. The clever Sherman Bawnder ducked down and snatched the rock from the man's hand without him even realizing it. He curled his eyebrows when seeing the Titanic continue to run. Then the criminal noticed the missing stone and Sherman Bawnder being free of pain.

"You think that's funny!" he shouted ready to travel the other direction. Ignoring the threatening words, Bawnder figured that commandeering a vehicle would be in his best intention.

He simply grabbed the car keys from a random civilian and then hopped into his red Lamborghini. He started up the engine and then drove to lose the incensed maniac.

The day was full of surprises. Sherman leered back to see the determined Titanic gaining up on him. The scoundrel stayed on Sherman's tail. He jumped. The sound of blustering steps on the concrete ended. Sherman glanced back. No one was there. He accepted that it was a close call; he was victorious in his effort.

Then the Titanic landed on top of the speeding car. The dent sank from the tremendous weight. Being as strong as he was, he punched the top. Then several more hits. His hand penetrated through the car roof and squirmed around to find Sherman's head.

Sherman sweated when seeing the hand come to grab him. He turned the steering wheel left and right to try and shake the Titanic off.

The agent called Tina who was still inside the museum and shrieked, "I need your help! Bring the jet and look for a speeding red Lamborghini!"

"Give me another description."

"For God's sake, I'm in the car and the Titanic himself is on top!"

"What street are you on?" Bawnder looked and said, "I'm on 34th street!"

"Okay, I'm on my way." Captain Tina hung up as Canavin asked, "Who was that?"

"It was Sherman. He needs our help." Canavin readied himself. He was about to leave the floor until he noticed Frankie and Vanessa still tased. When the effects ended, the two rose up.

"Where'd Zan go?" asked Canavin.

Frankie mumbled as if he was speaking an informal language. Celestica's words were clearer.

"He went after 'Optimistic'."

"You mean Derwin Grant? It's easier if you say that."

"Whatever. We need to help Zan."

"Zan's able to handle himself. It's the two of you that need help."

Celestica went to the exits and walked up the stairs to the roof where the ships were parked. Frankie followed and as for Canavin, he proceeded out the window and flew the remaining levels onto the roof.

As soon as he reached the top, he saw a new problem. The entire *Ark Eagle* jet was gone. All that was left were two working cruisers and one that was relatively destroyed. He remained speechless. When Tina made it, she experienced the same type of awe.

"Derwin!" the Captain screamed. Her echo continued six times.

"He stole the jet. The good news is that Zan's on his tail."

"I hope you're right! Otherwise Cyfreid's going to kill me." Canavin got inside his ship and ascended into the air.

"Where's he going?!" Celestica shouted, demanding an instant response.

"He's going to help Sherman shake off the Titanic."

"What on Earth are you talking about?" The Captain refrained from answering. The constant drama stirred enough thoughts within her to unfold surprises, ones to avoid writing in her AIA reports. Since there was one cruiser left that was in good condition, Frankie jumped inside, started it up, and flew off to assist the alien.

"So what are we going to do?" asked Celestica.

"What are we doing right now?"

"We're not doing anything."

"Well then…keep doing that."

Two cruisers soared in the afternoon sky and moved downwards to be above 34th street. When only seeing masses of people on each side of the road, their eyes found their speeding target.

"There!" shouted Frankie who got his voice back.

"Alright, let's descend more!" yelled Canavin. They lowered their ships and had a clear shot at the Titanic.

Many citizens witnessed the amazement and applauded. Some were photographers and journalists who agreed that this would be a great story to counter the success from Sherman weeks ago.

The Titanic punched another hole through the car roof and finally grabbed Sherman's head. Sherman bawled at the top of his lungs while he drove at a daring speed. He contacted Canavin.

"Shoot! Do it now!" He could feel his skull crush a bit. Sherman needed time to heal from the Titanic's thick fingers. The maniac brought them closer for a tighter hold.

"Now!" yelled Canavin to Frankie. The ships began to fire right at the Titanic's back. The blasts were broadened lasers.

The pain caused the Titanic to take his hand off of Sherman's skull and out of the car. He turned his attention to the two miniature cruisers.

Canavin and Frankie shot once again and with the villain turned to them, he was struck in the ribcage numerous times. The street was near its end; there was nothing more but an upcoming body of water. The flashes felt incessant, as if there was no end to the caustic firepower. They were at last enough to knock the Titanic off the speedy vehicle and onto the edge of the land.

"Now that's what I'm talking about!" Frankie enthusiastically hollered. With the trauma over, Sherman slowed down and parked the car. He looked at the Pixaliemain and breathed. His hand gently touched the top of his head and healed the damaged skull. Then he rubbed his forehead, just knowing that he was experiencing the worst headache ever.

The Titanic remained on the concrete floor with his eyes frantically wanting to close. When Canavin and Frankie got out of the cruisers, they proceeded towards him. Several journalists clustered around them and battled to ask questions.

Not being in the mood, Frankie and Canavin moved out of the annoying crowd. They came to his presence.

"Tell me the locations of the other 'Viles' as they are called," said Canavin.

The Titanic's eyes opened wide, inflamed with fright. He told the heroes, "He said he was going to kill me."

"What?" asked Frankie.

"He said he was going to kill me!" repeated the large man as he expressed more anxiety.

"Who?" asked Canavin.

"The Governor! He doesn't know where the other rocks are! He specifically said that if I didn't get this one, he would kill me!"

"Look, calm down. Cain isn't here at the moment."

"No! I won't die!"

The Titanic got up to his legs, jogged away from the heroes, and dove to splash into the prismatic ocean. Frankie and Canavin raced to the edge and witnessed the man's sinking hand.

Sherman Bawnder came out of the red Lamborghini and walked to the edge where Canavin and Frankie fixated their eyes on the sudden suicidal moment. He asked them, "So what did I miss?"

When the speechless Frankie pointed down to the ocean, Sherman realized the situation and said, "Oh…so that's how the Titanic sank."

Their attentions turned to Sherman as they shook their heads.

"You have the Pixaliemain?" asked Canavin. Sherman held the rock in front of him and noticed journalists coming close. He handed the substance over and watched them hop into their ships and ascend.

The reporters packed around him with camera flashes. They asked him questions about his sudden partnership with the Canavin Clan and their future plans.

"Listen, I'm not a part of the Canavin Clan," he explained.

"Then where did they come from?" asked one of the reporters. "What's this all about?" Some of the other questions were, "What was the Titanic planning all this time and does he have helpers?" "Does this have any relation to the crisis that occurred in Cleveland?" "Are you dating anyone?" The last question was asked by a wild woman.

Canavin and Frankie reached the top of the museum where Tina and Celestica sat down hopeless. He came out with the Pixaliemain. Upon seeing the azure gleam, the Captain clarified, "So you *are* immune to it."

"I wouldn't lie to you," Canavin responded. She held out her hand and expected the alien to give her the substance.

"I'm going to give this one to Cyfreid, if that's okay?"

Tina snapped. *"Absolutely not,"* her mind spoke with a cagey tone. The heart wished the opposite, her arm dropping down with true acceptance. She remembered the hero and what he taught her about Pixalian culture. Her loyalty lied between Canavin and the Commander, mostly towards Cyfreid and his hostile demeanor. Overall, Canavin had a good heart from the day she met him.

Trusting his words, she said, "Yes, that's okay." He got back into his cruiser and sat down to wait for Sherman to return from the press. Zan still had to stop Derwin Grant's voyage. Both would take too long. He called for the Captain saying, "Hey, I'm going to head back to AIA East."

"Are you sure?"

"Yes, I'm sure. To tell you the truth, I think we won!"

"What are you talking about?"

"Before the Titanic…well, the Titanic killed himself. But before that, he revealed to us that Governor X doesn't know the locations of the other pieces. As long as Valor and the others are successful, and Cyfreid figures out where the final rock is, we can pretty much call it a day."

"The Titanic was lying to you Canavin."

"I don't think so. You should've seen his face. I honestly think he was telling the truth."

The alien started the turbines. Frankie was about to start his engine until Canavin gave him a gesture that meant to stay put. Before the cruiser was able to levitate, Celestica ran to the ship. The glass seal opened.

"Vanessa, what is it?" he asked.

"Please be safe," she softly said. She held his hand with plenty of care and the Pixalian replied, "I will."

She took steps back. They witnessed the ship rise and fly away. The team now had three pieces, which gave them a notable advantage.

XIII

VERSION X

THE WORDS FROM THE TITANIC WERE apparently true. Governor Cain X was oblivious of the final two substances, which ultimately put the heroes in a favorable position. Tina thought about it and asked, "If Version X is out in Toronto searching for a sample, wouldn't it mean that Cain knows its location?" Frankie and Celestica pondered the idea. She had a point.

"Wait," said Frankie. "Canavin and I watched the Titanic drown. Why would he kill himself like that if it wasn't a vital mission? He clearly said that Cain would execute him. The Titanic desperately needed that piece."

"Unless," Celestica began. They awaited her response. "Unless Version X isn't working with the man we think."

Canavin was on his way back to AIA East. Alone at last, he thought about his old life being solo. Before the Canavin Clan, before Tina and Cyfreid, he had his unexpected spot on Shaw's most wanted list.

Canavin used to be a name of lobbing dread in the human population, even after saving a collection of lives. The warrior remembered the West Sector. Cyclohoma City, his precious home on earthly grounds, seemed to carry the memories of him and Identymous. The creature had to be stopped, no matter what. It wasn't about the Pixaliemain. It was personal. The sector was located near Los Angeles.

He desired to change his course. He glowered when being hungry for another shot at the despicable Pixalian.

Darkness filled the hero's soul like a raging torrent, for a good cause he believed.

No. Not now, not during the Pixaliemain circumstance. Perhaps another day, another time when things wouldn't be too risky. Canavin considered bringing the rock back to the base. He remembered that Captain Tina trusted his judgment. He also recalled Zan, who at the moment was still on a pursuit for Derwin Grant in *The Ark Eagle*. A transmission was sent.

"Zan, what's the status?" Within the cruiser that was still very much above New York, Zan answered, "Canavin? Optimistic is still flying in the jet. As for the pilot, I'm not sure what the insane man did to him."

"Just understand that Tina trusts that you have it covered."

"Why does she suddenly trust me?"

"Because I told her to have faith in you. Judging by her impatience, I'll say that she has already contacted Cyfreid for help."

"Tell her that there's no need."

"Actually, I'm not with her or Frankie and Celestica at the moment."

"Is the Pixaliemain secure?"

"I have it with me right now."

"Excellent. If I was you, I would bring that back to the Canavin Station where it will be safe." From those words, Canavin understood that it was a brilliant idea.

In Toronto, Team Valor, Silvert, and Titanium Titan walked out of the *Regime 5*. The seven of them witnessed the afternoon slowly shift to evening. The task was one that would take a while. Wherever the suspicious Version X was, Cyfreid's predictions were believed to be accurate.

Valor looked at the Torontonians and then back at his squad. "Something isn't right," he quietly said.

"This is craziness!" Titanium Titan shouted. "Cyfreid's out of his mind! What if this 'Version X' loon isn't here?"

Silvert clarified saying, "Well, the tracker was locked on to his position. He's around here somewhere, I know it."

If anyone knew Version X, it was Silvert, especially since Cain built the android counterpart. The silver man departed back inside the jet and looked on the tracking monitor. There was a red dot that resembled Version X and a green dot that resembled the exact spot of the *Regime 5*. Running out, he called the others.

"Version X is about a mile away from us," he said.

"Thank God for accurate tech," Breath-Stealer commented. The heroes envisioned their victory over the cyborg.

Their initial focus had to wait. Valor knew something wasn't right about the Toronto citizens that were around them. He gave a halting gesture, a signal to hush immediately.

"Wait." Their abnormal stance and their jerking limbs portrayed the absence of human character. Their clouded sight, the crass movements in their body that felt alive as if there were internal mammals digging for freedom. Each of them had a lazy eye along with hoary hair that fell when leisurely limping towards the heroes. They uttered many groans when their skin morphed to be murky grey.

Just by analyzing their odd actions, Silvert and the team inferred the obvious and annoying reality. Aliens were everywhere in sight. *Zombies.*

The sly soldier prepared his Valoric weapons to demolish the creatures. With her advanced vision, Evesdrop cautiously shouted, "Valor, look out!"

He twisted to witness more slow-moving aliens. The team came together to form a circle that was beneficial to their awareness of the incoming zombies. While they were anxious to defend themselves, Silvert cruised off in the distance. Titanium Titan asked, "Where does *he* think he's going?"

"For Version X you fool!" shouted Valor firing the static blasts from within him. As for Breath-Stealer, he did what his name was suited for. The spirit slithered into one of the aliens and then hastily escaped out of the body to cause it to drop down. He did this to as many creatures as possible, yet there were a lot to handle.

As he ejected too many flares at once, Valor waited until his firearms reloaded with the electrical fluid. He only took one deep breath for it to happen. After that, he was ready to continue shooting.

Fusion Fighter and Meditation used their abilities to a great extent. The spells from Meditation differentiated from one another, but still had the similar result of developing a great amount of mutilation towards the zombified citizens.

Evesdrop's strikes were quick and dramatic to make some aliens retreat. Her ability to avoid the creatures was exceptional enough for Valor to say, "Good job, Alicia!"

The bulbous eyes on her forehead blinked at the same time to thank the soldier. Valor rarely gave compliments, even to his teammates.

Titanium Titan attacked a band of zombies to aid Team Valor. His nunchucks helped the most as the spiraling metal caused intense squeals. As some tried to bite him, he clanked the metal at their fragile jaws. Hiro considered the task to be rather easy. He was too focused on Silvert and his awaited success of retrieving a Pixaliemain rock yet again. He yearned for his very own chance to succeed and receive a sufficient amount of admiration.

Seeing that Team Valor was too occupied with piles of the undead, the kung-fu specialist hurried himself into the jet and ordered the pilot, Draymond, to fly to the locked on Version X.

"Sure thing," said Draymond. He surprised Titanium Titan by opening the back hatch. Hiro spotted a scrambler bike made to travel at tremendous speeds.

"You got to be kidding me."

"Not a chance," Draymond replied. "It's also voice activated. I think you'll love it."

Titanium Titan leapt for the motorized beauty, but he forgot about Valor. The soldier ceased his fire. He ran to beat Hiro upon seeing the bike from behind. He hopped on and remembered that his pistols had connecting cords to his wrists.

After looking around for options, Valor screamed, "How the hell am I going to reach Version X?!"

He heard a voice from the motorcycle that said, *"Lock on: Version X."*

The bike raced out of the *Regime 5*, passed the alien raiders, and sped down the road. Valor had a difficult time staying on it. After a while, he got used to the speed and held his weapons up.

Titanium Titan couldn't believe it. He felt that nobody on the team gave him respect. Draymond also saw the situation and asked, "Do you still want me to lead you to Version X?"

Titanium Titan took a seat in the aircraft. He watched Fusion Fighter, Breath-Stealer, Evesdrop, and Meditation handle the heap of zombified citizens. He ordered Draymond to close the hatch. The way how they fought *together* was aggravating. His jealousy and selfishness boosted his negativity, making him feel even more insecure. The combatant sat down in misery and wished to be as talented as the others. The doubt he experienced soon ended as his anger rose. He shouted, "Bring this hunk of metal to Version X this instant!"

Draymond started up the *Regime 5* and soared away from the clashing monsters. The airstream flew back at the four heroes and their opponents.

They had to continue the fight; Valor would recommend it. With the jet now gone, they realized that there was no form of safety from the relentless zombies. Fusion Fighter took command over the other three fighters after he believed that it was Valor's consideration.

The dauntless Silvert continued his flight in the search for his immoral counterpart. After roaming over many streets, he found nothing. He began to lose confidence in the tracking system. Time passed and the shining hero thought about quitting the task.

Then Silvert slanted his head. A man running down the street in an auburn hood caught his attention. He descended to get a closer look. From afar, he recognized him; it was a silver mechanical face under the hood. The individual stopped and scrutinized the silver hero. He ran from his presence. Silvert followed him when knowing that it was the cyborg. The chase became more satisfying when he was able to notice a vivid light from Version X's hand. Silvert ascended for a bird's eye view of the escaping android. The *Regime 5* made its way behind him.

On the same street, Valor rode the speeding AIA scrambler. He knew that he desperately had to be careful of the other cars. He accelerated passed each and every vehicle and pulled the triggers. Each static flare missed; riding and shooting wasn't his forte.

Valor fired an abundant amount of times and received the same result. He couldn't believe his failure. He held up one pistol with the best look at ending the chase. He instantaneously shot the running machine.

The blasts struck Version X to send sparks flying. It was as if the hooded android was about to experience a malfunction. The effects were only temporary with the hated cyborg.

Valor's accurate shot was one to remember. He rode around the fiend. Silvert reached ground level and was ready to take the substance from his rival's machinelike hand. He did it fast to avoid the electric bolts.

"I'll take that," he said calmly to Version X being consumed by sparks.

Titanium Titan became more riled than he was in the past. Everyone had a provoking repercussion on his mood.

Silvert felt the opposite. The eminent hero saved the day again, with the help of Valor's perfect aim.

The static turned to swaying vapour. Version X looked at them and quickly departed without fighting.

"Where is he going?!" shouted Valor.

"I'm not entirely sure, but I'm willing to follow. How about you?"

"That droid is going to get crushed!" Silvert took the response as a "yes". The thought of bringing Version X to justice was completely irresistible. Within a short time period, they caught up with the menace and knocked him down once more.

His face was spine-chilling. It had a silver complexion with claret coloured eyes that resembled Cain X. The mechanical facial structures were added to cause discomfort. Silvert thought about telekinetically crumbling the face. *Would it really do me any good? What about the honourable way?* He chose to refuse using the ability.

"Who are you working for, Version X?" he asked although he felt that it was extremely redundant. The android spoke with a voice that was similar to his heroic counterpart. This was a part of Cain's original design.

Valor couldn't wait any longer. They figured that there was no point of waiting for a response since it was predicted that the contemptible drone worked for Cain X.

"Where is Cain?! What is his next move?!" The despicable Version X at last was ready to convey his message.

"I don't work for Cain anymore," the android said.

"Wait…what?" asked Silvert.

In a perceptive move, Version X threw down a gas pellet. When the vagueness withered away, the machine was gone.

Silvert was lost. Six years was the time frame that he knew Version X and understood his loyalty to the Governor. Never once did he think that Version X would've quit working for Cain.

"If Version X isn't working for the Governor, then who?"

After several minutes, the rock was brought back to Team Valor who successfully won against the zombies. This made Valor proud to call himself the leader of the four fighters.

All that was left was the *Regime 5* to arrive. Very soon, the massive aircraft landed in front of Team Valor and Silvert. The door opened and out came a ramp for the heroes to proceed. Valor and his group walked inside. Silvert began to do the same until he spotted Titanium Titan who wished to have words with him.

"Where are you guys going?" wondered Fusion Fighter.

"Silvert and I are going to have a walk," said Titanium Titan.

"Alright, come inside in five minutes."

"Did I mention that this was going to be a very *long* chat?"

Silvert was unaware of what was happening. Nevertheless, spending time with Hiro was in his best intention in order to end the ongoing *"hero contest"*. The others agreed to Titanium Titan's proposal under conditions that the two of them return as soon as possible.

The recently formed team of elite heroes now had the possession of four radiant Pixaliemain rocks. Zan Genrax was attentive to the sky-high voyage for Derwin Grant. As he was gaining on the drug lord's trail, the Pixalian had the perfect lockon position. He had to be careful not to cause too much damage. Derwin flew the aircraft directly up.

"You have to be joking," said Zan. He looked and saw nothing. He contacted the jet and said the words, "You *do* know that I will find you. And when I do, things aren't going to be pretty."

Derwin's face appeared on the screen.

"My 'precious' alien," he began. "You're correct about one little thing in your statement."

"And what's that," said Zan speaking back at the screen.

"You *are* going to find me. All you have to do is look back." Optimistic's revealing and fairly shocking words tormented Zan as he realized that he was being followed. Being the bait wasn't his way of saying that everything was under control.

Derwin frequently fired at Zan's cruiser. From within the miniature ship, the alien was able to feel the damages.

Zan began to improvise. He turned his cruiser around to be in attack position. Upon seeing this, Derwin laughed and degraded his logic.

"Are you really going to try that?!"

"Give me your best shot."

"Worth pleasure."

Derwin and Zan had each other as opposing targets. The nimble blazes collided, generating an amalgamated surge that expanded in the sky. The compelling outburst blinded Optimistic. When the smoke cleared, the man shouted, "Where did you go?!"

Zan crashed through a jet glass and picked Derwin up by the neck.

He dramatically flapped his arms up and down while being choked. At last, Zan allowed Derwin to catch his breath. He prepared his Pixalian rays just in case.

"I told you, things aren't going to be pretty."

Derwin held his hands high in the air and realized his probable defeat. Zan noticed the pilot in the corner who was tied up with his mouth duck taped. After Zan freed him, the pilot took out his handcuffs and arrested the drug lord.

"This isn't fair!" yelled Derwin. To get his own form of revenge, the pilot duck taped his mouth, only to hear persistent whining.

"Where's your cruiser?" asked the pilot.

"It's parked on the jet," said Zan very fond of his adlibbing skills.

"Very nice…I mean, for an alien."

"None taken."

"So where are we heading now?"

"Take us back to the museum. Tina and the others are waiting."

The jet was turned around. Zan and the pilot still heard the irritating sounds from Derwin Grant. The quicker they were to return, the quicker he would be behind bars.

Many minutes passed and the jet descended in front of Tina, Frankie, Celestica, and Sherman Bawnder who finished his moment of fame with the press. The presence of *The Ark Eagle* made Tina remember how even aliens were able to be trusted. She even disregarded the idea of contacting the Commander upon seeing that believing the team was the first step in a successful organization.

Since Celestica's ship was demolished, she entered *The Ark Eagle* with Captain Tina and Sherman. Frankie went into his ship while Zan detached his cruiser from the jet. The aircrafts soared with their amusing view melting in the apricot evening sky. Tina looked at her badge as it glowed bright from the lively warmth. She and the others agreed that their mission was now complete.

XIV

PLAGUES OF HATRED

WITH JUST ONE MORE PIXALIEMAIN TO recover, Commander Cyfreid understood that he had to act fast in order to finally secure the safety of the planet. The failure of his detecting system continued, which meant that soon he would have to rely on luck.

"Maybe I'm trying too hard. It's time I rest."

He refused to listen to the notion as it was too similar to the way Lynx would handle a situation.

Lynx had his navy blue helmet off and comfortably rested on the couch, stress-free and absent-minded. Shade-Master sat with him and added to making the Collaboration Hall very tranquil. The moment the other heroes reported their success, all the Commander could do was observe the cheery attitudes of the two gifted humans.

"I cannot believe the two of you! The last piece of a paranormal solid capable of destruction unlike any other is out there *somewhere* and you both have the nerve to—"

"Shush!" Lynx hissed. They continued to watch with their sight pasted to the news.

Lasher Labs, the primary facility where the first primordial stone was tested, was the key topic on television. The location of Lasher Labs was Los Angeles. There was an assembly of sightseers who examined Pixalian culture, or what humans believed to be accurate information.

Cyfreid remembered the Lashers. He missed them greatly, almost as if he wished to scuttle back in time and alter reality, just to see their faces once more. He loved them like his own family. The woeful Commander always used the famous researchers of the agency as a reminder that the danger of Pixaliemain had to expire. With Cain out of the way, Cyfreid desired the expected answer.

"Explain more about the Lashers," said Shade-Master. Cyfreid refused. He pointed at them both when his frustration began to grow. Then he waved his finger twice and glumly replied, "They're dead, just like I said in the meeting."

Shade-Master and Lynx took their eyes away from Cyfreid. His look suggested he was hiding something else— something beyond the Lasher story.

They observed the people on television that appreciated every artifact. None of them was the final piece to the puzzle. The Los Angeles citizens were grateful of the operators at Lasher Labs for allowing them to come to the event.

Lynx said, "Alright, I thought for sure that some stupidity would occur at Lasher Labs, but I guess I was wrong. Axel, change the channel. This one is dull."

"Are you considering that the Pixaliemain mission is stupid?" asked the Commander.

"Well actually Cyfreid, I think it is. How did the others do on their trips?"

"Team Valor successfully acquired the piece from Version X in Toronto. The Canavin Clan has the other one from New York. So that's four in total when counting the two that we already have. Soon, both squads will make it back here at base."

"You see! There is absolutely nothing to worry about. We got this man. Axel, please change the channel."

Shade-Master couldn't stop inspecting the area.

"Cyfreid," the realm-bender started. "Did the agency ever speak about knights?"

"Knights? I don't think so. What kind of question is that?" At last, he saw what Axel was referring to. Two pothelm knights with polished edged swords stood at the sides of the room, haughty and stable as if they were waiting for stringent orders. The sightseers believed that they were expensive mannequins. Cyfreid, Axel, and even Lynx after seeing their presence on TV, believed the opposite.

Some females moved their fingers to feel the armour. The crusty texture proposed the idea that the suits of the troopers were indeed, affected in war.

The heads of both knights lowered to the crowd. Both warriors directed their blades and rumbled with subsequent voices, "Halt, where is the Pixaliemain?!"

From viewing the knights on the screen, Cyfreid, Lynx, and Shade-Master shared the same reaction of everyone at Lasher Labs.

"Identymous *will* have his revenge!" the loutish voices claimed.

Astonishingly, appearing from a pallid blaze, three extraterrestrials arrived in the vast room. They wore cloaks of moroseness, very close to a cold midnight hue. Under their hoods were their scabby indigo faces. The cavaliers bowed down to the extraterrestrials. Some of the Los Angeles sightseers attempted to escape. One of the hooded Pixalians closed his claret eyes and recited a simple Pixalian scripture. Those that tried to leave were disintegrated into a sufficient amount of scattered fragments.

"Nobody leaves!" commanded one of them as glutinous ooze ran down his welts from battle. "You are all among us! We are the directors of the universal plagues."

"Universal plagues?" Cyfreid muttered when he watched.

The directors of the universal plagues looked at each other with hopes of confronting the humans. One of them held up an item with smoldering cobalt radiance. He stated, "We are in search for the other Pixaliemain stones! Where are the relics of the great rock of Xaliemer?"

None of them knew what the aliens were talking about. "I'm going to repeat myself one more time! Where is the Pixaliemain?!" His voice was more wrathful than before.

Cyfreid turned to his fellow heroes with his eyes unable to blink. He silently said the words, "I think we found what we've been looking for."

After he rose from sitting, Shade-Master and Lynx realized that 'relaxation time' was over.

"We're going to pay Los Angeles a visit," said Cyfreid.

"What do you mean *we*?" asked Shade-Master. Commander Cyfreid was close to leaving the room when he answered, "I'm coming with you."

He walked out and noticed Curtis Kareem pretending to wander. He denied the option of leaving him alone at the agency when knowing that there was a possibility of never seeing the hunter again.

"Curtis," he called, understanding that the codename wasn't necessary. Though, he always did prefer the acronym. "Are you coming?"

The depressed man was troubled by Cyfreid's presence. It took him a while to balance out the options again.

Stay here or leave for the mansion in DC.

Curtis remembered Tina and what she told him. And so, he nodded his head, indicating that he was ready for a trip with Cyfreid. The Commander smiled at Curtis. He was relieved that he was still able to choose *him* after revealing such heartbreaking secrets. Curtis always tended to find himself in frequent verbal fights with the Commander, but none of them had the subject of a long lost friend.

"Glad to have you stay with us, Sharp."

"It's Curtis!" he snapped.

"Okay there…" He chuckled, thinking Curtis fully forgave him. Then Curtis thought about the codename. Maybe it *was* perfect. After all, he was an alien assassin.

Lynx, Shade-Master, and Curtis followed the Commander down a hallway. He led them to a stupendous landing bay packed with jets, helicopters, and warships. They saw Stan speaking with various agents.

"Stan! You want to come with us to Lasher Labs?"

"Um, okay Cyfreid. Is it just to study more objects?"

"No fool. The last Pixaliemain rock is in Los Angeles within the gallery. It's with a bunch of ludicrous misfits who call themselves the directors of the universal plagues. Now prepare the jet!"

"Yes sir! Right away sir!" He ran to fulfill his responsibility.

"Crazy man thought he was actually going to get a freebie," said Cyfreid. Shade-Master and Lynx were very amused by Cyfreid's tone. Agent Stan came back and said, "The jet is now ready!"

"Good, now get inside!"

The heroes rushed inside and secured themselves with their seatbelts. When he noticed that there was nobody at the controls, Stan asked, "Who's going to fly this thing?"

"You of course. Why do you think you're with us?"

"Sometimes, I hate you."

"I'm sorry, what was that you said?"

"Nothing, sir!"

"That's what I thought." Even though Cyfreid purposely treated Stan with almost no respect, he was proud of the young man and his commitment to the sector. The agent sat down with Cyfreid at his side.

"Are you all ready?" he asked.

"Hurry up, would you." Within the bay, the back doors opened wide. The jet sped down the runway and flew away. The agents in the bay saluted the Commander's departure.

While inside, Cyfreid asked, "Is there any way this thing can go faster? Those directors could easily summon—"

"You've said it many times," explained Stan. "Don't worry, I got this one covered. For a while now, I've been having some meetings with galactic engineers. They've provided this very jet with a 'light speed generator'. Just pull that lever to your side since the system is pinpointed to the west coast. Hang on to something if you must." Cyfreid looked to his side and noticed a red lever.

They lived in the age where technology was at its finest. Aircraft were able to travel at the speed of light only within particular ranges. Before he pulled it, he told the heroes to strap on their seatbelts. After he noticed that everyone had already done that, he swallowed a huge gulp and then pulled the lever. The ship shot like a missile that was invisible to the naked eye.

The city was just like any other metropolis and Lasher Labs was only minutes away. They reached and they each ran out of the plane and through the entrance.

Commander Cyfreid, Agent Stan, and the three heroes marched into the auditorium that was filled with the petrified spectators. The directors were protected by the cavaliers.

"Now, who knows where I can find a sample?"

"I do," said Cyfreid as he approached the unnatural beings. "And how's about we make a deal. You let these innocent people go, and I'll tell you the locations of the remaining pieces." The dark shrouded creature that held the final Pixaliemain turned sharply to face Cyfreid.

"What is your name?" he asked.

"My name is Commander Cyfreid."

"Alright, Cyfreid of Earth. Reveal the other locations and I'll spare your people."

"Let them leave first. They have no power over you. They are weak and need time to calm their minds." Cyfreid exaggerated in order to change the directors' motives about the issue. After thinking about it, the creature called for the audience and said, "Humans, you are free to leave. Depart from us." Many of them obeyed, but some remained still. Cyfreid didn't understand. He asked, "Why do you want the rocks?"

"That is not for you to know," said another one.

"From what I can see, it seems like you don't want to free Xaliemer. You seem to be immune."

"We are indeed."

"What do you want with Identymous?"

"Identymous is one of us. And Xaliemer will be unleashed when the high power accepts."

"The high power?"

"We worship the leader of the universal plagues. There are ten in total. Xaliemer is one of them. We must build our kingdom on this planet. We will come another day when we receive the word to free the beast."

"Very well...Sharp, help these misfits out."

"Sure thing," said Curtis. He advanced to the third Pixalian and prodded his claws through the body. Upon removing them, the alien dropped down dead, saturated in his own plasma.

There was an abrupt shift of fear as Cyfreid calmly said, "You see, we humans can also be cruel. So let's do things my way. You give me the rock to keep and I'll make sure the two of you won't end up like your friend."

"I curse you Cyfreid of Earth! You will perish very soon!"

Sharp seized the last Pixaliemain from the confident creature and gave it to Cyfreid.

The directors of the universal plagues, each with their mangy chiseled faces that looked moth-eaten, faded with the mysterious knights in another startling flash.

"Wow, that was easy," Lynx said.

"Yea, too easy," said Shade-Master. The Commander and Agent Stan agreed. The animal that symbolically lurked inside of Sharp spoke to him, mouthing its urge for an exhilarating hunt. He snuffled in the aroma of eccentric creatures. The whiff was new to him. *Why?*

Cyfreid eyed the remaining crowd. They weren't too stunned from the beginning.

He was sure that the conflict of the possible release of Xaliemer was over. The team of heroes was a true achievement. All of them began to leave until one of the sightseers screamed, "What you have there belongs to me!"

Cyfreid and the others heard the voice. It was actually quite faint. The Commander's eyes squinted in order to get a good view of the person. He was within the strange clutter and looked very average.

"What did you say?" asked Cyfreid raising his tone.

"I *said* that what you have there belongs to me!"

"This rock?"

"Yes," said the man. His outer flesh died to resemble a crinkled raisin. Each section flaked off as easy as a banana peel. The grease of his dead skin surrounded the man. Its ghastly nature made them uneasy.

He was a vile Pixalian unlike anything Cyfreid had ever encountered. The Commander couldn't figure out why the beast would want the rock. Xaliemer was believed to be so powerful that Cyfreid met aliens who never wanted to see the monster again.

The predator possessed teeth of a shark and a scruffy exoskeleton close to the directors of the universal plagues. The difference was that it appeared to look more like a hefty bug parasite. Surprisingly, it wasn't alone. Many more creatures were tired of their uncomfortable looks. They ripped through the human shells and showed their horrendous form.

Agent Stan, Cyfreid, Sharp, Lynx, and Shade-Master remained steadfast, but not for long. A battle to prevent the parasites from coming in contact with the last piece was essential.

"Defend the rock...whatever it takes," said Cyfreid the moment he pulled out an AIA projectile blaster. The others were prepared for the worst, yet knew the importance of making sure none of the aliens came close to the Pixaliemain.

In Toronto, Silvert talked to Titanium Titan in a calm man-to-man chat. While they sat where there were barely any residents, the main subject of their conversation was none other than the dishonesty they showed to one another. It took time for Silvert to finally believe that Hiro Matsuo was trying to make things right again. This way, they wouldn't have a grudge that would continue to *tear* them apart.

Hiro asked, "Do you remember the time when you and I stopped those crooks from invading that family's home back in Washington?"

"Oh yea, I remember. It was our first achievement as a duo."

"Those were good times, Jamal. I can call you Jamal right?"

"You always used to. I guess it's fine."

"Ah…Jamal Vertison, otherwise known as Silvert. The greatest hero the world has ever seen." Silvert didn't want to take his sentence literally. He presented a puzzled look and said, "Okay, maybe I'm not the *greatest* hero…"

"You're not? I thought nobody could match up to the *glory* of Silvert. Maybe I was wrong."

Silvert became slightly angered by Hiro's words. He thought the talk was supposed to be a rebirth of a brotherhood. He asked, "What are you trying to imply, Hiro?"

"All I'm saying is that if you want to be the greatest, you have to make sure nobody stands in your way, including me. Well I'm guessing I was already in your way of true glory."

"Everyday I'm just doing what is right," said Silvert trying his best to recite Canavin's words given to him earlier.

"Of course, the *right* thing. Suppose you had to do the wrong thing to fulfill your success? Then what?"

"I will always do what I feel is right."

"Your heart can deceive you."

"And your mind can deceive *you*," said Silvert quickly as possible. He noticed something strange about Hiro, like he was very close to initiating something. Silvert said to him, "Hiro, where are you going with this?" The kung fu specialist laughed; it was a fake laugh but nevertheless, it had similarities to a real laugh. The titan looked at the necklace that was locked on Silvert's neck.

"I wonder where you would be without that chain necklace. Don't you wonder the same thing, Jamal?"

"Not a day goes by when I don't. It's an alien amulet…sort of like a medal."

"So you're a woman?"

"What the hell? No, it's just a medal."

"Only girls wear necklaces, Jamal."

"You clearly don't know anything about the 21st century, so just shut up."

"Fine. All I'm saying is that you wouldn't be successful without it. The necklace gave you these extraordinary powers."

"Yes you're right and I thank God for it!"

"How would things be if I had the amazing silver necklace? Then I'll be the hero of the ages."

"I am not the hero of the ages!"

"Of course not," said Hiro mocking him some more. "That's because you're not me."

"Shut up right now!"

"No!" His emotions switched. "I'm not going to shut up! You don't deserve the necklace, I do!"

"I got this chain on a private mission years before I met you! What makes you think that you deserve it?"

"Because I'm the better hero!" Those were the vital words signifying that the nonsense between them wasn't over.

"Really?! You think that you're the better hero?! Well guess what, titan! You were never a recruit for this team of *real* heroes!"

"What are you talking about?!"

"I'm saying that the Captain herself chose you because she felt sorry for you. The *great* Titanium Titan was never good enough to qualify for Cyfreid's alliance! You're a failure and always have been!"

"Take that back, Jamal!" Titanium Titan threw a punch at Silvert, who gripped the fist, twisted it, and hit him in the eye. It left an ugly shiner on his face; the blood flowed down from under his mask and onto his lip.

"Titanium Titan…can't even dodge a simple hit," teased Silvert. Hiro took a taste of his blood and then spat it directly in Silvert's face. Sickened by the nastiness, Silvert wiped it off, only to be kicked in the metallic mouth. It split to produce an open wound. His blood was dappled grey while in his silver form.

"Karma," said Hiro Matsuo. "It's a 'kick to the mouth' isn't it?" Silvert allowed for the grey liquid to drip down as he said, "Is that the best you got?"

"Actually I'm full of surprises." Titanium Titan took out the nun chucks and began to swirl them faster than ever before. He went at Silvert and clacked him with the nun chucks. A silver shard chipped off of Jamal's face. He became enraged when he saw the glossy piece.

"You're going to pay for that!"

"What's the matter 'tin man'?"

"It's silver you idiot!" The silver man shot his blasts right at Titanium Titan's chest to send him back and lose the nun chucks. Silvert approached and picked him up. He clouted his face to send him back down and he repeated with an ongoing pattern. The lifts and hits continued until Hiro stretched to vehemently clench the sparkly neck. It was hard to do it, but he managed. Very soon, Jamal broke away.

"Face it, Jamal! That necklace is the only thing that's keeping you from failing! But it won't matter."

"What are you going to do…take it from me?"

"You know, that's not a bad idea!"

"Good luck with that." Titanium Titan and Silvert walked in a circle and waited to see who was going to strike first. Silvert couldn't wait any longer. He ran for Hiro and was whacked again by one of the nun chucks. Another piece of his body flaked off.

"Remember Silvert, they're called *Titanium* nun chucks."

"Who gives a damn?!"

"Maybe you need to go back to school. The world doesn't need senseless heroes like you."

"That does it!" Silvert shaped his blasts into a sallow amalgamation. He ejected the beam and the energy rallied out like dominant wades to tear Hiro's suit to shreds. Seeing this, the small groups of people who were watching the grudge match ran in fear.

All that was left of Titanium Titan's red suit was the bottom half; the upper body was just bare skin. His mask still remained, as well as his fury. He took time to recover from the blast, but Silvert didn't stop there. He shot the beam once more. Hiro successfully dodged it and came up with an idea of succeeding. Desperately trying to breathe, he dropped his nun chucks.

"What's this? You finally give up?"

"Where I come from, a virile fight is done hand to hand." Titanium Titan held up his fists ready for combat. Having complete confidence in himself, Silvert smiled and said, "Man, I'm going to enjoy this."

They circled around with their arms in position. Each of them was sure to defeat the other. Matsuo saw the opportunity and made more grey blood drip from Silvert's mouth. Then it was Vertison's turn, but the reflexes by Hiro gave him the advantage. Hiro tried another time with an awfully rapid combination that amplified Jamal's pain. The silver hero had to prove that he was superior.

He displayed a feral expression and then gave Hiro everything that he had, exploding with firm and brash hits that made the combatant fall to the ground. Silvert refrained from stopping as he continued more and more. Finally, when believing that it was enough, he stopped and looked Hiro in the eye. The gaze spoke its own message that said their friendship was no more. Even though he was almost pinned down, Hiro gave a threatening laugh.

"What's so funny?!"

"What's funny you ask? This is!" He bashed Silvert down. Then, something came to his attention. He remembered the AIA shield he stole from the agency earlier on. He took a glimpse of it from his pocket, smiled, and then taunted Silvert some more.

"And to think…you actually thought you were capable of having a relationship with the Captain." Silvert rose up with a sullen voice. "I don't know what you're talking about."

"That's a lie if I didn't know one. But it's okay. After I'm done with you, she'll be *all* mine."

"If you do that then I swear I'll—"

"Titanium Titan and Captain Tina Truman. It sounds like a perfect couple to me."

"Shut up!" Silvert was fulsomely charged up with a bright ring of light around his body. The detrimental Silver Explosion was on its way.

"Poor Jamal. Are you upset?"

"Hiro! Don't make me do it!"

"Do what?! Unleash your precious *silver* energy? Pathetic...Tina wouldn't like *that*."

And then it happened; his sentiments enhanced the devastating blow. The rampant flames tinted with silver expanded to overflow the area. The entire field reduced to a barren wasteland. It took a while for the searing fire to smear in the dirt.

Silvert kept looking forward and noticed that Hiro was nowhere in sight. He agreed with himself that it was the most caustic Silver Explosion ever. He didn't even blink and was saddened by the fact that Hiro Matsuo was probably dead.

He was in an unwavering position, crouched on his knees with a metal face of dim hollows from the nun chucks. He noticed a tiny teardrop.

What he didn't know was that Titanium Titan activated the shield before the explosion. It was a holographic spherical protector. When deactivating the device, Titanium Titan watched Silvert who was a great distance away. The silver figure shifted back to his human form. Jamal kept staring forward. Hiro snuck close from behind. The titan was finally in reach. He jumped up and brutally kicked Jamal's right temple hard with his metallic boot. Jamal's eyes broadened. He hopelessly fell to the ground with the side of his head buried in the dirt. He gently closed his eyes.

"Who's the better hero now?!" screamed Titanium Titan. Jamal remained knocked down, eyes shut, body still.

"Get up Jamal! I'm not done!" The titan looked at Jamal; the way he stayed there; the fact that there were absolutely no movements.

"Jamal! I said get up!" Once again, there was no response. The titan admitted to himself that the kick to the temple was a little harsh. He quietly said, "Jamal?" With no answer, Hiro became worried. He knelt down, stared at the human body, and repeated his words, "Jamal…Jamal?" Then, when fearing the worst, he listened for heartbeats. *None.*

"Oh no," he said. "Jamal! Jamal, wake up!" The inner wrath went away. All that he felt was sadness and guilt. He let his hatred control his actions and now, Silvert was down, not even breathing.

"Jamal! Silvert c'mon don't do this! Answer me please!" He tried cardiopulmonary resuscitation, but even that was unable to bring Jamal Vertison back.

"No! Jamal!" And it was finished. The dirty deed became a reality, but was never meant to be real. The thought strayed around his mind. All of this derived from his envious personality and made him sense complete acrimony. He shrieked out at the world saying, "What have I done?! Please come back!" Those words, in fact no words at the time, were able to revive him. Hiro stood up to behold the *now* pronounced dead, Jamal Vertison. Silvert was gone. No more.

Hiro began to cry; the tears were almost endless. He was selfish, conceited, worthless, rubbish, malicious. Hiro Matsuo was a *murderer*. And that wasn't even the horrible part. He was in a very insecure position; he had to reveal the news to Team Valor. He picked up the heavy body and looked at Jamal one more time. Hiro's ways disgusted him, presenting no sense of heroism whatsoever. He even compared himself to some of the foulest and spiteful villains he fought in the past. To his realization, he wasn't much different. He contacted Draymond with an upset voice.

"This is Titanium Titan. Bring the jet to the location of my communicator."

"Sure, is everything alright?" Draymond asked. With one strong arm holding Silvert, Hiro said, "*No…everything is wrong.*"

"Well what happened?"

"Just…I don't know. Just get to my position."

"Okay, I'll be there very soon." The transmission ended and Hiro was unsure of how he was going to explain the tragic situation. Then another thought came. They didn't have to know exactly what happened, at least not Team Valor which was led by a shrewd soldier who basically had guns as hands.

He didn't wish to keep it a complete secret. It was necessary for him to own up for his mistakes. He knew exactly who to tell, although it would mean the end of him being on the team. This happened to be none other than Captain Tina.

XV

PENITENCE

THE CURIOUS PILOT RODE THE AIA SHIP

to Titanium Titan's exact location with Team Valor aboard. Prior to this, the pilot had already phoned the base explaining the good news. Still, Titanium Titan had some unfortunate news to tell them. Draymond looked down at Hiro as he understood that his theories were correct. The voice of Hiro *did* indicate that something was out of the ordinary, and when seeing Hiro hold a black man who wore a galactic chain necklace, Draymond became dismayed. He turned and looked at the four recruits in a way that made them realize the problematic concern.

As the plane landed, the members of Team Valor stared out the window with sadness. The tears of Meditation and Evesdrop sprinkled down. The others walked out and insisted to find the meaning of the situation.

"What happened here?" Breath-Stealer asked softly. With the top half of his suit ragged and gone, Titanium Titan soundlessly walked into the jet and placed Jamal on a medical bed. Valor, Fusion Fighter, and Breath-Stealer followed him. He asked the question a second time. Titanium Titan answered, "He's gone. Silvert is gone."

"But how?" asked Fusion Fighter.

"It wasn't my...it was Version X," he said in order to hold back the truth.

"Version X? But that makes no sense. Valor told us that he escaped."

"He came back. It was an ambush. I didn't know until he arrived from behind and fought us both. Silvert used his

Silver Explosion, but even that wasn't enough. I had to leave to avoid the blow. When I returned…I found him like this."

They sighted the body of the dead man. Draymond also took another glimpse. They detested the fact that Silvert had to go out in such a way by one of his arch adversaries. When the others couldn't stand the tragedy, they turned their heads, yet Valor kept looking.

"So what do we do now?" asked Evesdrop. "I mean, are we really going to let that *thing* get away with this?"

"There's really nothing we can do," said Draymond.

"Hell no, we need to do something about this," added Breath-Stealer. "There 'ain't' no way I'm letting that robotic trash wander around after taking the life of one of the world's best. We're hunting Version X down!" They all agreed until Valor finally spoke, "Revenge is not the way."

"Says the guy with pistols who's always looking for a fight!" The soldier stared the ghost down with plenty of seriousness. After, he looked at Titanium Titan and said, "Silvert has fought Version X almost as many times he has seen the Governor. And if there's one thing I know, it's that he's a guy that is used to winning."

"I did everything I could to aid him," the liar said.

"He's used to winning on his own. You out of all people should know that." He walked over to Draymond and ordered him to take off. The aircraft flew away from the city of Toronto, and very soon the Commander would have to be notified about the loss of Jamal Vertison.

In the city of Los Angeles within the alien infested Lasher Labs, Cyfreid and the others fought boldly to protect the Pixaliemain. He understood that this was considered to be the most significant piece. The bug-like creatures were all over the heroes. They snarled like revolting wild beasts and some attempted to bite the heroes. So many of them went for Cyfreid, but were instantly shot down. More swarms arrived and before they knew it, the entire floor was crammed with the monsters.

"So this is what the directors meant when they said our lives were over," said Cyfreid.

"I think they meant your life!" shouted Lynx. "These slime balls are killing me!"

"Let's hope you mean that figuratively," said Shade-Master opening wormholes one at a time and kicking the beasts away.

Lynx's agility was his advantage, but with only a few areas to run, he decided to continue using his lightning strikes. He stretched both arms out and shocked the aliens that were in his way. As a result, they began to shriek aloud and excruciatingly shake. The precious Pixaliemain rock was metres away from unleashing the beast as some of the parasites were beginning to recite the dreaded ritual.

"Cyfreid!" screamed Stan.

"Yes I know! Everyone retreat, there's too many of them!" There were a lot of exits to choose from. The idea was to split up. Racing for the safety of the planet, they each came near their exits. Nonetheless, they were too late as more raucous bugs blocked them from escaping.

"What species is this?!" cried Stan.

"I'm not sure," said Cyfreid. "I have never seen such creatures so anxious to free Xaliemer."

"They must be his kind! We don't know what he looks like!"

"Yea and I don't want to find out!" With no escape route to take, the Commander and his group were doomed to a traumatizing existence of an unknown species that was capable of terminating their lives. The plan of retreating was still the only option and with that in mind, Cyfreid risked the safety of the world and fired at the creatures to make way. Agent Stan assisted him in the action with absolutely no sense of surrendering to the repulsive vermin.

Sharp's belligerent slashes were intensely necessary. While thrusting his jagged fingers, he saw the creatures heal their lacerations.

"They regenerate!"

"Keep attacking! I know you have it in you!" Cyfreid was trying to give him some motivation. This way, the hero's negativity towards him wouldn't be so obvious.

As of the moment, Sharp demanded to bring his true internal animal to full effectiveness. He gave a thundering roar, exposing absolute bravery and assurance. He battled with all of the beasts in his range. He was hasty with each slash. For every wound the creatures healed from, he made two more after that. One of the outsized parasites gripped his arms.

"Let go of me! What are you beasts?!" The answer was a lurid wail that showed the common type of predator it was. Seeing that the alien wouldn't let go, Sharp moved his body weight forward and then landed on the beast. He swiftly pulled away from the grasp and raised his hand. With all five claws, he sliced the entire creature in half.

The animalized hero got up, dusted himself, and agreed that it was a job well done against that alien. He walked a couple of steps and turned back to witness both halves mutate into new beings. Their regeneration capability was spine-tingling.

"They restore themselves no matter what! I...I don't know what to do anymore! I just wish these things can explode and—"

He stopped with the perfect idea. He saw the Commander and tried to get his attention.

"Cyfreid!"

While he blasted the most beasts while holding the galactic stone, Cyfreid answered, "What is it Curt?! I'm sort of in the middle of something!"

"Do you still have that detonator with you?!"

"Yes, but do you really want me to kill all of us?!"

"Not exactly, we're going to escape before it detonates!"

"How do you figure?! These things won't let us leave!"

"Oh they will. I doubt they're intelligent life forms. They only want what looks like the Pixaliemain!"

Cyfreid was cluing in to the brilliant plan. He was enlightened to see that Curtis Kareem was thinking like the assassin he was. He told Lynx and Shade-Master to come near as the strategy was about to be put into effect. Cyfreid gave the alien rock to Shade-Master and he took out the thermal detonator. He received the attention of the aliens and shouted, "Hey, you want this don't you?!" He was cautious—only a tad. He held up the device and pressed a combination of buttons. It would take a minute to obliterate half of Lasher Labs.

The detonator began to flash in order to trick them into believing it was the light from the Pixaliemain. The aliens admired the beauty of the orbicular device.

"If you want it then go get it!" The Commander tossed the detonator to the center of the auditorium. Every savaging alien galloped to the middle and leaped for the so-called Pixaliemain. They piled on top of each other and had the same goals in mind. The exits were clear for Cyfreid, Stan, and the team to leave.

"Now let's go! Move it before we're dead!" They ran like track runners out of the auditorium and darted down the short stairs to call every person who stayed inside.

"The place is going to explode!" yelled Lynx at the top of his lungs. They all trusted his judgment. With almost no time left, they made their way out. They continued to run a good distance.

Behind them, just like it was predicted, half of the building exploded. Luckily, the team didn't suffer. There was a bloated mushroom cloud and a scrunching fire. The battle against the unknown species was finished. Hordes of people outside were very glad that they listened.

"We better inform the fire department," said Shade-Master.

"Right, I'll get on that right away," said Cyfreid. He saw that Shade-Master had the rock safe and sound. As he grinned with the realization that the Earth was saved yet again, he took out his phone. The phone rang before he was able to punch in the numbers. He looked at the caller identification. It said Draymond. He said, "Yes, what is it Dray?" Cyfreid expected that Draymond was going to ask him where he was, but instead the pilot's words voiced depression.

The corners of his smile fell. His face began to mold, first looking ecstatic and victorious, but now vapid, thwarted, and desolate. The heroes and Stan saw the transformation of his expression.

"Okay," said Cyfreid as he spoke with Draymond. "Yes, I know…I understand. Over and out."

"What did he say?" Stan asked. Cyfreid tried to hide some of his emotions. He didn't want to answer, but knew he had to anyway.

"Cyfreid?" asked Shade-Master. "Are you okay? What did that guy say?"

Cyfreid took a profound breath. He couldn't believe the news. He looked at each of them and sensitively said, "We got a man down."

Back among the blissful clouds, Draymond flew the *Regime 5* into the AIA East landing bay with uncountable operatives. A dense mist filled the area the second the seal opened. Titanium Titan held the dead body of Jamal Vertison as he walked out.

Captain Tina, Sherman, Zan, Celestica, and Frankie already reached the base moments ago. Seeing Hiro carry Jamal from the garage to a medical center within the floating station was not what they had in mind of good news.

Tina sobbed from viewing the scarred body; she recently got to know Jamal, and now she will never get a chance to know him more. She was meant to be rather merciless, inflicting penal decrees to inimical creatures. This on the other hand, was something entirely different. She cared for Jamal, a lot more than she expected.

Valor and his companions walked out of the ship and showed complete composure by holding their feelings. The large pack that was comprised of Team Valor, Zan, Celestica, Frankie, Draymond, Sherman Bawnder, and Captain Tina, all paced for the medical center. As Hiro reached first, he told the AIA paramedics not to give up their efforts. He placed the body on the bed and watched them hook Jamal to an electrocardiograph.

"Anything?" asked Hiro. There was an endless beep from the machine.

"I'm sorry…"

They were heartbroken. Out of all of them—even more than Captain Tina—Titanium Titan felt the most agony when being the only one who knew the truth. The guilt began to taste his insides, bit by bit, as if the sensation was alive and squeezed his heart tight. A part of his soul started to mock him, just like he mocked Jamal. It cackled at him and said he was pathetic, and it was right. He wished to take everything back; the words he said, the hatred he conveyed from who knows where, but nothing was able to stop the reality. He was anguished and knew that he should be.

With everyone in the room, eager for just one heartbeat to show on the monitor, Hiro tapped Tina and quietly asked if he could speak to her in private. She tried her hardest to compose herself as they left the medical center. Hiro walked far away from the others with Tina following him. It was so far, that the Captain rubbed away her tears and asked the man, "What's going on?" Hiro looked around for any witnesses. He spotted some cameras and then understood that the devices didn't pick up sound.

"Okay," he started. He had no idea how he was going to explain it, seeing how much Tina revealed her sadness about the issue. He continued with, "Silvert was a great man. Actually, he was a really great man…and as of right now, I'm starting to miss his *greatness*."

"As am I," she inaudibly stated.

"Jamal and I fought so many scoundrels when being as what you might call a tag team duo."

"Yes, I know. That's why…Hiro you actually weren't an official recruit for this team. It was my idea to make you a part of all this."

"Yes, yes I know. Jamal told me."

"He told you? I didn't expect him to do that. How'd you take it?" Her voice was finally easier to hear. Hiro strolled around the hallway and tried to think about his next words.

"Not so well," he said. He looked away to avoid facing the Captain, which made her realize that something was wrong.

"What do you mean not so well?" she asked back.

"A tag team…has its ups. But it also has its downs. I guess in this case, the *downs* overweighed the *ups*."

"So you didn't take it that well, that's okay. All I want you to know is that you'll always be a part of this team." Her words only made things more difficult. She caringly touched him on the shoulder and explained how amazing of a hero he was. He couldn't accept that; he wanted to, but could not. Hiro turned away from her once more and looked outside. The sun was going down and evening was now becoming night. He looked back at her and said, "I'm not the hero you thought I was."

"What are you talking about? I saw everything you did. I mean, just think about the way you took down that cavalier."

"It was mostly Silvert. He did most of it. In fact…he *deserves* most of the credit. I can't believe I'm just realizing that now. Tina…I'm no hero. Not after today."

"So is that what you wanted to tell me? That you don't believe that you have what it takes? You fought for Jamal. Draymond told me the whole story. We're going to find Version X."

"Version X…didn't kill Silvert." Once again, he pushed his gaze away from her and walked to face the large windows. She was confounded by the news she was hearing. She didn't say another word and waited for Hiro to explain the truth. While waiting a short moment and still looking away, he was ready to reveal the honest and tragic circumstance.

"I did," he finally said. The Captain was mystified and trapped in a world with distress combined with anger. She tried to tell herself that she heard it wrong.

"What did you just say?" A silent awe came upon her when noticing Hiro's bruised eye under the mask.

"It was me. I'm responsible for the death of Jamal."

Her eyebrows dropped. She softly breathed through her mouth, having the words formulated in her mind, but dying out in a cool breeze. She kept her jade eyes on Hiro.

He turned around and saw her face stuck with the expression of calmness. Her look remained that way for a while, not even blinking as if she was a frozen pillar.

"Tina?" he asked quietly. As soon as he said her name, the Captain slapped Hiro in the face; it was a horribly brash whack that caused his cheek to slightly swell up. Then she thought that one hit wasn't enough and so, she gave him another spanking to the other cheek. She was livid and also hurt when seeing that the tears were coming back.

"How could you?" she said with an upset tone. Hiro didn't answer immediately. As for the slaps, he knew he deserved them.

"How could you?! How could you lie?!" Hiro scratched his head, ready to explain the story.

"I...I was *jealous*. We got into a fight to see who the better hero was. And...I took it too far. I kicked him in the temple out of pure anger. But when noticing how he wouldn't get up, it got me worried. I tried to bring him back but..."

She began to cry and had a heart that now felt completely empty.

"Tina," he continued. "The only reason why I'm telling you is because I knew how you felt about him. What I did was wrong...which is why I'm leaving the team. For my actions...I-I am sorry."

The Captain walked away from him. She smeared enough tears and replied, "You are done...done! And it doesn't stop there. Before you leave, you're going to tell everyone what you did." She walked off, trying her best not to let any more feelings out. Hiro was hushed and ashamed. He understood that she was correct. The right thing to do would be to tell everyone. The truth had to get out. He felt that it was time to depart. He bleakly walked to the landing bay. Then, he and spotted a cruiser.

Valor saw Tina when she made it back to the medical center. With his pistols detached, he approached her and gave her the alien rock. She took it, not even smiling for the acquired piece.

"Where's the one that you guys got from the museum?" he asked.

Her eyes opened wide. She looked around and then told him, "Oh my goodness, I gave it to Canavin. Where is he?" Tina repetitively called his name and then asked the others, "Do any of you know where Canavin is?"

They all shook heads explaining that they haven't seen him at all. She marched into the massive landing bay and searched for the alien's cruiser. It was nowhere in sight. She asked more of the agents and received the same results. Tina put her trust in him, but it seemed like she was having bad luck when doing that to others.

The alien-hero changed his mind. He decided to set his course for the west sector to confront Identymous once and for all. The location was Cyclohoma City, which was not too far from Cyfreid's squad.

The alien eyed the prominent base. He remembered everything about it. The pungent thoughts showed that nothing *good* really came from the west sector. It was a corrupted agency since it was last led by Professor Shaw, and judging by the mysterious Identymous, he predicted that the organization stayed that way.

The very moment he landed the ship, Canavin forcefully jumped out and faced the past that he wanted to forget. He stood before the entrance doors; there was usually advanced security, but not this time.

"Hello?!" he called for a response. There was no voice. His infiltration of the west headquarters had no purpose at the given time. The fact that nobody was there meant that the answers to the Identymous mystery were still vague. The armoured Pixalian carefully sauntered down the prison cell hallway to see rotten and stomach-turning inmates to his left and right. Some of them constantly groaned his name. This was common; he was the reason for most of their imprisonment.

He ignored the voices and made way to a very familiar room. It was Professor Shaw's creature test center: a place where aliens were fused with humans.

As Canavin stepped forth and saw all of the test tubes, beakers, and samples of Pixalian DNA, he heard a jarring sound with his antennae. At first, he thought it was the security system. Then, he went to Professor Shaw's monitor. It was an alerting mechanism that showed a map of Cyclohoma City.

"This is odd," he said. Then he noticed how the view of the map zoomed in closer to a location just beyond the metropolis.

"That's it." He was now certain that the view was coming from a satellite. He expected that it was one of the same satellites that his team overheard Cain X speak about in Chicago.

He ran out of the room, down the prison hallway, and back out the doors to his cruiser. He knew exactly where to go. It was a foreign and isolated field just outside of the town. It would take about five minutes to reach.

From an exceedingly high bird's eye view, he saw the headquarters. Several agents from the corrupted sectors of AIA West and AIA Central showed their devotion.

Most importantly, there was Identymous. He was a bizarre looking creature with olive green skin and a face that lacked a mouth, though he was still able to speak. He had bear claws for hands. As for his forehead, there was a circular dial that possessed different options of changeable aliens.

Canavin activated the cruiser's cloaking, making his ship and himself become completely invisible.

He watched as Identymous conveyed information to the central agents. He was able to hear every word spoken from the shape-shifter at such a high height.

They were talking about the satellites; their efficiency and whether they were able to handle the heat pressure. It was the same subject that he heard earlier.

More events rose Canavin's tension. There was a black car that arrived in the area and Governor Cain X walked out. Then a warship flew by and descended to the dirt covered surface.

It was an AIA Central aircraft, and to Canavin's surprise, the villains of Cain's alliance made their way to front their leader. The various mutants saluted Cain along with the main assets: Bloodblast, Dark-Shallow, Corometheus, Gold-Mine, and Avinotch. The sufferers who weren't there were Professor Shaw, Derwin Grant, the burnt Gustavo, and the recently dead Titanic. Cain and the rogues moved towards Identymous.

"The Pixaliemain," said the creature. "Where is it?"

"I'm afraid I don't have it. I trusted that pathetic and overweight numskull to retrieve it! He failed me!"

"The Titanic was never a true asset to your team," Identymous replied. "Now, where can I find a sample?"

"It's Cyfreid's team of super fools! They have it!"

"What of the other pieces?"

"I don't know where the other ones are. He and I hid them all those years ago, but unfortunately, he has the advantage. He knows where at least one is…and they probably already have it."

"Then I can't get your machines to work. The Pixalians from my kingdom can never be under our control without something as massive as the great and powerful Xaliemer."

"I understand. My team and I are going to have a little *talk* with those so-called heroes."

"Cain, there's something else you must know. There's a new species that arrived on this planet. I can sense their presence."

"Are they in the way of us reaching our goal?"

"I'm not so sure. I know that they're regents. They're highly indestructible."

The Governor looked at his alliance and then back at Identymous.

At last, it was night. As he almost accepted a defeat against the heroes, Identymous's senses began to act up again.

"Shush," he told everyone.

"Shush what?" asked the Governor.

"I said shush. Everyone, quiet down."

They figured that he was serious and so, they cooperated. Whispering to the creature, Governor X asked, "What's going on?"

"I sense him."

"Who are you talking about?" Identymous waited for only what he could feel. Then he said, "Canavin."

Everyone prepared themselves for battle. The Governor was anxious to know when the alien was going to strike, and it made Canavin edgy as he sat in his imperceptible ship.

"Where is he?" Cain X questioned with his gun in front of him. Identymous kept observing. He brought his head up to the darkness.

He noticed the cold colour of the night and then listened closely. There was a faint sound; he listened again. He concluded that his instincts were correct as he compared the sound to that of a cruiser.

He pointed his finger and cried, "Right there! Shoot right there!"

The Governor and the agents of the two sectors obeyed and fired at the position. The gunshots hit the ship with some trying to protrude through the exterior. He didn't know how much of the bullets the aircraft could take.

When deactivating the cloaking and revealing his presence, Canavin attempted to fly away from the scene. He only got far enough to be a short distance until the Governor shot the ship's stern, making it plummet and crash-land.

The alien coughed from inside with his cruiser nearly damaged.

"I have to get away from here!"

It was too late. The agents fenced his ship with each of them brandishing their weapons. The top glass seal opened and before Canavin raised his arms to accept defeat, he charged himself with Pixalian energy. The brightness degraded when Identymous and the Governor came near.

"I wouldn't do that if I were you, Canavin," said Identymous who grabbed his communicator.

Canavin was furious with Identymous. This was his chance, the perfect opportunity for the scum's head on a plate.

Canavin couldn't understand why he was thinking this way. Honour, trust, faithfulness, and courage; each possessed no meaning at the time. If his father was still around, would he approve? Or would he immediately stop him in a fierce instant and say, *"No Canavin. This is not you. Remember my teachings."* Canavin knew the answer and was starting to regret his choice of soaring to the Pacific.

"I sense something else," the wicked Identymous added. And then the thought hit Canavin: the Pixaliemain. It was in a compartment within his cruiser.

"It's something, something…a sample of the rock! He has it!"

Everyone was stunned, especially the Governor. He couldn't believe how Canavin himself would provide him with the substance necessary to make all extraterrestrials under his control—only as long as they weren't immune to Xaliemer's power.

Canavin gulped. It was never a part of his intentions to risk the world. He had personal reasons for challenging Identymous. He admitted that he was different. The dark personality—something that was never believed to be within him—had its upcoming consequences. He began to doubt himself with villains bringing him out of the cruiser. They locked him in handcuffs that even he couldn't break free from.

"Where's the Pixaliemain?" asked Identymous. With an obvious silence from Canavin, Identymous ordered Gold-Mine and Dark-Shallow to search the ship. Canavin sweated just like he did back on Star-Pix in the throne room.

Dark-Shallow and Gold-Mine hurried themselves. They peeped at a dynamic blue radiance escaping from a compartment. Gold-Mine opened it and leered with pleasure. The light threatened everyone's eyeline to emphasize its immensity.

"At last!" shouted the Governor as Gold-Mine placed the rock in his hand. He saw that Identymous was ready to perform the ancient hex.

"Identymous!" Canavin cried out. "Don't do it! Xaliemer's too powerful! You'll be controlled too!"

"I'm afraid that's not true," the creature stated. "Thanks to the technology provided by Cain, Xaliemer will not have any effect on me. As I speak right now, there are a number of satellites orbiting above the planet. You see Canavin, you out of all the Pixalians on this planet should already know that I'm a shape-shifter." Cain X stared deeply into the vast light. He mischievously smirked and handed the substance to the alien.

"Identymous don't!" shrieked Canavin, trying to free himself from the unbearable handcuffs. The portentous being's eyes shifted crystal clear, like beaming sapphire elements. He spoke the words of the 'Reading of Xaliemer'. Each word derived from a Pixalian language that only Canavin was able to interpret. His father's very spell; his father's hard work; it was close to its end.

Canavin almost endlessly roared the word, "No!"

Identymous continued the reading. While remaining to shout for the life of the world, Canavin's veins popped out. His muscles ached; his heart pattered for safety; his tense nerves brought dread to his guts that felt useless. The stress made him wish he was able to end it all, the proper way. Not like this.

The villains, agents, and the Governor were ready. Questions collected in their heads. How big was he? How destructive? Did he possess any furtive capabilities?

"Identymous!" Canavin aggressively hollered. "You must not do this! Please, you have to stop the reading! Don't give in!" The attempt was meaningless. And with the final phrase to be said, it was already too late. He finished the hex.

"Oh no," said Canavin low and fearful.

The ground tremendously rumbled. Clumps of dirt shot directly up from the shuddering field.

"Earthquake!" screamed Corometheus. The agents from the despoiled sectors panicked. They held on to whatever they could. The rock itself shook in Identymous's palm.

"Yes! It's happening!" The illuminating Pixaliemain levitated on its own. The others were amazed; Canavin was greatly troubled. He lowered his head with shame and said, "Father…what have I done?"

All of the pieces of the full Pixaliemain rock vibrated terrifically. At AIA East, the three rocks performed the same action of levitating. It shocked Captain Tina and the others as they knew that someone failed. The situation made everything worse when the heroes continued to look at Jamal's body. Everything was a disappointment.

The rocks trekked out of AIA East, sharply creating dazzling azure streaks in the nighttime sky and very soon, making their way to the location of the completed ritual.

In Los Angeles, Cyfreid and the group watched their acquired piece bounce around. It floated and zipped away to leave the mystic trail. They were speechless until Lynx asked, "What just happened? Did we fail?" Cyfreid's heartbeat paced faster. He looked at the four of them with misery.

"No," he said. "But someone else did."

Cain X laughed aloud when seeing that at last, his dream was able to come true. Five years of waiting, all for this approving moment. Canavin, the perceived hero of the ages, had so much remorse when watching all five of the Pixaliemain stones arrive.

They came together and compressed like a puzzle. Then with the combined luminosity, the sweltering glow consumed the entire sarsen. A malevolent spirit was produced and mounted its way to be free. It shaped itself to the outline of a figure and finally grew into the biggest, most wretched and demoralizing abomination that destroyed thousands upon thousands of Pixalians many years ago.

Xaliemer was unleashed.

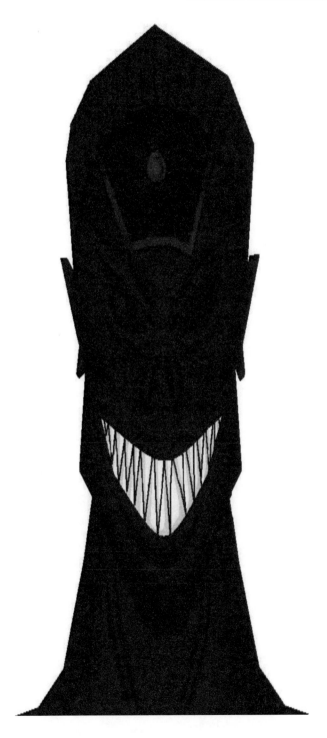

PART 3

THE MASTER DEFENDERS

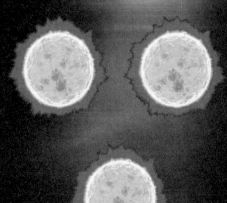

XVI

OWNING UP

THE PIXALIAN NIGHTMARE RETURNED.
This time, the location was Earth. Canavin lifted his head sky
high and watched Xaliemer.

The beast was a little taller than a fifty storey building.
Luckily, his legs were not too close to them. Identymous was
honoured to be in the presence of an abomination that has done
things that only he could imagine himself doing.

Everyone saw the colossal alien: his head was formed
like a venomous marauder, having eyes of dreaded vehemence
and large razor-sharp tusks. He was more like an alien
humanoid, lofty and slender from afar. One of the main traits
about Xaliemer was that he could only communicate with
aliens through the mind. He had an outstanding vision that was
capable of seeing the smallest objects. His body had multiple
shades of blue, black, red, and green.

Xaliemer remained steadfast upon the earthly ground
within the range of humans and two Pixalians, Canavin and
Avinotch. Cain X became quite confused. He didn't
understand why the creature didn't shriek out anything or start
going on a ferocious rampage—not that he truly wanted the
monster to do it.

Every single person was quiet, tense, frozen in position
and not even wanting to twitch a muscle. They held their
weapons out for safety.

"What's he doing?" the Governor whispered to
Identymous. The alien answered saying, "He's going through a
critical examination process. Right now, he doesn't know
where he is."

"Can he see us?"

"Obviously yes. Once he realizes that this isn't Star-Pix, he'll begin his wrath. Cain, now is the time to initiate the operation."

"At last, my plan is complete." Cain X reached inside of his black jacket and took out a miniature apparatus shaped like a remote control. He aimed his hand to the stars and pressed one of the buttons that made a shrill buzzing.

When the sound ended, everyone looked up and saw how certain stars illuminated more than others. They weren't stars, but instead the satellites that the Governor put so much time, money, and effort to have produced.

Up in space, the satellites—more like doomsday devices—turned to face the planet and were locked on to Xaliemer's location. They loaded up the energy and emitted tapering emerald coloured beams that all aimed for the same target.

Back on ground level, the agents, villains, and Canavin watched as the rays hurtled down to electrocute Xaliemer.

The formidable giant yowled with a daunting voice of a lion. His movements slowed down; the controlling process was working. And soon, with the combined power of the rays, Xaliemer slept.

"Finally, the power of Xaliemer…in the palm of my hand," said Cain as he admired his remote. The different buttons on the device were options that would send a signal to the monster's mind, making it so that Xaliemer would obey the Governor's every order.

The beams continued. The agents and rogues became more pleased. The Governor turned to the captive Canavin and said, "You see Canavin, I told you and your team that we had this under control. Now it is time for the main part of this amazing reality."

"What do you mean?" said Canavin fiercely. Cain called for Identymous and told him that now was the time. He backed up and got a good look at Xaliemer. He spread out his arms and the circular dial carved on his forehead spun around.

Before anyone knew it, Identymous began to grow. His height increased like never before. The people were astonished as their necks began to strain from looking directly up. Within five frightening minutes, Identymous grew so large that he was the same height as the beast. His body seemed to resemble that of Xaliemer.

It was true; it was the exact thought that Canavin feared. Identymous had now shape-shifted into Xaliemer, making the others somewhat anxious to leave the premises that now had two brutal abominations.

"No," said Canavin quietly. Cain guffawed with the prized remote.

"I *think* what you mean is 'yes' my *friend*. Xaliemer is under my control. If you were smart, you would put the pieces together and realize that I control all these pests on the planet."

"Cain! You don't understand!"

"But I do understand! In fact, I did my research. I know that you and that companion of yours are immune to Xaliemer. So, suppose you escape and bring Cyfreid's alliance…it will mean nothing. Identymous will defeat you all. Although it's not like it really matters. I have an army of AIA agents from two sectors and a team of unique individuals. Basically, your precious crew better stay out of my way."

The rays were still focused on Xaliemer. They didn't harm him, but still had effects that put him to sleep. While watching the beams, Dark-Shallow noticed one of them turn off for a second and then turn back on. He addressed the issue to his boss saying, "Did you see that? One of the rays turned off for a moment."

"You're overreacting," said Cain X. Accepting this, Dark-Shallow began to mind his business until he noticed that the same action happened again with a different beam.

"Sir, it happened again."

"Didn't I tell you that you're imagining things? Nothing happened."

"But sir, I know what I saw and it—"

"One more word out of you and you'll be in Identymous's stomach. Now be quiet and wait 'til the satellites give me the amount of power that I need to fully control Xaliemer." One of the beams stopped completely.

"What! What's going on?!"

"Sir," said an operative. "The heat pressure might be two much for the satellites to handle."

"No it's not!" he hollered back. "It's fine! I just need some more time, that's all. There's no way I'm going to let one streak determine—"

Before he could finish his sentence, two more beams stopped and then continued.

"Cain," said Canavin. "What he says is true. Your devices will be destroyed."

"Why do you speak like that?! You're supposed to be the *hero*, the one who's always thinking positive!"

"I'm sorry," said Canavin shaking his head. "But it might…it might be too late."

A satellite in space exploded when being unable to survive the heat pressure. After that, another was destroyed. Very soon, it was unfortunate for them all. The bursts were rapid twinkles from where they stood. The years of production were wasted. Xaliemer still slumbered. It gave the Governor and the monstrous Identymous some hope.

"You see," said Cain who was saddened by the loss of his satellites, but confident that the process worked. "Everything's fine."

Suddenly, Xaliemer opened his alarming eyes and roared out in anger. He took his first step on the planet and looked around for the fully combined Pixaliemain sarsen. The mighty boulder levitated and in an instant, Xaliemer disintegrated the entire rock that Canavin's father trapped him inside. Pixaliemain ceased to exist.

"Great God of mercy," said Dark-Shallow. Hearing that, Xaliemer snarled again and levitated the dark magician.

"Help! Help me! Shoot at him!" His voice became fainter the more he was lifted. They wanted to shoot, but were too frightened. As Dark-Shallow floated and finally faced the gigantic head of Xaliemer, he was promptly crumbled into plenty of particle fragments.

"Orders sir," said one of the agents who couldn't stop shivering. Cain hesitated when not finding any solution except for one.

"Run!" he cried as if he was screaming *above* the top of his lungs.

Everyone sprinted like never before. The beast considered them to be ants. He telekinetically raised them up, cluster by cluster, and executed them within seconds.

A number of AIA agents were elevated and collapsed to create sky-high speckling explosions. Some villains suffered the same tragic fate.

The survivors separated themselves by scattering in different directions. Within minutes of short wheezes and yelps, all who remained alive from Xaliemer's wrath was Cain, Gold-Mine, Avinotch, Bloodblast with his repaired bazooka, and Canavin.

The Xaliemer representation that was Identymous tried to end the beast's harm. He shouted for the monster saying, "Xaliemer! Why don't you focus on me instead of them?!" Xaliemer faced Identymous as if he was looking through a mirror. He said his first words with Identymous through his mind.

"Who are you?" Xaliemer said with a profound voice.

"I am you."

"There is no way," he said back. "What planet is this?"

"This is the planet which *humans* call, Earth."

"Earth? So this is the *rock* that was near Star-Pix. Did I succeed in slaying the Pixalians?"

"Yes, you have won," Identymous fibbed.

"Then why do I sense millions of them lurking on this very planet?"

"What you detect is for me to handle. I am this world's plague. Please leave this world for me to destroy."

"No...there is only one plague and that is me."

"There are ten universal plagues in total. I told you, I am you."

"Lies! There is only one Xaliemer!"

The monster lifted his counterpart high above him. In order to save himself, Identymous returned to his original form. He skydived to the ground and cowardly ran away in fright much like everyone else did before they were demolished. Identymous listened for Xaliemer's words.

"You're just like them! Small, weak, and easy to crush! In time, this world will be mine to control." Out of everyone there, Canavin knew how much time that would take: approximately forty eight hours.

He noticed how his cruiser was still in good condition. He refused to wait any longer. With his hands locked in the handcuffs, he ran for his only ticket to escape.

Nevertheless, it was too late. The abomination levitated him and very soon, he heard the dark, cavernous voice inside of his head. Xaliemer stated, "You are rich in energy only I know of. I sense that you ought to be a Pixalian. Is that true?"

Canavin was smart enough to remain silent and continued this when Xaliemer decided to split only the handcuffs.

"You look very familiar," Xaliemer said. "What is your name?" Canavin realized that the beast was most likely confusing him for his father. Since the battle on Star-Pix occurred before his birth, Canavin took a heavy gulp and answered Xaliemer.

"My name is Canavin."

"Canavin. The power I sense within you is stronger than most. You are a potent Pixalian. I can feel it."

"Are…are you going to kill me?"

"You are immune and I don't know why that is. You may be strong, but I do not see you as a threat. Therefore, I offer you with a choice. Join me in the destruction of this planet and I will spare your life. Or you can fight me and die. It is your decision, but either way, this world the humans call Earth will be no more."

"The humans did nothing to you."

"Not yet. They are a corrupted race of imperfection."

"Are the Pixalians any different?"

"No, that is why they are dead. Their remains seem to be here." Canavin was soundless. He knew that the surviving Pixalians from Xaliemer's terror rebuilt their lives to make Star-Pix a rich and organized kingdom. His silence made Xaliemer ask him once more what his decision was. The floating Canavin thought about it and gave his response.

"The answer is no."

"Then you are of fault like the rest of them. You will perish." Still being under Xaliemer's psychic force, Canavin felt that everything inside of him was getting weak. His organs tightened. His racing heart started to shrink in size. He recognized that his energy was at its maximum capacity, and to aid his thought of survival, the hero shot Xaliemer; the Pixalian energy caused no harm.

Canavin still sensed that his life was about to end. He screamed aloud and emitted several blasts at Xaliemer to finally cause some sort of pain. At last, he was free from the levitation.

He descended all the way down to his cruiser, hopped inside, and constantly talked to himself.

"This ship has to function!"

He caught a chill running down his back as he saw Xaliemer standing there, ready to destroy the cruiser.

Xaliemer telekinetically picked up the ship. Canavin tried everything he could to get the systems to respond. Seeing that nothing was functioning, he aggressively knocked on the panel.

"Dammit, just work already!" At last, the computers turned on and the amount of fuel was satisfactory.

"Next stop, AIA East!" He tried to fly away, but the force of Xaliemer was too strong.

"C'mon, c'mon!" Canavin opened the glass seal and repetitively shot his blue rays. Xaliemer turned his large-scaled head away. The warrior closed the seal and flew off in the distance to be extremely far from the empty land outside of Cyclohoma City.

Inside of the cruiser, the shouts of Xaliemer became hard to hear. Canavin was far enough. He looked back and then forward to admit his actions. The nightmare was because of his fraudulence. He knew that not only would the Captain and Commander be outraged, but the members of the Canavin Clan. His saw the compartment where the enemies found the Pixaliemain. Seeing it open made him shout long from inside of the starship screaming, "Why!" It was the loudest he ever shouted.

Trust was the main component in securing a space rock from the dangers that skulked on Earth. Canavin had to reveal the news to Captain Tina and the other mournful heroes. As the ship traveled at the speed of light and managed to make it to the headquarters, Canavin returned to his human-like self, almost as if he was giving up his abilities. He came out with every agent watching him. They were desperate, anxious, and saddened by something.

"Where's the Captain?" he asked them.

"I'm over here," said Tina who came to the armored humanoid slowly. Canavin didn't want to look at her face. She was troubled as were the rest.

"Follow me," she said shedding a tear. She brought him to the medical center where the heroes stood.

"Look who finally made it," said Valor. The body of Jamal was brought to Canavin's attention.

"What happened?" he said as his voice became still.

"Jamal's gone, Canavin," said Evesdrop. Canavin put his head down in despair. The negative revelations weren't over. He remembered the ones who were on the Toronto assignment.

"Wait," he began. "Where's Titanium Titan?" Everyone thought that he went for a walk, but Tina said, "Titanium Titan…quit."

"He quit? Just like that?"

"I'm afraid so. And I think we won't be seeing much of him anymore. In fact, it seems like this team doesn't follow commands like they should! Every time it's the same thing, and we really don't have much *time,* do we Canavin?" Her sadness was now bitter resentment.

She shouted, "What happened?! You specifically said you had it covered! You better have come here to say your father's precious possession is safe!" Almost as if he was speaking with full shame, Canavin stated, "It...it was disintegrated."

"Disintegrated...by who Canavin?! But I guess that's a really stupid question to ask!"

"Look! I didn't know it was going to end up like this! I'm sorry okay! I failed you, I failed my team, and most important of all, I failed all of humanity! I found Identymous and I was about to confront him, but he...he unleashed Xaliemer."

"All for just bringing a lone creature to justice. I didn't expect this from you Canavin."

"He wasn't alone! Cain was there along with the remaining 'X Viles' and several agents from two AIA sectors. His satellites were destroyed!"

"Was it worth it Canavin? Did you get what you wanted?"

"He sensed the Pixaliemain! I was held captive! There was nothing I could do! But it doesn't matter now. I will take responsibility for my actions. Just remember one thing Captain. The pieces of the rock of Xaliemer belonged to my father. You and Cyfreid should've been wise enough to give it to me years ago. That's where you failed."

Canavin was about to leave the room. Breath-Stealer said, "Uh, guys...you might want to check this out."

There was a television screen within the medical room and on the current channel was Marvelous Munroe starring Alyssa Munroe. The show was broadcasting live from Cyclohoma City. She said, "This is Alyssa Munroe live from Cyclohoma and this is an urgent broadcast. People all over the city are panicking, all because of what appears to be a giant, I mean really giant, extraterrestrial in the distance that is making its way close."

The camera cut to the huge creature that was none other than Xaliemer. He was far from Alyssa. His presence on Earth made Tina wonder where Cyfreid was located. The news reporter continued to speak.

"I've seen crazy things from the crisis eight years ago. But this brings *insanity* to a whole new level. We don't know how this occurred. Some civilians say that it just appeared as if it was magic. The forces that are going to attempt to stop the threatening creature to mankind are now on their way and it seems like all agencies are being considered. All that the people of Cyclohoma can do is pray that—"

Tina turned off the television. She contacted the Commander.

"Cyfreid, where are you?!"

"As of right now, I'm in Los Angeles."

"Los Angeles? Wait that's not too far from where—"

"Yes I can see that our worst fear has been realized. So tell me, Miss Truman…who the hell failed?!"

"Canavin. It was Canavin."

"My God, you have to be joking. Our field leader? How?"

"It's a long story. I'm just tired of hearing bad news."

"Tina," he began upon recently hearing something unfortunate. "Tell everyone that they are not needed by AIA East anymore. The team is no more."

"What? How come?"

"I don't know. It wasn't my idea. Somebody from a different sector and of a higher rank than me found out that we were collecting heroes and announced it to the council. They're shutting it down."

"Wait, the only person who could do that is Cain X, but after we defeated him back in Chicago, we informed the council of his ways. Who else could it be?"

"I'm not sure. Maybe they hired new personnel to run AIA Central. I'm sorry Tina. Tell them immediately." He hung up.

Canavin didn't hear a word from Cyfreid. Still, it was clear that the message wasn't good. He left the room, only focused on the mission of facing Xaliemer

He didn't know how it was possible, but he cared for Earth and refused to let it suffer like Star-Pix did years ago. Celestica followed him outside and to his ship.

"Wait!" she wailed for his attention. "Canavin, what are you doing?!"

"What does it look like," he replied. "I'm going back."

"You can't!" she yelled grabbing his body and forcefully hugging him. "Please don't! You'll die!" Canavin gradually took her arms off of him.

"What other choice do I have?"

"Canavin, please! I care for you!" He smiled at her and looked deeply at her beauty without her mask.

"Thank you," he said. "But I'm on this planet for a purpose. And that's to protect humanity. If that means the death of me...I'm willing."

"No, Canavin don't."

"Goodbye Vanessa."

Canavin placed his hand on her cheek and then departed from her to go inside of his ship. She shouted, "Wait!"

He turned around to be surprised by an ardent kiss. Her soft lips pressed fondly to emphasize the times they shared together. They believed that those cherished moments were over. After she took her lips off of his, Canavin's antlers and gold face returned.

"Be safe," she said once again. He nodded, but couldn't promise her anything. The ship ascended from inside of the landing bay. Agents saluted him from down below. Canavin gave one final look at Celestica, the one he loved so much. He flew out and everyone witnessed his cruiser vanish. Celestica viewed the sky the longest, wishing that the beloved Pixalian was still at her side. She wept slightly while making it back to the others.

"This is outrageous!" Frankie shouted. "We finish Derwin Grant and then now I have to hear about this nonsense. I was expecting something like a welcome back party."

"Where exactly is Derwin?" asked Valor.

"Our team of operatives sent him away to a different sector where he will be placed under permanent lockdown," Tina said. "But there's something that I need to tell you all." She was about to convey the ill-fated message. She asked, "My God where's Canavin this time?"

"He left," said Celestica entering the room. "He's going to face Xaliemer, alone."

"What?! No! What's he thinking?" Zan screamed.

"Then I guess that's his choice," Tina replied. "I'm not responsible for his actions…and I'm not your Captain anymore."

They all wondered what she was talking about. Valor added, "You were never my Captain. Nobody's my Captain but me."

"Tina, what are you saying?" asked Meditation.

"While I was talking to Cyfreid, he told me…that this organization of specialized individuals is being shut down. We don't know who, but there's a new leader of AIA Central. You are all ordered to leave the headquarters and are forbidden to encounter Xaliemer. Right now the government is through with powerful beings. For all they know, all of you could be aliens. The United States forces have it covered. I'm sorry for all of the trouble."

She walked close to the bed and knelt down as she fixedly gazed upon Jamal's body.

"I'm sorry Silvert," she said tenderly. She rose up without saying another word. Her feelings were similar to theirs. The sorrow of everyone combined. The pistol wielding Valor began to laugh.

"What's so funny?" asked Sherman. His laughter ended and he immediately shook his head, displaying their lack of sense.

"All of you tend to forget. I don't take orders from anyone else but myself, especially not some stupid council."

It was a strange moment, but Valor motivated each of them. They looked at one another cleverly. Those words were intended to change their ways of thinking.

Tina smirked at them and asked, "Well then…who's up for a fight against Xaliemer?" The heroes stood up with courage, ready to risk their lives in order to save Cyclohoma.

The sight gave the Captain gladness; they were the right team for any circumstance. Her leader, Commander Cyfreid, predicted that Xaliemer could be released and did everything in his power to prevent it. Now they were faced with the ultimate test of determining whether or not they were truly called: the best of the best.

"Follow me," she said. She brought the nine of them to a tech lab. She opened a safe and provided them the access to holographic shield generators—the same kind that Hiro slyly stole.

"What are these?" Sherman asked Tina.

"Well they're shields, Sherman. If I'm correct, they should generate a blockage from Xaliemer's power. Each of you will receive one to keep for the mission."

"In order to activate this," said Valor. "I would have to detach my weapons, am I right?"

"You're telling me that the great Valor himself needs a shield generator? You're fine."

"I was testing you, woman." After receiving the advantage of the defensive devices, Captain Tina led them to the landing bay where the AIA agents stood and waited for orders.

"Okay people," she began. "The council has ordered the AIA East team of heroes to avoid getting involved with Xaliemer's rampage. I say, screw it! We are not like the other sectors. We are unique and capable of many things, including defeating a force as powerful as this beast. I need everyone's assistance for the attack. We will maneuver in the skies at approximately one hundred feet above the giant. While directly overhead, await further orders."

The agents along with the heroes nodded. As for Valor, he simply said, "Whatever."

"There is one more thing I forgot to add. It's not guaranteed that y'all will make it back alive. Some…will possibly die. So if you wish to opt out now, please let me know." They all remained to show their loyalty to the Captain. The same reality of probable death was upon the heroes. They didn't flinch one bit.

"We will fight beyond our last breath…if that's possible," said Sherman. It was easy for the indestructible man to say. Frankie added, "If we don't, tonight it's Cyclohoma City. Tomorrow, it's the world."

"One alien can do all of that?" an agent asked.

"Yes," stated Zan. "He does it by interfering with the minds of the other creatures on this planet. Whether we help or not…many people are going to die tonight. And worst of all, Cyclohoma has the greatest population of Pixalians in the world."

"Then we must leave this instant," Tina said. "Alright team, let's finish what was started!"

Two warships were currently in their possession within the abundant bay. The agents went in one and the heroes in the other. Draymond was asked to pilot the warship with the heroes.

Then Tina stopped. Her admiration for killing creatures degraded. The absurdity of her job and the cold-hearted thoughts all started to wane. The predator from Detroit flashed before her again, menacing, looming through her, disturbing her sentiments. Its malignant fangs, the coarse maroon eyes and the flooded craters were recently beginning to startle her, like swarms of lice crawling under her skin.

The words, *"All hail Xaliemer,"* stridently shrieked in both her ears. Her inner assassin felt afraid for the first time since she joined the agency. Normality was evident.

Tina brought her projectile blaster along with her pistol at its capacity with bullets. This was truly a war. Death against Xaliemer was the negative thought. For some reason, she said that it was worth it, all for her hobby of slaughtering aliens, just like how creatures killed her parents.

The heroes went inside. A nurse ran by and asked, "Where is Captain Truman?"

"I'm right here. What is it?" The nurse handed her a silver necklace and said, "If you want, you can keep it as a good luck charm." Tina gaped at the attractive silver light and wanted to keep it. She would receive magnificent teeming power. Then she thought once more. The silver necklace was a sign of his heroic life, and therefore, it was not right for her to have it. Jamal wasn't the hero he was because of the necklace.

"No," she calmly said to the nurse. "He was meant to wear the necklace to his grave. Put it back on him at once. That's an order."

"Yes ma'am." She left her sight. Draymond got word from the other warship that it was time for take off. They strapped themselves tight. Some of them said prayers as it was possibly their last. Draymond tilted his head back.

"Is everyone ready?!" The notification was given. It was time to leave the headquarters.

"Have caution for what you'll see," said Tina.

"Initiating takeoff in five, four, three, two, one..."

Draymond's warship rose from off the ground and led the way out of the large doors followed by the other ship filled with the brave AIA agents and soldiers. The ships were painted black and blue with the credited AIA logo on their sides.

Draymond flew to a great length and then stopped to engage the light-speed system.

"Brace yourselves, this is going to be fast," he explained. They were ready for battle. The ship streaked through the clouds and the other one followed.

After half a minute, the team made it above downtown Cyclohoma. Even from such a high height, Valor and the other heroes were able to see the dispersed citizens. And the loathsome creature himself was seen in the distance: Xaliemer. He was bigger and more obnoxious than what they had expected. His height increased to be one hundred storeys. The people in both ships were the most traumatized they had ever been in their lives.

"My God!" cried Draymond. Even if they wanted to change their minds, there was no opting out now.

XVII

A TRUE DEFENDER

ALREADY AT THE SCENE OF THE BEAST
was Canavin who landed his cruiser not too long before Tina, Valor, and the others arrived. It was against what they were told, but Cyclohoma deserved every force necessary. Commander Cyfreid didn't accept the council's command. He along with Agent Stan, Sharp, Lynx, and Shade-Master made it to Cyclohoma City with the abomination present.

"Okay," said Lynx. "Now what? I mean, that thing is huge!"

"Consider this to be your last training simulation," said Cyfreid.

"Last training simulation? We never had a first!"

"Well make sure you'll see the day when you do. This team is not over yet! The AIA council will regret their words."

"How are we going to destroy that thing? If we don't act fast, it'll reach the city."

Xaliemer was firmly fixed. It got them to question what the alien was focused on. He was concentrated on the return of the Pixalian who escaped from his wrath: Canavin. He was able to sense him, wherever he could be in the city.

"We need everybody! Do you hear me?! That means the FBI, the CIA, all the sectors from the AIA, the Army, the Air Force, the—"

"Lynx!" Sharp screamed. "Quiet! Look up in the sky would'ya." He looked up and saw ships that belonged to every organization he spoke of."

"Oh…what a coincidence."

There was an abrupt clamor from behind. As much as a predator he was, Sharp was sure that aliens were near.

"We are not alone!" The agents took out their weapons and Sharp, Lynx, and Shade-Master were prepared for more beings to fight.

"Where are they?!" asked Shade-Master who was sure that it was another attack.

"Why don't you look around, fool?"

Shade-Master and the rest of them realized the number of people who slowly enclosed them. Cyfreid recognized their Pixalian origins. As their human bodies flaked off of them, they went for the group.

Sharp sounded a vicious growl and began to shred. Everyone else joined in the severe battle against the Pixalians. One of them said, "You humans will be exterminated. I am the great power. This world now belongs to me." Another Pixalian said the same words and then after that they all spoke simultaneously.

"It's Xaliemer!" said Cyfreid putting the hints together. "Xaliemer is controlling them!"

"Really, you think?!" replied Sharp understanding the obvious. With similar tactics from before, Curtis showed no mercy. He sliced as many as he could with much hatred.

Some were innocent; not all aliens were immoral. It meant nothing. Xaliemer's curse was strong and there were too many of them. Lynx aided with his lightning strikes, and Shade-Master had to be cautious. The master of many realms was running out of dimensions to choose from. Axel had to be careful when opening them. He didn't want to provide an escape route for trapped aliens and criminals.

An alien hopped onto Cyfreid. It looked less vile than the others. All Cyfreid could do was hear its words of torment.

"Give up and submit to the almighty power."

"Not a chance!" he exploded. His gripped the alien's arms and threw it away. After tumbling over, it leaped for him again, but was tricked into jumping into another realm. Shade-Master locked it shut. The Commander gave him a nod to appreciate his assistance.

"You're welcome," he said. "But I only know so many dimensions. I don't want to use them all up and free past nightmares."

"Then you don't have to," Cyfreid told him. "How good of a fighter are you?"

"I'm pretty decent, I think."

"Well your decency must become that of a pro. Incoming threats await their defeat!" There were more monsters where that came from.

"Lynx! How are you surviving?" the Commander asked. Lynx sacked a creature and responded with a raised tone, "Barely! But I'm going to live, no worries!"

"Just like in Los Angeles, we cannot fail!"

"Yea I got you! But do you have any more of those detonators? I can really use one right now!"

"Sadly no! Just give them everything you got!"

"Man that sucks! What kind of Commander are you?!" Cyfreid ignored him. At times, he felt sorry for some of them that were labeled as a non-threatening species in the archives. The pressing invasion overwhelmed their character.

Agent Stan stood back to back with Cyfreid, being somehow rational with another chance to prove his capabilities. As if it was some sort of training exercise, their accuracy was surprising beyond belief. The galactic beings from far and near were executed with effectiveness. If it wasn't for Xaliemer's spell, Cyfreid agreed with himself that he would spare the lives of some of them.

"Cyfreid, it's no use!" Stan desperately said from behind him. "We shouldn't be doing this! The main focus is Xaliemer! Certain Pixalians have their own rights too if you don't already know."

"I agree with every word," Cyfreid said as he shot one more down; he told himself that would be the last, for now.

"Everyone retreat and follow my lead!"

After he finished impaling his harsh claws into what looked like a perilous extraterrestrial, Sharp groused and hurried for Cyfreid. Lynx and Shade-Master came near and followed. They ran down the street side by side. From their left and right, they sighted the revulsion of the city. Controlled creatures of diverse alien backgrounds were haunting the dismayed public, breaking into apartments and stores, and producing fires of disheartenment—all saying the chilling words of the freed giant. The heroes ran faster and Lynx looked back to notice more of them in search for blood. They increased the speed of their fleeting legs. The small group soon found themselves with nowhere to run as the savages bordered them.

The circle of fright got smaller. Sharp checked to see the flustered citizens. Some didn't survive from the menaces, making the animal crave the death of the aliens regardless if they were under Xaliemer's spell or not.

They stalked closer; the shaky team got cold feet. To their left, they heard whirling wind. A shriek from an alleyway raised a bizarre moment of bravery.

Strangely, it came from Titanium Titan spinning his metal nun-chucks. His presence was a sign that it wasn't time to quit. They all brawled with spirit to defend not only themselves, but the people of Cyclohoma. Every alien was thrashed, mainly by Hiro's aberrant bravery. The final squeal died from a fully gashed body. Hiro and the fighters had a chance to catch their breaths. Lynx walked over and thankfully patted Hiro on the back.

"Nice of you to drop by," he said. "Where are the others? We could use more heroes like you." Hiro put his head down in shame.

"I'm no hero," he stated almost soundlessly. They were completely unaware of his past acts of detestation, as was everyone else except for Captain Tina.

When Tina gave him specific orders to leave the facility but to first tell the team the truth, he ignored her judgment and made his way west for Cyclohoma by secretly acquiring an AIA cruiser.

"What do you mean you're no hero? You just came to our rescue, killed most of those *things*, and saved a good number of people. In my book, that's a hero. I know one when I see one." Lynx patted him once more to show his gratitude.

"Thanks," said Hiro having a smile on his face. "I appreciate your words."

"No problem man." Sharp approached them and specified, "When you two are done with your little love fest, we need to find a way to get closer to Xaliemer!"

"You actually want to get near him?" Titanium Titan wondered.

"I'm going to tear that beast limb by limb! I don't care if it takes me weeks to do it!"

"Well unfortunately we don't have that amount of time!" shouted Cyfreid. "He's too powerful, you'll die!"

"You got any better ideas, *Commander*?"

"Curtis, I won't let you. You're one of my best!" Sharp's propensity to ruminate violently was put on hold. All he could think about was the slim chance of Cyfreid actually caring about him, like an opaque brotherhood that was never really observable. At last, he understood that Cyfreid really was not a bad person.

"Well," Curtis began. "If your words are correct, and I'm truly one of your best, then let me prove myself." Complete shock went through them, being ignited by Sharp's lethal request to see the dire face up close. They awaited Cyfreid's response.

"Okay," he said to his once beloved pupil. "We need mobilization to get near him quickly. Once there, I'll let you aid the additional forces. But don't say I didn't warn you."

"Where are we going to get vehicles?" Lynx asked. "If I were you, I'll just take the jet. It sounds easier."

"The jet's too big as are the Army's strategies of attack. We need something small, something that Xaliemer won't see coming, or at least won't focus on."

"Leave that to me," Titanium Titan said. He traveled through another alleyway that led to a different street. Sharp, Cyfreid, Stan, Lynx, and Shade-Master picked up on the notion of following the kung fu specialist. Running down the alleyway, they saw Titanium Titan standing beside the AIA cruiser.

"What in the world? Who gave you the approval to fly this? You're not authorized to pilot AIA tech."

"Let's just say I borrowed it. Sharp, you think you can fly this heap of metal?"

"Well yea. I spent years working for Cyfreid."

"Well then *she's* all yours. Try and come back alive."

"If I die, Xaliemer dies with me!" They agreed with each other that Sharp was foolish.

"I think that's just his way of saying he'll try his best not to die," said Lynx. Curtis hopped into the cruiser and returned his claws to fingers. He found the controls to be quite familiar. Cyfreid walked over to the ship and said, "Strike him from behind, always! If he's too concentrated on the Army, that'll give you a strong advantage."

"I understand," said the relentless Curtis Kareem. It was easy for Cyfreid to say that Curtis was a man of pluck, wrath, and slight serenity.

He flew the ship away from the hysterical screeches. Shade-Master, Titanium Titan, and Agent Stan attacked more aliens. The Commander confined his view on the departing cruiser until Lynx, still with his annoying mouth, said, "Man…he's truly a goner."

Turning his head, Cyfreid became displeased with the comment. He helped the others with the static recruit.

Sharp sat in the cruiser and remembered Cyfreid's words to strike from behind. He saw Xaliemer eliminating every ship that flew close, as if the ruptures began with simple thoughts that manifested brutality. He was a force unlike anything Sharp had ever encountered. That didn't change his mind. Sharp had to rush before he was seen. The ship sped through the skies and avoided the eruptions.

From the top of an edifice not too far from the overhead battle, there was Canavin who stood up with gallantry, willing to risk his life in order to give humanity a sense of hope. He could see everything from his stance. The Army ships were destroyed with soldiers parachuting out, but even they were shattered in the attempt to escape. Canavin knew that deep down, he was a powerful humanoid. Xaliemer could only come close to separating his particles. He was ready—ready to defend or die trying.

He ran with heroic force and jumped to glide in the air and fly towards the massive Xaliemer. He reached the humongous face of malice, the vile teeth, and the fact that Xaliemer was nothing but abominable. Canavin's head began to ache the moment Xaliemer infiltrated his mind. The beast's company stung his daring passion. He somehow felt the existence of miniature spirits loitering around inside, snickering like gremlins. The action caused him to scream with agony.

"So, you've decided to come back for more?" He spoke with an abysmal tone. Canavin was aware what he had to do. He had to reveal to the monster his species—the kind of alien he truly was. He slowly reached for his mask and then, he took it off and dropped it. The mechanical mask, his symbol of heroism, pitifully fell down and disappeared from his sight. He showed his gold face to Xaliemer.

"You!" Xaliemer scolded. From outside of his mind, all Canavin heard was a nasty roar. "You look just like him!" The beast was referring to Canavin's father, the one who led his own team of honorable individuals to take him down. For many years, Xaliemer wished to seek revenge on any creature whose skin was gold, especially one that had three antlers. Canavin had almost the same appearance as his father. He thought that this way, Xaliemer would focus his rage only on him instead of everybody else.

The sacrifice was one he wanted. Canavin was furious. He felt his scabbard and then took out Pixcalibur, believing that it was most likely his last time. The blade was bright as ever and in perfect condition for a fatal match.

"Xaliemer! This will be the last time you harm an innocent race!" He zoomed for the massive face and repetitively sliced off pieces with stressful aggression. Xaliemer tried to reach for Canavin, but the warrior was too small. He was a giant that refused to be slain. The rumbles got brasher with every hit Canavin gave. The hero was certain of his choice of defending a planet that he was able to call his home.

"You killed my people! But you won't do the same to the humans!"

"Your people?!" wondered the crude voice inside Canavin's head. "You sound like the king!"

"I *am* the king!" Canavin lied, although, it wasn't so much of a lie. He was simply just holding back the full truth.

"Then die with these things you call *humans*!"

"I'll live to see your death! But if the worst happens, I will not die in vain!" To Xaliemer's surprise, Canavin caused him to bleed. It was nothing more than his version of a paper cut. Nonetheless, just noticing it was discouraging for the beast.

"Enough!" Canavin developed a dramatic headache, very worse than a painful migraine. The torment continued as he was risen up and was unable to escape Xaliemer's force. With Pixcalibur in his right hand, Xaliemer caused Canavin to let go of his dear weapon. The blade of glory was lifted beyond his head. He looked up with no other thought except retrieving it. He couldn't move from the invisible grasp. And with his eyes on the prize, it left him.

Pixcalibur was dematerialized. The particles floated down like pixie dust. Without an effective weapon, Canavin thought that he *was* now going to perish.

Xaliemer raised the tiny body. Canavin caught some of the dust of the once powerful rapier.

"Now it is Canavin's turn," Xaliemer thought. The alien panicked for the first time facing him. When he was high enough, he could feel the inside of his body shrink. He was losing blood without even seeing the fluid drain out.

Canavin's breaths were condensed, each one shallow and wilder than the other. His faith was the fuel that kept him from dying quickly. It made him feel only a little bit better. He felt the very Pixalian energy rushing out from within.

"Stop!" Xaliemer held nothing back. Canavin noticed his arms crumple like a prune. The wrath was expressed to an even higher extent. With so much hatred for Canavin's background, he continued to suck the life out of the pathetic being.

Resonant blasts disturbed Xaliemer. He lost all concentration with levitating Canavin.

The assaults came from the cruiser. Curtis Kareem developed a sense of a magnetic force engulfing the ship. The systems were failing; the circuits sparked with failure. The metal interior was collapsing. Jumping out was the only option. Intense flickers hovered over him.

The overriding alarm was too much; now was the time. Curtis Kareem tried every switch to open up the top hatch. The ceiling of the ship was closing in onto his head. He pierced his fingers through it, hoping that he could create a fat gap for escape. The sweat vexed his eye sockets and ran down his face from the demoralizing area.

From what he was able to point out, he only had seconds before he would be flattened. With one more breakage, he could see the night sky. He repeatedly made more holes until he formed an opening that was big enough to make his evacuation. Sharp climbed through and jumped out of the AIA cruiser that straightaway exploded.

Skydiving and almost swimming in the air, he made his way for Xaliemer's body. His claws extended. He was ready for the fight of his life. Sharp landed to remain high above the city with his tines jabbed deep inside of the abomination's skin. He scaled his way up and then determined the right place to attack. Sharp grimaced with a weighty scream and urged both hands inside, rasping portion after portion, as if he was digging for a striking treasure. The residue from Xaliemer's flesh didn't bother him.

He wiped away some of the space substance and looked above at Xaliemer's churlish face. The plaguing monster grew a smile. Xaliemer couldn't communicate with Sharp—since he wasn't an alien—but the man was able to infer what was going to happen. He was elevated by the incredible force.

Good things were able to come from good deeds. When Sharp saved Canavin from Xaliemer, Canavin did the same. The Pixalian was charged with some remains of his inner power. He went with the same tactic and fired his volatile rays at Xaliemer from behind. The energy penetrated only slightly through his crusty coating. Xaliemer lost focus on Sharp.

Curtis yapped for assistance as he fell from the scary height. With the monster's body too far for him to clench, he was sure that this was the end. Then he was caught and began to fly unexpectedly. When being completely muddled, he looked up and was enlightened.

Fusion Fighter carried him and flapped his pterodactyl wings. More sightings of the heroes enlarged Curtis's mood. Draymond's warship stayed above the monster. Team Valor along with Sherman Bawnder, Frankie, Celestica, and Zan jumped out and landed on Xaliemer's shoulder. Breath-Stealer, Fusion Fighter, and Meditation flew there.

"Fusion Fighter, get me closer!"

"Whatever you say, we'll cover you." The pterodactyl glided towards his team's location on the monster's body. He landed safely and awaited Valor's orders.

"Kill this beast," said the soldier. They all sensed his legitimacy.

Captain Tina Truman was still inside of Draymond's warship. She watched the United States reinforcements arrive. Some of the soldiers were surprised to see famous heroes on Xaliemer's shoulder. Xaliemer's concentration was on the flyers that circulated his head. He didn't worry about the ants on his shoulder. He focused on the warship.

Tina felt the interior walls closing in. She called for Draymond saying, "We have to leave now!" The pilot refused to listen.

"Draymond, let's go!" The crucial event continued.

"Draymond, the doors! Let's go right now, I order you!"

"Don't worry about me, you go."

"No! Be smart and let go of the controls. There's no surviving inside of here. C'mon!" Draymond's hands were tightly gripped on the yoke. He calmly said, "Tina…jump."

"Not without you Draymond! Let's go!"

"Tina…just jump. They need your help."

"What? What are you trying to say?! Don't do this! Come on!"

"I got it covered. Save yourself."

"Draymond!" With almost no room, she shot the glass seal, soared out, and activated a parachute for safety.

Her head rose up and witnessed the dented ship divide in a flaring blow. Draymond's full body tumbled out to be scalded in flames. Tina knew that some people wouldn't make it back, but never predicted Draymond to be one of them.

She trusted that his life would be remembered with great honour. He was an experienced AIA pilot and respected the lives of others. Tina landed on the shoulder and saw them looking at the falling parts. She bit her lip with an itching impression from the cause.

"Draymond?" wondered Breath-Stealer.

"He didn't make it out in time," said Tina. Valor brushed by her, greatly holding both pistols high with green voltage flooding the cords.

"Well we're not going to let him die in vain! Everyone shoot this damn thing!" They unveiled the repulsive blasts. Valor was sure that his energy would be enough to defeat the beast, even though he stood only on its shoulder. Xaliemer refused to allow the earthly pawns to prevail. He uttered an acrid roar to ruin their stance. Only Canavin heard his words from the other side.

"Enough!" said the abrasive voice resonating over the hastening people down below.

Xaliemer, the cause for the deaths of thousands of Pixalians, proved to humanity why he was the ultimate ruling. He raised his arms; the heroes held on tight. In front of everyone—the heroes, the army soldiers, and the reinforcements of the agencies that made their way to the conflict—buildings near the beast broke from the ground and ascended in the air with plenty of scared citizens.

Tina and the team all froze from the peculiar atrocity, becoming almost obsessed with his horrific ability. People stopped their cars, aliens continued their rampages, and Canavin among every single person who was watching, mourned inside of his body. It reminded him of his father's kingdom.

"You humans have a lot of potential," said the voice. "Some of you differ from the others and have power related to the Pixalians. Now you all will share their fate! It is finished!"

The buildings leveled off with one another side by side. Stunningly, they were each wiped out to combine the explosions and scatter plunging bricks. The innocent people were promptly killed in a sharp blink of an eye. An inflated haze formed in the nighttime darkness. Canavin and the other heroes lost their sight temporarily; it returned after a short while. The laughing creatures raced down the many streets and found more human flesh to calm their appetites. The dead population showed the fighters the abomination Xaliemer truly was. The consequences lived on as the remaining soldiers dissolved to pieces while retreating.

Even the Department of Defense was running out of options. The rise of Xaliemer went global.

Tina linked contact with Cyfreid. She said, "Oh my goodness, he just wiped out almost a quarter of the city! Cyfreid, did you just see that?!"

"Of course I saw it! And what are you doing here?!"

"What does it look like? I'm trying to save Cyclohoma!"

"Are the heroes with you?"

"Yes they are…most of them."

"Tina, the council gave specific orders that—"

"You gave me a job! A job to defend the planet from alien threats! Open your eyes Cyfreid! What does this look like to you?!" From down on ground level, Cyfreid smiled and took a brief look at the heroes he was with. They found more Pixalians to battle and they protected the lives of civilians.

"You didn't let me finish *Miss Truman*. I was going to say that the council gave specific orders that we stand down. But I declined to listen. I formed this team, so what I say goes! So wherever you may be, fight with honour! This is your team too! By the way, where are you?"

"I'm currently on the enemy's shoulder."

"Oh…well um, try not to get killed."

"Unfortunately, there are no promises!" She ended the transmission and gave her share of ways to harm Xaliemer.

Xaliemer refused to worry. He only tried to end Canavin's life. The gigantic being swung his arm at Canavin. He fell down a long way and crashed deep into the concrete road, causing high and soundly ripples.

The world famous Canavin coughed and tried to recover from the devastating shock. He watched Xaliemer terrorize more buildings and enterprises. The hero rubbed his face and was alarmed. There was blood, so much that some people confused him for a red alien instead of a bright yellow one. After wiping all he could, he noticed a lot of grazes and contusions. He was weak and looked in the distance to see what appeared to be familiar faces.

"Canavin!" Lynx yelled. "Guys look, it's Canavin! He's hurt!" They finished their creature opponents and came to aid the field leader. Commander Cyfreid moved his strict glare towards him and said, "Man, you better have a way to defeat this *thing*! And I mean you better! Because I don't know how *you* allowed this to happen!" Canavin coughed out the redness and stared angrily at Cyfreid.

"You better watch what you say. I'm doing everything I can to end this." Cyfreid nodded for his unnecessary words; now wasn't the time to be a faultfinder.

"I'm sorry. It's just that…I care so much for Earth."

"And so do I," said Canavin. "And I will find a way to stop him, whatever it takes."

"Wait a minute. How did you say your father defeated Xaliemer?"

"It was some type of a spell." Immediately after Canavin said that, the Commander held on to the alien's shoulders and stated, "Canavin, you *must* possess the same ability as your father!"

"But I don't!" Canavin unfortunately said. "Most of my powers came from my mother and I never knew her. She died after I was born."

"The keyword is *most* Canavin! Please, you have to be a spellbinder of some sort!"

"Cyfreid, I just…I just can't I'm sorry."

"What about Meditation?" Titanium Titan asked.

"Trust me, Meditation won't be that powerful. She is still a mere human. I wish I had the ability, but I don't." They put their heads down with discouragement.

"Well then," the Commander said. "I guess that's it. That is, unless anyone else has a strategy?"

"Canavin, maybe you do have the power but you don't know," said Shade-Master. "I didn't know I was a master of different realms until I was eighteen."

"Really?" said Lynx. "You never told me. That's pretty sad." The moment wasn't a funny one, mainly since Cain X, Bloodblast, Gold-Mine, and Avinotch arrived.

With no hesitation, they surrounded the villains, outnumbering them six to four. Canavin met with his cousin standing face front, bestowing a sullen silence at his unexpected appearance with him doing the same. Commander Cyfreid grabbed the Governor by the collar.

"Why Cain?! Is this the future you had in store for the planet?! Tell me how this is helping us!" The event wasn't the way how the Governor thought it would be. At first, he actually thought that he was doing the planet a favour—minus the crimes he committed and the bribery of remaining the head of AIA Central, but not anymore.

"Cyfreid…I was going to change the world. To control the alien slime that lurks on this planet, like him!" With hatred, he pointed at Canavin.

"Canavin has proven his loyalty! Do you realize that the most well-known hero on the planet is an alien?!"

"Aliens must all die! Their abilities are unknown!"

"Well you're right about one thing," said Canavin aggressively. "Our abilities *are* unknown." He turned to Cyfreid.

"I really don't know how I'm going to do it, but I'm going to try anyways."

"I knew you wouldn't give up on us," he replied. Cain was lost.

"Wait, Cyfreid what is he talking about?"

"He's talking about saving the damn human race! I believe he has a spellbinding power."

"What? Him! I don't believe it!"

"And that's the problem with you crooks these days! Y'all lack faith. Faith is believing the unimaginable!"

"Canavin," said Avinotch. "Do you really think you could do this?"

"Right now, I have nothing else to think of. Xaliemer's control on the Pixalians is crucial to stop. I'm going to need everyone's help with this matter. We must work together."

"Work together with you *people!*" shouted Bloodblast. "Not a chance! Who do you think I am?"

"I think you're Bloodblast. You're an alternate version of Valor. And I know that even though the two of you have different views, you both understand that teamwork is necessary for better results." The anti-hero looked at the other fiends. He agreed to help the heroes. Avinotch accepted and then it was Gold-Mine. All three of them pledged to assist them in the attack. Cain X was too frustrated with his enemies, especially Cyfreid.

"Cain," said the Commander. "Own up!"

"Fine! I'll help. But don't think that this changes anything, Cyfreid. Or should I say, leader of AIA East."

"Whatever you say, leader of AIA Central. Oh wait that's right…you're not anymore."

"Hey Cain," Lynx began. "Why are you known as *Governor* X?"

"That's a private story. Only your friend Silvert knows. Is he currently fighting Xaliemer?"

"No," said Canavin. "You won't be seeing him anymore." Titanium Titan kept quiet.

"Oh…if only I had the privilege to do it."

"Do you want me to shoot you right now?" asked Cyfreid with the muzzle of his gun pressed hard on the Governor's chest.

"Okay, okay. Look let's just get this over with. What's the plan, oh great alien *hero*?"

"We are all going to make our way directly above Xaliemer's head by using Cyfreid's jet. Stan over here will be our aviator. Once we're high enough, Lynx and Bloodblast along with the jet's weaponry will provide us with the necessary ammo. Xaliemer won't see it coming."

"Then what happens when he decides to look up?" Gold-Mine asked Canavin.

"No matter what, you must survive long enough until I can think of the proper incantation to cast Xaliemer away from Earth." Shade-Master faced the alien-hero and said, "It has to be similar to the ritual the other Pixalians try saying to unleash him, but backwards or something. I don't know. I'm just trying to formulate ideas."

"Actually, that's not a bad theory. I'll consider it. Cyfreid, where did you park the jet?" Canavin and the others could only watch as the Commander shook his head with disbelief.

"What's wrong?" Titanium Titan asked.

"My jet. It was parked on top of an enterprise, a certain building that Xaliemer just demolished!" Everyone, the heroes and the rogues, felt Cyfreid's emotional pain.

"We'll find another ship!" Canavin shouted to bring back hope. "Trust me, this war belongs to the humans!" They were surprised to see how an alien could care so much for humanity. Cyfreid was gratified to have him as a member of the team. He touched Canavin on the shoulder and smiled.

"No," he said. "Human or not, this war belongs to the *heroes*." The anger that the alien kept was now lost or possibly saved for another match against Xaliemer. He was a hero, a true defender.

XVIII

FAITH OF OUR MASTERS

THE INFLUENTIAL XALIEMER DIDN'T USE words of persuasion to get the creatures of the Earth to listen to him, but relied on mind control, posing as each and every alien that resided in Cyclohoma City. Canavin and Zan were the lucky ones, or perhaps not in terms of who was receiving the most impairment. Zan, who also had inner Pixalian energy much like Canavin, emitted it to his full potential. All that was brought to the war from Frankie, Celestica, Tina, and Sherman Bawnder were their popping bullets that penetrated the first layer of the surface. Valor's pulse blasts caused the most damage—or what they considered to be damage.

"I'm going to call for backup," said Sherman Bawnder firing bullet holes in the shoulder.

"What do you mean?" the Captain asked.

"I'm referring to the squad that helped me in Cleveland."

"Sherman, we just saw some agents along with many other forces die."

"Not my squad," said Sherman being so sure. Tina didn't understand. She thought that all of the operatives of the specialized departments had already joined the battle, simply to be perished in heart-aching fireworks. She still saw more soldiers spiraling out into burning clusters. The primary fear continued. Tina's limbs became numb; insensible; dazed from the unceasing trauma from Xaliemer's dark and noxious spirit.

She imagined the condition to be different, to be something with more intelligent methods of securing their safety. When she trained with Cyfreid in her months of displeasure, the man used to remind Tina of her audacious personality. He planted an austere, puckish identity that was meant to assist humans from the Pixalian offenders. Tina admitted that she relied on him too much. He was her hero, and his teachings had to live on through her. She obviously refused to be blown to smithereens like the others. The female assassin had to develop a way to be indestructible, just like Sherman. She told Sherman to contact his squad since his faith in their survival didn't wear off. He quickly called them.

"Hello," he started. "This is Sherman Bawnder, I repeat, this is Sherman Bawnder. Does anyone copy?" Tina heard nothing except fuzzy static. Sherman repeated himself.

"Does anyone copy?" At last there was a response.

"This is agent Luke Crimson, over." Agent Luke Crimson was one of the main members of his force. Even when Sherman was interviewed on Marvelous Munroe, he said that he hoped for another chance to work alongside the agents. This was the perfect moment.

"Agent Crimson, this is Agent Bawnder speaking."

"Agent Bawnder? Sherman, where are you? Have you been informed about the disaster that is occurring in Cyclohoma?"

"Agent Crimson, I'm living it right now."

"You're in Cyclohoma? So am I!" The excitement wasn't too grand. Sherman witnessed more warships break apart. A massive fragment came for Tina. He snapped and pulled her away fast. She ogled down the piece from the close call. Sherman continued to speak to Luke.

"Where's the rest of the unit?"

"We got two men down. The rest of us are okay." It was a relief; losing two men wasn't that bad of a result. There were nine agents in total to make his squad. Seven troops remaining meant that his team still had an awaited success. He said, "Unite the survivors and meet me on the enemies left shoulder."

"Yes sir, we'll be there shortly."

"Over and out, Crimson." It was a positive note that help was on the way. He persistently shot the alien surface.

The voltage that Valor provided was becoming too much. The abomination focused to draw all attention to the one who was shooting such an impressive substance. He closed his eyes and formed pestilent phantoms to help search for the source. They wailed aloud until they found the cause. The specters soon vanished; their smog covered the others. The great Xaliemer knew the answer.

He telekinetically raised Valor. The gunman floated high and faced the beast. He insisted on continuing his fearless yet violent behaviour. Valor aimed the weapons at the spitefulness; each blast shot faster than the other.

"Die you beast!"

Fusion Fighter and Meditation flew up to Valor. His swiftness in shooting and the obsession with the monster's death as a sign that meant, *"Don't help me, I got it covered."*

Xaliemer pounded his foot for another step. The ground quaked again, much like during his sinful summoning. He concluded that everything about the soldier was quite similar to the other humans on the planet. Their suspected powers were not so much from internal traits, but more external. They carried artificial weapons to satisfy their avenging cravings. Xaliemer happily grinned, revealing the keen tusks and now knowing the truth.

To end the incoming electrifying blasts, Xaliemer targeted his thoughts on Valor's pistols. The cords that connected to his veins detached and the soldier could only watch as his valuable weapons fell beneath him.

Captain Tina checked her utility belt. Valor was almost not even a threat without the pistols. She had an extra shield generator. She called for Breath-Stealer.

"Hurry!" she screamed. "Give this to Valor right away!" The spirit slithered his way up. Tina was wrong; she should've given Valor the shield from before. His abilities were overestimated. It shouldn't have been the case when facing the most devastating plague.

Breath-Stealer's task of ultimately saving Valor was one he wanted to live long enough to tell his kin. With the defensive device, DeMarcus reached the same height; he was able to hold objects while in his spectral form.

"Valor! Catch this!" He threw the device far enough and the cunning Valor held it. He activated the shield right before Xaliemer's dematerialization process. Valor was now thankful for his team more than the battle of the zombie-like aliens.

The protective holographic sphere had Valor at its center. Xaliemer couldn't harm him. Fusion Fighter descended down to catch the Valoric pistols. The pterodactyl yelled, "Valor, deactivate your shield for a moment!" Xaliemer still had him levitating.

Valor eyed the prize. He deactivated the shield, but at the same time, Xaliemer's force let go. Valor dropped like a descending missile. He was surprised to feel the wind blow even with his helmet on. Fusion Fighter flew downwards and handed Valor back the weapons. While he fell, he wielded them and the cords attached once more to charge up his blood flow. Under the helmet, he gave a crafty smile and fired like a maniac, building a continuous downward stripe of potent holes on the monster's chest.

The sight was epic for the team and everybody else. The many citizens watched the battle from down below. They cheered aloud with great joy as they knew for a fact that the blasts came from the heroic Valor. They were glad that Team Valor was in Cyclohoma defending their alien infested city.

Xaliemer took hammering steps back when trying to resist the Valoric energy. Tina and the alliance crouched to stay put and not roll off. As he saw that Valor would not stop, Xaliemer reminded himself about his capabilities. He became quite surprised by the humans. More incoming ships fired at him intensely. One of them was piloted by Luke Crimson.

"They never fail me!" Sherman shouted with excitement. "I told you my crew is different!" Tina raised her eyebrows being impressed. The enraged Xaliemer began his madness once more. From different locations, wherever people looked, buildings levitated again to be ripped in ruins. Tina couldn't stand it any longer; it was all from their inability to end the threat.

"This is outrageous! That's the second time he did that! People are dying and the blame is going to be on us!" The Captain only made everything else worse, but it was a needed frustration.

"We are giving him everything we got!" Sharp screamed. His slashes were beginning not to do any good. He was tired and then he remembered his vow he gave earlier.

"There has to be an easier way," he said almost noiselessly.

"I know," said Tina. "I'm glad to see that you chose to stay on this team, Curtis. It's what Cyfreid would've wanted."

Curtis put his head down to remember his anger towards the Commander—how close he was to grazing his face. The attempt wasn't right, and now he knew it deeply. No matter what, Cyfreid was a companion. His head rose up and he was completely energetic to show why he was one of Cyfreid's best. His claws grew even longer. The Captain was alarmed and then she smirked affectionately.

"Hold nothing back," she stated. As for the impressive and free falling Valor, Fusion Fighter swooped over, caught hold of his shoulders, and tenaciously carried his body as Valor shot with accuracy. Together, they glided in the air and tried to make one full trip around Xaliemer. The beast swung his arm much like he did with Canavin earlier. Fusion Fighter and Valor were forced to experience a fall that was capable of ending them for good.

"No!" the Captain shrieked. The countless ships were more like flies from what Xaliemer saw. They were all destroyed; Sherman's group of experienced agents jumped out and parachuted down. None of them were crumbled.

Agent Luke Crimson led the agents to where Sherman and the others stood on the monster. He didn't receive the name for no reason. He wore a red leather jacket with a black leotard underneath. His height was about the same as Sherman's.

"Crimson!" Sherman called. "I'm glad that you and the others made it." The other agents were each similar in appearance.

"Now do us all a favour and help blast this thing!"

"I wish I could," said Crimson. "But we have to get off this massive creature right now!"

"Why do you say that?" Sherman asked.

"Because from what I saw, this is no ordinary alien! It's not safe up here! The best way is to take it from the skies!"

"Crimson, did you not see what it can do? Any defensive tactic the United States throws at this beast gets obliterated approximately every ten minutes. The napalm attacks are not even working!"

"Since that you're the boss, I'm going to trust your decision. But remember Sherman, even though you claim to be untouchable, that doesn't mean that a day will not come when you meet death." Sherman was still. He wondered to himself, *"Was it really possible for me to die?"*

"Sherman!" Tina shouted. Her piercing cry caught the attention of the agent and his group. They saw the Captain gawking with her finger pointed across from where they were.

There were several vast pore openings on Xaliemer's neck. Gruesome predators scuttled out of them. They made their way to the shoulder.

"Great God of mercy!" said one of the agents. "Those things just came out of his neck!" Curtis Kareem refrained from his jabs in the skin and focused on the incoming beings.

"Stay behind me!" he said charging for them. Each predator represented a small version of Xaliemer, having the same physical appearances and skills.

Sharp's extended claws made their first move. The telekinesis forced Sharp to float. He was thrown away from the body and traveled an equivalent of one hundred storeys.

"No!" Tina screamed, weeping for the many people that were thrown off from the high height—Valor, Fusion Fighter, and now Sharp. Their survival was unknown. The Xaliemer creatures approached Frankie and Celestica and performed the same action of tossing them away. The last to remain on the shoulder was Sherman Bawnder and his crew, Breath-Stealer, Meditation, Evesdrop, Zan, and Tina Truman whose faith was damaged. Her fear grew larger to be so great that it corresponded with every alien she has ever killed.

It was dark. Curtis's eyes were tightly shut. He somehow survived the fall. The mask was slowly coming off. He tried his best to keep it on. His torso was ratty; his elastic army-green gloves were tainted with plasma like never before. Curtis heard some movements, the sounds being uneven. He opened his eyes and then narrowed the sight. He found himself on a road with aliens of all backgrounds surrounding him.

His index finger protracted to a sharp tine. The hunter attempted to shuffle up. He couldn't do it. The fight was too much, too tiring. They came closer to their chance of the beloved beating. Before he could get up, they were too close. He was ready to admit the suspected truth. It was over. There was no way to defeat Xaliemer, one of the most destructive universal plagues. He was sorry for his team and most importantly, he was sorry for Commander Cyfreid. He closed his eyes again, thinking that it was for the last time.

More noises were apparent. He couldn't pick up on what they were exactly. He wondered if it was the afterlife, a heavenly field where the roads were gold, the grass edges richly lined that had playing children and angels singing praising melodies. Then Curtis thought he was somewhere else; a cruel, ruthless realm of the dead where the sounds were whippings from merciless demons that recalled every horrendous event.

He thought again, and then realized that the whole concept of him even thinking should be impossible. If he was dead, his mind shouldn't be working. He listened closely. The sounds were understood to be rather violent. Curtis was not dead after all. Opening up his eyes, he saw every alien defeated on the road. He slowly rose up, seeing the brutal lesions of the dead bodies. His inner animal could only wonder, "Who came and did all of this?"

In a split second of anxiety, Sharp was held by the neck from someone behind him. The grasp was firm with almost no air seeping through his throat. He was thrown into a local business store and crashed through the glass windows. The people inside who hid from the aliens ran away. Some of the glass shards were wedged inside of him. He quickly took them out. Sharp turned around to be shocked by a returning nightmare.

It was Brute-Spine. His broad hatred was beyond what Sharp encountered in Chicago.

"I told you that no matter where you lurk on this planet, I will find you! It's impossible to escape me! Now I have finally tracked you down!" He sprinted and picked Sharp up. He threw him out of the store and back on the street. Sharp couldn't believe it. He didn't expect Brute-Spine's scent to be that effective at chasing prey.

"How did you find me?! I left you in Chicago after the elevator dropped!"

"Nothing can escape Brute-Spine!" He proved how a nightmare was able to dramatically haunt someone.

"Gary, listen to me! You have to—"

Sharp was picked up and squeezed. He could hear his cracking bones from inside that were close to being fully fragile. Some were still healing from his last match in Illinois.

"Gary!" Sharp's voice became fainter. Brute-Spine laughed blatantly with a vengeance.

"At last, you will die!"

"Gary, please don't! I did nothing!"

"You're a monster! Is that not my job?! To destroy them all?!"

"No Gary…you're the monster."

"Shut up, Curtis!" Brute-Spine squeezed tighter. Sharp had no gaps to move. It seemed as if the hero couldn't survive one day where he didn't feel like he was going to die. With no options of offense standing, Sharp continued his attempts at trying to talk the brute out of it.

"Listen Gary! You need to stop now! This is not you!"

"This is exactly me! I know it!"

"No! No you don't! Don't you remember? You're my best friend, Gary Herman! Even yesterday, you said that Gary is no more, but now you insist that you *are* him!" Brute-Spine became silent. Then he continued his contradictions.

"No...there's no Gary!"

"Yes there is, you just agreed you were him! Fight it Gary, fight it now! Don't let this *thing* take over you!" The grip loosened completely. Brute-Spine held his head with a paining sensation. He was confused. The voices in his head were louder than they should've been.

"Stop!" he yelled at the top of his lungs. Sharp was free and in front of his lost friend.

"Yes Gary! You're doing it! Fight it!"

"No! I can't! Ah!"

"Yes you can, don't doubt yourself! I know you can hear me! Let go of the hatred!" Brute-Spine tried to let go. Gary Herman was inside there somewhere. He clamped his head the tightest he could and tried to focus. Brute-Spine took his hands off and stared at Curtis.

"Gary?" Sharp asked hoping for his friend to return. He held Sharp by the neck again and shouted, "Gary Herman is dead!" He used both hands to lift him. His fat thumbs pushed harder. Sharp was unable to swallow any gulps. He creaked a doleful voice saying, "Gary."

"He's dead! Brute-Spine is all who remains!" Sharp was saddened by those hurting words.

"When I'm done with you, I'm going to finish Cyfreid!"

"Brute-Spine," Sharp said softly. "There is something that I want you to understand."

"What is it Curt?!" Sharp tried to catch his breath, but there was no way to do so. While suffocating, he recited the words of Captain Tina Truman.

"The Commander has made mistakes, but just because Cyfreid may seem wretched...that doesn't mean he's a bad person."

"Why do you insist on being loyal to him?!"

"Because," said Sharp. He finally swallowed a gulp. "Because he's my friend."

His brotherly feelings for Cyfreid were expressed. It scared Sharp as if his own claws were used against him, shredding parts physically and emotionally. He knew it was true. Cyfreid was always there for him. Brute-Spine couldn't accept it. He pressed his thumbs to meet the other fingers.

Sharp jabbed every claw in his arms to be free. He jumped and had enough airtime to speedily cut his face. The nocturnal animal snarled ferociously with his mouth fully moist and his spikes sparking in the cold night. He felt that if Gary was gone, then this was his retaliation. The monster that took over Gary Herman had to be punished. Whenever Brute-Spine tried to strike, Sharp got him first and stopped at nothing.

Xaliemer's uproar was boosted. More Cyclohoma citizens changed to ashes. Aliens were still hungry and Canavin believed that he was the key to ending it all.

Having recently making a temporary allegiance with the last villains of the 'X Viles', their search for the proper sky-fighter continued.

"Maybe I can call Tina for some help," said Cyfreid.

"Good idea," Canavin replied. Cyfreid spoke into his communicator.

"Tina," he started.

"This isn't the right time, Cyfreid! I'm in the middle of fighting a bunch of Xaliemers!"

"Yes I know Xaliemer…wait a minute, did you just say a bunch of Xaliemers?"

"Yes! There are many of them! They just crawled out of his skin!"

"Then this is worse than I thought. Do you have access to a ship of any kind?"

"No we don't but…" She remembered Sherman's agents. "Actually, yes we do!"

"Send a team to pick us up. Our coordinates are—"
The transmission ended unexpectedly.

"Tina? Tina?!"

"What happened?" asked Titanium Titan.

"The channel was cut off."

"We got to move right now," Shade-Master insisted. Governor X stopped Cyfreid and the others from continuing to walk.

"I can call some more AIA Central troops," he told them. Cyfreid crossed his arms.

"How many times do I have to remind you that you are fired from AIA services?"

"And for what Cyfreid? You know, you used to be different."

"I was never like you and never will be. And besides, you can't call a single person anymore. I'm sure that whoever their new leader is won't approve of anything from your mouth."

Cain kept quiet when understanding that Cyfreid was correct. Canavin led the group down the roads to get them closer.

The Xaliemer looking aliens mimicked the very powers of the original. The members of Sherman's crew fought courageously. Survival wasn't promised in the war, as Tina quoted from the start. Sherman was punctured, resembling the corpse he used to be that scampered its way to the surface. The regent was ready for more.

His gladness was from his lack of experiencing death. His moves were nothing compared to the aliens. They were learning; their brain capacity was increasing to realize how humans fought their opponents. A creature stopped one of Sherman's punches and rotated his arm, nearly snapping the bone. Agent Bawnder bawled out a distressful mourn and stepped back. Tina wished to help. She had to defend herself from three Xaliemers.

Sherman's agents came to her rescue. Tina's gun was running out of ammo. She decided to switch to her projectile blaster.

"Why do more keep coming?!" she asked as more of them crawled out of the big pores.

"It's just like on Star-Pix," said Zan. "From the stories I heard growing up with Canavin, my people referred to them as Xaliemites!"

"More like gigantic termites if you ask me!" Tina looked back and saw one of Sherman's team members die before her. Another went down in total misery. A Xaliemite gripped Tina by her waist and opened its mouth wide for a nasty bite. Her legs quavered to try and escape the seizing choppers from meeting her face.

"No!" yelled Sherman. He astoundingly tackled the beast. Tina landed on her back. *Another close call.*

She saw the match that now included Sherman. The remaining agents fronted her to shoot at the other predators. Still down, Tina took a look at the battle. The Xaliemite died with blue substance flowing out. She got up and ran towards Sherman.

"Are you alright?!" she asked loudly.

"Tina," he began. "I don't think I'm going to make it out of this."

"What are you saying? Don't say that, you're indestructible!"

"I...I know, but right now I don't feel that way." He coughed out a load of the substance.

"I need you! Stay with me!"

"Okay. Okay then...I'll try." It was xenophobia that almost got the best of Sherman. Captain Tina helped him to his feet.

Zan, being the last of the Canavin Clan to stay put on the shoulder, was now expected to have the most kills with Meditation, Breath-Stealer, and Evesdrop. He was a Pixalian of strong force. The power amazed all of them and made simple handguns seem obsolete in nature. Every tactic was still needed to defeat all of the Xaliemites. Luke Crimson rallied his troops and together, the bullets and the Pixalian light blasts made an almost never ending offensive power, sounding much like a machine gun. Zan knew the way to stop the aliens.

"Someone needs to head over to the neck and shoot at his pores. It's the only place where the Xaliemites are coming from!"

"Can't you do it?!" Crimson shouted back. "Since you seem to know so much!"

"Alright, but you need to be able to handle the Xaliemites without me!"

"You might want to hurry up!" The Pixalian flew to reach the neck fast. There were many holes and Zan didn't know where to start. He blasted one, and then another, and many more after that. With all of the pores closed and bruised, he returned to lead the agents to victory with the fighters as assistance.

The fight continued for minutes until it was finished. The haunting Xaliemites were defeated with convulsing hands. The casualties had insufficient luck from the battle. Sherman's squad was shrinking in numbers.

Agent Crimson took out a small gadget from his red jacket.

"What's that?" asked Tina.

"It's a homing beacon that signals a receiver built inside of the ship." The unharmed ship remained high above Xaliemer. Within seconds, it returned to their level and the top seal opened.

"Alright everyone get in right now, and bring the bodies too. This is not going to be a good sign for their families."

Tina and Meditation helped Sherman inside. Zan and the survivors carried the dead operatives. Crimson started up the system and was ready to depart from Xaliemer. Nothing was working. They needed to interpret a proper plan. Xaliemer noticed the ship and turned to his left. He opened his exhaling parasite mouth.

"Go now!" Breath-Stealer said. Agent Crimson flew away; it wasn't far enough. The air pressure from Xaliemer's roar caught hold of the ship and blew them away. Crimson lost control and the ship spun around as it descended. Everyone kept their heads down.

"I don't have any control! There's nothing I can do, we are going to crash!" Even from ground level, the people of Cyclohoma City saw the event—a rolling dot in the air—and were completely worried. Aliens arrived and chased the huge crowd away to end their watch.

Xaliemer was pleased with his success. Cyclohoma City was now his to rule. The abominating force demolished more skyscrapers than before. The burning city bared its own identity as the underworld.

"Pull up!" Evesdrop shouted with her front eyes open and the others closed.

"What do you *think* I'm trying to do?!" Crimson gave it more effort. There was no triumph from the fall.

"Crimson!" the injured Sherman Bawnder said to catch his friend's attention. "It's up to you! Our lives are at stake at this very moment! You must pull up!" Crimson couldn't argue with a word from Sherman Bawnder. He tried to interact with ships that could've been nearby.

"Mayday, mayday! This is Agent Crimson from the Bawnder unit! We are going to crash and we need assistance. Does anybody at all copy?" Upon hearing no response, the distressed agent remembered that they were all dead. He meditated briefly to avoid the drama of the passengers.

"Okay," he quietly said. He tried once more, this time straining his muscles. In a short time, the ship successfully leveled in the air.

"There we go!"

"Now that's the Crimson I remember," said Sherman. The other agents exhaled and their heartbeats returned to normal paces. They looked through the window to see the fireworks of the buildings. Xaliemer was in good condition, practically a perfect state, like the fresh transcendent figure that climbed out of the glowing sarsen. Hell was on earth. Only certain humans were branded as slaves, which was actually a blessing compared to the crushed majority. Captain Tina and the rest were aware that their fight against him was futile.

Alyssa Munroe, the news woman of Marvelous Munroe, was currently inside of a helicopter. The cameras were rolling.

"The top and tragic story for tonight is the invasion of a monster that I have never seen in my life. Civilians all over Cyclohoma are in a state of siege because of the aliens. This…this just might be the end of the city, trapped in an alien apocalypse that's able to spread to nearby towns in the west region. We have witnessed several people die, and word is unknown about the terrifying falls of great protectors like Valor and Canavin. We don't have any way to end the threat."

Many people around the world were informed and anxious for the survival of Cyclohoma. From back at AIA East headquarters, the staff bit their lips. Others gave up hope and agreed that Xaliemer simply could not be defeated. Two members were inside of the medical room.

"If the Commander dies, then what?" asked an average janitor.

"The Commander won't die," said the main nurse. "He's better than that. And so are Miss Truman and the heroes."

"Yes, but what if you're wrong? Who knows, they're probably dead right now."

"I'm going to access the jet's communication system."

"Okay. But if there's no response then I quit being a janitor."

"Don't you have some place to clean?!" The nurse's voice rose to a point that made the janitor scatter away. She shook her head and accessed the system.

"Is anyone there? Draymond?" It was a failure. The nurse looked back at the television only to hear more from Alyssa Munroe.

"Several ships that orbited the monster were destroyed, thus disrupting the attack process. Lost forces include the FBI, CIA, and fighters from AIA sectors including that from the east headquarters. God, if this is truly the end of the world, please forgive us for our sins."

The nurse broke into tears that flowed down her uniform. The janitor returned and asked, "Any luck?" When seeing her cry, he said, "Okay, then it is official. I quit."

"Leave! Or else I'll find someone to fire you!"

"Lady, did you not hear me? I said I quit. Besides, AIA East is pathetic to me. I have a family to protect in the capital." The janitor dropped his broom and departed, never to come back. Still with tears, she remembered the one thing Tina told her to do: put the silver necklace back around Jamal's neck. She told herself that she had to obey the Captain. Walking to the bed with Jamal on it, she moved his head forward and put the chain necklace on. She spoke to the dead body.

"It's heroes like you that this world needs. And I pray to God that the team will triumph. You were and will always be remembered as a protector of nations. And we should never seek revenge on our enemies. Instead, we should change them. Change the way they act, the way they see things. The only way for people to get rid of their enemies is to make them their friends." She delicately held Jamal's hand.

"Thank you Jamal. Actually, thank you *Silvert*." The nurse walked out looking at the monitor, the endless sound of the straight line. Then she looked at the ceiling, but truly believed she was staring at the Lord in Heaven. She grinned and left the room.

Times were officially tough from the alien apocalypse. Hope was still able to found with the power of faith. And even in such a dispiriting circumstance, the future was not determined. With nobody to stand foot in the medical area, the electrocardiograph symbolized the unusual and yet, the impact of confidence. It beeped.

XIX

WE'RE THE MASTERS NOW

PIXALIANS FROM ALL OVER CYCLOHOMA
were greatly feared thanks to their minds being heavily under
the control of Xaliemer's massive force. Most of the alien
species were feared from the start. The people could only rely
on those who fought for justice like Canavin.

An hour passed from his meeting with Cyfreid's group
and Cain's rogues. The concerned hero was running out of
options. He was able to fly to attack Xaliemer alone again;
some backup would increase the chances of winning. To make
matters seem even more disrupting, Canavin and the group
spotted a familiar creature—one to truly blame for the dire
situation. *"Identymous."*

He sat on the side of a street where no possessed
extraterrestrials seemed to wander. While running down the
same road, Canavin shouted, "It's Identymous!"

Shade-Master, Titanium Titan, and Lynx saw the
villainous being for the very first time and were disgusted by
his physical traits. Canavin rushed faster than anyone else.
The aiding villains moved the slowest. He reached near and
Identymous tried to leave immediately. The creature was too
late. Canavin was swift and fierce. He brought Identymous to
the road and threw a punch. With the sinister alien wounded,
Canavin forced him to stare at the freed Xaliemer.

"Look! That's the monster you unleashed! The reality
is facing the city! Many people are dying and it's all because
of you!" Identymous, who now feared Canavin, was also fed
up with the cruelty the beast portrayed.

"I know," he simply said. "If only there was a way to
stop him."

"There is! I believe there's another ritual to destroy him for good! Do you know what it could be?!" Canavin's dark scars were enough to tell the creature how serious he was about the issue. With all of the cautiousness of the heroes and villains circling around, Identymous gave a bogus laugh that expressed his thought of failure.

"There is no ritual," he said. "He can't be stopped."

"What do you mean he can't be stopped?"

"I'm sorry, Canavin. And I'm sorry for all of you."

"Yea, well I'm not accepting your apology," said Titanium Titan. He readied his nun chucks.

"Hold on there," said Canavin. The Pixalian warrior willed himself to uncover the truth. He said to Identymous, "Tell me, how is it that you are not controlled and yet, you said the words of the reading of Xaliemer?"

Identymous peeked behind Canavin to see the frustration from all of them. The remaining members of Cain's alliance were furious with him. His sight shifted back to Canavin who had no other way of attacking left but the energy within him. He missed Pixcalibur. If he had it, he agreed that he would use its mighty supremacy on Identymous. He needed to fill that hole, that heavy twinge of a blamed deed. Identymous saw the energy signature around Canavin's body, spangled cerulean just like the stones. The creature was the target in the eyes of everyone, including Cain X.

"Okay, okay people! I...it just so happens that I knew the reading of Xaliemer before you all searched for the Pixaliemain." Canavin couldn't believe the words.

"You mean to tell me that you were—"

"Immune from the very beginning...yes."

"But why Identymous? How?" Everyone wanted an answer.

"Xaliemer was trapped inside of the Pixaliemain rock, the same your father sealed him in. I knew that in order to unleash him, I would need a sample piece. It's impossible to just say the hex from anywhere and not have the spirit of the beast nearby."

"So when you unleashed him, you were never under his spell?!"

"No Canavin, I wasn't. I was reciting from memory. Xaliemer had nothing to do with it. And...I lied. There is a ritual to defeat him. But it would only work if there was a—"

"Pixaliemain sample," said Canavin sadly.

"Well what are we waiting for?!" screamed Cyfreid. "The Pixaliemain rocks couldn't have traveled that far. We just need to find one and—"

"They were all destroyed!" Canavin shouted with melancholy. Cyfreid was thunderstruck. His jaw slightly came down. He respired out for a while and asked, "Did you just say they're destroyed?"

"All of them. They're all gone." In the time of despair, Identymous said, "Well then that's that. Pixaliemain is an ancient rock. Its effects are linked back to Canavin's father. And I doubt Canavin is the *same* person."

"You doomed us all."

"No Canavin, your father doomed us all. He should've just destroyed the rocks all those years ago."

"You're going to blame this on him?! After everything that *you* did, you're going to say it's his fault?! What's the reading Identymous?!"

"What did you say?" he asked pretending he misheard.

"I said, what's the reading?! I know that you're familiar with it!"

"Canavin! It won't work without Pixaliemain!"

"Just tell me now!"

From the sides of good and evil that all revealed plentiful sins, they never heard Canavin scream like that to anyone. Identymous was always known to be a trickster. Before Identymous was able to make his decision, Shade-Master bellowed, "Aliens, and they're in great numbers!" They stared down the road and saw a full army of controlled ethnic Pixalians.

"Oh shi—" said Lynx being too much in awe to finish. There were eleven of them counting Identymous and nearly two hundred marching monsters. Identymous tried to escape until Canavin stopped him and said, "Oh no you don't! You got us into this mess so you're going to fight like a soldier!" Identymous was afraid of Canavin and the incoming alien army. The affliction was too much. He shook his head, unsteady from an emerging seizure.

"Yes…this is how I die," said Lynx. "They're going to write it in the papers. Slaughtered by alien troops."

"At least you have agility! All I got is bare knuckles because I'm running out of realms to send these things!"

"Wait a second!" Canavin cried out. "Say that again!"

"At least you have agility."

"No, after that Shade!" Canavin was beginning to catch on to an idea that could actually work.

"I said that I'm running out of realms."

"That's the answer right there! You need to send Xaliemer to a different dimension! One that's not inhabited by anybody! Is there a world you can think of?"

"Well…yes but I doubt I can make an entrance portal that tremendous in size." The army was reaching close.

"Not only that," said Cyfreid. "But if he could, the attractive pull could suck half of the city."

"Cyfreid," Canavin calmly said. "What other way is there?" The question amplified the urge of ridding the world of Xaliemer once and for all. Cyfreid couldn't think of an answer.

"I don't know," said the Commander. Canavin already predicted his words. He touched Shade-Master on the shoulder and said, "I need you to make that portal. Please Shade-Master." It was a moment that Axel would never forget; the greatest hero in the world, asking him for help.

"But the size for that is too—"

"Never doubt yourself, especially not now. The city needs you. And a matter of fact, I need you."

When joining the team, Shade-Master considered himself to be a minor. He was never qualified for the team, much like Hiro Matsuo. The leading Commander Cyfreid wasn't familiar with him before they met. This gave him the confidence to embrace the time of need. He said, "Alright Canavin. But I need some time to develop the passageway."

"We'll give you time! How long do you need?"

"Approximately half an hour." Canavin hoped that wasn't accurate. He wanted the period to be shorter.

"Okay," he said. Accepting the required timeframe was difficult. He promised to make enough time for Shade-Master; unfortunately, it had to wait.

The predators reached them. Their front ranks provided the most revulsion. The merged groups were prepared for battle. Cyfreid and Cain X made the first move by shooting concurrently. Deep within their frames of mind, it reminded them of old times they shared. They showed no affection towards the aliens and certainly no fondness for each other. When some of the aliens died from the offensive ammo, one creature gave a signal for the others to halt. They were intelligent from Xaliemer and what he learned about the imperfect human race.

"What just happened?" Titanium Titan asked. Nobody wanted to answer. They observed as every creature pulled out weapons that belonged to all of the fallen agencies.

"Everyone watch out!" screamed Canavin. No matter how hard they tried, there was nowhere to hide from them. Bullets from all over the street were more flamboyant than imaginable. The creatures' knowledge grew to such an extent, that they finally understood what the firepower of human technology was capable of doing. Bloodblast refused to go out like a pawn. He fired his bazooka to destroy a sufficient amount of them.

"Good shot!" yelled Lynx. With his silent juncture, Lynx realized that Bloodblast wasn't pleased with the group. To have the same glorifying satisfaction, Lynx electrocuted his amount and smiled at Bloodblast to boast.

Titanium Titan was set with a vital test. This was the time for him to be efficient with his combat skills. He wasn't trying to prove anything to anyone. There was a certain alien that wouldn't keep its eyes off Hiro. As the titan spun his nun chucks, the creature snatched them from him. It was smarter than the others when being a humanoid with a lot of potential. Its lack of physicality surprised Hiro the most. The alien ran away holding the metal weapons into a smoky apartment building.

The distinctive nun chucks had a background meaning; the gift of his wise, plangent sensei of many talents. Most people would ignore the situation, but not Hiro Matsuo. He insisted on retrieving the weapons, though it was considered to be reckless. There was no telling what the result would be. Titanium Titan went into the building in search of the atypical and unpredictable predator. Canavin and the others were too busy to worry about him as they each confronted the galactic army, squadron against squadron. From inside, Hiro focused to sense where the alien could be creeping.

It wasn't a large apartment, having a simple stairs, an elevator, and a total of eight floors. Hiro searched high and low and found no alien. He calmed himself down and meditated. The sound of pattering footsteps hovered up the creaking stairs, higher, so much to a point where the answer was clear. He was sure of its location. It was at the pinnacle, as he expected.

Reaching the level, he looked around and the creature stood as if it was waiting for his arrival. Titanium Titan smiled and thought of the things he was going to do. He ran and attacked only to see that the alien dodged his strike. It was hasty much like him. Hiro made a second move and was too slow. His temper—like everyone's from time to time—rose again. Titanium Titan shrieked to catch the creature's attention. Immediately, he grabbed his nun chucks and fought. The alien kept speaking Xaliemer's words. It said he was nothing, a failure, a misfit, a misguided soul, and a murderer. Hiro stopped and couldn't imagine how Xaliemer was familiar about his actions. What he didn't know was that the beast was very experienced at playing mind games. The hesitant Hiro paced back with sudden shock.

"How did you know?" The monster was a caliginous bat with fleecy texture that had stubby ears mixed with Pixalian antennae. It jumped on Hiro with its overawing mouth stretched wide to make its way into his chest. The titan pushed off the predator and ran to reach the roof.

He took his time to rest until the threat returned. It gradually advanced and continued to say words that attacked Hiro's mind. They were personal and related to his childhood, his days learning from his sensei, and quotes from opponents he faced. It was too much for Hiro to bear.

"Stop!" From the body of the humanoid, Xaliemer was literally picking pieces of memory and emphasizing the negative thoughts at a rate that was able to easily demoralize Hiro. It was a struggle to contest the monster. Every time Hiro wanted to fight, the creature would recite words he tried to forget. He agreed that it was enough and charged at the alien until it unexpectedly had the voice of Captain Tina Truman.

"What are you doing?!" the alien yelled. Hiro stopped.

"Tina?" he said. He was losing himself and forgetting what was true and untrue. He saw that it was clearly an alien species, but Xaliemer was intellectually powerful. It was almost like a dream, a sense that nothing was correct but he still went with it anyways.

"Why would you do that?" said the predator.

"Why would I do what?" asked Titanium Titan.

"How could you?! How could you lie?!" The expressed tone was one hundred percent the same as Tina's voice. The dreaded phrase of his mistake crippled him perfectly.

"I said I was sorry!"

"That's it! You are done! Do you hear me?! Done!" He disapproved of living through it again.

"Shut up!" he yelled coming back to proper thinking. He fought the creature and at last got precise hits. The voice of the alien returned back to the parasite screeches, coming from a beast of the night. Hiro was sure that the creature was going to die, especially after what happened.

Minutes passed and he still found himself in the match. The alien had added characteristics; he mimicked constant moves and created ways of defending them. There was no way to stop it unless the source was destroyed, and from the negativity that Identymous showed, it seemed like it was nearly impossible.

The bloodsucker was surviving the most. It had the least amount of welts on its body. Hiro was terribly sore by his opponent whom he refused to clarify as worthy.

After time, it got the best of Hiro and made him step too far back to the ledge of the apartment. There was no way to free himself of the predator except for jumping. Its face up close was like prodded daggers that twisted his reactions. This time, it possessed the voice of his old sensei.

"You are beaten," it said with the judgment of sagacity. Trying harder than before, Hiro spun his nun chucks fiercely. The attempt meant nothing as the monster took one step forward to cause Hiro to take a step back.

He fell and gripped the ledge with one arm. He looked down and witnessed the battle he should've never left.

"You will never become a *true* hero," said the creature with his sensei's tone.

"Please stop this!"

"You must let go, Hiro. Let go of everything, your past and your future. Focus on what is right. Take that leap of faith. You must let go of the ledge." With the intense mind control, Xaliemer was bright. He knew that Hiro looked up to his old master and would obey him.

Hiro insisted on not falling for the trick again. He strongly held on until it took his hand and dangled him from above. Hiro scoffed at the thing and even with his mordant outcry, the alien sneered. There was no forestalling what it was going to do. Hiro was dropped.

He thought to himself, *"Was this what I deserved?"* And his final answer was 'yes'. It was his epiphany. He wasn't fit for a task that involved saving the city or the world. The doubts were returning at the critical life-threatening point. The fall was too great; he wanted to yell for help, but what would it do? His death would be his way of truly admitting that he was sorry for the wrong he has done. His sorrow would be enough to kill the grief of Captain Tina. He felt that she along with the rest would be better off without him. Hiro closed his eyes while he fell, saying a farewell to his once appreciated life of heroism.

In the situation of low self-esteem and pity, there was a savior. The trail was faster than what was imaginable, being a thin darting flash of light. It was silver. It passed by and caught Hiro to save his life. Titanium Titan opened his eyes and saw the bird's-eye view of the rapid moving city. Everything was inaccurate with facts. He wondered what the cause was. He glanced back and his heart nearly stopped. It was not *what* saved him, but instead it was *who* came to his rescue. The excitement enabled him to shout with confusion.

"Silvert?!"

Jamal Vertison was back. After the miraculous beep on the electrocardiograph, there were multiple heart contractions. Jamal began to breath and woke up to hear the grievous news of the calamitous Cyclohoma City. With him being the only one in the medical center, he shifted to his silver form and left the headquarters at full speed west. An hour later, he saved Titanium Titan.

Silvert landed on a separate street and Hiro was lost and began to ask questions. Silvert explained everything. Hiro was joyous to hear Jamal's voice once again and wished to make it up to him. He embraced his presence and sniveled with tears.

"I...I thought you were dead. I'm so sorry Jamal! I was wrong to hurt you! You deserved better than what was handed to you!"

"Hiro, listen I—"

"You shouldn't have saved me. I was completely jealous and impatient for my success. My actions should lead me to prison."

"Hiro, just hear what I have to—"

"I'm so sorry! Just...just take me in! A person like me needs to be behind bars."

"Hiro, would you just shut up for a moment?!" He finally got Titanium Titan's awareness.

"It was also my fault. I threw the first punch, remember? And from my Silver Explosion...it could've been your death. And for that Hiro, *I am sorry.*" Hiro was calm. Jamal's lively complexion resembled an alleged bright future for both of them.

"So how's about we put aside our differences and save the planet…even if it's our last time doing it."

"We'll do it together," said Titanium Titan. "Just like old times." The union of the duo returned, and it was nothing short of a miracle.

Curtis Kareem continued his long lasting battle with Brute-Spine. It was a sweet hour of punishment with complex perforations that the brute would never forget. The fight reached the same street of the battlefield of invading aliens and the unity of heroes and villains.

Sharp was too focused on his blood-spattered adversary when he accepted that Gary's spirit was long gone. Lynx sighted the match and recognized Brute-Spine.

"Hey!" he cried out. "Isn't that the man we met in Chicago?" Shade-Master killed a Pixalian creature and turned to see the fight.

"Yea man, I think he is!"

"Let's go help Sharp! We owe it to him!" Before he was able to run, Cyfreid stopped him. He also recognized Brute-Spine and was the only one who knew about his past.

"Trust me," he said. "That's Sharp's fight. He has it covered. You definitely don't want to get involved." Lynx and Shade-Master looked at each other being faintly bemused.

"Whatever you say," said Lynx. "Besides, he looks like he's going to be the victor."

"He will be. I can guarantee it." The Commander's faith in Sharp made him penitent for his actions. He left the decision for Sharp to make: defeat Brute-Spine or confront Gary from inside. The options were totally up to him. He only required Sharp to make the right choice.

The fury was past its supposing boundary. His growls enriched the grisly landscape. Sharp wouldn't back down.

"Curtis!" Brute-Spine said bursting out trepidation. "Please stop! Just stop fighting!" Sharp backed away, his claws anxious to continue. He asked, "What is it, Brute-Spine?!" He refused to refer to him as Gary Herman.

Brute-Spine was toppled over. As overweight as he was, the large man rose up. The red battle scars were slit open. They drained on his body, growing the agonizing mood.

One of the invading aliens from the ongoing battle ran down the road behind him.

"I just wanted to tell you that—"

"Brute-Spine, watch out!"

The intense and earsplitting scream caused Cyfreid to refrain from shooting and twist around to see Curtis among a deplorable occurrence.

The creature had an arm shaped like a spear. With it as its advantage, the alien impaled Gary's rough spine and stuck the spear out from the front.

"No!" Sharp screamed. The monster took its spear out and the heavy Brute-Spine dropped down. Sharp was almost too frozen to move. Even when he ferociously fought Brute-Spine, Curtis never wanted him to die. His actions were meant to prove a point.

He faced to the murdering alien. Sharp knew that it was controlled by Xaliemer. He didn't care whether or not it would be the same result if the creature wasn't under the influence. Sharp looked at his hand; the tips of the claws sparkled. He removed the smeared gloves to see his molded fingers. The bullets luckily shot passed Cyfreid as he watched from afar.

The spear creature was up against the sharp-clawed man. As the alien charged for him, Sharp thought about everything that occurred and said, "This is for you Gary!" He ran with his bare hands in front of him. Then he dashed to travel directly through the body of the monster. He came out and was covered with the foul residue. He watched the creature die on the road.

Sharp rushed for Brute-Spine and shouted, "C'mon, stay with me Brute-Spine! Be brave!" Brute-Spine refused to perish before saying his final words to Curtis Kareem. He looked at him and smiled; it was the first time Sharp saw him give a smile that actually meant something. Sharp listened closely for his whispering message.

"I'm...I'm sorry Curt."

The voice was more poignant than before, moving the animal of Curtis to sleep, figuratively giving a fair, gracious touch to his heart. It wasn't the same obnoxious voice. It was a voice Curtis missed so dearly—the voice of Gary Herman. He closed his eyes for the last time.

Curtis Kareem, the animalized man for rupturing predators, cried for his friend. His feelings were a mixture of sorrow and joy. The sorrow was for the loss of Brute-Spine and the joy was the realization that Gary Herman was truly deep inside of the body all along. He wiped away the tears only to find Cyfreid behind him.

"Let's go," said Cyfreid who witnessed everything. "We have to help the others."

"He was there all along. Gary was still there."

"I know, Curt. I know." He looked at the saddened Sharp and said, "I need you in this battle. Can you help me?"

It was a relative question when compared to the one he gave back at the mansion. Although Sharp lost his best friend, Cyfreid was a friend as well.

"Yes," he said. "I can do that."

"Good," said the Commander. They ran to help the others. Their success was the only thing on their minds.

Valor woke up. He found himself on top of a building. He looked to his side and saw Fusion Fighter. Xaliemer destroyed more edifices. Some of the falling bricks blocked the paths of the scattered people.

"Mark…Mark wake up," said Valor.

"W-what…what happened?"

"We must've fallen asleep after that drop."

Fusion Fighter's foggy sight cleared up and noticed floating buildings explode.

"You mean to tell me that we slept through this?! And we're on top of a building that could've been demolished?!"

"I guess so. It looks like we just got lucky."

"Where are the others?"

"I'm not sure, but I'm going to do something that I never would've imagined me doing."

"Okay, what's that?" Valor took out his communicator.

"I'm going to contact Cyfreid." He sent the transmission and the Commander gave him his coordinates. Fusion Fighter clamped onto Valor's shoulders and flew him to the destination. It was not far from where they were. They arrived and observed a war on the street. Valor fueled his inner static ammo.

"What the heck is wrong with Cyfreid?! He never mentioned this!" While Fusion Fighter carried him, he shot at the creatures from above.

Silvert descended on the road with Titanium Titan. Hiro drew out the nun chucks while Silvert blasted the monsters to their demise.

Cyfreid along with Cain and the two factions stopped, being fortunate enough not to get shot. They began to ask themselves if they were seeing the ghost of Jamal. Silvert looked at all of them and asked, "Are you people going to just stand there or are you going to fight?!" His commanding words were words of enlightenment from the heroes' perspective. Cain X—Silvert's prime adversary—was surprised how the hero didn't ask questions as to why his group was around Cyfreid and the others.

Valor and Fusion Fighter landed and helped in the battle. The gun-wielding soldier stood beside Canavin and Silvert. The Pixalian smiled at his heroic companions. He remembered his theory at the headquarters. The war was enough to tell him that it was worth a shot.

The three of them combined the incredible luminosity from their blasts: the silver strikes, the green Valoric Energy, and the blue Pixalian rays. The prodigious flare destroyed alien troops among several more after that. They kept firing and the rays helped the team more than ever. Aliens from all over were falling, their squeals flooding the air. Some retreated from the contrasting beam. The miraculous success continued when some of the heroes looked up to see a descending aircraft. The seal opened and Agent Crimson ran out along with the rest of the team, including Frankie and Celestica.

Cyfreid said to Cain, "That's *my* team." The Governor ignored him and fired his bullets beside the villains.

Avinotch saw the same traits of his heroic counterpart as he did in Chicago, only now the former Prince of Star-Pix encouraged more destruction. He contained necessary rage for the safety of Earth, the second home for Pixalians.

Avinotch stood in the front ranks beside his cousin to increase the Pixalian firepower. Bloodblast did the same for Valor, and Gold-Mine helped Silvert.

With his thoughts still on the death of Brute-Spine, Sharp had an intellect to avenge Gary. He felt that every alien was to blame. Nearby, there was Lynx, Shade-Master, and Commander Cyfreid. Calling them his friends was an honour.

A freakish monster leapt like a cheetah towards Lynx. Sharp shouted, "Lynx watch your back!" He looked behind him and electrocuted the creature to a burnt crisp. Sharp and Shade-Master were impressed.

"You know," said Sharp. "I could've saved your ass if your reflexes were not as quick." Lynx had a sullen glare.

"And get my thighs stabbed? I don't think so." Sharp smirked and hewed the monsters that came close.

As Tina and Sherman—who was fully healed from his fight with the Xaliemite—fought with Celestica, Frankie, and Zan, the Captain noticed the presence of Titanium Titan. She shot down an alien humanoid and ran towards him to yell, "What in God's name are you doing here?!"

"Look Tina! I'm not here to listen to you ramble on about my mistakes! I'm here alongside the greatest heroes to save the planet! So if you're going to kick me off this squad, fine! But right now, stay out of my way!" His response made Tina understand his recent change in behavior. Hiro realized that this was bigger than him. He added, "And another thing, Jamal's alive."

"What? Silvert is—"

"Just look ahead, *Miss* Truman." Her eyesight traveled beyond the predators and her heart skipped a beat when seeing

Silvert with Canavin, Valor, and the criminals. It was strange according to her since she just noticed him now. She desperately wanted to approach him although it wasn't the right time. She continued her role in the war.

After seeing his precious 'X Viles' aid the three heroes, Cain X agreed that his team was no more. From Gustavo to the Titanic and the others, he considered Bloodblast, Avinotch, and Gold-Mine to be dead. He saw everyone's contribution and decided he was not welcome. The Governor slowly paced back into a dark alley and fled away.

After a while, his departure became noticeable. Cyfreid approached Captain Tina. Being with her in the battlefield resembled the last night when they constantly shot at the corrupted AIA opposition.

"So what do you call this?" asked Tina.

"I call it a war of saviours and predators!"

"That's the obvious. Is it anything close to what you've experienced before?"

"Not a chance!" The Commander and Tina were very accurate with their shooting. As the last of the galactic assemblage fell in defeat, Tina noticed that the deaths were in the same area where the Governor used to be. She asked Cyfreid, "Where's Cain X?" Cyfreid looked around and accepted the facts.

"He must've run off."

"I guess nothing ever changes!" She rolled to her side and shot from that angle. Ever since joining AIA East, not a single day was normal.

Xaliemer had to be stopped at once before an arrival of another threat of life forms. From all of the creatures they killed, it was as if the team was cleaning up the Cyclohoma alien population. It was dedicated teamwork: Cyfreid assisted Captain Tina, Agent Crimson was alongside Sherman Bawnder and the three Canavin Clan members, Team Valor was with the remaining agents, and Sharp helped Lynx, Shade-Master, and Titanium Titan.

The group of six that provided the major contrasting beam of unavoidable energy saw only ten more creatures in front of them.   Judging by the faith the heroes had in their teammates, they concluded that it was a job well done. The ten aliens scurried away, but Avinotch and the villains didn't stop. They chased after them before Canavin, Silvert, and Valor were able to show their gratitude.

With only several aliens remaining, the heroes defeated them all except one. The last Pixalian found Identymous. The dark monster crept behind him, slinking low and steady for his attack.   To Canavin's surprise from watching the trickster, Identymous was sliced from that position.   Cyfreid shot the extraterrestrial in the forehead upon noticing the unexpected situation. He blew away the gun smoke.

Canavin hurried himself towards Identymous; as of the moment, he felt sympathy. The circular dial spun again, trying to find a noble Pixalian peer to become. It was too late. The dial slowed down. The carved head bent low. Canavin saw ink markings on his head that he never noticed. The tattoos were a code. He pulled Canavin close. The quick breathing made it difficult for him to speak. He knew that this was *his* time. Canavin thought he was going to hear some words of motivation from the creature. In a sense, it was.

Identymous spoke in the ancient Pixalian language that was used many centuries ago. When he finished, the depraved Identymous rolled his head over with his sight fixed on the dead creature, and then diminishing to a final distorted vision. Identymous died.

From within his mind, Canavin translated the words to English:

Pixalian force, Pixalian plague.
Your days of wrath shall perish with thy soul.
For The One exceeds all powers of Star-Pix.
All life that has been bought with a toll.
All idols of the thousand realms.
For it is written in the scrolls of life,
that any soul that believes,
shall have access to end a beast's might.
Therefore, I seal you in this rock, never to be free.

Unless called by a reading from the masters of the universe.

I rid the world from this plague. Your spirit shall flee.

This was none other than the reading to reverse the spell of Xaliemer's power. Canavin was right. Identymous knew about it all along, but tried to hide it from him, just like how he was immune from the beginning. Canavin figured that there had to be a legitimate reason for him revealing it. And then the hope of the survival of the humans struck him instantly.

"Could there possibly be another sample of the Pixaliemain?" he thought deeply. He was sure that there were none left. All that remained were glitters of particle dust.

Time was running out. Sooner or later, he among the others would find themselves in another death match against aliens. It was uncertain that all fifteen heroes will survive if the thought was to come true. Regardless of the sudden revelations, Canavin agreed that now was the time to execute the original plan of trapping the beast in another realm. He signaled the team including Agent Crimson and Sherman's operatives. Cyfreid looked around and asked, "Hey, where's Agent Stan?"

Canavin and the heroes didn't recall seeing him at all. He was gone some place and it was questionable whether he simply left or suffered a tragic death. They were scared for him, but as of the crucial moment, they had to forget about it. Too much was at stake.

"Everyone, come here," said Canavin. They gathered around. Some were confused and others were quite aware of what was going on. Canavin smiled at each and every one of them when being contented by the fact that none of them died. The team was back together. Their survival was a complete blessing.

The gold alien stretched out his arm and placed his hand in the middle of the crowd. The other heroes did the same to signify their union. The last to show his commitment was Silvert, who everyone was honoured to have back. The process was the same when they fought the 'X-Viles' in Illinois. And Canavin said the same inspiring words.

"We're the masters now."

They each nodded and the unique alliance of AIA East was ready for one more attempt to save Cyclohoma City and in turn, the world.

Luke Crimson led them to the ship. They took their desired seats, except for Canavin, Silvert, Valor, Fusion Fighter, and Shade-Master. The field leader gave them strict orders.

"What's going on?" asked Silvert.

"Axel is going to open up a portal that would be large enough to send Xaliemer to a different realm."

"Okay, elaborate some more."

"You're going to take Shade-Master to a height far from the beast. But be sure to watch him! It's unknown if Xaliemer would demolish the building you place him on. From there, Axel will open the portal."

"Got it," said Silvert as he took Axel's hand and flew away from them.

"So what do we do?" asked Fusion Fighter.

"You guys are with me. We'll fire directly at Xaliemer in order for him to step back in the realm."

"Wait, directly at him?"

"Yes, because our new aircraft is going to give a surprise attack from above." They agreed to the cause and watched the ship levitate and fly away. Canavin directed his dark eyes to them and said, "The world is counting on us right now. Failure is not an option." Valor inhaled a deep breath, being almost bottomless. His static flowing blood was powered to motivate his maximum potential in the war.

"It never was an option," he said. The pterodactyl picked him up and flapped away to Xaliemer's location. Lastly, Canavin ascended and was packed with so much indignation that was necessary for the ultimate confrontation of good versus evil.

XX

DEFEND

THE DEFENDERS OF AN INNOCENT CITY

were destined to become the saviours of the planet. Canavin believed it with all of his might. Seeing the rage monster from afar, he accepted the only way that they were going to hand him his death.

Faith.

Faith combined with hard work was the ultimate ticket to success. Canavin contacted Commander Cyfreid who sat inside of the aircraft.

"Don't attack until my signal," he said. Most times, Cyfreid didn't accept orders. In the grave event when the rigid command came from the mouth of the one and only Canavin, he agreed.

Minutes passed and Canavin entered Xaliemer's reach. The face turned to the small Pixalian fly, still baffled why he wasn't speckled ashes like the other organizations. The spiritual energy always seemed to blow life back into him. The universal plague commuted through his mind.

"Why must you come back yet again? You and your *humans* are dead…never to return."

Xaliemer eliminated nearly half of the city with nearly half of its human population. Canavin spoke to him in order to buy some time.

"What makes you think that you'll possibly win?" he taunted. Xaliemer guffawed with all of his sinful passions added.

"Look around! This kingdom is in ruins! Fire fills the nation and I am the king of the humans and the ruler of all Pixalians! What makes you think that *you'll* possibly win?!

You're weak! As an individual, you are nothing!" Canavin leered from his claim.

"I will defeat you," he calmly said.

"I control each organic species! I am an army!"

"You haven't met my army."

"Your faith in survival is your downfall."

Fusion Fighter arrived with Valor and Silvert. Valor desperately wanted to shoot until Canavin told him to hold his fire. Little did Xaliemer know that Shade-Master already began his task.

A wormhole was commencing its formation from behind. The midpoint flourished to become a round ingress for dark substances, looking like a shaded eye of vast wonders. The beast had absolutely no phobia, seeing that he already faced them. The mere difference was Silvert and he didn't have grand predictions for his capabilities.

"This is what you call an army?" said Xaliemer in Canavin's mind.

"Not exactly," said Canavin cleverly. Out from above, Luke Crimson shot at Xaliemer's head; the back doors opened and everyone contributed using their armaments. The blending firepower included lightning, bullets, and mystic rays. As Xaliemer saw them, Canavin, Valor, and Silvert combined their illuminating forces. The offensive power had a resilient effect, although it was not as damaging. Xaliemer was still colossal like a brooding alien Goliath, and the team only hoped to initiate the portal backup scheme faster.

Shade-Master struggled. It was becoming too much for him to stand. The realm-bender's refusal to quit allowed his muscles to strain from the process. Thinking back to all of the realms he knew, he figured that this was indeed the last one. Any other realm would be too dangerous to open. The area he wished to send Xaliemer was a forsaken domain of heaped steam. Its sky was dim much like the night of the battle. The realm was perfect to trap Xaliemer. All that Axel needed was more minutes.

As the heroes contended with Xaliemer, the beast tried to focus his telekinesis. The constant moving served as a problem for the primeval giant. Canavin and his companions continued the beam as they aimed for Xaliemer's eyes. The force of the ejection caused them to move back in the air. The three of them expressed an amalgamated anger. The blinding light nearly provided Xaliemer with a reeling aftereffect. The surviving citizens praised them for their valiant efforts.

Xaliemer despised failure. His force caught hold of the flying aircraft. Crimson was unable to fly from the magnetic pull. He shouted with woe. Sherman came and said, "Relax, I need you to focus. Concentrate the same way you did before." The others from within the ship calmed themselves down as well. Raising the nerve-wracking pressure wasn't needed.

"I can do this," said Luke. He used all of his strength and with the help of Canavin, Valor, and Silvert with the vibrant blast, he successfully moved the ship away.

"Once again," Sherman began. "That's the Crimson I remember." Luke Crimson flew above Xaliemer to execute the strike. The dire situation was the fear of allowing the magnetic pull to happen again. If Xaliemer was to use it again, he felt that he might not be able to avoid the attraction. He had to try something.

From above the monster, Agent Crimson signaled the others. Captain Tina found a different pistol on a dead operative's utility belt. She lined herself with the rest, winking for the best shot.

"I hope these bullets can fly that far..."

Either way, her blaster always functioned as a plus. Her brown hair flexed back from the wind. The maroon eyes of the lurid creature of Detroit returned yet again. Her mouth was dry; her abrasions were slowly restoring. She licked her lips like a predator and said, "Oh the hell with it!"

The merriment and insanity resumed, slaying the views of the red-eyed soul for good. Tina and the others fired again at the beast. Canavin and the two heroes motivated the beam to a new level. The monster actually took steps back.

"It's working!" yelled Canavin. "Keep at it!" Even when the gigantic humanoid had the equivalent height of a hundred storey building, the beam of three prevalent blasts and the added mocking from the sky made the creature worry. He remembered the hatred he had for Canavin when believing that the armoured alien had some sort of relation to the one who recited the sealing spell. He saw the leadership traits that Canavin possessed and agreed that he had to be the team's admired *master*.

Instead of trying to focus his powers on every living thing that moved in the assault, he focused it all on Canavin. The hero had Silvert on his right and Fusion Fighter holding Valor on his left. Xaliemer aimed for the center and shockingly sent Canavin flying away from his teammates. There was no point of trying to disintegrate him since the monster already tried on occasion with his last rounds.

Canavin's sudden travel left the other heroes dumbstruck. With their best weapon out of the way, it was easier for Xaliemer to concentrate. The beam ended; the chaotic rein was back in disastrous action. While roaring to the skies, Xaliemer was really shouting, "Nothing can stop me!"

The degree of the sound of his words traveled far from the city and roved around Canavin's three antlers. He found himself back at the scene of the unleashing, the wasteland from out of the scorching metropolis. He limped up and felt sorrow for the world. That was his last attempt, and Xaliemer still beat him to the punch. And on the more hurtful note, he had more discomfort than his former match. He looked at the area in front of him, remembering where the villains held him captive, where Identymous said the reading, and the exact position where the plague stood on earthly soil. He figured deep inside of himself that perhaps Earth was going to suffer the same fate. Xaliemer was right. Faith somehow meant nothing. With Cyclohoma City as the preliminary point, Xaliemer's rein would spread like wild fire. Canavin squatted low and put his head down to see the dirt.

"I failed. I'm...sorry." It was over. He closed his eyes.

Having his eyes tightly locked, what was supposed to be completely dark was not. In actuality, it seemed that there was a light. Canavin opened his eyes and saw a tiny illumination about ten meters ahead. He got up fast. His foot was eager to pace close. He took one step and the light excelled brighter. He trusted its brilliance. Running to see what it was, Canavin beamed exultantly.

The miracle that he speculated, the one way to defeat Xaliemer, it was fronting him. The revealing light was sky blue. It was none other than the last relic from the disintegrated Pixaliemain rock. The size was nearly the same as the five broken pieces his team was asked to search for.

He was sure that the whole rock was particle dust. It turned out that he missed the sighting of just one miniature stone.

Canavin picked up the rock and held it to form a fist of bravery and celestial fervor. He had the two puzzle pieces of ending the conflict: the reverse-spell, and now a Pixaliemain sample. He looked back at the inflamed city. He saw the size of Shade-Master's portal that still wasn't big enough. Canavin had to hurry in order to proceed with the new plan.

Shade-Master screamed; the pain of trying to enlarge the gateway was intensifying. Opening the gateway was supposed to be the easy part as compared to closing it. Matter began to feel the portal's pull when cars, street signs, and animals were swallowed into the blackness. Humans believed they were going to lose their limbs from the amount of running. Xaliemer felt no pull. He threw a glance over his shoulder and then turned completely around. He thundered with hindrance and levitated Shade-Master. The portal started to close.

"No!" Shade-Master yelled when trying to keep it open. He felt that the tendons were going to snap from his trembling muscles. Shade-Master desperately cried for help.

Silvert swooped down and flew to his rescue until being trapped in the same situation. They floated and rolled in the air. Everything began to shrink internally as if their bodies were going to disappear.

"They're in trouble!" shouted Meditation. Celestica was there and looked at Frankie.

"This is really not good," she said.

"I know," he replied. "I can't stand this. I mean, with Canavin now gone—"

"Please don't say that. I know that he's alright."

"Okay, I really hope so. We need to help Axel and Silvert."

"I'm on it," said Agent Crimson. When saying that, the ship itself shook back and forth.

"What's happening?!" asked Evesdrop.

"I don't know! I'm having some difficulty! The systems are not responding whatsoever!"

Xaliemer enabled a quake to occur on the aircraft. The ship vibrated everywhere. The fighters were timorous and lost their balance. The force threw off their accurate aim of attack.

"Close the cockpit doors, now!" Tina screamed. The juddering motion improved and Crimson reached for the button. The heroes heard a thump. They looked at the agent and saw that the radical motions made his head hit off the main controls. Sherman and Titanium Titan moved closer.

"Crimson, wake up!" shrieked Sherman. He was knocked out. Tina threw her arms up to complain.

"Well that's *perfect*! Now who is going to—"

"I'll fly the ship," said Titanium Titan. The Captain laughed.

"You...fly the ship?! You really think I'm going to let you?"

"Tina, please! My friend is in danger! I must help him!" He was referring to Silvert. She agreed to his wish, although remained fairly insecure about it. He sat in the commanding seat and Sharp sat on the passenger side. Hiro closed the back doors and rebooted the systems in an instant; the Captain was impressed. She asked, "How did you do that?"

"I didn't only learn combat back in my homeland." He moved the ship a considerable distance away.

"What are you doing? I thought you said—"

"Just let me do this!" After the ship was far enough, he brought it back and increased the speed. The others held on to anything they could from inside. He readied the blasters and shot at the beast from behind. Numerous beams penetrated Xaliemer's back.

Silvert was free and when the master of many realms fell, Silvert caught him and flew to the top of another edifice. He continued the process.

The aircraft zoomed by and Jamal was able to see Hiro exchange an expression that meant their friendship was now eternal. The look was Titanium Titan's way of returning the favour earlier when Silvert saved his fall. Still, Hiro felt that it was not enough for owning up.

With Crimson remaining unconscious, Titanium Titan was the new aviator for the assault. Cyfreid and Tina momentarily admired his success.

Very soon, the twirling portal became a perfect fit to send the rampant plague inside forever. Silvert arrived next to Valor and Fusion Fighter and wondered if Canavin was ever going to return.

The alien zipped for the demonized city and arrived at the battle scene. He hid the Pixaliemain behind his back and his notable return left Xaliemer stupefied. He was in the range of the others who knew he was a survivor. The strong headaches started from the monster's words.

"The plagues of the universe would be worthy to have such a persistent opponent like you, Canavin." Xaliemer at last read the hero's mind to know his deep secrets. From Canavin's perspective, Xaliemer said, "If I cannot defeat you physically, then I'll have to do it mentally."

Xaliemer lifted Silvert, Fusion Fighter, Shade-Master, and Valor. The portal shrank in size. After that, he caught hold of the aircraft that held the perturbed agents and heroes.

"If you do not submit to me, I'll kill every single one of them!" Titanium Titan tried to exit the pull, but failed with his efforts.

"Why can't you escape?!" Tina shouted. Titanium Titan took his hands off of the ship's yoke and said with shame, "Why do you think?!" Tina shook her head to accept defeat along with the others. One of the agents told the other operatives, "Abandon ship!"

"No, don't!" shrieked Cyfreid, Tina, and Sherman. Although they showed much concern, some of the agents refused to listen and jumped out. The result of them was shimmering particles that gradually scattered down.

"No," said Sherman seeing it was too late. Lynx took a peek and stated, "Okay…don't jump out, check."

Now was the crucial period for Canavin to say the reading that Identymous revealed. The ritual had to be performed fast before more of the squad decided to take their unwise chances. Before he was able to recite the arcane phrases his father said all those years ago, Xaliemer subconsciously intruded his mind.

He haunted Canavin with memoirs of lost regal ancestors that only he was aware of and tried to forget. The worst one included his father being slaughtered to death. With the creature's power being so effective, Canavin saw the visions in front of him. The distress continued throughout everyone. The heroes sensed desperation and predicted their deaths to be very soon.

His mind began to sting like he was being electrocuted. With one hand clamping on top of his head, Canavin used the other and revealed the Pixaliemain.

"What?!" shouted Xaliemer. They were all lost and wondered where Canavin found the substance. Ignoring the constant throbbing veins, Canavin began to say the redeeming incantation.

Xaliemer was aware of it, believing it was some sort of déjà vu moment from Star-Pix. He screamed aloud to try and throw off Canavin's concentration. The shaft of vivid sapphire light around Canavin's palm increased with every ancient word that was said. Xaliemer, who was now too focused on the alien who could end his rein, tried to make Canavin suffer the same fate as the hundreds he had already crushed. Zan, the only other alien on the side of justice, called for the others in the ship. Titanium Titan and Sharp opened the back doors.

"Everyone shoot at Xaliemer! Now is the only time!" Frankie and Celestica followed his commands and watched as Zan gave the first hit with the Pixalian energy. Then, there were several bullets, light strikes, and electrifying blasts from Valor and Lynx. Silvert grabbed hold of Shade-Master and this time, brought him within the aircraft. He didn't quite understand what Canavin was doing, but decided to go along with it anyways.

The portal was shrinking at a fast rate and Canavin was sentences away before ending Xaliemer's terror. Canavin looked straight at the beast and said them loud and clear.

"I rid the world from this plague! Xaliemer, your spirit shall flee!"

The words caused Xaliemer, the abomination of Star-Pix, to frightfully scream. From all over the city, there was a thrilling radiance. Survivors stared in wonder and also with excitement. They were thankful when seeing that the monster that wrecked their precious city was in vain. The team of heroes protected their eyes. Cyfreid grinned, noticing that his vision was finally complete. The city of Cyclohoma and added to that, the world, saw that its days were not over. The gigantic hundred storey body of Xaliemer yelled as its arms broke off. Before they landed, they quickly crumbled into discrete particles. The remainder of the body's exterior flaked away. The skin dematerialized in the night. Xaliemer's face was a wretched skull that had eye sockets with green haze—just like the cryptic knight. The body returned to an ornate wraith and was forcefully sucked into the Pixaliemain rock carried by the warrior. Canavin's pulsations became more apparent in order to handle the massiveness. He was pushed back with the spirit around him that flowed into the stone. Canavin held on tight and looked up in the sky. He couldn't conclude it, but his soul felt the presence of his murdered father. The face was pleased with his hard work. As the final remains of the spirit went inside, Canavin heard Xaliemer speak to him internally.

"Why must you accept the humans?!" he asked again.

"Because," said Canavin looking at the team. "They accepted me."

Canavin witnessed the portal in front of him closing. He sneered at the rock and then in an instant, threw it to be drawn inside of the realm. After that, he flew inside.

"What's he doing?!" asked Valor. "Is he crazy?!" Before it was able to fully close, Cyfreid shouted, "Axel, start opening the realm!" He tried but it was of no use.

"I can't!" he hollered.

"If he doesn't get out, he'll be lost!" Silvert soared to the ship and said, "I'm going to help him!"

"No don't!"

Jamal flew away into the portal to aid Canavin. Fusion Fighter got strict orders from Valor to follow.

From inside of the realm, there was a gas-like texture and there wasn't a single living thing in sight. The quietness of it all made Fusion Fighter get chills. The heroes sighted Canavin who stared at the rock as if he was having a communication with Xaliemer. The vexatious spirit pestered him. Upon saying his final words to the beast, Canavin saw that he was not alone.

"Canavin, let's go! The portal is closing!" yelled Silvert.

"Not until we destroy this rock," he responded. "I need you two in order for this to work."

"Why?!" cried Valor. "The threat is over now. We need to leave!"

"The threat isn't over. As long as the sprit of Xaliemer is alive, there's a chance that he'll come back. And that's even if it's from another dimension. I won't allow that to happen. So are you going to help me or not?"

Pixaliemain was a strong substance and it required all of them to contribute to the firepower. Valor and Silvert saw the shrinking view of the city from the other side. They both agreed, but needed to complete the task as quick as possible.

Canavin, Valor, and Silvert, the world's most supreme heroes, merged their blasts for the final time to rid the universe of Xaliemer. The Pixaliemain rock floated in the distance, and the heroes shot the beam. It took a while for the outside to fleck off. At last, it snapped. The core exploded like their version of a nova. The fire came their way and it was expected by Canavin.

"Now let's go!" the alien said. They turned around and the portal was just big enough for each of them to escape. Fusion Fighter, who carried Valor, made it out first followed by Silvert. They waited only to realize that Canavin didn't come out as fast as they thought.

"He's not going to make it," said Silvert sadly.

Suddenly, with not much room, Canavin forced his way out to save himself from the fire and to save his earthly home, Cyclohoma City, yet again. As he flew out, Silvert, Fusion Fighter, and Valor agreed that they were honoured to have the Pixalian as their field leader.

Hiro lowered the ship to their level. Tina, Cyfreid, and all of the heroes and the remaining agents clapped for Canavin. The bravery he showed was far greater than what was previously imagined. Canavin smiled from the applause and clapped himself. He thanked the association of unique people for their efforts. They were with him the whole way and even when Canavin made the biggest mistake of his life, they still fought by his side to defend Cyclohoma from the most vile alien.

Now, the dreadful Xaliemer was forever gone. The dark spirit was erased from existence and it was all thanks to a defending alliance.

Aliens all over the town were in a world of confusion. They stopped their rampages to try and think about their sudden exposure to the humans. They didn't know what they were doing and wandered around to find their human coatings. As they thought about it hard, many more AIA reinforcements arrived. They landed their cruisers and aircrafts and unloaded hundreds of troops to arrest the creatures. Their lack of knowing their actions only made it fair for the aliens to be brought to the AIA Court of law, where the council will decide their punishments.

Many local firefighters were able to put out the crackling fires that filled the city without any meddlesome extraterrestrials.

Canavin and the rest of the team landed safely and watched as the AIA soldiers from numerous sectors arrested every exposed alien they could track. It was a job well done. Agent Crimson woke up and gasped.

"What happened? Did we win?" he asked. Tina and Sherman Bawnder looked at each other and then laughed. They explained how he banged his head and slept through the final event of beating Xaliemer.

"You mean I missed the entire thing?" He was a little discouraged.

"Yea, you missed it," said Lynx approaching them. "But don't worry, I filmed the *whole* battle for you. You see, I swooped in and used my incredible lightning strikes to blast the pathetic creature to the never ending realm of—"

"Okay, there's no way I believe a word from your mouth."

"Whatever man, but it was epic!" The witty Lynx stepped out of the aircraft along with the others. The Sun rose to symbolize the success from their struggles and that everything was now right. They breathed in the fresh air. Canavin watched the Sun and smiled. Disrupting his personal moment was Celestica, someone who made him smile even more. She looked at his gold face and said, "Your father would be proud."

"Thank you," he replied. She grabbed hold of his cheeks and kissed him out of love. Lynx watched and was concerned how a human can kiss an alien, even if it was Canavin. He said, "That's really disgusting." They expressed mirth and everyone embraced one another by sharing hugs and handshakes of gratitude.

Canavin shook the hands of every person. When he got to Tina, she saluted him before he could salute to her. She said, "You're the true captain." Canavin smirked.

"I'm only the field leader...Captain Tina Truman." He walked off. Tina approached Silvert who was speaking with Valor. When noticing her, he asked to be alone. Valor nodded and greeted his four heroic companions.

"Hey," said Tina. She didn't know how she was going to explain herself. She said, "I thought for sure you died. But now that you're here, I guess I finally have the chance to tell you something important."

"What would that be, Miss Truman?"

"Silvert," she started. "I…I want to say that I—"

"Let's talk about it at the headquarters." She instantly exhaled. Silvert walked away and already knew how she was going to finish her sentence. Commander Cyfreid saw everything and was proud of his pupil. Then he remembered about his other previous student: Curtis Kareem.

"Sharp," he called. "Get over here."

"What is it Cyfreid?" he asked.

"A deal's a deal." Cyfreid pointed at an AIA ship that just landed on the street. A pilot came out and waited for Cyfreid's orders.

"I don't understand, what's going on?"

"I'm taking you home. You're going all the way back to your mansion in DC." Sharp watched as the ship's seal opened. Now was his chance to return to a life without danger, aliens, and imbeciles who just had no clue when to shut their mouths. He was happy, but only briefly. Curtis Kareem learned so much from the experience, that he developed a totally new way of thinking.

"Hold on Cyfreid," he said. "The past couple of days have been traumatizing and filled with anger, hatred, and the loss of a good man. Although I could return home, I'm not going to. You see, if it wasn't for you, I wouldn't have learned the truth about Brute-Spine. And most importantly, I wouldn't have met these remarkable people. Their abilities are beyond what I expected. So, I'm going to stay with them."

Cyfreid was puzzled. He thought for sure Sharp wanted to be back in his comfy bed, but now he was seeing someone completely altered. He said, "Well actually since Xaliemer is defeated, there's no real point of having you all together." He signaled all fifteen heroes.

"The project is over people…that is, if you want to return to your homes across the nation?" They thought hard about it. Some of them were too hesitant to speak until Valor stepped forward and said, "I usually don't like taking orders from you Cyfreid. However, my team wants to stay so I guess that means I'm in."

"I'm in too!" shouted Lynx.

"So am I," said Shade-Master. Soon, all the heroes agreed that this wasn't going to be a one time deal. It was settled that they would remain an alliance until further noticed.

"Except for one condition," said Valor.

"What's that?" said Cyfreid.

"We become our own unit. Remember, you called us for this stupidity. That means you're going to rely on us."

"If that is your wish, then I accept."

"And, I want to be the field leader." Cyfreid thought about it.

"How's about second-in-command?" Valor grinded his teeth and said, "Fine…close enough."

Canavin slowly walked down the street alone and recounted all the events that occurred in the last couple of days. He walked with gladness and stumbled upon a metal object. He looked down and grew a smile.

It was his mask. The reflecting sunlight was glorious, giving him gratification of the survived mission. Even when thinking he was going to die, he lived from Xaliemer's rage. He picked it up and dusted it off to see that the heroic symbol appeared almost brand new. At last, he put on the mask. Now, his armour was complete.

From behind him, there was Gold-Mine, Bloodblast, and Avinotch. He thanked them for everything.

"I sense good in the three of you," said Canavin. "It might be really deep, but I sense it somewhere."

"I'm not even going to listen to a word you said," stated Bloodblast.

"I think what he's trying to say is that we did what we had to do," Gold-Mine commented. The hero and the three heard a wind-swirling propeller noise. A helicopter lowered and Alyssa Munroe came out to greet the heroes. After, the Cyclohoma press with several news photographers came with their questions. Alyssa Munroe of Marvelous Munroe was the fastest to front the team.

"Guess that's the press," said Canavin. "Why don't you three come along? It'll change the way people view you." His cousin watched the crowd down the road. If he chose to go, it would be a new starting point in his life, but he wasn't willing.

"No," he said to Canavin. "Besides, that's *hero* stuff. You go ahead, Canavin. You deserve it." Before Avinotch was able to lead the two away, Canavin stretched out his arm.

"Once again, thank you," he said. The two aliens shook hands. Avinotch turned with his crew and then said, "Oh, and one more thing. This isn't over Canavin. I look forward to fighting you another day."

"And I'll be ready," Canavin solemnly replied. The three of them departed and the grudge between Canavin and his cousin was still very much alive.

Agent Crimson was tapped by Sherman Bawnder.

"Ah, the press," said Sherman. "Just like our efforts in Cleveland."

"Actually man, I'm going to head off."

"Wait, what? But the people are here to honour our bravery."

"I know. But you're the one they want to hear from. Besides, the troops and I got business to take care of in Orlando." The last of the agents entered the ship.

"Are you sure?" asked Sherman.

"I'm positive. Now go on and enjoy yourself."

"Hey, I'm supposed to be giving you commands, remember?"

It was Sherman's way of saying farewell to his friend. Crimson went inside. The ship rose up and then flew away.

There were constant flashing lights as pictures were being taken, heroes were signing autographs, and voices battled each other to try and receive the top story from the recently formed team. Some females even asked Titanium Titan for his signature. At first, Hiro was lost; something like that hasn't happened for a while. He agreed and fulfilled the wishes of the fans. Silvert was amazed.

"This is your time to feel special," he told him.

Alyssa Munroe swayed back and forth as the camera rolled. She was trying to find the hero that Cyclohoma was blessed to have. When finding him, she ecstatically shouted, "Canavin! Get over here!" The Pixalian warrior came near and stood in the center of the heroic crowd.

"This is Alyssa Munroe of Marvelous Munroe," she started. "After a crucial battle of the alien race, the terrifying monster that threatened the good people of Cyclohoma has been defeated by this outstanding group of recognizable heroes from our proud country. Before me stands none other than the alien we have come to love and respect, Canavin." She brought her microphone close to him.

"Tell me Canavin, you've saved the world once again and this time with the help of a larger crowd. The chaotic apocalypse is over thanks to your team. So I just want to ask, *what* are you heroes called?" The other reporters brought their microphones near as well, anxious for the alien's important response.

Canavin didn't know what to say. He looked around at the others and then back at Alyssa. He thought about the battle against Xaliemer, who was indeed the master abomination. Xaliemer was now defeated not once, but twice. His father lived the first battle, being the leader of the specialized team, the Star-Pix Defenders. Now, Canavin's victory was very relative to that of his father's since he used the reverse spell to trap the beast. Commander Cyfreid, Captain Tina, and the rest left the name up for him. And then, he knew exactly what it should be.

"We're the Master Defenders," he said uplifting the people. Not only the press, but the survivors of the war encouraged the Master Defenders with an applause they would remember for a lifetime. Their hard work has paid off at last.

Cyfreid pondered it briefly. He thought, *"If these heroes fought off a savage giant and won, then what other threats could possibly succeed over them?"* From what he could infer, the answer was *nothing*. He knew that if they really wanted to remain a team, they would face trials. As long as they face them together, that made them more than a team. It made them a family.

Alyssa Munroe spoke with her enthusiasm saying, "Well there you have it, the Master Defenders! The saviours of the world!"

When the cleanup of the city continued, and when injured civilians were brought to safety, Commander Cyfreid and Captain Tina brought the team all the way back to AIA East headquarters by using the reinforcement jet. Canavin was able to find his cruiser in the exact spot where he parked. He traveled safely with the victors.

Even when entering the front doors, staff members praised their success. The group returned to their relaxed life of the base. Within the Collaboration Hall, they sat and were offered drinks to celebrate.

Curtis resided in his new room that had his name, *Curtis Kareem,* displayed on his door. He rested from the trauma until he heard a knock on the door.

"Who is it?"

"It's Tina." He opened the door and the Captain handed him a wrapped gift. It was rectangular and thin.

"Cyfreid wanted me to give this to you," she said. Without saying a word, Curtis took the gift and thanked her. Tina walked inside and sat on his bed. Curtis placed the gift on his desk.

"That was some battle wasn't it?" said Tina.

"Yea. To be honest, I didn't think I was going to make it back."

"None of us did." There was silence between them. Curtis sat down beside her. He brought his hand up without the claws. It trembled slightly. He felt nervous for some reason. Then he remembered the first day he met Tina, when she was proving herself to be an elite fighter. He still had feelings for her. The animal inside remained asleep. He placed his hand on her soft cheek. He felt warm and Tina didn't move one bit. Curtis came near, really close. He slowly moved his lips on Tina's. They kissed long and after a while, he placed his arms around her and they rested. The lips were locked with the other until Tina turned her head away.

"Wait," she said.

"Come on," Curtis whispered back.

"I can't."

"Why not?" Tina got off the bed and walked to the door. She said, "I won't."

"Tina, I said I was sorry."

"You abandoned us, Curtis."

"I was mad at Cyfreid, not you."

"That's not what I meant." She walked towards him and said with a serious tone, "You forced me to kill him. That's why we can't be together again."

"I told you, he was destined to be evil."

"And you're still so sure? My child was not destined for that. As the father, you should've had more faith in him." Curtis didn't say anything. Tina added, "Look, I love you. I will always love you, but not like this. There's someone else on my mind right now. You and I are Tina Truman and Curtis Kareem. We're alien slayers. No more, no less." She kissed him on the cheek and Curtis understood that it was the last kiss. He knew what he did was wrong and always tried to forget the past. He accepted Tina's words. Regardless, he cared for her. He looked at the gift from Cyfreid.

"What could it be?" he wondered. He opened it with no hassle, and there he sat, touched by what faced him.

It was a portrait of him, the Commander, and Gary Herman before he was scientifically altered. It was an old portrait when remembering the date to be sometime just months after his first submission to AIA East. While looking at the way they stood together, he thought about his old life with Cyfreid and concluded that it wasn't that flawed after all.

Curtis Kareem relaxed on his bed and flipped the frame. On the back was writing that was recognized to be Cyfreid's.

He wrote:

I have my flaws and I've made my mistakes. Most of which I cannot undo. But regardless of the people and experiences you face in life, you'll always be known as one of mine. Never forget that Curt. Never forget. Your ally, Cyfreid.

Tina Truman took her respective seat in the Collaboration Hall beside Silvert. They were quiet about their attraction. She was on Silvert's right side while Titanium Titan sat on his left. The combat specialist rose up to get everyone's attention.

"Everyone," he began. They all turned their heads to face him. "I have an important announcement to make. In fact…it's a confession."

Immediately, Silvert grabbed hold of his arm and anxiously whispered, "Hiro what are you doing?"

"They have to know the truth Jamal," he whispered back. Tina heard every word. The whispers continued.

"It's alright Hiro, don't worry about it."

"I must let them know. It was my fault. Now I'm being responsible for my ways. Besides, they say the truth will set you free."

"Yea, it'll set you free alright…free of the headquarters. They're going to send your ass away." The rest of the team was confused about what they believed to be a bickering of whispers. Titanium Titan saw all of them staring and waiting for his response. He had a strong feeling that Jamal was right. Lynx asked, "What's your confession?" Now very troubled, Titanium Titan said, "My confession, right. Um, my confession is…I wanted to tell you. How do I put this? When we arrived here—"

"He just wanted to say," began Silvert interrupting. "That before he arrived at AIA East, he wasn't fond about this team. He felt that he was not welcome and that he was a minor. However, now he found his inner hero. This is all because of the days he spent with you guys, the people he can call his friends." Silvert directed his eyes at Titanium Titan.

He said, "And I'm proud to call him my friend." He poured a glass of Tina's favourite wine and picked up his drink.

"A toast, to the Master Defenders!" Everyone shouted the team name and drank. Hiro couldn't believe it. He was saved yet again by the man he once hated. He turned to him and pleased the hero.

"Thank you. I owe you big time." Silvert finished his drink and gave a crafty smile.

"You're right...you do." Hiro had to admit that Silvert's words startled him. Whatever that meant, he would have to own up, and for the first time, he was willing.

Cyfreid found Canavin in the landing bay. The alien was seen going into his cruiser.

"Canavin, you're not going to celebrate with the others?"

"I have some things to take care of back on Star-Pix. Actually, I'm in search for answers from King Flern."

"Well then, safe travels. Your service today will be remembered until the day I die."

"Let's hope that's not too soon." Canavin came out of the ship and shook the Commander's hand to give a farewell until he was to meet him after his talk with King Flern. Before Canavin entered the ship, Cyfreid asked, "Why did you care so much about confronting Identymous?" Canavin was quiet, hiding the answer briefly. In fact, it was a long story. He summarized it to the Commander.

"Well...he was my father's enemy. The Pixalian that murdured my father was sent by Identymous. And I'm sorry. I was so fixated on what he was planning, that if it wasn't for me going to his operation, this apocalypse would never have occurred. Many humans died because of my anxiousness. I'm only telling you this because the team was your idea. And I don't belong." Cyfreid nodded his head left and right.

"That's not the Canavin I assigned for the mission. Just because you made one mistake, doesn't mean you should punish yourself for it. Don't forget Canavin, if it wasn't for you, we would've all died. You saved our lives and the world. This wouldn't be a *master* alliance without you. You're a master…you're the field leader." Canavin promised himself never to forget that. He agreed and went inside of the cruiser.

"Wait Canavin, there's one last thing I want to ask you." The alien listened closely. Cyfreid said, "When we had that meeting and I elaborated on the assignment, I said that if Xaliemer was to be unleashed, it would be the greatest invasion the world will ever encounter. But then you said it won't be the greatest. What did you mean?"

Canavin took in a deep breath and stated, "There was a story about a certain race of imperfection. Their flaws included jealousy, greed, lies, and violence. It was very relative to the Pixalians, but these people had a gift. Their gift was a saviour, a man who had three elegant forms. His task was to save the race of imperfection by allowing himself to be plagued by them. His name is, The One. He completed his mission, giving all the people a chance for the ultimate opportunity. All they would have to do is submit to The One's spirit. I have no doubt in my mind that this was the planet he walked on and humans are the very people he died for. Soon he will return, which will make it the greatest invasion. This invasion only requires one thing and that's faithfully honouring The One. When that day comes, every man, woman, child, and hopefully any Pixalian that does this shall be granted with the ultimate gift…eternal life. So tell me Cyfreid, are you ready for it?"

The Commander was fully aware of who Canavin was referring to. He calmly said, "I will be."

"Make it fast," said Canavin as he started the ship's engine. "Time's running out."

He zoomed out of the headquarters and Commander Cyfreid felt the rush of the wind. It was the pleasure of the arrival of a new chapter; a new life; a new team. His sight was fixed on the soaring cruiser, the delighted spectacle that embraced hope, courage, and abundant faith. Cyfreid stared long until the ship disappeared into space with a swift blaze. He gently said with all of his heart, "God bless the Master Defenders."

Cyfreid returned to the room and saw Captain Tina laughing with the others. Their enjoyment was truly his fulfillment. After pouring a delightful glass of "Dark Essence", she saw his proud smile. He gained the Captain's notice with his fist analogy, holding up his hand and clenching it into a fist. She smirked and did the same.

As individuals we are nothing, but together we are powerful.

The season of summer is so brilliant and so captivating for a cheerful population. The playing children, the lovely birds, and the gentle breeze continued to enhance the soothing atmosphere. Should the tender environment be put to question? Now, this *was* one of those times. Even after the crisis, the answer stands as a flat out "no". Cyfreid and Tina agreed that it was all because of the union of fifteen brave heroes the world will remember forever: Silvert, Sharp, Titanium Titan, Zan, Frankie, Celestica, Lynx, Valor, Breath-Stealer, Meditation, Evesdrop, Fusion Fighter, Sherman Bawnder, Shade-Master, and Canavin. They are:

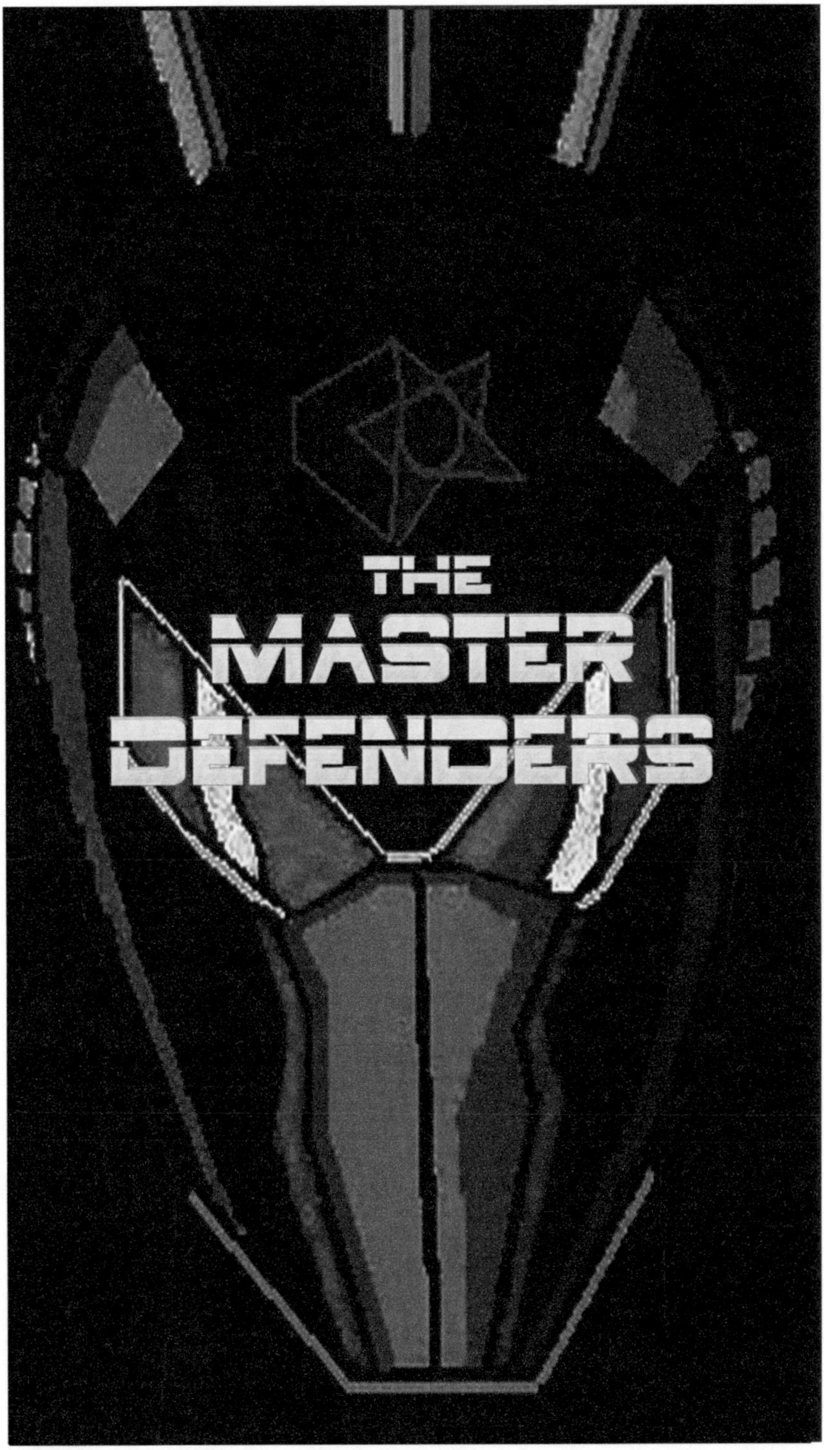
THE
MASTER
DEFENDERS

EPILOGUE

AFTER THE CITY OF CYCLOHOMA WAS restored, AIA troops found the fugitive, Governor Cain X. He was accused for the same standards as before. The former head of the central sector was held in a prison chamber. That night, Cain sat in his cell and felt misery. Maybe, just maybe, if he would've stayed in the fight, he might have been credited. It was too late for that now.

Cain felt the presence of someone. He knew he was not alone. It was dark, but he felt it. With his senses having the proper familiarity, he said, "You really think I don't know my own creation?"

Revealing himself out of the blackness was the android, Version X. He didn't say anything to his creator.

"Have you come to rescue me?" Cain asked. Then, another man arrived behind Version X. His face was hard to recognize when being shielded in shadows.

"No, he hasn't," said the man.

"And who might you be?"

The man took out a monitor. On the screen, it showed Agent Stan who was locked up somewhere in the facility. It only amused the Governor.

"Why do I see Cyfreid's dear Stan behind bars?" The person spoke with a dark voice.

"He's been charged."

"With what exactly?"

"Assisting an alien." He displayed a picture of Canavin. Cain chuckled and replied, "You do realize that the picture you are showing me is Canavin, right? Everyone loves him."

"You and I have something in common, Cain. We both agree that all Pixalians should perish from this world. That includes ones like him."

"So why are you telling me this?"

"Because I want you to tell me who authorized the specialized alliance called, the Master Defenders."

"Well who else…Commander Cyfreid of the east sector."

"That man needs to be dealt with. We can't just have aliens pose as heroes. It corrupts the minds of the public."

"Have you been living under a rock? Canavin has been on the front pages since the year of the crisis." The man looked at Version X and then back at the Governor.

"I want you to know that your job belongs to me now. I'm the new head of AIA Central."

"You came here to mock me? I mean, you even brought Version X who I should remind you, was created by me!"

"He made his decision to join me."

"What are you planning?"

"Word has it, there's a new species that made its way on Earth. They possess an intriguing structure and they can regenerate from almost anything. The cause of their arrival is none other than a group of galactic masterminds called, the directors of the universal plagues. I can set you free, only if you provide me with the species' DNA. And I want the Master Defenders…dead."

Cain thought about it deeply. The man added, "I have a way to destroy those *heroes*."

"For God's sake who are you?!"

"Let's just say I have a new way of thinking after that little accident at Lasher Labs." Cain's eyes opened wide.

"William," he said. "William Lasher." The man cackled as if he was humoured. However, he was the complete opposite.

"No Cain," he said. "My father is dead! And so is my mother! So do we have a deal or not?" Cain was partially frightened. He knew the name of the man he was dealing with. Nevertheless, he was unaware how he survived such a horrible attack.

"Hank?" he asked softly. The sinister man, Hank Lasher, smiled with his hopes to end Cyfreid's defenders for good.

MASTER DEFENDERS

CANAVIN

CYFREID

CAPTAIN TINA

GOVERNOR X

CURTIS KAREEM

JAMAL VERTISON

CHARACTERS DESIGNED BY MATT SHANKS

MASTER DEFENDERS

TITANIUM TITAN

PROFESSOR SHAW

VALOR

IDENTYMOUS

DRAYMOND

BRUTE-SPINE

[TITANIUM TITAN BY MALCOLM BHANKS]

CHARACTERS DESIGNED BY MATT BHANKS

MASTER DEFENDERS

COROMETHEUS

THE TITANIC

DARK-SHALLOW

GUSTAVO

OPTIMISTIC

KING FLERN

CHARACTERS DESIGNED BY MATT SHANKS

MASTER DEFENDERS

AVINOTCH

AGENT CRIMSON

BLOODBLAST

GOLD-MINE

VERSION X

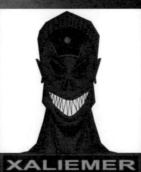

XALIEMER

Matthew Wayne Bhanks developed his artistic skill at the age of five when he drew his first imagined character called *Super Can* which later became *Canavin*. Throughout his childhood years, he and his brother imagined a number of different fictional characters. By creating background stories for each character, Matt became more enthusiastic about storytelling.

Master Defenders is his first published novel.

MASTER DEFENDERS
FICTION
MATTHEW BHANKS
MB ENTERTAINMENT
MB BOOKS
Copyright © 2013 All Rights Reserved.

ISBN: 978-0-920233-68-9

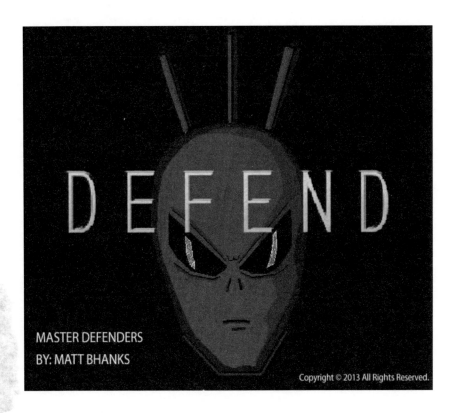

MASTER DEFENDERS
BY: MATT BHANKS

www.masterdefenders.com

Facebook.com/MasterDefenders

MASTER DEFENDERS 2
COMING SOON